"Written by Kerry Anne King with humor and heart, *A Borrowed Life* is the story of Liz, a woman who finds herself at a midlife crossroads and bravely decides to reinvent her life by taking a giant leap outside her comfort zone. At times hilarious and cringe inducing, heartbreakingly sad and bursting with joy, Liz's unpredictable journey will have you gasping at every turn. I loved this book!"

—Loretta Nyhan, bestselling author of *Digging In*

"Kerry Anne King's *A Borrowed Life* is both beautifully written and unflinchingly honest. A cautionary tale about the insidious ways we allow others to keep us small, it's also a lesson on the enormous power of love and friendship, and how the people in our lives can lend us strength as we grow, cheering us on to live our best lives and be who we are truly meant to be. This story with its wonderful cast of characters is one that will grab you by the heart and refuse to let go."

—Barbara Davis, Amazon Charts bestselling author of *The Last of the Moon Girls*

"Life has a way of coming up with surprises, even for people who know themselves to be settled. In Kerry Anne King's latest wonderful novel, Elizabeth is a mother and dutiful pastor's wife, serving the needs of her family and the church. But when Thomas suddenly dies, Elizabeth embarks on a journey of self-discovery that awakens her to life's joys and losses, risks and magic. With *A Borrowed Life*, King has written a heartrending, page-turning novel that zips along with twists and turns, humor and poignancy, and will have you cheering (and gasping) as Elizabeth-now-Liz rediscovers the meaning of freedom and creativity and love."

—Maddie Dawson, bestselling author of *Matchmaking for Beginners*

"In *A Borrowed Life* Kerry Anne King cleverly delves into a forty-nine-year-old woman's unexpected coming of age. Newly widowed, after a twenty-six-year marriage to a man who controlled her thoughts and actions, Elizabeth becomes Liz and takes complete charge of her life, exploring her world as never before. Making decisions that bring her happiness, often at the temporary expense of her inflexible adult daughter, Liz discovers life is not linear as she contends with unexpected roadblocks. King's storytelling gifts have us completely engaged until the last page is turned."

—Patricia Sands, author of the bestselling Love in Provence series

Praise for *Everything You Are*

"Hopeful at its heart and sincere to its core, *Everything You Are* is a testament to the power of connection."

—*Booklist*

"*Everything You Are* is a fresh, imaginative story about the power of dreams and our hunger to be who we really are. Kerry Anne King orchestrates a fluid, emotional, and wholly original tale of families, secrets, and the power of our gifts to free us. I loved every magical word."

—Barbara O'Neal, author of *When We Believed in Mermaids*

"Real and raw, King's *Everything You Are* is a gorgeous tale of life told between those lines too often blurred. Love and sorrow, regret and hope are woven into every aspect of the story by music—not just any music, but the magical kind that leaves both creator and listener, for better or worse, irrevocably changed."

—Terri-Lynne DeFino, author of *The Bar Harbor Retirement Home for Famous Writers (and Their Muses)*

PRAISE FOR KERRY ANNE KING

Praise for *Other People's Things*

"This is a really well-written book with interesting plots that interwind. The characters of Nicole and Hawk are great and I wouldn't mind more adventures with these two. Hopefully this will be a potential series of books. A great fall read."

—Red Carpet Crash

"Fans of Nicole Baart's *Little Broken Things* and Janelle Brown's *Pretty Things* will appreciate King's razor-sharp voice."

—*Booklist*

"*Other People's Things* is a mesmerizing novel with an unforgettable, indomitable heroine. Kerry Anne King is at the top of her game, weaving humor and magic and reality into a story that shines with surprise."

—Maddie Dawson, *Washington Post* bestselling author of *Matchmaking for Beginners*

"Woven with suspense, family drama, magic, and just the right touch of romance, *Other People's Things* is an utterly compulsive read. With a compelling cast of characters and a delightfully imaginative plot, readers are taken on a journey of self-discovery as a young woman struggles to embrace her unique gifts and find her place in a world that has already made up its mind about her. King's emotionally honest storytelling and wonderfully flawed protagonist remind us that people aren't always who we think they are—and that some curses might actually be blessings in disguise."

—Barbara Davis, bestselling author of *The Last of the Moon Girls*

"A funny, unexpected, magic-touched read with plenty of twists and turns, and a *Legally Blonde*–esque courtroom finish! Loved it!"

—Susan Mallery, #1 *New York Times* bestselling author

"What a fantastic read! A beautifully written novel with a cast of flawed but lovable characters and a plot twist I didn't see coming. Highly recommended."

—Soraya M. Lane, Kindle bestselling author of
The Last Correspondent

Praise for *A Borrowed Life*

"King's fans will love this tale of rejuvenation."

—*Publishers Weekly*

"In this vivid and triumphant tale, a woman loses her controlling husband and discovers she's been tightly contained in a cocoon for decades. Learning who she is, one step at a time like an unsteady toddler, means challenging everything and every relationship in her life—and grappling with surprises that will turn her world upside down. Is she Elizabeth, the tight-laced pastor's wife, or Liz, the thespian who has a point of view all her own? Earthy, unpredictable, and wildly enjoyable."

—Barbara O'Neal, *Wall Street Journal* and *Washington Post* bestselling author of *When We Believed in Mermaids*

"Watching Liz Lightsey come back to life after years of letting her identity slide away is a treat. *A Borrowed Life* shows Kerry Anne King at her empathetic best, writing a tale of passion, meaning, and growth at any age, and leaving this reader touched and delighted!"

—Kelly Harms, *Washington Post* bestselling author of
The Bright Side of Going Dark

"Writing sensitively about characters struggling to overcome tragedy and loss, Kerry Anne King has delivered a beautiful, soulful novel that hits all the right notes—especially for music lovers. It will leave you with tears in your eyes and sighs of contentment when you reach the satisfying, emotional conclusion. A richly rewarding read."

—Julianne MacLean, *USA Today* bestselling author

Praise for *Whisper Me This*

"Rich in emotions and characters, *Whisper Me This* is a stunning tale of dark secrets, broken memories, and the resilience of the human spirit. The novel quickly pulls the reader onto a roller-coaster ride through grief, mystery, and cryptic journal entries. At the heart of the story is an unforgettable twelve-year-old, who has more sense than most adults, and her mother, Maisey, who is about to discover not only her courage, but the power of her voice. A book club must-read!"

—Barbara Claypole White, bestselling author of *The Perfect Son*

"Moving and emotionally taut, *Whisper Me This* is a gut-wrenching story of a family fractured by abuse and lies . . . and the ultimate sacrifice of a mother's love. King once again proves herself an expert with family drama. A triumph of a book."

—Emily Carpenter, author of *Burying the Honeysuckle Girls* and *The Weight of Lies*

"Kerry Anne King writes with such insight and compassion for human nature, and her latest novel, *Whisper Me This*, is no exception. The families on which the story centers have secrets they've kept through the years out of concern for the damage that might be done if they were exposed. But in the end as the families' lives become intertwined and their secrets come inevitably to light, what is revealed to be the most riveting heart of this book are the gut-wrenching choices that were made in terrifying circumstances. One such choice haunted a mother throughout her lifetime and left behind a legacy of mistrust and confusion and a near-unsolvable mystery. Following the clues is an act of faith that sometimes wavers. There's no guarantee the end will tie up in a neat bow, but the courage of the human spirit, its ability to heal, is persistent and luminous throughout the pages of this very real and emotive story. I loved it."

—Barbara Taylor Sissel, bestselling author of
Crooked Little Lies and *Faultlines*

Praise for *I Wish You Happy*

"Laugh, cry, get angry, but most of all care in this wild ride of emotions delivered by Kerry Anne King. Brilliant prose inhabited by engaging characters makes this a story you cannot put down."

—Patricia Sands, author of the Love in Provence series

"Depicting the depth of human frailty yet framing it within a picture of hope, *I Wish You Happy* pulls you in as you root for the flawed yet intoxicating characters to reach a satisfying conclusion of healing. King's writing is impeccable—and her knowledge and exploration of depression and how it affects those it touches makes this a story that everyone will connect with."

—Kay Bratt, author of *Wish Me Home*

"Kerry Anne King's Rae is a woman caught between the safety of her animal rescue projects and the messy, sometimes terrifying reality of human relationships. You'll never stop rooting for her as she steps into the light, risking everything for real friendship and love in this wistful, delicate, and ultimately triumphant tale."

—Emily Carpenter, author of *Burying the Honeysuckle Girls*
and *The Weight of Lies*

"Kerry Anne King explores happiness and depression [and] the concept of saving others versus saving ourselves in this wonderfully written and touching novel populated by real and layered people. If you want to read a book that restores your faith in humanity, pick up *I Wish You Happy*."

—Amulya Malladi, bestselling author of *A House for Happy Mothers* and *The Copenhagen Affair*

"It's the horrible accident that forms the backbone of the plot at the beginning of *I Wish You Happy* that will take your breath and have you turning the pages. The hook has a vivid, ripped-from-the-headlines vibe, one that will have you wondering what you would do, how you would respond in a similar situation. But there are so many other treasures to find in this story as it unfolds. From the warm, deeply human, and relatable characters to the heartbreaking and complex situation they find themselves in, this is a novel to savor, one you will be sorry to see end. Sometimes funny and often very wise and poignant, *I Wish You Happy* is a reading journey you do not want to miss."

—Barbara Taylor Sissel, bestselling author of *Crooked Little Lies* and *Faultlines*

"Kerry Anne King has written a novel that will grab you right from page one and then take you zipping along, breaking your heart and making you laugh, both in equal measure. It's a lovely story about how we save ourselves while we try to save those around us. I loved it!"

—Maddie Dawson, bestselling author of *Matchmaking for Beginners*

Praise for *Closer Home*

"A compelling and heartfelt tale. A must-read that is rich in relatable characters and emotions. Kerry Anne King is one to watch out for!"

—Steena Holmes, *New York Times* and *USA Today* bestselling author

"With social media conferring blistering fame and paparazzi exhibiting the tenacity often required to get a clear picture of our lives, King has created a high-stakes, public stage for her tale of complicated grief. A quick read with emotional depth you won't soon forget."

—Kathryn Craft, author of *The Far End of Happy* and *The Art of Falling*

"*Closer Home* is a story as memorable and meaningful as your favorite song, with a cast of characters so true to life you'll be sorry to let them go."

—Sonja Yoerg, author of *House Broken* and *The Middle of Somewhere*

"Kerry Anne King's tale of regret, loss, and love pulled me in, from its intriguing beginning to its oh-so-satisfying conclusion."

—Jackie Bouchard, *USA Today* bestselling author of *House Trained* and *Rescue Me, Maybe*

"King's prose is filled with vitality."

—Ella Carey, author of *Paris Time Capsule* and *The House by the Lake*

IMPROBABLY
YOURS

ALSO BY KERRY ANNE KING

Closer Home

I Wish You Happy

Whisper Me This

Everything You Are

A Borrowed Life

Other People's Things

IMPROBABLY YOURS

YOURS

A NOVEL

KERRY ANNE KING

LAKE UNION
PUBLISHING

Text copyright © 2022 by Kerry Anne King
All rights reserved.

No part of this book may be reproduced, or stored in a retrieval system, or transmitted in any form or by any means, electronic, mechanical, photocopying, recording, or otherwise, without express written permission of the publisher.

Published by Lake Union Publishing, Seattle

www.apub.com

Amazon, the Amazon logo, and Lake Union Publishing are trademarks of Amazon.com, Inc., or its affiliates.

ISBN-13: 9781542035477
ISBN-10: 1542035473

Cover design by Faceout Studio, Lindy Martin

Printed in the United States of America

For Sandi: we can't get it wrong, and we'll never get it done, but it's always an awesome ride.

Prologue

Blythe

Mom says magic isn't real. She says a girl turning six is too big to believe in such foolishness. Nomi says it's not foolishness at all and what Mom doesn't know won't hurt her. I'm going with what Nomi says, at least while I'm at her house.

She makes it easy to believe our games of let's pretend are real. She looks just like a storybook fortune-teller, with her bright colored turban and the golden hoops dangling from her ears. Silver bracelets clink on her wrists when she moves. I'm dressed up, too, in one of Nomi's silken nightgowns, my wild red hair covered by a scarf.

Between us on the tea table sits Nomi's big snow globe, pretending to be a crystal ball. She has been gazing into it, looking for my fortune, long enough for me to drain a cup of milky tea and finish every crumb on my plate. Now I can't wait another single minute.

"What do you see? Tell me! Tell me!" I say, bouncing up and down in my chair.

Nomi frowns but doesn't look up. "Seeing the future is not like turning on the television. Hush now. Be patient."

She shakes the globe, the snow swirling up into a small blizzard. Her eyes narrow. "Ahhh, there you are," she says in a different sort of voice. I stare as hard as I can, but all I see is the swirl of snow and my own face, all twisted and strange in the curving glass.

I put both hands over my mouth to keep from spilling out my questions and breaking the magic.

"I see you, surrounded by water—"

"Am I swimming?" I lean forward with my nose almost touching the globe, trying to see what Nomi sees.

"You are not swimming. You are on an island. You are searching for something."

"Like Treasure Island, *you mean? I'm hunting for treasure, right? When do I start?"*

"Hush now," Nomi says again. "Let me focus." She turns the globe slightly, her bracelets clinking. "I see a birthday cake. I am counting the candles . . ."

That means another birthday. Today I am six, and I'm right here with Nomi, so maybe it will be next year, when I'm seven. Or even when I'm ten, although ten is so old it's almost impossible to imagine, even for me, and I'm a pretty good imaginer.

"There are, oh my stars, there are thirty candles," Nomi says.

"Thirty!" I squeal. "But I'll be old! Thirty is too old to go treasure hunting."

"Thirty is a perfect age," she says. "The age for finding yourself."

"Uh-oh," I say, hearing the front door open, followed by the rapid click click click of my mother's footsteps.

"What exactly are you two up to?" she asks, click-clicking into the room. She always wears high heels and a soft blouse and a pencil skirt, and perfume, something that is part flowers and part vanilla and something deeper and darker that I don't have a word for.

I run over to hug her so maybe she won't be mad. "Nomi is telling my birthday fortune! I'm going to go to an island and hunt for treasure. When I'm thirty. Only I'm sure that's wrong because that's way too old, don't you think?"

"Not so very old," Mom says. Her arms go around me, the sleeves of her blouse cool and crisp, and her lips press against my cheek. She straightens up and says, in a different voice, "I wish you wouldn't put these wild ideas in Blythe's head, Mother. She spends altogether too much time reading fairy tales. I've asked you not to do this."

Nomi sighs, and all at once she's just Nomi again, dressed up for let's pretend, and the crystal ball is just a snow globe. "Aren't you early, Lyndsey?"

"Late, actually," Mom says. "You've lost track of time again. It's five o'clock. Time to get Blythe home for dinner."

"And cake?" I ask.

"And cake. Although it looks like you've already had more than enough sugar for one day."

"We had tea," I explain. "A cream tea, with strawberry preserves and clotted cream and scones. Just like the queen of England. And then we played fortune-tellers, only I can't ever see anything in the crystal ball, so I couldn't tell Nomi's fortune, but she told mine."

"Let's help Nomi clean up," Mom says instead of scolding, because even though she isn't happy about the crystal ball and the cream tea, she loves me and Nomi anyway. Besides, it's my birthday. So we clear away the tea things and Nomi wraps up the snow globe and puts it away and we go home to my house for dinner with Daddy and baby Kristen, who isn't quite a baby anymore and is old enough to eat her cake this year with a fork, instead of trying to bury her whole face in it like she did last year.

After dinner, when Daddy is getting his car keys so he can drive Nomi home, I pull her down close to me and whisper in her ear, "How will I find the island, Nomi?"

"It's magic! You'll know."

"But what if I don't?"

"We'll make a treasure map, darling girl. That way you'll know exactly where to go."

Chapter One

Blythe

Alan's alarm goes off at 6:25 a.m., Pink Floyd's "Money" pulverizing my pleasant dream into particles as fine and unreclaimable as beach sand.

Morning is not something on which the two of us agree. I firmly believe it's the best time for half-lucid dreaming, while Alan's alarm is precisely calculated to launch him into his daily routine of treadmill, shave, shower, and breakfast, followed by a day devoted to his life plan of becoming a young millionaire and retiring at forty.

I roll over and cover my head with my pillow, my body heavy with sleep, waiting for him to leap out of bed, wide-awake and supercharged, so I can drift back into slumber. Instead, he slings an arm over my shoulder, moves the pillow, and plants a kiss on my cheek. "Wake up, sleepyhead."

I burrow deeper into the bed, trying both to recover the disrupted dream and to avoid the inevitable but unwanted happy birthday wishes I assume are coming my way. I should know better. My birthday—and the fact that I am turning a most reluctant thirty—is not what's on Alan's mind. He yanks the pillow away from my clutching hands, smooths my hair, and says, far too cheerfully for this hour of the morning, "You have a big interview today, remember?"

When I groan and grab for the pillow, he rolls across the bed, taking it with him.

"Come on, Blythe. This is important. This is opportunity. You want to be psyched and ready, and you do not want to be late."

He's wrong. I *do* want to be late. In fact, I want to skip the whole day: the interview, and work, and the family birthday party, and the ring that I have reason to believe Alan might have bought for me, and very possibly the rest of my life.

Thirty is a signpost that has wakened me to the truth that I am on a train headed for the wrong destination, traveling down a mountainside without brakes, gathering momentum at an alarming rate. I got on board trying to make my mother happy and I stayed on board trying to make Alan happy and it's way too late to jump off now.

Alan tugs at the covers. I know from experience that he's not above stripping them right off of me and carrying them out of the room with him if I don't get up. So I sigh, huddle into my robe, and head for the kitchen and coffee. At least the coffee maker has already done its thing, thanks to Alan and his schedule, so I pour myself a mug and carry it into the living room, where I can curl up in a corner of the couch and attempt to soothe myself with logic and caffeine.

I tell myself that today is just another day. That thirty is, quite simply, the sum of twenty-nine plus one, and that one is such a tiny number it doesn't even count. Aside from the interview and the family dinner party and the possible marriage proposal, there is nothing inherently worse in this day than any other day of my life.

When that doesn't make me feel better, I remind myself that there are three hundred and sixty-five days in a year, that if I live to be eighty that's twenty-nine thousand and two hundred days, and in the vast scope of that, what difference does this one day make?

But this equation adds up to old and decrepit and dead after a lifetime of doing things that I don't really want to do. That's life, Mom says, but I can't help thinking there should be more. I want vibrant colors and passionate feelings. I want the sort of love that makes time stand still. I want to do something that matters in the world. And I really, really, really want a touch of magic and adventure in my life.

When Kristen calls, I almost don't answer, but she's more persistent than both Mom and Alan put together, and I know I might as well get it over with now, rather than waiting until she's tried ten times and we're both thoroughly annoyed.

"Happy birthday!" she chirps.

"Why is it that everybody in my life is a morning person?" I lament, slurping the last of my now-tepid coffee.

"You're grumpy because it's your birthday. Get over it. It's just a number."

"Yeah, wait until you turn thirty. I'll remind you of that." Kristen is three years behind me. Twenty-seven still has edges and attitude and hope, especially for the successful sister, the one who figured life out when she was twelve and never wavered.

"Whatever," Kristen says. "Now, on to more important things. Mom is freaking out about your birthday party already."

"I told her I don't want a birthday party."

"Yeah, well. You know you're having one, want it or not."

"I'll be there."

"Be on time. Set an alarm on your phone or whatever."

"I said I'll be there."

"Blythe." Her tone shifts to its most managerial and condescending. "We both know how you are with time. Set an alarm right now, while I'm on the phone. I'll wait."

I hang up on her. Sometimes I love Kristen to death. Sometimes she makes me crazy. We have what I think of as a Schrödinger relationship. Schrödinger's claim to fame is this idea that if you were to put a cat in a box with holes in the lid and gas the poor thing, the cat might be either alive or dead, and therefore is both at once until you open the lid and it either jumps out at you . . . or doesn't. Kristen and I are like that.

Any time I pick up the phone or open a door, we might be on speaking terms, or we might not.

As for Schrödinger, I think he was an animal-torturing sociopath to have even come up with this idea, and yet he's famous. His mother would have been proud, unlike mine, and what kind of fairness is that in the world?

Alan sweeps into the room, dressed for work in immaculately pressed pants and a sports coat and a perfectly knotted tie, smelling of toothpaste and shampoo and expensive aftershave. "You should be early. Hop in the shower now, so you have plenty of time. Set an alarm."

"I think I'm old enough to manage my own schedule," I retort, irrational enough to be hurt that he hasn't wished me a happy birthday. Just because *I* want to pretend today isn't happening doesn't mean that *he* has any business forgetting. He smiles and kisses the top of my head, immune to my morning snarkiness.

"Set an alarm. I'll see you at dinner."

Fueled by large quantities of coffee, I review all my notes on Blake and Lomax Inc. and the job requirements of the position I'm interviewing for, still in a state of shock that I managed to land an interview at all, given that I'm well short on the experience and qualifications being asked for.

I applied because Alan pushed me. He's getting set to launch his own property development company within the next five years, and our plan—his plan, honestly—is for me to develop skills and experience as a property manager so I can head up that portion of the new firm when the time comes.

Even though I've applied for the position and set up the interview, I know deep in my bones that I am not the woman for this job. I've muddled along okay as the sort of real estate agent who sells family homes, primarily lower-end properties to first-time buyers. I like people, as long as they don't come in large groups, and I love seeing their happiness when the deal is closed and they know they get to move in.

But I'm not good under pressure and I really, really hate wearing a suit and heels and I'm pretty sure negotiating high-level deals will give me hives. Real, splotchy, itchy blemishes like the ones that popped up in college during an ill-fated accounting exam.

I dress carefully in a skirt and blouse, tame my hair in the chignon Kristen taught me how to do, and even put on makeup. With a deepening feeling of dread, I realize that if I get the new job, I'll be expected to dress like this every day. Even though I haven't put on my shoes yet, my feet start aching at the very thought of spending days in heels.

"Easy, toes," I tell them. "Maybe we can work out a deal. Platform soles. Something."

My feet are not buying the story, the ache turning into a sharp pain in my big toe. A bunion, probably. Disfiguring and disabling. Wings begin to flutter frantically in my belly. My breath feels tight in my chest. I can hear my heart beating, way too fast, can hear it surging in my ears.

Hopefully, I stare at my face in the mirror, searching for the splotchy red bumps that would give me an excuse to call the whole thing off. *I'm so sorry, I've been taken ill. Plague, I think. I'll need to reschedule.* But the only blemishes on my pale skin are the irrepressible freckles, still visible under the makeup. My curls are already escaping from the combs and pins. I've managed to get a coffee stain on my blouse.

Almost time to go.

I fix my hair. I put on the only other blouse I currently own that works with this skirt. When I consult the mirror again, I think I look more like I'm going to a funeral than a job interview. So be it. It's too late to go shopping, either for clothes or a different life.

Feeling faintly dizzy, I stuff my feet into the offending shoes, grab my phone, purse, and briefcase, and head for the door. At the last minute I return to the bedroom and pick up my good-luck pendant, a raven sitting in a silver tree, and fasten the chain around my neck. The *you-need-to-leave-now* alarm goes off on my phone and I lock the door behind me and head for my car.

"Somebody die?" a thin voice asks.

I look over my shoulder to see our elderly neighbor, Mrs. Fleming, sitting on her front lawn in one of two Adirondack chairs, coffee in one hand, a book in the other, basking in the warmth of the late-June sunlight.

"No. Job interview," I tell her.

"Oh dear. So much worse," she says. Sarcasm, surely, but her face is serious. "Death is a quick exit. The wrong job goes on forever. Take advice from an old woman. Run away."

"Too late to run."

"Is it?" she queries, then adds irritably, "Oh, never mind. What do I know? Only what I wish I had done, that's all."

"You wish you had run away?"

"I did run away," she says, her lips turning up a little at the corners. "I just waited too damn long to do it. Take my advice. Run now."

Could it really be that easy? Get in my car and drive off into the sunset?

I tip my head back to let the sun warm my face. White, puffy clouds float serenely in a blue sky. A sparrow flits down to the ground near my feet, pecking happily at seeds hidden in the grass.

But then a cloud covers the sun and the light dims. The little bird chirps, and when I look down it cocks its head, peering up at me out of one beady black eye, begging, I think.

"I'm sorry, I have no crumbs for you," I say. It chirps again—a bird curse, probably—and flutters away.

"Run," the old woman advises.

"Maybe I will," I tell her, but I know I won't. I'm a people pleaser, and there's no escaping that. I don't want to let Alan down or disappoint my mother or inconvenience the people at Blake and Lomax.

By the time I park in front of the building—an intimidating plate-glass and steel structure that doesn't share space with any other business and even has its own perfectly paved parking lot—I'm a nervous wreck.

I drape my purse over my shoulder, grab my briefcase, check my face one last time in the mirror.

No hives, but three curls have already fought their way loose from confinement and there's a tiny smear of mascara under my left eye. Nothing to be done about any of that now.

I clip-clop into the lobby, feeling awkward in my heels, my skirt too tight around my knees, as if I'm playing a role, pretending to be somebody who isn't me at all.

"I have an appointment," I say to the narrow-eyed receptionist sitting behind a desk made of green-tinted glass. Her lips curve into the facsimile of a smile, and a matched set of perfectly plucked eyebrows arch up inquiringly.

"Blythe Harmon," I say, borrowing Kristen's business voice. "I have an interview."

"Just a moment," she says in a tone even colder than my icy hands. Her fingers click a mouse; her eyes scan a computer screen. "Right. There you are. I'll let him know you're here."

Just as she pushes a button, my own phone starts ringing. For a brief and very strange moment I think she's called me, but her frown reconnects me with reality. I dig the offending item out of my purse and scramble to silence it, but then I look at the caller ID. Melanie.

She knows I have an interview this morning. She wouldn't call if it wasn't important.

"I'm sorry," I tell the receptionist. "I have to take this."

Stepping away from the desk, I turn my back and hit answer. "Make it quick, Mel, I'm about to go in for my interview."

"I know! I'm so sorry! I've already called everybody else and it's just awful and I had to see if maybe you might be able to help." Mel sounds close to tears and my own throat tightens in sympathy.

"What's happened?"

"Some guy's cat had kittens and he wants to surrender them."

My sympathy gives way to annoyance. I glance over my shoulder at the woman at the desk, who taps the watch on her wrist with a meaningful glare. I hold up my finger to signal just one minute, and say into the phone, "Well, that's good, right? I can help with that when I'm done here. An hour, maybe?"

"But that's the thing! He said he'll drown them if we don't come out right now. And I suggested other shelters and he said he does not have time or patience and he's already gone out of his way. I think he was high, honestly, and seriously, Blythe, we have to save the poor little things!"

Helping at the shelter is the closest thing I have to a life's purpose. The only reason I don't have a house full of rescue animals is because Alan claims he's allergic. I'm pretty sure he's not, and that the truth is he just can't handle chaos, schedule disruptions, and small housekeeping issues like potty accidents and furballs.

I don't want to let Mel down and I can't bear the thought of drowned kittens. But the chances of getting another interview like this one any time within the next decade is approximately zero.

A chorus of helpful voices insert themselves into my head.

> Alan: *I'm sorry, honey. I know you love animals, but you can't save them all. This interview is part of the plan. Our plan! Don't let me down!*

> Dad: *Oh, honey. Poor kitties, but your safety is more important. This kitten guy sounds dodgy.*

> Mom: *Seriously? Grow up, Blythe. Life is sad, sometimes. These kittens are not your responsibility. You've made a commitment to this interview. Honor your word.*

"Blythe?" Melanie says. "Can you? Possibly?"

"Can't you go? This is really important."

"I can't! I'm expecting two surrenders in the next hour, Blythe. And there's a couple here looking to adopt and I have to show them around."

I can feel the receptionist's laser glare burning circles into my back. I can even smell smoke.

Still, maybe I can do both things. If there's one thing at which I excel, it's making concessions. I remind myself of all the other interviews of my life, the ones where I sat waiting for five minutes, ten, half an hour, for the interviewer to get around to me. Probably the interview team is still getting coffee, laughing with each other over my résumé.

"Text me the address and phone number," I say. "Be quick."

"You got it."

My phone buzzes almost immediately with the information and I hit the kitten drowner's phone number while I glance back over my shoulder to check on the receptionist. She's been joined by a silver-haired gentleman, and both of them are now staring at me.

My wish for the interview to be late has not been granted.

"Who's this?" a voice demands, overly loud and making my eardrum crackle.

I take a step toward the people waiting for me, filled with a dire foreboding that the man is not some lackey, and that he must not, under any circumstances, hear me discussing kitten drownings when I'm already—I glance at the big clock behind the receptionist's desk—five minutes late for this interview.

"This is Blythe Harmon, and I am the woman who is going to solve your problem," I say into the phone, channeling confidence and reaching for the words that will solve two problems at one time.

"You are?"

"I am. However, I am in a very important meeting, so you're going to have to trust that I'll be there to resolve the issue as soon as I can."

"Listen, I told that other—"

"I completely understand. The situation is absolutely unacceptable. Do you feel we need to get law enforcement involved, or will we be able to settle the issue between us?"

"The cops?" The voice rises. "What do you want to call them for? It's not illegal to surrender animals—"

"No, of course not," I say, clicking up to the desk. "As long as that's what you actually are prepared to do. I would prefer that we settle this ourselves. I should be there to meet with you by two at the latest. Will that work?"

"Yes, I guess—"

"Wonderful. I will see you then." I hang up the phone and smile apologetically at the people waiting for me. "I'm terribly sorry about that."

The man smiles warmly and holds out a hand for a shake. "Not to worry. Business crises do not always have convenient timing. Buddy Lomax."

Wait, what? *The* Buddy Lomax? Multimillion-dollar empire builder Buddy Lomax? Where's the midlevel PR person I was expecting? My brain flatlines. Mr. Lomax is still waiting, hand still outstretched, and I grip it with my own, desperately, like somebody who has fallen off a cliff and doesn't want to plummet to the death waiting below.

"Blythe Harmon," I gasp stupidly, as if he doesn't already know who I am.

He laughs, as if I've been witty rather than an idiot. His eyes are keen, but the crinkles around them might be shaped more by laughter than meanness. His handshake is firm, professional with just a hint of personal warmth. I'm surprised to realize that I like him.

"Come with me, Blythe Harmon. We're right this way."

"This is a beautiful building, sir," I say as he leads me across the lobby and punches the button for the elevator, which immediately begins descending toward us in a clear glass tube that makes me think of a hamster cage.

"Do you really think so?" He turns his head to look directly at me, his eyes probing, and the truth spills out of my mouth before I can stop it.

"I think it's very impressive, but I guess I like older places. With history. And personality."

He laughs again and gestures for me to step into the elevator first. "Personally, I think this is a very ugly building. But it makes a statement."

The elevator sucks us upward and spits us out on a mezzanine, and Mr. Lomax leads me directly into a glass-walled conference room, furnished with a glass table and stylized, uncomfortable-looking chairs. A young woman in a suit smiles at us both. "Mr. Lomax. Ms. Harmon. There is water on the table. Can I get you anything else? Coffee? Tea?"

I shake my head, knowing the last thing I need is more caffeine. My hands are already vibrating, and my heart is pounding so hard I'm afraid it's visible through my rib cage. "Not for me, thanks."

"We're good, Amanda, thank you." The woman nods and walks out, closing the door behind her.

I suppose the closed door might make for soundproofing, but otherwise it doesn't really make much difference, because I can still see people moving around outside. They can see us.

"Makes me feel like a goddamned fish in a bowl," Mr. Lomax says, frowning. "Anxiety provoking. There's open, and then there's too open. I miss walls. Have a seat."

I sit gingerly, discovering that the chair is every bit as uncomfortable as it looks. I lay the folder I'm carrying on the table, and slide it toward Mr. Lomax. "I've brought an extra copy of my résumé, in case you'd like to refer to it while we talk."

He ignores the folder, pouring a glass of water for me and another for himself from an ice-filled pitcher, before settling himself where he can look me over at his leisure. His lips quirk up into a smile, and he says, "Whatever the big question is that you are dying to ask, Blythe Harmon, please do spit it out."

Obviously I'm doing a very bad job of hiding my confusion, which is normal for me. Mr. Lomax's directness invites my own, so rather than tell an unconvincing mistruth, I blurt out, "I wasn't expecting you to conduct the interview, to be honest."

He laughs. "This isn't an interview, my dear. The position is yours already."

"It is?"

"I'm a very direct man and I don't see the point in tying up my staff in an extensive interview process when we all know I'm going to hire you in the end. So I've cut directly to the chase."

"I don't understand," I say faintly, afraid that I actually do.

Mr. Lomax crosses one leg over the other knee. "Your credentials, I'm afraid, would never have been sufficient to get you through the hiring process, although I do see that Alan is right about your people skills. How you handled that client on the phone. Your directness with me. Very refreshing."

Good with people is something I'm not. Animals, yes. People, no. What he witnessed was a desperately trapped version of me pretending to be my sister. Who would probably be great at this job.

Alan knows all this. He never thought I was really capable of landing a position like this on my own. He's set me up to be some sort of goodwill employee. It's the same old story on repeat for all my life. *Blythe simply doesn't measure up.*

I feel like I've been dropped in a mud puddle and kicked in the ribs. My breath hitches in my chest. I feel heat rising in my cheeks, the dangerous prickle of encroaching tears.

"Don't look like that, Blythe Harmon. I'm not trying to insult you, just speaking the truth. I'm sure you're perfectly competent and capable. And the minute young Alan asked if I could get you in, of course the answer was a given. His father and I go way back. I owe him a favor."

I pick up my glass of ice water and drink, hoping the shock of cold will drive back the encroaching tears, cool my face, help me hide my humiliation.

"Alan hadn't mentioned that," I say when I set down my glass. I'm relieved that the tears have receded, and I'm able to look Mr. Lomax in the eye.

"Ah, I see. Wanted you to feel it was your own achievement, did he? Well, I'm sorry I've burst that bubble. But surely you must see this is easier than a dog and pony show. You'll start next week. All you need to do is sign the papers." He slides a folder across the desk toward me. "Everything is here. You can go over them at your leisure and drop them off at reception. Could you do that by Monday, do you think?"

I swallow hard and nod, unable to find words.

"Excellent." Mr. Lomax smacks the table with the flat of his hand, then gets to his feet. "Thank you so much for coming in. It's been a pleasure. Amanda will show you out."

He pushes a button, and the woman in the suit appears almost immediately, like a genie summoned by the smallest wish.

"Escort Ms. Harmon down to reception, please, Amanda," Mr. Lomax says.

"Yes, of course," she answers with a smile that seems like it might be real.

"Say hello to Alan for me," Mr. Lomax tells me, shaking my hand again.

"Thank you, sir."

And that's it. Feeling slightly disembodied, as if I'm moving through a dream, I follow Amanda to the elevator. We ride in silence to the ground floor. As soon as the door opens, before I can stop myself, I break into a run, heels and all, hell-bent for freedom.

Chapter Two

BLYTHE

Compared to my non-interview, the kitten surrender is a piece of cake. Yes, the neighborhood is a little dodgy, but the man meets me at the curb with a cardboard box, answers all my questions politely, and signs the forms. His words are slurred and his eyes are blurry, but that's his business, so long as he doesn't hurt these adorable babies.

The rest of the day speeds by in a flurry of activity, while I get mama and babies checked out at the vet and settle them into the shelter. Then, since I'm already there, I help with some other chores, which includes playtime with a group of older kittens ready for adoption. They are delighted to have some human company and I am delighted to have the distraction.

They've played themselves out and fallen asleep in my lap when Kristen calls.

"Where are you?" she demands.

"What time is it?"

"Almost five, dimwit. Everybody is here. Except you."

"I'm sorry. I lost track of time. I was—"

"Just get here, okay?" The line goes dead.

I stow the kittens back in their cages and run out to my car, doing my best to make up for lost time. As I drive, I make a wish for a nice little traffic jam. Nothing too tragic, of course; I don't want anybody to get hurt. Just a friendly fender bender, preferably involving multiple vehicles. Barring that, perhaps a small earthquake and a sudden sinkhole. I'll settle for any twist of fate that will tie me up for a couple of hours so I can miss the party.

But the universe is set against me. Traffic moves along smoothly, all the lights conspire to turn green, and far too soon I'm driving down the street where my parents live.

The driveway is bumper-to-bumper with cars and I nudge my Toyota in behind Alan's gold-toned BMW. Kristen is watching for me from the open gate to the backyard, and sashays out to my car, all sleek perfection in a tailored black skirt and high heels. Her hair, expertly cut and smoothly styled, holds the gloss of polished mahogany. Her elegant face, with the sculpted cheekbones and Audrey Hepburn eyes and bow-shaped lips is, as usual, expertly made up.

"About time you got here," she fusses. "Also, my God, you're a mess." She runs her manicured fingers through my hair, which completely escaped from confinement hours ago, then surveys my face with a frown. "You've got mascara all over."

She glances at the rest of me, her eyes widening with horror. "Oh my God. There's cat hair all over your skirt. You've got a giant run in your nylons."

"I get it. I'm a mess. Does it matter?" I protest as she pulls a makeup-remover wipe from her neat and organized purse and swipes beneath my eyes. "It's just family, right?"

"Trust me. You'll thank me later. Here. We don't have time to do your makeup, but at least put on some lipstick. And you have one of those sticky roller things in your car, I know you do."

Kristen would never show up rumpled and covered in fur to a party, family only or not; she never leaves her house without looking like she's ready for a photo shoot. If we hadn't shared a room growing up, I'd be tempted to believe that she wakes up looking like this, magically protected from puffy eyes and ridges in her face and mussed-up hair. As for me, according to Mom, I was born messy.

My sister knows all this about me and has pretty much given up on trying to save me from myself, so her current behavior confirms my suspicions about the true nature of this party.

"It's not just family, is it? How many people are actually here?" Either my words are garbled by the need to hold my lips still while Kristen applies the lipstick and blots me, or she chooses to ignore my questions.

"That will have to do." She slots the lipstick back into its appointed place in her bag, runs the sticky roller over my skirt, then grabs my hand and drags me toward the garden.

A shout from approximately a thousand voices goes up as we walk through the gate. "Surprise!"

I startle appropriately and scream a little, more from the volume assault than from surprise, since I'd guessed such an event was in the works. I just hadn't expected it to be on the size and scale of what I'm seeing. The yard is full of people. Mylar balloons are anchored to tables full of food, all sporting messages like "Happy Birthday" and "30" and even "Over the Hill" all in black. An actual string quartet seated under the maple tree starts playing "Happy Birthday," and everybody sings, while I try to figure out what to do with my face and my hands.

Large gatherings, even when it's just family, are not my idea of fun. In this case, family is here, all right, but so are a bunch of other people, some of whom I only dimly recognize. Aunt Bella, my Nomi's best friend and an honorary part of the family, waves with one hand from over at the food table, supporting a full plate with the other. Dad's brother, my uncle Pete, nods, his hands occupied with a glass and a wine bottle. There are two people from my real estate office, and a cluster of old high school friends who wave and cheer. My family doesn't know the people in the shelter, who I'd actually be happy to see, so none of them have been invited. Thank God Alan's very proper parents have moved to LA.

Kristen keeps on dragging me forward into the center of the yard, and even though we've left the gate open, I know it's too late to escape. My conversation with Mr. Lomax lingers hot and raw in my chest, and I'm in no state of mind for a party.

I look around for Alan, torn between my abhorrence of conflict and my need to ask him what the hell he was thinking and my fear of what the answer would be. But maybe there's a perfectly valid explanation, a misunderstanding. Alan is very good at explaining things that I've gotten wrong.

Before I can go in search of him, Mom gets her hands on me. She looks lovely and eternally youthful in a yellow sundress that flatters her slim figure and dark hair, and I can't help thinking that she looks more like Kristen's sister than I do.

"I thought you'd never get here," she reprimands, attempting to tame my flyaway curls under the guise of a motherly caress. I resist the urge to squirm away, not entirely sure she didn't spit on that hand first, the way she used to do when I was little and she hadn't yet given up on my appearance.

Dad, refreshingly rumpled, pulls me into a warm hug. "Happy birthday, little Bee."

"Thank you, Daddy." I lean my forehead against his chest, breathing in his comforting smell of soap and books and the same aftershave he's been wearing since before I was born. He is a sanctuary, as always, but I know I can't stay here—everybody has been waiting. When I step out of his arms to dutifully mix and mingle, something else is clearly afoot. The guests have not headed for the food table. They aren't chattering with each other or coming to hug me. They've formed a circle, apparently awaiting some sort of entertainment.

Dad pats me and retreats to stand by my mother. Mom looks expectant. Kristen, pensive. Dad, misty-eyed. What do they want from me? Am I expected to give a speech? Where *is* Alan, anyway?

And then the string quartet begins to play "Unchained Melody." The sliding door that leads from the patio into the house opens, and Alan steps out. All eyes follow him as he moves gracefully toward me. It's not uncommon for eyes to turn toward Alan. It's not just that he's tall and dark and has the face of a big-screen hero, it's the way he moves, as if he owns the earth he walks on. Also, at the moment he's wearing a tuxedo and carrying an enormous bouquet of red roses.

I know, because I know Alan, that if I count them, they will number thirty.

He knows I love roses and that red is my favorite color. Any normal woman's heart would melt, but mine has something wrong with it. Instead, I think of Snow White and the poisoned apple, also beautiful and red. I think about cages and closing doors. My eyes flick toward the gate and freedom, but Alan has reached me. He holds out the roses and I take them into my arms while he bends his head and kisses me.

It's the sort of kiss that ought to be right up there with the five pure and passionate kisses referenced in *The Princess Bride*, but my heart, still not melting, starts beating its metaphorical wings against my rib cage. And when our lips part and Alan drops onto one knee and holds out a diamond so big every jewel thief within a hundred miles must feel an internal shiver, all I feel is despair.

"Blythe. I knew when I met you that you were special, a rare treasure. I wanted you then, I want you forever. Will you marry me?"

I feel as if I'm floating above my body and looking down on us all. Alan on his knee, holding out the diamond. Mom with her hands over her heart and daydreams of grandchildren in a vivid thought bubble over her head. Dad with tears on his cheeks. Kristen fixated on the diamond. And me, my arms full of roses, the inevitable *yes* stuck in my throat.

Any woman would be lucky to have Alan. When we met during our freshman year in college, I was flattered and swept off my feet by his good looks and charm. Since then, one tiny bit at a time, so imperceptibly I didn't realize what was happening until I woke up one morning and knew the truth—I have fallen out of love with him. But I didn't know what to say, or how to end a relationship that has become a habit, so I've drifted along on Alan's momentum and now here we are.

All I can think, looking down into his upturned face, is that he doesn't think I'm enough, that he called in a favor to get me the job he thinks I should have but will never be qualified for. I wonder whether he really loves me, or if I'm just built into his plans now, woven into the empire he's building.

The music fades and falls into silence as the whole world waits for me to spit out the word that will seal my fate. Of course I will say yes. The kind of love I dream of, the many-splendored thing that will make time stand still, doesn't exist any more than a magic door into another life. As I open my mouth and shape my lips, a wizened old man steps through the open gate, a balloon bouquet tugging him upward, a large, brightly wrapped package weighing him down.

Jostling his way through the circle of guests, he proclaims, in a carrying and theatrical voice, "I'm looking for Blythe Harmon."

So, instead of *yes*, I hear myself saying, "That's me."

"We're kind of in the middle of something here," Alan objects. "Do you think this might wait?"

"To be honest, this gift is a little heavy," the old man says. "And I'm on a schedule. If I could just—"

"By all means, put the package down. And then step back, if you would." Alan's tone is sharp and impatient. There's a faint crease between his eyebrows that looks a bit like pain. I suspect that the one-knee position isn't exactly comfortable.

"Right over here," Mom says, taking hold of the balloon man's sleeve and trying to tug him toward the gift table.

He doesn't budge. "I have a protocol. First, I sing. Then I give the gift directly to its intended recipient." He turns to me. "You're Blythe?" Again, I answer. "That's me."

"Oh, good. I would hate to disrupt the wrong garden party. Could you maybe take the balloons?"

I look down at my arms, already full of roses. "Here, hold these for a minute," I say, shoving them at Alan. He glares at me, not moving, and I set them gently on the ground and straighten up to accept the balloons. These are not Mylar balloons with slogans printed on them; they are the big, round, brightly colored globes of my childhood. They feel alive, tugging at the strings that hold them.

"Blythe," Mom says, in a voice of correction, and I glance back down at Alan. His face is flushed, his jaw tight. I don't blame him. He, Alan Longwood Stewart III, descended indirectly from the actual royal line of Stewarts, has offered his hand to me in marriage. On his knees. In front of friends and family. With roses and music and an outrageously shiny ring. And instead of an enthusiastic and heartfelt *yes*, I've allowed myself to be distracted by a bunch of balloons.

I've humiliated him, I realize, guilt and insight showing up late to the party, even as a little voice whispers that maybe it was a tiny bit presumptuous to ask me in front of God and everybody. Desperate to salvage the situation, I channel my devious self, the one that rescued me earlier this morning.

"Alan," I squeal, attempting to clasp hands that are full of balloon ribbon to my chest. "Oh my God! Did you arrange the balloon man, too? What a delightful surprise!"

He doesn't confirm or deny, but he does get up from his knees. I've given him the opportunity to save face, even though he and I both know if he'd been the one who arranged for the balloons, the delivery person would look considerably more glamorous and would have known better than to interrupt a proposal in progress.

The balloon man clears his throat. "If I might? There is a song." He clears his throat again and launches into "Over the Rainbow." The musicians glance at each other, shrug, and join in. The old man has a beautiful tenor voice, and despite the way Alan's arm remains hard as granite beneath my hand, and even though I know we're going to have a horrible fight later, I'm transported.

By the second verse, I'm wiping away tears with the back of my hand and hoping that my nose won't run. But it does, of course, and a polite sniffle doesn't take care of the problem, so I'm obliged to rest my head on Alan's shoulder, then put my arms around him and bury my face in his chest, blotting away all inconvenient moisture on his shirt.

"Seriously, Blythe, *now* you're crying?" he whispers in my ear.

"It was Nomi's favorite song," I explain, the absence of my grandmother suddenly a cavernous emptiness, even though she's been gone for nearly twenty-four years. She loved this song, and she loved balloons. We once spent an entire day blowing them up, filling her apartment with bright shapes and colors that drifted and floated and clung to my hair and hands.

"That was beautiful," I tell the balloon man when the song is over. "Thank you so much."

"Yes, thank you," Alan says, in a tone that makes it clear he's not thankful at all. "Now, if you are done? Perhaps we could get back to—"

"I'm glad you enjoyed it. I need to see Blythe's ID."

I stare at the balloon man blankly. He stares back.

"Just give Blythe the damn package and get out of here." Alan has transitioned into King Alan, as Kristen calls him when he runs out of patience and begins tossing out commands. I can imagine the crown on his head, the sword in his hand. Only this time, the grass stain on his knee and the wet patch on his shoulder, left by my snot and tears, mar the effect.

"I need to confirm that you are Blythe Harmon before I can deliver this gift," the old man insists.

"Oh, for God's sake!" Alan exclaims, rolling his eyes.

I fumble my driver's license out of my purse, and the old man checks out my name and birthdate, glancing from the photo to my face and back again, as if he's TSA or border patrol. Apparently satisfied, he intones, "Blythe Harmon, on behalf of Naomi Katerina Balfour, please accept this delivery."

And then the brightly wrapped present is heavy in my arms and the old man is walking away out of the yard. The gate slams shut behind him.

I'm frozen, unable to move or think or even feel. It's not like my grandmother can just order up a gift and a singing telegram from her grave. In fact, she doesn't even have a grave; she was cremated.

"Wasn't that the strangest thing ever?" Aunt Bella asks, her voice sounding far away. "But he did have a beautiful voice, don't you think? Naomi wanted that song for her funeral. Remember that, Lyndsey? But you weren't having it."

A half-forgotten memory surfaces, dragging me back to another birthday, the year I turned six, the last one before Nomi died. The year she pretended that she saw a vision of me on an island on my thirtieth birthday, hunting for treasure.

"Blythe," Mom's voice says, sharp edged enough to cut through the memory and my paralysis. "You have guests." She reaches for the package in my arms.

I've got one hand full of balloons, but my other grabs on to the gift, protective and possessive.

"Perhaps we could get back to the moment that was unfortunately interrupted," my mother suggests, with a warning look at me. She loves Alan, she wants grandchildren, and I'm out of compliance with the script for my life.

"By all means, let's see what's in the mysterious package first," Alan says.

I glance around the circle of bystanders. Curiosity is killing me, but I'm also aware that I've just committed the worse faux pas of my entire life, which is saying something. Mom's lips are pressed tightly together in disappointment and disapproval. Dad looks bemused and tolerant, as if I'm an adorable toddler who has done something outrageous but he can't find it in his heart to be mad. Kristen, who has gathered up my discarded roses, looks vaguely triumphant. Uncle Pete has given up on the extra steps required to walk back and forth to and from the drinks table and has settled into a chair with a bottle of Chardonnay in one hand and his glass in the other. Aunt Bella has begun circling the dessert table in a shark-like fashion, eyeing the cake and the champagne bottles in the ice bucket. The other guests are trying to look everywhere other than at me and Alan.

"Oh, sweetheart, I'm so sorry." I turn toward Alan and try to hug him, but between the package and the balloons I don't have an arm to spare and end up with my forehead pressed awkwardly against his chest. When he doesn't put his arms around me and hug me back, I tilt my head to look up at him.

The expression on his face is that of a noble martyr, eyes fixed on a distant horizon, a brave man bearing with courage the trials and tribulations of the moment. It's a very affecting look, marred by the fact that from this angle I can see his nostril hairs and the white flake of a tiny booger clinging to them.

"I'm sorry," I say, again, this time including everybody. "You know me—they should have left me with the circus that time I ran off to join up." A couple of people laugh politely. Mom frowns repressively. Uncle Pete gives up on the glass and drinks from the bottle.

"Congratulations. You have ruined everything," Alan whispers. "I've been planning this for months." Then, louder, for the benefit of the crowd, "I hope you've all been thoroughly entertained. Good evening."

Head high, shoulders stiff, he marches across the yard without a backward glance at me. His dramatic exit is ruined by the latch on the gate, which the balloon man has closed behind him. It always sticks if you haven't mastered the exact trick of it. He attempts it once, twice, then starts rattling the gate in a frenzy of pent-up anger and frustration. Kristen, her arms full of flowers, rushes to his aid. She lays a soft hand on his shoulder, says something, low enough that I can't hear it, and his hands drop to his sides. She manages the latch on the first try and follows him out of the yard. I look around at the shocked faces of the guests, knowing it's up to me to say or do something, anything, but my mouth and throat are so dry, even if I could come up with some meaningful words, I wouldn't be able to speak.

Aunt Bella saves the day. She draws her cigarette lighter out of her pocket and methodically lights every one of the thirty candles on my cake, while we all watch in silence. Then she begins to sing, her voice lonely but determined on the first line of "Happy Birthday." The string quartet tries to join her, but she's badly flat, and when everybody else joins in, the effect is appropriately discordant and awful.

Following my cue, I move into position beside Aunt Bella. When the song ends, I already know my wish, but as I blow out every one of those tiny flames I hold no hope that it will come true. A gust of wind tugs at the balloons and I look up at the bright-colored globes jostling each other, pulling at their tethers, and on an impulse I open my hand and set them free.

Up, up, up, they rise, dancing on the current of the wind, carrying my unspoken wish for a little magic along with them.

"Blythe!" I can tell by the decibel level that this is not the first time Mom has called my name. "Would you like to cut the cake?" My eyes come back to earth to see her standing beside me holding out a knife, with an expression in her eyes that indicates she's close to wanting to carve some sense into me, if such a thing were possible.

"Take the knife and give me that package," she orders.

I see from her expression that if I don't surrender the gift she will try to take it from me, and if it comes to a tug-of-war, I will not win.

Besides, I've made enough scenes for one day, caused enough trouble, so I let her carry it off to the gift table and try to focus on serving out the cake.

Kristen, who came back into the yard halfway through the murder of the birthday song, fetches vases and water for the roses. Then, in an unexpected act of mercy, she brings me a glass of champagne.

"I'm guessing you need this."

I pause in the act of plating cake to take an inappropriately long swig. The bubbles tickle in my throat and nose and I barely stifle a sneeze.

"Is he okay?" I whisper, under cover of the clamor of voices.

She shrugs. "He'll live." Then she bumps her shoulder up against mine. "Hey. He might even forgive you in a week or two. Have another drink. I'll refill you."

Another good long swallow of champagne makes me feel lighter, as if the bubbles are floating me up into the sky to join my balloons. Good as her word, Kristen brings the bottle over and refills my glass, and hers. "You should maybe eat something," she says, also bringing a plate full of fancy hors d'oeuvres.

I poke sadly at a canapé nestled next to a shiny mound of caviar. "You sure there are no chips and dip?"

Kristen shakes her head. "With champagne? You have no appreciation for the finer things."

She's right. I never have been fond of caviar and pâté. Too shiny, too wet, too much like what lies inside a body and ought to stay there. My stomach twists alarmingly at the glistening food on my plate. "Please, just take it away."

Kristen shrugs and starts eating it herself. I turn back to the cake and serve myself up a huge corner piece, piled high with swirls of chocolate frosting. The first bite is so sweet it makes my jaw ache. I wash it down with champagne.

By the time Mom calls me over to open gifts I'm floating several inches above the ground and Kristen has to tow me over and sit me in a chair. I scan the table for my balloon-man package, the gift from beyond the grave, but I don't see it anywhere.

Mom hands me another package, rectangular and flat, wrapped in shiny gold foil. I turn it over and over, fumbling hopelessly with the tape.

"This is hard. I think I need another drink," I say to Kristen. I meant to whisper but a general laugh goes up from the watching spectators and I realize I've spoken aloud.

"I think you've had enough. Just tear it," she advises.

So I rip off the paper, blinking at the object in my hands—a framed photograph of a tropical island. "Very pretty," I say. "Thank you. Who is this from?"

Kristen hands me a card. I open it and stare at the words, in Alan's handwriting: *How does this look for a honeymoon?* Inside the card are two plane tickets to Bali for December 25.

Even with all the alcohol on board, my hands start shaking.

"I'll get you another glass," Kristen says. She's back in a minute with refills for both of us.

I open the rest of the gifts on autopilot, making what I hope are appropriate noises of thanks and appreciation, but barely registering the contents.

"Last one," Mom says, and I jolt to something almost adjacent to sober as she finally drops the balloon man's gift into my lap.

I'm no longer sure that I want to open it, at least not in front of a crowd of bystanders. *It can't possibly be from Nomi,* I remind myself. It has to be a gag gift. Except that the balloon man and his formalities and the way he presented it to me were all very convincing.

"Come on, Blythe, we're all curious," Aunt Bella calls out. I narrow my eyes at her in sudden suspicion.

She and Nomi shared a taste for whimsy and woo-woo, along with an offbeat and sometimes twisted sense of humor. Arranging a singing telegram from beyond the grave is exactly the sort of prank she might pull. If so, it's not her fault that the balloon man arrived in the middle of Alan's carefully planned grand romantic proposal, and if opening the gift will make her happy, well, somebody deserves to enjoy this day.

Holding my breath, I tear off the paper, revealing a plain white cardboard box that offers no clue to either its contents or who it's from. Kristen impatiently lifts the lid, and when I sit staring, frozen into immobility once again, she hands the contents to me, one object at a time. First, what looks to me like a cookie jar made of polished black stoneware with an iridescent finish and a varnished wooden lid. A raven is carved into the wood. Also, the jar is obviously full of something heavier than cookies. Finally my eyes find the brass plaque engraved with the words *Naomi Katerina Balfour, 1948–1999.*

"Dear God," Mom says, in a tone of total shock. But nothing ever rattles her for long, not even the unexpected sight of her mother's cremation ashes, and she turns on Aunt Bella. "What kind of sick joke is this? We scattered Mom's ashes the week after she died."

Aunt Bella shakes her head. "Don't look at me like that! Her attorney picked up her ashes and brought them to me. Talk to him about it."

"There's a letter," Kristen says helpfully. "And some sort of drawing."

I set the urn reverently on the ground beside my chair, just in case it really does contain Nomi's ashes and not the contents of some trickster's fireplace. Kristen hands me a yellowing piece of paper, a letter. I squint to decipher an uneven cursive, faded with time.

Dearest Blybee . . .

Tears well up at the old pet name, a muddling of Blythe and my middle name, Beatrice. Nomi is the only person in the whole wide world who has ever called me that. Kristen, ever prepared, hands me a tissue and I wipe my eyes.

"Sorry," I apologize, and read aloud for everybody to hear:

> *Dearest Blybee,*
>
> *Here you are, safely arrived at thirty, and finding out, I suspect, that it's not such an old age to be after all. I do hope Ted got everything right for you. He's a good sort, but he is a lawyer and they can be such stuffy old bores about legal things, don't you think? Did he remember the balloons? Did he sing "Over the Rainbow"? He should have gone into music instead of law with a voice like that; he'd have been a much happier man.*
>
> *How is your mother? Having a little fit right now, isn't she? If she's reading over your shoulder, tell her to take a breath and lighten up. She never could take a good joke.*

Mom makes an odd little bleating sound. I glance up from my letter in time to see her face crumple before she turns to hide it in Dad's shoulder. He puts his arm around her and strokes her back. Shocked at this unprecedented public display of emotion from a woman who rarely cries, and certainly never in public, I hesitate, not sure if I should go on reading out loud.

"Might as well finish it," Dad says.

I clear my throat and continue.

> *Tell her not to fret about the ashes. These are the real ones. If you all scattered what Ted gave you in that nice big field like I requested, there are happy dog spirits playing there now. You'll be wanting to know the why of this, and here it is.*

Blythe, darling, I want you to take my real ashes and bury them at the place indicated on the map that accompanies this letter. There's some money set aside for your travel, and another item or two that I asked Ted to keep in trust for you. He also has official documents in his possession and will give you access to your money. Go see him. His card is attached.

My love to Lyndsey and Kristen and your father, and anybody else from my family if they're still alive and hanging around.

Love, Nomi

A shocked silence follows while Kristen produces a sheet of paper from the bottom of the box.

"This can't be right," she says, "but there's nothing else."

"Let me see."

And then, as I look at the paper she places in my hands, I'm sucked back into an undertow of memory so vivid it takes my breath away.

Chapter Three

BLYTHE

Nomi has moved from her apartment into our spare room and spends most of her time in bed. It's a fun bed to play with, because it has buttons that make it go up and down, only Nomi hurts too much to want to play that game for very long. There's also not very much room for me, even though she's bent up her knees, because the bed also bends in the middle so her head can be up, and that makes her slide down toward the foot.

I miss the big bed at her house, the one with lots of room for both of us, and the puffy duvet that feels like floating on a cloud. And I miss the old Nomi, having her all to myself without Kristen or Mom or a nurse popping in all the time. But Nomi has something called cancer, something awful enough that it makes Mom cry when she thinks nobody is looking.

So now Nomi lives with us, but she's extra tired, because of being sick, and she sleeps a lot, and some days she says things just hurt too much for her to play a game, even let's pretend, and she'd rather watch TV or maybe have me read to her. And now it's fall, so I have school again, so we hardly ever get to spend time together.

But today Nomi is having a good day. She's been teaching me card games, and I've just won Crazy Eights and I want to play again. But Nomi sets the cards in a neat stack on the wheeled table that can swing over the bed, and says, "We never drew a treasure map so you'll know where to find your island."

"But I don't need a map," I protest. "The crystal ball knows where I'm going. And you're coming with me."

"I think maybe you'll need to go alone, when the time comes." She smiles, but I can see that it's the way I smile when I've skinned my knee and I'm trying not to cry. Her eyes are all shiny, like maybe she has tears that want to come out, but she's holding on to them, hard.

And now I have tears that want to come out, too, and I squeeze them back. "But I don't want to go alone!"

"Well," she says. "Thirty is a long time away, isn't it? Years and years. You'll be all grown up and going somewhere alone won't be so scary. Besides, it will be fun to make a map, won't it?"

I want to make the map at Nomi's house. I want her to be dressed up in her fortune-teller clothes, the turban and the earrings and the bracelets on her wrists. She's wearing a boring nightgown, and her head is bald and she's not wearing any makeup or jewelry. I don't believe in the island anymore, not when Nomi just looks like a tired old lady.

"We're extra-good pretenders, you and me," she says, as if she understands what I'm thinking. "Get some paper and crayons."

So I fetch some paper and my crayons and climb back up onto the bed. I put the paper down on the table and dump out all the crayons in a rainbow of color. They smell warm and happy, almost drowning out my sadness and the sharp smell of sickness.

I take a minute to sort out my colors. Blue for the ocean, brown and green for the island. I pick up the brown crayon to start the island, but then I put it down again. My teacher told me last week that I need to let things be their real colors, which means the colors that she thinks they should be. And then she showed me how I could start making things look more like their real selves when I draw them, and I noticed that my pictures don't really look like our real house, or real people, which I guess I knew before but didn't know it mattered.

There's a twisty feeling in my tummy. "I don't know how to draw a treasure map."

"Of course you do," Nomi says. "Start with the island. What shape do you think an island is?"

"My teacher says—"

"Has your teacher ever seen this island? I don't think so. It's whatever shape you want it to be."

And so I draw a shape on the page. It looks kind of like an egg, and Nomi says that is perfect. I use the brown crayon for the outline, because of dirt and rocks, but then I color it in green, because trees and grass. It wants more colors, so I put some flowers on it. I make blue water all around, filling the paper all the way to the edges.

"That's lovely," Nomi says. "Only I think there ought to be a tree—a really big tree that marks the place where the treasure is buried. Now, where do you think the tree will be?"

Before I can get sad again—because how do I know where to put the tree without the magic ball to show me?—she says, "Here's another way to do magic. Close your eyes."

I squinch my eyes up tight, blocking out the room with its up-and-down bed, and the tiredness of Nomi's face and the nakedness of her scalp. I feel her fingers tucking a crayon into my hand.

"Remember pin the tail on the donkey?" she asks, and I do, because we played that game once with little Kristen, only we used tape and not pins so nobody would get hurt. The donkey looked silly with a tail on its head and one sticking up from the middle of its back and we'd all laughed.

"Eyes closed, just pick a spot on the paper and make an X," Nomi says.

"What if it's in the water?"

"Then that's where the treasure is. Treasure is in water lots of times."

"Mermaids!" I say.

"Yes. Or sunken ships. Wherever the crayon lands, that's the perfect spot."

"What if I miss the paper?" I laugh, though, thinking about the third donkey tail that ended up nowhere near the donkey.

"I'll hold the paper," Nomi says. "And if you're going to miss I'll move it. That way we're both doing the magic. Okay?"

So Nomi puts her two hands on the edges of the paper, and I close my eyes and bring down the crayon and carefully make a big X. When I open my eyes, the X is right near the water on the skinny end of the island.

"Draw the tree," Nomi says, and I do, giving it lots of branches. And then, because a tree like that should have a house, I draw one in beside it.

"One more thing," Nomi says. "You need to know how to find the island. On a map, there's something called latitude and longitude, and they are magic words that go together with numbers to say exactly where to find something."

I love the sound of the words, but I know I can never spell them.

"You write them," I say.

"They are kind of big words for crayon, how about if I use a pen? Can you find me one?"

I get the pen from the nurse's clipboard and she turns the paper over and prints the big words in careful capital letters on the back.

"Now we need the numbers," she says. "Hand me the cards. We'll choose our numbers from the deck."

She shuffles, then hands the cards back to me and says, "Deal out six, all in a row. That will be our first number."

I lay the cards out in a careful row, and then I turn them over, one at a time, and Nomi writes them down on the paper next to the word that she says is latitude. Then we do it again for longitude.

"Perfect," Nomi says, lying back against the pillow. "There you have a treasure map. Would you mind leaving it here for me to look at, since you won't be needing it for a while? We could tape it up on the wall."

Even though I want to take it with me, to help me daydream about pirates and mermaids and what the treasure will look like, I will do anything to make Nomi happy. And, even though Mom got mad when I taped pictures on my own wall, and said I was going to hurt the paint, I run for the tape and stick the picture up on the wall beside Nomi's bed.

"That's perfect," she says, but her eyes are closed now and she's not even looking at it. "Why don't you read me a story?"

"Blythe?" Kristen's voice queries, and I'm not sitting by Nomi's bed, I'm in my parents' backyard, with a whole crowd of people staring at me.

I touch one finger to the map, clear my throat, and say, "Nomi and I drew this map together. I'd forgotten all about it. I can't imagine how the balloon man came to have it."

"Is this really a place?" Kristen asks.

I laugh, drunk, overwrought, and close to the edge of hysteria. "Oh my God. Not even close."

Mom straightens up and steps away from Dad, smoothing her hair. "Surely you are *not* taking this seriously, Blythe. You can't take her ashes to a place that doesn't even exist."

"There's a business card," I murmur, turning the thick, creamy card stock over and over in my fingers. "Like she says in the letter. Theodore Wilcox, attorney at law. He must be the Ted she's talking about."

"A fake lawyer!" Mom says decisively. "A prank. Like those ashes."

"Well, it wouldn't hurt to make a call. Just to be sure."

"My opinion doesn't matter, of course," Mom begins, and then she remembers the guests, who are all still staring, rapt with attention, as if we're performing a stage play for their enjoyment.

Kristen rises to the occasion, lifting her champagne glass and addressing everyone in a carrying voice. "To my sister, Blythe—may the rest of her life continue to be full of unexpected twists and surprises!"

The tension breaks, with a round of clapping and cheering.

"There's still plenty of food, and champagne," Kristen continues when the applause dies away. "Eat! Drink!" The musicians start playing something lively, and people drift away in little clumps, talking animatedly among themselves. I fold the map and the letter and tuck them into my purse for safekeeping, along with the business card, and the secret that I've kept to myself, the postscript at the end of Nomi's letter:

PS: I'm counting on you. You promised.

~

Hours later, I've far exceeded both my drinking limit and my tolerance for stress. My head feels light and buzzy and is beginning to ache. I'm just sober enough to realize that tomorrow is going to be hell, and the thought of Alan is like a heavy rock dropping into a very deep well, which happens to be situated in my belly. Going home to him is incomprehensible. Staying here so Mom can lecture me is just as bad.

"Come home with me," Kristen says, holding my hand in the way that only happens when our inhibitions have been drowned in alcohol. "I'm Ubering. You can sleep on my couch." I feel close to her in this moment, like we're allies and friends. But experience has taught me that our emotional connection will follow the curve of our blood alcohol levels, and if I go with her, we will awake to mutual hangovers and get into a fight.

I've already got a lifetime of making up to Alan to contend with, and the last thing I need is to be at odds with Kristen.

"I'll just sleep here."

"Oh, honey, the bed isn't made up," Mom says.

The pain in my head begins to pulse behind my eyeballs. I wonder if maybe there's a little more champagne left somewhere, to help delay the inevitable reckoning, but the caterer has already very efficiently cleaned up and the tables are bare.

"I'll sleep on the couch. All I need is a blanket and a pillow."

"Nobody is sleeping on my couch like a vagabond," Mom says. "You need to go home."

My mother loves me. I know that she'd make the bed up for me in a minute if I really needed a place to stay. She wants to make me go to Alan, to apologize, to get back on track with the life that she has planned for me.

"How about I make the bed," Dad says. He puts his arm around my shoulders, warm and comforting. "Come on, little Bee. You've had a big day." He guides my unsteady feet away from Mom and Kristen, and I lean against him as if I'm a child, letting him support me up the stairs, Nomi's ashes clutched against my chest.

When we get to the bedroom, I stop at the doorway, not wanting to go inside. Even though it's been repainted and has new curtains and the hospital bed is long gone, I can still see Nomi lying there, cold and dead and not Nomi anymore.

"Go wash your face," Daddy says, very gently. He kisses my forehead. "I'll make the bed. Here, give me those."

I surrender the ashes and stumble into the bathroom. Washing my face feels like a difficult task, but Mom will definitely not appreciate makeup all over her clean pillowcase, so I make myself do it. There's ibuprofen in my purse and I swallow some with a glass of water, hoping it will help take the edge off the coming hangover.

When I go back to the room, the linens on the bed are turned back. The overhead lights are off, and the bedside lamp glows softly. Nomi's urn sits on the dresser. Daddy is waiting for me. He puts his arms around me, tucking my head under his chin.

"You're a lot like your Nomi," he says. "The two of you were peas in a pod, always making magic out of the ordinary."

"I think I've forgotten how," I whisper into his chest.

He laughs and drops a kiss on the top of my head. "I suspect it's like riding a bicycle. Get some sleep. Your adventure will wait until tomorrow."

"But Mom," I say. "And Alan. And the new job. And—"

Dad puts his hands on my shoulders and steps back so he can look into my face. "What was that nickname Nomi had for you?"

"Blybee," I murmur, smiling at the memory despite my pounding head and my guilt and confusion and worry.

"Brave Blybee," he says, with mock seriousness. "Rest now. Tomorrow you shall pursue this new quest."

I hug him, hard. "I love you, Daddy."

"I love you too, little Bee. Always and forever. Go to sleep. Your path will be clearer in the morning."

Chapter Four

Blythe

Despite my father's pep talk, when I wake I am as far from Blybee the brave adventurer as a human could possibly be.

The light filtering in through the blinds is intrusive and far too bright. My mouth tastes awful and my stomach is wobbly. I picture my brain swelling against my skull in protest over all the cells I killed with alcohol last night, my IQ dropping by the minute.

Lying flat on my back, knowing that sitting up is going to make everything even worse, I fumble blindly on the bedside table for my phone and squint at it to read the time. Nine a.m., which means Mom will be up shortly with a lecture about facing up to the consequences of my actions.

Worse, I have a series of text messages from Alan, which apparently began last night after the party.

Alan: Where are you? Are you coming home?

Alan: Couldn't be bothered to let me know your plans? Guess I know where I stand.

Alan: I'm WORRIED. Your parents aren't answering,
either. Do I need to call hospitals?

Oh dear God. I close my eyes and will myself to sink back into
unconsciousness, but my bladder has gotten in on the morning's misery agenda and there will be no going back to sleep. After I visit the
bathroom, splash water on my face, persuade my stomach to look at
ibuprofen and a glass of water as a gift rather than a full-on assault, I
flop back down onto the bed, the wreckage of my decisions and failures
tumbling in and out of my poor, swollen brain.

Nomi's ashes are sitting on the spare-room dresser and I'm supposed
to bury them on an imaginary island. I have a new job that I am not
qualified for and do not want. I'll be a goodwill employee. Everybody
else who works there will know it and hate me for it. As for Alan . . .

Mad and hurt as I am that he got me into that mess, what I did to
him last night was worse. If I had any guts at all, I would have told him
how I feel right after Kristen confided that he was looking for a ring.
Instead, I'd buried my head in the sand and pretended that everything
was fine and we could just carry on as we were indefinitely. I never even
dreamed that he'd propose in front of an audience.

God, what a mess. I'm too hungover to talk to him now, but the
least I can do is send him a message. Something eloquent and apolo-
getic, words that will not only convey how deeply sorry I am but also
soothe his wounded pride and comfort his hurt. I have no such words.
The best I can come up with is:

So so so sorry. Not enough words to apologize. Only excuse, I
was pretty buzzed and crashed. Not in my car. Into Mom's spare
room bed.

I add a couple of crying face emojis and hope it will be enough.
Of course, it's not. He sends back:

KRISTEN let me know you were safe.

Of course she did. My wonderful little sister, so considerate, so, so, so . . . perfect. It's a very good thing I didn't go home with her last night. I wonder if she's been back here yet to get her car, whether she's downstairs right now with Mom, both of them waiting for me so we can all discuss my shortcomings over coffee and breakfast.

As if I've summoned her, the phone starts playing "True Colors," which is Kristen's ringtone. I decline the call. And then I turn the phone off, because if she's called once she'll keep calling until I answer.

"What am I gonna do, Nomi?" I ask the urn on the dresser. Not surprisingly, she doesn't answer. With a groan, I lever myself upright in the bed, my head now pounding with a vengeance, and grab my purse up off the floor, fumbling around in its depths for the map and the letter and the business card.

But my hands are unsteady and my eyes are still blurry and I finally dump the entire contents out onto the bed. A mini roller for pet hair, a can of kitten formula, coffee shop receipts, dog treats, rental property keys, a rose quartz crystal, a baggie of sage that I like to burn in empty houses to cleanse the energy of previous owners or unpleasant prospective buyers.

Sorting out the items I want, I scooch back and lean against my pillow while I have a better look. The map has cracked along the lines where I folded it last night. I hold it carefully, squinting my eyes so that the house and the tree and the big red X are blurry, as if maybe some secret message will reveal itself. Nothing. I read the letter again, listening for Nomi's voice in the words, lingering over that postscript and the promises she extracted from me before she died.

Finally, I examine the business card. It is substantial, elegant, textured like linen. The words THEODORE WILCOX, ATTORNEY AT LAW are embossed in ornate gold letters. If this is a prank, somebody spent good money on it. Grabbing my phone, I search the name, and it pops

up immediately under an ad that reads: **ARDEN & WILCOX LAW FIRM,
SERVING SPOKANE FOR THIRTY-FIVE YEARS.**

"Very tricky," I say out loud to Nomi's ashes. "You outdid yourself
with this one. But we both know the island and the map aren't real."

My hand goes to the pendant I didn't take off last night before
falling into bed, fingers stroking the smooth obsidian that is the raven,
running over the branches of the silver tree, summoning up memories
of all the make-believe games Nomi and I played together. Fortune-
tellers. Treasure hunts. Fairy-tale quests. This is just an unusually elaborate game of make-believe.

And I'm completely willing to play along and find out where it
will take me.

Even though it's Saturday and no bona fide attorney is going to be
in the office, I dial the number on the card, figuring I'll leave a message.
When a man's voice comes on, right away, saying, "Arden and Wilcox,
Ted Wilcox speaking," I choke on a mouthful of my own saliva and can't
talk for a minute, caught up in a fit of coughing.

"Sorry," I manage to wheeze. "This is Blythe Harmon? I have a
card with—"

"Blythe. Could you come in this afternoon?"

"So soon?"

"Would you rather wait? Another twenty years, perhaps?"

"No, today is fine. I'm just surprised. It's Saturday. Isn't it? Please
tell me it's Saturday." A fear strikes me that I'm caught up in some weird
fairy tale and I've slept far longer than one night. No wonder Alan is so
upset. No wonder . . .

"I've been holding on to this bequest for well-nigh twenty-four
years," the voice on the phone says. "That's why you have my personal
cell number. I can work on a Saturday. Two o'clock?"

"Okay. Yes. Two o'clock."

"You have the address?"

"It's on the card, right?"

"It's on the card."

He hangs up. I let my gaze travel from the phone, to the business card, to the map, to the letter. I glance up at myself in the mirror, and there I am. Still me. Pale and disheveled, wearing my father's "Best Dad Ever" T-shirt, my red hair spiraling in wild curls, mascara circles under my eyes.

There's a firm tap at the door, followed by my mother's voice. "Blythe? Are you planning to get up sometime today?"

"Go away, I'm sleeping," I answer, deliberately muffling my words into my arm.

"You are not. I heard you talking on the phone just now."

"Well, why did you ask then?" I hurl back, wincing as the volume of my own raised voice slices through my pounding head.

The knob turns and the door opens. Half past nine on a Saturday, and Mom could glide into a high-level business meeting without so much as a touch-up. I watch her take in the sight of me, her scapegrace daughter, who could fit right in under the overpass, asking for handouts. Her gaze travels over the map and the letter and the contents of my purse.

Her eyebrows rise, her lips press together, and I brace myself for the lecture about what a mess I am, and how if I would drink moderately I wouldn't suffer a hangover, and more importantly, about how I don't deserve Alan and what was I thinking to treat him that way?

But she doesn't say anything. She taps across the room in the heels she always wears—even at home, even on a Saturday—coming to rest in front of Nomi's ashes. The fingers of both hands settle lightly on the urn, and she just stands there, head bowed, breathing like maybe she's crying.

"Mom?" I clear a path through the junk on the bed and get my feet on the floor, thinking maybe I'll go to her and . . . what? Put my arms around her? Offer comforting words? We're not like that, Mom and me. I stay where I am, squinting against the intrusive light. Mom turns to me and I'm glad I didn't follow my impulse. Her face is calm, her eyes dry. She's still my self-contained, practical mother.

"You can't take this seriously, Blythe," she says. "I'm sure Mother meant well, but she was very ill when she wrote that letter. Confused. Maybe delirious."

"The attorney seems to be legit," I say carefully. "I Googled the law firm. Maybe I should see what he has to say."

She thinks about this for a minute, then nods. "I guess it makes sense to talk to him. Maybe I should go with you."

It's the sort of offer I can't refuse. She is, after all, Nomi's only child. Which means, if any of this is real and not an elaborate and twisted joke, Nomi should have given *her* the ashes and the special bequest. I remember the unexpected sight of Mom sobbing into Daddy's shoulder and think maybe she's feeling hurt and left out.

"Give me the card. I'll call and make an appointment on Monday," she says in her well-that's-settled voice.

I open my mouth to tell her that I already called, that I'm going this afternoon, but something inside me rises up in rebellion. This is my treasure hunt. My last gift from Nomi. If I let Mom come with me, she'll organize all of the mystery and magic right out of it.

The old familiar sensation of panic, a bird beating its wings against a cage, starts to rise in me, and then I hear myself saying, "Okay. That will be great, you calling on Monday."

My unplanned evasion startles me right out of my panic as I ask myself the question: *Did I just lie to my mother?*

She holds out her hand. "Where's the business card?"

I shrug. "Somewhere in this mess. I spilled my purse."

"I see that. Well. Clean it up and come get some breakfast. Kristen's here."

She walks out, closing the door behind her, and I start cramming things back into my purse, half in a daze.

"Please," I whisper to Nomi's ashes as I set the map and the letter on the dresser beside them. "Please let this be real."

Chapter Five

BLYTHE

My first thought as I park in a small lot in front of Arden & Wilcox, Attorneys at Law, is that Mom would approve. Everything about the business speaks of money. There's a tasteful and elegant sign on the window that lets you know you're in the right place but doesn't scream at you to bring in your sordid ambulance-chaser lawsuit. The flower beds are well tended, the Japanese maples are artfully pruned. A pleasantly musical chime announces my arrival into a waiting room that is worthy of a photo shoot for a glossy magazine.

Even the air smells good, infused with a soothing fragrance that invites me to take a deep breath and sink into one of the cushy leather chairs. Before I can sit, though, I hear a door open and an elderly man appears in the hallway.

"Blythe," he says. "Thanks for coming in."

I stare at him. He stares back.

"But you're the balloon man," I blurt out. "I was looking for Mr. Wilcox."

"Ted Wilcox at your service," he says, as if there's nothing unusual about a lawyer delivering a singing telegram. "Come on back to my office."

"I have so many questions," I say, following him down a dark paneled hallway hung with framed oil paintings, our footsteps muted in thick carpet. His office is more of the same—thick carpet, a heavy wooden desk, the same boring but probably expensive paintings, a bookcase filled with heavy tomes that make my eyes tired just looking at them—all the things that justify the comment in Nomi's letter about attorneys being stuffy.

But there is one feature that utterly redeems him. A different sort of painting, large enough to commandeer a whole wall. The subject is water and sky and a single tree, but it's really all about light. There's the clear, brilliant, unfettered light in the sky, and then the limpid reflection of light from the water and the green, muted light filtering through leaves. I'm drawn to the painting so strongly I want to step into it, like it's a door to some other world.

"Beautiful, isn't it?" Mr. Wilcox asks in a hushed voice, coming to stand beside me.

"Who is the artist?"

"An unknown. This is his masterpiece. The others are interesting, but they lack . . ." He waves his hands expressively. "Whatever this is. Well. We have things to discuss. Have a seat."

I sink into the buttery softness of a leather chair facing his desk, while he takes a seat behind it, adjusts his glasses, and peers at me as if he's trying to read a story in my face.

"You are very like her, you know," he says. "It's remarkable, really. But I'm sure you've heard that before." He clears his throat. "So, to business. First, let's talk about money. There is a trust fund in your name that is now worth approximately five hundred thousand dollars."

I blink. Close my mouth, which has fallen open. "Pardon me? I don't think I heard you correctly."

"Five hundred thousand," he repeats, enunciating carefully.

Right. Sure. The faint buzz of anticipation I walked in with dissipates in a cloud of disillusionment. "Very funny," I say. "Absolutely hilarious. Did she put you up to this?"

His face is calm and serious. "This is not a prank," he says. "Here. Look at the paperwork."

He slides a thin stack of papers over to me. The top sheet bears what looks like an official header for Chase. Skimming the document, I see the words *in trust for Blythe Harmon* and an account balance of $522,000.67. It certainly looks real. But it can't be.

"You're telling me that I now own half a million dollars?" I ask, my voice thick with skepticism.

Mr. Wilcox shakes his head. "Not exactly."

"See! I knew it." I start to get up out of my chair. "I'm done playing whatever game this is."

"It's not a game," he says. "You don't own it *yet*. There is a condition to the trust."

I sink back down and stare at him across the desk. "Of course there is. Don't tell me. I must marry a beast, move into his enchanted castle, discover his secret, and kiss him with a true love's kiss."

"Nothing quite so exotic," he says. "Although I'll admit that it is, shall we say, unorthodox. There is, by the way, another trust for your sister, which she can access when she turns thirty. Both were funded with your grandmother's life insurance policy and have grown very nicely under my care, I must say."

"Does Kristen also have to complete a quest to get her money?" I ask.

"Your sister's only quest will be to come down here and sign the relevant papers. But we are talking about you. All of the money will be transferred into an account in your name as soon as Naomi's ashes have been laid to rest in the place marked by the X on the treasure map."

"The map you gave me yesterday."

"Yes."

I draw a breath. My head aches. I feel a little dizzy. Digging my fingers into the pressure point at the base of my skull, I say, very patiently and a little cautiously, because I know that delusional people can become violent when challenged, "There's a problem with that, Mr. Wilcox. The island on that map does not actually exist."

"Tell that to the people who live there," he says.

Definitely delusional. Which means, despite the official-appearing letterhead, the money is as imaginary as the island. I dig in my purse for the evidence of reality, unfolding the map and laying it out on the desk between us. "I drew this," I tell him, tapping my finger on the tree. "I closed my eyes and scrawled an X. And you know where these coordinates came from?" I turn the paper over and tap my finger on the latitude and longitude. "Cards. I drew cards off of a deck and Nomi wrote down the numbers."

"And yet," he says. "Here. I'll show you." He turns his computer screen to face me and slides the wireless mouse and keyboard across the desk. "Pull up Google and search the coordinates."

Humoring the lunatic, I do as he says. To my absolute shock, Google obligingly brings up a series of results, all for a place called Vinland Island. I click on the Wikipedia link and discover two entries: one detailing a region referenced in Viking literature, another a modern-day island. I focus on the second and discover the following facts:

Vinland is a small island in San Juan County, Washington, located in the San Juan Islands. The population was 119 at the 2010 census. Previously known as Calvert Island, in 2004 its name was changed to Vinland, namesake to an elusive land mentioned in Viking historical records. The island's name was changed as part of a civic initiative to convert the entire island into an exclusive tourist destination. Its best-known feature is an annual summer treasure hunt, which brings in visitors from around the world.

Vinland is not serviced by the San Juan ferry system and can only be reached by water taxi, private boat, or plane. Only residents and registered guests are permitted on Vinland.

"All very interesting, but it's not *our* island," I say, clinging to my disbelief. "It's not the island on my map."

"It is the island that matches the coordinates, and therefore the island where you will take your grandmother's ashes."

"So I go to this Vinland Island. And I bury Nomi's ashes. And I get half a million dollars," I say, dripping sarcasm for the benefit of the camera that must be recording this interaction somewhere.

He clears his throat. "Well, yes. However, there is one more . . . condition." His eyes shift away from mine and he adjusts a stack of papers on the desk in front of him.

"Well?" I ask, after a long and awkward silence. "Are you going to tell me what the condition is?"

"It's a little more involved than just finding the island," he says. "You'll locate the tree—"

"The tree that I drew by the X that I marked with my eyes closed, in a featureless child drawing of a map? That tree?"

He looks pained. "That's the one."

"And I'll know that I've actually located it how?"

"Something is buried beside it. You'll need to find it. She wants her ashes buried in that exact location, with whatever it is that you find there."

"What is it?"

"I'm not at liberty to say."

"You can't really expect me to act on this," I protest. "It's all so . . . far-fetched."

"Think of it as a vacation," Mr. Wilcox suggests. "Take the summer to explore the island. You'll need somewhere to stay."

He slides another sheet of paper across the desk, this one a computer printout of a Google ad for Frieda's Treasures Vacation Rentals: LIVE YOUR ULTIMATE ADVENTURE. HUNT FOR BURIED TREASURE ON THIS EXCLUSIVE ISLAND PARADISE. EXPLORE OUR PRISTINE BEACHES AND MYSTERIOUS SEA CAVES. CONTACT FRIEDA JOHANSEN FOR MORE INFORMATION.

"I can't just take a whole summer off!" I object. "I'm supposed to start a new job this week. I'm supposed to get married."

"Well, the choice is yours, of course," he says. "If you want those things—the job, the marriage—you do not have to go. Perhaps you are less like her than I thought you were."

"What is that supposed to mean?"

He ignores my question. "Whether you accept the quest or not, she also left you this." Bending down, he lifts a large box from behind his desk and sets it in front of me. My fingers trembling with a mixture of excitement and trepidation, I open the box.

My hand flies to the base of my throat, where my heart seems to have relocated in an anatomically impossible shift, the other hand covering my mouth so it can't fly right out of my body and escape.

There, nestled in a bed of cotton wool, is Nomi's snow globe.

"It's a beautiful item," Ted says. "Unusual. Possibly worth money to a collector, if you don't wish to keep it."

Breath held, I reach in to lift the globe and set it on the desk. It's big, maybe even a foot in diameter, and the glass is perfect—no waviness, no flaws, no seams. Unlike every other snow globe I've ever seen, there are no miniature figures or buildings inside it, only a layer of pure white snow. It sits on a frame made up of four silver feet, heavily tarnished by time and neglect.

Reverently, I let my fingers rest on the glass, cold to my touch, even though the office is warm, as if the snow is real and affects the temperature. I close my eyes and see Nomi, the purple scarf wrapped around her head, the gold rings in her ears, pretending to tell my fortune. Tears prickle against my closed lids, squeeze out, and trail down my cheeks.

Mr. Wilcox clears his throat. "I see it holds memories for you."

Maybe it's the tears, but when I open my eyes, the room looks different. The large painting of the tree is suffused with rainbow colors and the entire room seems filled with light. Nomi looked into this very snow globe and told me that I would go off to search for treasure on an island when I was thirty, and now here I am, about to do exactly that.

Chapter Six

FLYNN

I'm in the water, deep enough to feel the pressure of it on my eardrums, my body. The hiss of my oxygen tank is regular and comforting, and I move easily through the depths. But it's too dark. For some reason I haven't brought a light. Savannah swims beside me, and she's forgotten her oxygen tank and wet suit. When we get back to the surface, we'll need to talk about that. The hulk of a wrecked ship emerges through the dimness ahead, a gaping and jagged hole in its side.

Even though it's dark, I catch the glimmer of a sinuous body swimming in slow circles, just inside that gap, and try to call out to Savannah to warn her. Shark! But I can't make any sound and she swims away from me, directly toward sure and certain disaster. I try again, yanking the respirator out of my mouth, screaming now, but no sound comes out. I flail after her, the water slowing me down, holding me back, and then my eyes fly open and there's a ceiling above me.

I'm lying in bed, gasping for breath. There is no ocean, no sunken ship, no sharks. But the pounding of my heart, my fear that I've taken Savannah to her death, does not abate. Bright light floods into my room, but it was after two when I fell into bed last night. Even though I didn't have a single drink, I feel hungover. I check the time—nearly nine already, and there's so much to do today. I'm behind before I even begin.

Groaning, I drag myself out of bed, pull on a pair of jeans and a T-shirt, while flashes from last night's fiasco with Savannah come back to haunt me.

It started with a reasonable request, or at least one that I thought was reasonable. On Giselle's advice, I even fed Savannah pizza and ice cream before making it. She didn't say one word to me during the whole meal, her entire attention fixated on some novel she was reading. When I finished my own ice cream, hers was half-melted in her bowl.

I cleared my throat, leaned back in my chair, and said, "Could we talk for a minute?"

"Talk if you want, I'm listening." She turned a page.

"I need you to start telling me when you leave the house and where you are going. I'm not good with you running off whenever and wherever you feel like."

She went stiff. Her eyes stopped moving, but she still kept them on the book. "Mom let me."

"Savannah. Please. I know I'm not your mother, but I'm doing the best I can."

She did look up then, fixing me with the sort of glare only a teenage girl is capable of. "Who's Mike?" she asked, a question not even remotely related to the topic.

"Just a guy I know. Why?" But I felt the adrenaline spike, a sensation as if I was free-falling, and even before she told me, I knew how badly I'd fucked up.

"I heard you on the phone last night," she said. "He's some expedition guy, and you told him you couldn't go because you were stuck here with me."

"Savannah—"

"You should just go on your stupid expedition. I don't need you. I could stay with anybody. Giselle or Glory or even Old Nick would be better than you." Her voice betrayed her, cracking on the last word. She shoved back her chair, snatched up the book, and stomped out of the room, but not before I saw her face crumple and the tears start to flow. Total massive fail.

I can't imagine anything I can do that would be worse than letting her hear me say how much I don't want to be here on Vinland, that I feel trapped and suffocated and maybe even resentful about missing out on the expedition of a lifetime. What she didn't hear and what I don't know how to tell her is that I would do anything for her, give up anything for her, even tolerate this accursed island for her. Not only do I not know how to say it, I've done a shitty job of showing it.

Both Giselle and Glory have reminded me, one gently and with tact, the other bluntly and without, that Savannah is a gifted child, well beyond the meaning of the word *precocious*, that her tongue is every bit as sharp as her intellect, and that I'm the logical target for an anger born of a grief she doesn't know how to cope with. And still, I've allowed myself to be provoked into one battle after another.

I need to talk to her and try to explain. Now. Before breakfast, before I get sucked into the chaos of a day on Vinland during treasure-hunting season. It's Sunday, but that does not mean a day off. Summoning all my courage, I walk down the hallway to her room, running lines through my head of what I might say, and promising myself that if I have to, if it will help, I'll tell her something about my own childhood and why I was so desperate to get away.

But Savannah isn't in her room. Her door is open, as is the window. A cold, damp wind blows in, straight off the sound. Norman, the raven she's raised from a baby, stares at me balefully from his perch, making it clear that he doesn't approve of me any more than his mistress does.

"Shoo," I say, waving my arms at him. He croaks something I'm pretty sure is a curse, spreads his wings, and launches himself out into the morning. I close the window, shivering, wondering whether Savannah even slept here last night. The bed is made. Despite the various furred and feathered creatures that reside here with her, her room is the one place in the house that is consistently clean. I check their cages out of habit. The rescued mice are busily chewing up a toilet paper roll. The injured bunny is curled into its nest, asleep. The baby squirrel chitters at me, twitching his tail. All of them have food and water.

Damn it. This is the exact behavior I was trying to talk to her about. It's been going on for months. She'll be gone in the morning when I wake up. She'll come back to the house late at night. And she'll never tell me where she's been or what she's been doing. Sure, the island is relatively safe. No islander would hurt her, and all the guests are carefully screened, but there are other dangers. Trees to fall out of. Cliffs to fall off of. Cold, deep water to fall into.

Worry swells into irritation and drowns my remorse. I stumble blearily down the stairs, squinting against the bright light in the kitchen. Dirty dishes are still on the table where I left them, Savannah's ice cream a scummy puddle of goo.

"Savannah?"

No answer. I can feel the emptiness of the house, but I still walk through the rooms looking for her. It wouldn't be the first time she spent the night on the couch. But she's nowhere to be seen. I open the door and step out onto the back porch. Sure enough, her bike is gone.

I go back in the house and call her on the radio.

"Savannah. Report in."

My own voice echoes back at me from another radio docked in the charging station on the kitchen counter, the radio she's supposed to carry with her whenever she goes out. Damn it all to hell and back again. How on earth did Frieda do this? Manage a child—this child—while running a business, cleaning and cooking and paying bills and whatever else it takes to keep a household functioning?

As far as I know, Savannah's father has never been in the picture. Twelve years ago, I received a birth announcement at my PO box, a necessity given my nomadic lifestyle, along with a short note from

Frieda saying that she missed me, but telling me nothing about where or with whom Savannah was conceived.

Neither one of us were much for romantic commitments, but Frieda at least nailed the responsibility thing, taking over the family business, looking after our needy and fragile mother, and raising Savannah while I roamed around the world, following my every whim. I've lived in small apartments between expeditions, no pets or even plants to hold me down, with as few adult responsibilities to my name as I can manage. I've cobbled together a career around my twin passions for scuba diving and treasure hunting. I've taught scuba-diving classes. I've helped out the police when they've needed eyes on the bottom of a body of water. I've been on the underwater end of gold mining in the Bering Sea. And once or twice, when I was really lucky, I got in on a real treasure-hunting expedition involving sunken ships.

Six months ago, when I got the news that Frieda was dead and Savannah orphaned, I returned to the island I swore I'd never set foot on again, and tried to step into my sister's shoes. I've fallen short, repeatedly, and my latest failure is epic. Savannah is still running wild, and now I think I've lost any possible leverage to contain her.

I need to talk to her, but first I have to find her. Shoving my feet into a pair of sneakers, I stride over to the Coffee Dragon to interrogate Giselle. There's a line at the counter ten people deep, but Giselle waves me up to the front of the queue, cheerfully shouting to the crowd, "Flynn, here, is Viking bred and born and the savviest treasure hunter in these here parts. Keep an eye out for him, ladies and gentlemen, if you wish to leave here richer than you came!"

Unfortunately for me, I do happen to come from Viking heritage—Norwegian on my mother's side, Swedish on my father's. I'm tall and sturdily built, my eyes are blue, and I've always worn my blond hair long. To make it worse, I've got a scar that begins above my left eye and carries on down over the cheekbone. So even though I've absolutely and categorically refused to don a costume or alter my appearance to play to the tourist trade, I look the part.

In any case, Giselle's speech is entirely unnecessary—all Vinland guests attend my metal-detecting class, so they know exactly who I am.

A middle-aged woman with a black pirate hat nearly covering her eyes queries, "Where's the best place to start? Over by the rocks on the north shore, right?"

"You kidding?" an elderly man argues. He's got binoculars slung around his neck and wears a T-shirt portraying a bloody tangle of wolves, ravens, and sword-wielding, scantily clad Viking-helmeted women. "I did research. It's going to be in one of those sea caves. That's where the original treasure was found."

"Right now, if I don't get coffee, blood is going to flow," I growl. I am only half joking, but everybody laughs, with the exception of the man in the blood-frenzy T-shirt, who looks like he wants to strangle me with the strap on his binoculars. His name escapes me, but I know he's a retired history professor who has been here since the start of the season even though he seems to hate the whole game and holds forth on the historical inconsistencies of Vinland at every opportunity.

I don't hold it against him; this is something we have in common. I absolutely detest the bastardized alternate history the town council has created for Vinland, even though I understand what is driving the narrative.

In my childhood the island was known simply as Calvert, and it was well on its way to being largely abandoned.

Young people were leaving to get mainland educations and not coming back. The fishing industry took hit after hit and was no longer profitable. Small family farms, dwarfed by mega corporations, couldn't do more than provide a subsistence living for their owners. More and more houses were standing empty, abandoned by those who'd moved on to find a living elsewhere.

Everything changed the day Ricky Lawson, an adventurous teen-ager, discovered a treasure stash in a sea cave you could only get to by boat during low tide. The kid mistakenly thought he'd found a Viking treasure trove, even though experts later asserted that the gold, silver, and jewelry were undoubtedly of Spanish origin, and that there was no reason to believe Vikings had ever so much as dropped anchor in the harbor. But Ricky's exuberant report of the find hit not only regular news channels but the tabloids, and the misinformation stuck.

A couple of years later, after an influx of inconvenient amateur trea-sure hunters began roaming around the island digging holes, the Calvert Island Council hatched the idea of transforming the entire island into a treasure-hunt resort. They talked about Leavenworth, a small commu-nity that lucratively rebranded itself as a Bavarian-styled village. They talked about Stehekin and cruise ships and Disneyland. And they came up with Vinland, a resort based loosely on Viking mythology, shame-lessly mixed with pirate lore.

The Coffee Dragon is a prime example. A wooden gangplank leads up to an outdoor patio, shaped more or less like the deck of a ship, marked on one side by a dragon-headed prow, on the other by a curv-ing tail. Each wooden table bears a centerpiece shaped like a horned Viking helmet. Stuffed parrots and ravens dangle indiscriminately from an elaborate rigging that would never be able to hoist a sail.

During the summer, tourists fill the place, inside and out, dressed in a mishmash of Viking and pirate hats, eye patches, and "Vinland Treasure Hunter" T-shirts. No paper coffee cups here—all beverages are served in stainless steel mugs, artificially tarnished in an attempt to resemble silver. I once pointed out to Giselle that Vikings actually drank from the hollowed-out horns of cattle or goats. "Well, *that* sounds prac-tical," she'd said disdainfully, and that was the first and only time I suggested that she go for authenticity.

Now, she beams at me approvingly, her round face flushed and damp with perspiration.

"What can I make you, Flynn?"

"Just coffee. Black. Nothing fancy."

She waits me out, knowing from experience that I'll cave eventually, and order off the menu handwritten on a blackboard behind the counter. I sigh. "Fine. Raven's Blood, unadulterated. To go." She taps in the order and turns away to fill my mug.

"Hey, Giselle, one more thing," I say, low, when she hands me my order of Raven's Blood—aka dark-roast coffee, black. "Savannah has gone missing again. Have you seen her?"

"Poor child," she clucks. "Licking her wounds somewhere, no doubt."

"Poor child, nothing," I snap, and then, before Giselle can reprove me for my hard heart, I hold up my free hand in a *don't shoot me* gesture. "Did said poor child stop in here to lick said wounds?"

Giselle sighs. "Stopped in for coffee and a scone. Don't fret so, Flynn. She'll come home when she's ready."

"Her mother might have been okay with the free-range program. I'm not."

"Maybe pick your battles?" she suggests, patting my hand and looking into my eyes.

"I really messed up, Giselle. She listened in on a phone call and heard what she shouldn't have heard. I need to talk to her."

"What did she hear?"

Ashamed, I don't answer, but what Giselle reads in my face makes her sigh again. "Not that she said where she was going, but you might check Improbable House."

A dark knowing settles deep into my bones. Six months today since my sister fell off the roof of that accursed place and died. Of course that's where Savannah has been hanging out. The only surprise is that I didn't think of it myself.

Giselle and I exchange a long, meaningful glance, and I lift my coffee in a silent salute. As I make my exit, the tourists part for me like I'm King Canute.

What do I do with the child? I ask myself, not for the first time. I'd suggested grief counseling shortly after I arrived and was rewarded with a withering stare and the flat statement that I couldn't make her go and certainly couldn't make her talk. I didn't push it then, thinking that time would start to heal her. But realizing she's haunting Improbable House changes everything. Surely it's morbid and unhealthy for her to be spending so much time at the scene of her mother's death.

I consider hopping in my cart and going out there right this minute to tell her what I think, but I know myself well enough to realize that I'm way too emotionally wound up to attempt it now. Stuffing down my worry and guilt and bewilderment, along with a not very mature need to win this war for the sake of winning, rather than what would be good for the child, I go back into the house to drink my coffee and try to wrap my mind around the day.

I settle into my desk in the office of Frieda's Treasures, looking over the books and preparing for the usual flow of tourist complaints. *My faucet is leaking, the toilet is plugged, I haven't found any treasure yet, can you show me again how to work my metal detector?*

The chime on the door dings and I glance up, braced, wondering what it will be first.

Only it's not a tourist who stumps scowling into the office. It's Old Nick.

I can't imagine the man has ever been Young Nick—he's been Old Nick since I was a child and long before that. Nothing about him has changed in the years of my absence. Same twisted, badly scarred face, one side drawn up tighter than the other, a patchwork of shiny pink-and-white skin. Same missing eye, the socket covered by a drooping eyelid. Same thin, wizened body. Same hitching gait and dragging foot. Same hook hand, straight out of a Peter Pan movie.

And definitely the same seething bitterness and sarcasm that terrified me as a child. My beleaguered mother capitalized on my fear and used Nick as a cautionary tale. "If you don't mind me, if you run off, if you don't do your chores, Old Nick will get you," she would say.

Nick owns and operates Odin's Trading Post, the establishment that supplies groceries, hardware, and other necessaries to islanders and tourists alike. He's also the owner of Improbable House—the place where my sister died—and several other rental properties that Frieda's business maintains and leases on his behalf.

"What's up, Nick?" I try to sound pleasant but fall utterly short.

His one good eye sparks with malice. "'What's up' is that I don't want that child of yours poking around Improbable House."

"She's not hurting anything," I say, even though I absolutely agree with him.

"Something might hurt her," he says ominously. "It's my property, Flynn. She's trespassing."

My temper flares and I say nothing, knowing I'll regret any words that pass my lips.

"Frieda wasn't the first of your family to come to harm out there," Nick growls. "I'd think you'd want to make her the last."

The old fear, always vigilant beneath my skin, stirs at his words. *Nobody knows,* I remind myself, as the secret buried at the core of me begins to thrum against the confines of my chest. Nobody knows, now that Frieda has crossed to the other side.

"That sounds like a threat, old man," I say.

"Think of it as a warning. Keep Savannah away from there, or I'll do it myself." He turns and hobbles out of my office, slamming the door behind him.

I stare after him, breathing hard, as anger rises in answer to my fear. Unjustified anger at Nick, who is completely within his rights. Anger at Savannah, who doesn't listen to a word I say or follow a single one of my requests, or give me half a chance to get this right. Most of all, anger at myself, for fucking up this whole situation so absolutely and completely.

Precisely at that moment, when the rage has filled me to the point where I'm about to burst, the office landline rings. I should let it go to voice mail, but all my good sense walked out the door with Nick. I answer, the disembodied voice on the other end providing a perfect target on which to vent my rage, and then, unexpectedly, offering the solution to Savannah and Improbable House.

Chapter Seven

BLYTHE

"Have you talked to Alan yet?" Kristen studies the menu with great concentration, as if she's really considering the selections and might order the special or maybe even the pancakes and bacon instead of her usual egg-white omelet and fruit cup.

"I have not." I keep my eyes on my own menu. Unlike Kristen, I make a game out of having something different whenever we meet at IHOP. Today, however, it's a little hard to focus.

"And you're going to do that when, do you think?"

"As soon as he responds to the last five text messages I sent him."

Yes, I'm avoiding Alan. Partly because I don't know what to say to him about the future of our relationship. Partly because I'm afraid he'll talk me out of going to Vinland, and talk me out of the call I plan to make tomorrow, turning down the job with Blake and Lomax.

Kristen remains riveted to her menu, which is not at all normal Kristen behavior.

"Why don't you just spit it out?" I suggest.

"I have no idea what you're talking about." She does look up now, eyes too big, too innocent.

"Are we ready to order?" the waitress asks. She's angled toward the next table already, her body ready to move. The place is crowded and understaffed and she doesn't need a game of wills between me and my sister complicating her life.

Kristen opens her mouth to say we need more time, but I cut her off.

"She'll have the veggie egg-white omelet and the fruit cup," I say. "I'll take the number seven." I don't even know what the number seven is, but I don't think I've had it before. It doesn't matter, anyway, because this breakfast meeting is not at all about food.

As soon as the waitress hurries off, Kristen asks, "What's up with you?"

I stare back at her, and her eyes actually fall away from mine. I know her guilty look when I see it. "Why don't you tell me what Alan said when *you* talked to him," I suggest. "Also, why do I suddenly feel like I'm in high school again, with you as go-between?"

"Okay, yes, I talked to him." Kristen makes an infinitesimal adjustment to her knife, which is already perfectly aligned with her plate.

"I need you to stay out of this," I say. "It's my life. He's my . . ." I run into a problem with word choices and stop. He's my what? Not my fiancé, although that ring is probably not entirely off the table, if I grovel properly. My boyfriend, my lover, my security blanket. Maybe he's not my anything anymore.

Kristen finally meets my eyes. "He is *devastated*. He's waiting for you to come home and talk to him in person."

"Oh, come on, Kris. Devastated? Alan? His pride is hurt and he's pissed that his plans didn't work out."

"I wouldn't wait too long," she warns. "He's so far out of your league you're not even playing the same sport. You might want to keep him happy."

"Thank you so much for the vote of confidence." I'm used to Kristen but the words still sting. I'm already well aware that Alan is good-looking and intelligent and born to be wealthy. The subject of what exactly it is he sees in me has been hashed over by my mother and sister at length and they've never come to a satisfactory conclusion, other than that opposites attract.

Nobody has ever questioned what it is I see in him, of course, because it's obvious that he's a dream catch. When we first met, I couldn't believe that he'd fallen for me, the two of us caught up in a romance that felt like it ought to be a movie. Never mind that we had little in common, that he was driven by money and success and I was not. What did any of that matter when he smiled that smile that melted me down to my toes, looked deeply into my eyes, whispered endearments in a velvet voice?

I suppose the real question is: Why did I fall out of love with him? Nothing big, nothing vital, just a host of little things that chipped away at my starry-eyed adoration. The day he told me he was never going to want a cat or a dog—too messy, too needy, too time-consuming and allergy-inducing—and suggested I consider a fish tank or a plant, if I really needed to nurture living things. The day he suggested, very kindly, that I might consider upgrading my wardrobe. The day he spoke with animation and admiration about Kristen's attitude and how she could not possibly fail at reaching the success she was aiming for. The way we somehow furnished the house to his taste, not mine; the friends and business associates he brought into my life, with whom I have nothing in common.

The day he displayed his complete no-confidence vote in my abilities by arranging the job he didn't think I could get on my own.

"Don't get huffy," Kristen says. "What are you going to do?"

"I'll talk to him. Just stay out of it."

Our plates arrive. Apparently, I have ordered biscuits and gravy with two eggs and a side of bacon. Kristen's eyebrows go up.

"How can you eat that?"

I'm actually asking myself the same question, but only because I didn't specify the eggs and they are fried solid instead of runny the way I like them, but I'm not in the mood to give Kristen any kind of satisfaction, so I take a big bite and wash it down with lukewarm coffee.

"How can you eat *that*?" I gesture with my fork at the pallid, rubbery thing on her plate.

"You'll die of cholesterol before you're forty," she retorts.

"As it turns out, a certain amount of fat is good for you," I point out. "You should eat the whole egg. Yolks are full of antioxidants, vitamins, omega-threes . . ."

She shudders. "And calories. Back to Alan—"

"I am not discussing Alan."

"Fine then, what are you going to do about Nomi's ashes?"

"I'm taking them to the island and burying them. As she asked."

"To the fictional island you created when you were a child."

"As it turns out, there's a real island at those coordinate points. In the San Juans, not far from Orcas Island. I saw the attorney yesterday. There's even money set aside for me to go, so why not?"

"Three reasons," she says, ticking them off on her fingers. "Alan. Your new job. And just because there's a land mass at those coordinates, it doesn't mean it's a real island. I mean, okay. Yes. It's real but not *the* island. Not the one you drew in that stupid map."

"How do you know that?" I ask. I was about to tell her that Mr. Wilcox has money in trust for her, too, but now she *has* annoyed me and I figure she can find that out for herself.

She stares at me as if I've completely lost my mind. I smile at her in the way I know pisses her off and say, "Right island or not, I'm going as soon as I can figure out a place to stay."

"How hard can that be? Check Vrbo. Look for an Airbnb."

"It's a themed resort destination, very exclusive. No Vrbo. There appears to be only one contact point for lodging, as a matter of fact."

"And?"

"I called. Nobody answered and I left a message."

She rolls her eyes at me. "Call back! It's already summer, and I bet those places fill up fast."

"It's Sunday. They're probably closed."

"Right in the middle of tourist season? Are you kidding? They are open. And you need to get this over with so you can get on with your life," she says. "Drive to the coast, spend the night on the mainland, go to the island and scatter her ashes, then drive back. You could go next weekend so it doesn't interfere with the new job. Or with making up with Alan. Hey, I could go with you. We could do it together. Maybe Mom should come, too."

I look at her in dismay. I've been daydreaming about this as a magical adventure. Just me, brave Blybee, off on one of Nomi's quests. A week, at least, exploring a mysterious island, not some there-and-back trip taken over by my mother and my sister.

Kristen says, in a low voice, "She was my Nomi, too, not that she ever drew treasure maps with me."

"Because you were three!" I protest.

"Old enough to draw a crayon map and play pretend."

Something in her voice wakes me up for the first time to what should have been obvious, that Kristen is sad about Nomi, too, and maybe she even feels left out that she wasn't included in the bizarre ashes bequest. I've always felt jealous of her, my perfect sister, but besides this thing with Nomi, I know Kristen would love to have the job I'm about to turn down, is probably asking herself how I landed it when she's applied for similar positions herself and didn't get an interview. As for Alan, I've seen the way she looks at him sometimes, as if he's a star in the sky that is just out of reach.

"She got cancer then and there wasn't very much playing," I say gently. "I'm sorry you missed out on her, Kris."

Kristen shrugs. "She could have still included me in this little treasure-island game."

Love for my sister floods me, followed immediately by guilt over my own selfishness, and I sigh as I release my fantasy and invite her in. "Of course you can come, if you like, but here's the thing; it's a tiny bit more complicated than just scattering Nomi's ashes any old where on the island. You'll need to take a week off work, at least, maybe two. The lawyer suggested I clear my entire summer."

She stares at me, eyes wide. "A couple of weeks? Why on earth would you stay so long? What about the job? What about Alan?"

"Because it's a treasure hunt, Kris! Mr. Wilcox says I need to use the map to find the specific place on the island where Nomi wanted to be buried. And there's absolutely nothing to go on, other than apparently it's next to a big tree, which is next to a house. So it might take a while."

Kristen waves her fork at me. "Are you serious right now? I mean, I can see that a couple of days would be fun. But weeks? A whole summer? I couldn't possibly take the time off. You can't do this, either, Blythe. You'll lose everything you've worked so hard for."

I blink at her, struck with the epiphany that I don't want any of what I've worked for, and that this weird bequest from Nomi offers my only chance at escaping a life I wish I had never created. Finding a place to stay on Vinland is imperative. I need to finish breakfast and get back to my search.

"Are you planning to eat any of that omelet?" I ask. "It's getting cold."

Kristen pokes at it with her fork, glances over at my plate, and unexpectedly grins. "Are egg yolks really good for you?"

"They are. Want one?"

She nods, and I fork the egg up onto a piece of toast and transfer the whole thing to her plate. It's half-cold already, but she makes a rapturous sound as she takes the first bite. "Love yolks. Haven't had one in forever."

"It's not about health, is it?" I venture.

She shrugs. "Looking good doesn't just happen by itself, contrary to what you may believe. There is work involved." And then she suddenly seems to realize she's being vulnerable, because she launches back into the offensive.

"You need to decide what you're going to do so you can talk to Alan. It's not fair to leave him hanging like this. Call that rental place. Do it now."

Her urgency combines with mine and I pull up the number programmed into my phone, cross my fingers, and hit call.

A male voice answers almost immediately, sharp with irritation.

"What do you want?"

My brain function screeches to a halt. "Is this the wrong number?" I ask, thinking I must have somehow programmed in the wrong digits.

"Do I sound like a psychic?" the voice retorts. "How should I know what number you were dialing?"

My thumb hits disconnect. Kristen shakes her head at me. "Why are people such assholes about wrong numbers? We've all done it. Just look it up and try again."

"But it's not the wrong number," I protest, remembering. "I programmed it in before I called last time. And I got a recording for Frieda's Treasures Vacation Rentals."

But Kristen is searching her phone, not listening to me. "Here we go," she says, and hits call. I can hear her cell ringing from across the table. Hear the same voice answer, this time with a thin veneer of impatient politeness. "Frieda's Treasures Vacation Rentals. What do you need?"

"If you're done being an asshole, I need to make a reservation," she says.

"I'm never done being an asshole," the voice says. "So I guess you're out of luck."

Kristen's face reddens. The two little white dents appear in her nose, the ones that show up when she's pissed but maintaining control.

"Let's skip the personality problem and just book a date," she says.

"Kristen!" I protest, reaching for the phone, but she shifts her body to keep it out of reach.

"Anything special in mind?" the voice asks, with an edge that says he can think of a few things, none of them pleasant.

"What do you have available for Tuesday?" Kristen gives me a thumbs-up and a nod, as if I can't hear the whole conversation.

"As in, this Tuesday?"

"Would Wednesday be better, then?"

"Ma'am, we're booking into next summer already."

Kristen covers the phone and says to me, "I told you."

In that moment, I know with utter clarity that I need to go to this island, and I need to do it now. Not next year. This year. This week, not next week. This is my one chance to shift the trajectory of my life. If I don't go now, I'll make things up with Alan. I'll accept the job he got for me. And then it will be too late to break the spell.

"I really only need one night," Kristen says. "Surely you have some sort of opening. What's the soonest you have available?"

"Next summer." Irritation comes through the phone loud and clear. "There are a limited number of properties, and they are booked well in advance. Also, the minimum booking is for a week."

"That's ridiculous!" Kristen snaps. "Listen. I know how this works. You have cancellations. You have rooms in reserve."

"Clearly, you have no idea how it works," he says. "If you want to reserve something for next summer, I still have two properties available. If not, I suggest you try another island."

Kristen's tone turns to pure ice. "Surely there's somebody more helpful I could speak with. Your supervisor, perhaps."

He laughs. "Sorry to disappoint, but you've reached the top of the food chain. Also, we're able to be selective about who we rent to, and I don't think we're going to be able to accommodate you next summer, either."

I lunge across the table, get my hands on Kristen's phone, and tear it away from her.

"Hi," I say, in my most conciliatory voice. "I apologize for my assistant. I'm the one who needs a place to stay for a few days. I wonder if I could possibly speak with Frieda? Or leave her a message, even?"

"Frieda's not . . ." He clears his throat. "She's not taking messages right now. She's . . . on vacation."

"Could you possibly give me a number for another place I could stay? I've looked online but this is the only agency I could find."

"Sorry, I handle the bookings for all of the vacation rentals on the island."

I drop the attempt to sound empowered and resort to pleading. "But it can't wait until next summer! My grandmother died, and that's where she wants me to bury her ashes. Please tell me there's some sort of option available."

"You could do a day trip," he concedes, his tone marginally softer. "We're not far from Orcas Island. You could take the ferry there and overnight in a hotel. I can get you permission to hire a private boat or plane to get you here for the day."

Tears are threatening and I can feel the tightness in my throat and know my words are going to be wobbly. "Her wishes are . . . complicated. I need a few days. Are you certain there's absolutely nothing? A waiting list, maybe?"

I hear a rhythmic tapping sound, his fingers or a pen on the desk. "Well," he says, drawing the word out as if he's thinking out loud. "There is one possibility."

"Really? Who do I talk to?"

"I have a property that is . . . It's been taken out of rotation because it needs some work."

"What's wrong with it?"

"Nothing, really. It's just run-down. The roof leaks. It needs new shingles. The landscaping needs attention."

"I'll take it," I say, without even asking how much it's going to cost. Kristen is shaking her head so energetically she's going to give herself whiplash, but I ignore her.

"When were you wanting to be here?" he asks.

"As soon as possible. This week?"

"The water taxi operates once a week," he says. "On Thursdays. Bookings are seven days, minimum. In on Thursday, out on Thursday. Will that work?"

"Is it possible to book through to the end of summer? I don't know how long I'll be."

There's a space of silence, during which I imagine him miming hanging himself and mouthing *just kill me now* to some appreciative coworker.

"That's a long time for burying ashes."

"It's complicated."

"Let's do week to week. I'll give you a discounted rate to compensate for my personality disorder and any inconvenience you'll experience if we need to do repairs while you're there. Give me your email and I'll send you the information. Payment for a full week is required in advance. Also, we do a background check on all island guests, so there will be another email asking you to agree to that."

I give him my name and my email address and hang up the phone.

"You're really going to do this," Kristen says. "A wild-goose chase. Risk losing everything. I bet Nomi never thought for a minute you'd take this all seriously!" She leans forward and lays a hand over mine. "Really, honey. I love you, but you have this overdeveloped conscience and it gets you all wound up in knots over stuff that doesn't even matter. I know you loved her, but she's dead and you have important things to worry about. Your career. Your relationship. Just lay her to rest somewhere and let it go."

I grin at her. "I want to go, Kristen. It's an adventure! It will be fun."

She releases my hand and shakes her head. "Well, go if you must, but Alan isn't going to wait for you forever."

Chapter Eight

BLYTHE

As it turns out, Alan isn't going to wait for me at all.

When I open the door to the house we bought together, the sound of a Sunday afternoon baseball game fills my ears. Alan's in his recliner, a bottle of Sam Adams on the table beside him, the remote in his hand. Based on Kristen's description of his devastation, I half expect him to be disheveled and unshaven, but he's showered and shaved and sleek as always.

He glances up at the sound of my footsteps, then his eyes go right back to the television as if I'm not standing there looking at him.

"Could we talk?" I ask, raising my voice to be heard above the excited commentary of an announcer explaining how a double play was the greatest achievement of the twenty-first century.

"Hang on a sec, would you?" Alan asks, and turns the volume up to catch the replay. After we've watched the infielders complete their miracle from five different angles, I move to stand directly in front of his chair, interposing myself between him and the TV.

He finally presses mute. "Thought maybe you weren't coming home," he says. The hurt in his face, his voice, stabs through me, and I drop to my knees in front of his chair.

"I never meant to hurt you," I say. "It was so beautiful, what you did. And I know I ruined it."

"I planned it for months," he says. "Orchestrating everything. Guests. Music. The food."

"I know." I put my hands on his knees. When he doesn't pull away, I lay my palm against his jaw, feeling the muscle clenched tight.

"You made it look like you didn't care," he says. "In front of all those people."

"I was surprised," I tell him. "By the party. The people, and the music, and you asking me to marry you. I was all off balance, and then the balloon man—"

He covers my hand with his and laces our fingers together. His eyes gaze deeply into mine and I tip my head down, letting my hair screen my face.

"The real problem is, you don't love me." His voice snags in his throat, as if it's caught on something sharp.

"I do love you," I protest. "You're part of . . . of everything I am." But I still can't look at him.

He releases my hand and cups his under my chin, tipping my head back up and forcing me to meet his gaze.

"I'm not talking that kind of love. I'm talking the kind of love where when I ask you to marry me, your face lights up with joy. Where no balloon bouquet in the world would tear your eyes away from me."

There's nothing I can say to that. He drops his hand. My skin feels cold in its absence and I shiver.

"You know how I am with crowds and surprises," I say desperately, feeling like I'm free-falling into an abyss with no light, no bottom. "Maybe we could, I don't know . . ." My throat closes up and I sit down on the floor, blinking back tears.

"Exactly." It's not much of an answer.

"Now what?" I ask, after a long silence during which I have time to remember the whole job interview fiasco and that I was mad at him, before the tables got turned and put me in the position of being in the wrong.

"Since you hate crowds and big gestures so much," Alan says bitterly, "let's try this. Look me in the eyes right now. Tell me you love me absolutely. Tell me you want to marry me. I'll apply for a marriage license tomorrow, and on Thursday we'll get married in your parents' backyard. Family only. Screw the big wedding."

"Thursday?" My eyes fly open and I stare at him in dismay. "So soon?"

"My point," he says, his voice hard. "You don't want to marry me."

"It's just that I . . . Did Kristen tell you? About what Nomi asked me to do?"

"What does that have to do with us getting married?"

"I need to bury Nomi's ashes like she wanted. I made reservations to go to the island on Thursday."

"It's been how many years since she died? Forgive me if I don't understand the rush. What about your new job?"

"The job you got for me as a favor?" There's an edge in my voice now, my own hurt and anger clawing its way upward through the layers of guilt.

"Is that what this is about? You're pissed because I helped you get the sort of job some people would kill for?"

"I'd like to think I'm capable of getting a good job on my own. I'd like to think that *you* think I'm capable of getting a good job on my own."

"Seriously?" he asks. "Nobody gets a job like that on their own, Blythe. It's all about who you know. Besides, come on. It would take you years to build the sort of résumé that would score you a job like that."

The last thing I want to do in this moment is cry. I want to be angry and self-righteous and empowered. But the tears are stronger than I am. They show up, fill my eyes, spill over onto my cheeks.

Alan's expression softens. "Hey," he says. "I'm sorry if your feelings were hurt. But that's just the way life is. Sometimes you're like a child, and it's time you grew up. Like now. Make a decision. Live with the consequences. Do you want the life we planned or not?"

There's truth to what he says, which just makes me feel worse. I swallow hard, but my voice is still wobbly and small when I say, pleadingly, "Couldn't we wait just a bit? I'll go to the island, and when I get back I'll look for a job that I'm more suited for and then we can see where we're at, you and me?"

He laughs, a sharp, dry sound with no humor in it. "Sorry, Blythe, but this is it. Final offer. Marry me on Thursday, or you and I are done."

"Don't," I say, and I'm not even sure what I mean. *Don't make me choose, don't ask me again, don't love me, don't let me go.*

Alan sees the decision in my face before I know I've made it. He picks up the remote and unmutes the TV, even though I'm still right in front of him. I've been dismissed.

He's never employed this tactic on me, although I've seen him use it on others. I'm invisible to him now. We're done. Wordless, choking back sobs and powerless to control the tears pouring down my face, I get to my feet and retreat to our bedroom. I fling myself face-first onto my pillow, but my tears immediately dry up. I feel constrained and self-conscious. Like I'm hired help and the bed doesn't belong to me.

Which is when I realize that we are really over. There is no going back from where we are.

I get up from the bed and begin selecting things from the closet and drawers that I'll want to pack for my adventure. It doesn't take me long. When I'm done, I automatically reach out to smooth the covers where I've rumpled them, but then stop, feeling like if I smooth the spread and fluff the pillow, I'll erase all traces of myself, that this room won't remember me and it will be as though I've never existed.

So I leave the imprint of my face in the pillow as evidence that I was here and lived this life, and roll my bag down the hall. I pause by the living room. Alan is still watching TV and doesn't turn his head toward me. So I keep moving, leaving my key on the table just inside the front door as my answer to his final offer.

Chapter Nine

FLYNN

The customer-facing office for Frieda's Treasures is attached to the house, but the true heart of the business is located in a nondescript, tin-roofed building on the far edge of town, heavily screened from casual eyes by a tall hedge. Inside is office space and a storage area containing supplies that range from cleaning rags and buckets to hammers and nails and even lumber and shingles. There are also two dormitory rooms, each with six bunk beds, along with bathrooms and showers, which house the mainland college students who work with us in the summers.

Glory is sitting behind a desk cluttered with logbooks and files haphazardly stacked around a computer and an office phone, but she's not looking at any of it. She's eating a Viking Dog, her blue-jeaned legs propped up on an empty chair, her dark eyes trained on the view outside the window. She looks like she's daydreaming, doing absolutely nothing, but I know better.

She was Frieda's full business partner, and since my sister died, she's been running the bulk of this complex operation—both staff management and the warehouse—without ever looking hurried or harried or any of the things I feel right now. Whatever Glory does, she does with full focus. And right now she's focused on food and the view.

"We should set up a picnic table outside for days like this," she says, in that deceptively soft voice with the Salish lilt.

"It's raining," I point out, a fact that has done nothing to help my mood.

"Exactly," she says. She watches me as I take off my jacket, shake water off of it, and hang it on a hook to dry. She dunks her dog in a pool of ketchup and takes a bite, savoring it, before she adds, "It's not personal, the rain. Although if there ever were a mood to call a storm, you're wearing it."

"Savannah," I say. "Fake treasure hunts. This godforsaken island. Rain. Monday. You name it."

The smell of hot dog and mustard and ketchup wafts into my nostrils and I realize I never did eat breakfast. I gesture at the little cardboard ship that the dog came in. "I'd think you'd really hate this Viking shit. Like they were ever here. We should be celebrating your people."

"My people are perfectly happy not to have this island full of fake wigwams and powwows, thank you very much. Better smarmy Viking shit. I think you're hangry, Flynn. Here. Have one."

She takes another bite, then gestures with her chin toward another dog on her desk. I'm feeling childishly contrary enough to say no, just to feel more like a martyr, but I can't do it. Much as I hate the Viking spin, and even though I'm at odds with Nick, who makes them, I've got to admit he's onto something. The dogs are more sausage than wiener, and the old man smokes them over some special blend of wood chips that imparts an extraordinary flavor. Stone-ground mustard and ketchup are the perfect complement.

Glory's sneaker-clad feet thud down onto the floor from the chair, and she shoves the extra dog in my direction. It's an invitation I can't resist, and I squelch over, my boots squeaking on the wooden floor. I lower my body into the chair and take a delicious bite.

"Wanna tell me why you are walking around in the rain that you so hate?" she asks.

I take another bite, taste buds exploding with the perfect flavor blend, and start to feel a little bit better. "Savannah drove off with my golf cart."

"At Improbable House, is she?"

"You know about that? You might have told me." I put down my dog and glare at her. Everybody on this island apparently knows that my niece is haunting that house, and knew long before I did.

"It's no secret, Flynn. She's been out there pretty near every day since Frieda fell."

The implication is clear that I should have known, would have, if I'd been paying attention. This new evidence of my total failure as a competent guardian heats my already simmering irritation to a full boil.

"Am I the only one who doesn't think it's healthy?" I growl. "She needs to be stopped."

"You have a plan for that?" Glory's lips twitch upward in amusement. "Gonna need to be a very good plan."

"I've rented out the house."

Glory's smile vanishes. "Does Savannah know?"

I shake my head. "Just set it up yesterday. I haven't told her yet."

"Coward."

I grit my teeth and bite back a retort. Keeping my voice as level as I can, I say, "Look, a woman called the office. She needs to be on the island for a week or indefinitely. Improbable House is empty. Savannah needs to break her obsession with her mother's place of death. Win-win."

"Hmmm," she says, turning away from me and waking up the computer. "You let me know how that works out."

"Glory! Just say what you're thinking."

"I'm thinking that the child is grieving and the house is where she grieves best."

"And I'm thinking that spending so much time there is morbid," I retort. "Also, that we are running a business and the house could be making some money. Six months is plenty long to leave it empty."

"Well, clearly you know best," Glory says. Her tone is calm and without inflection, but it would take an idiot not to recognize the sarcasm.

"It's done. The contract is signed. The guest has already paid."

Glory, apparently immersed in spreadsheets, doesn't respond. I raise my voice, as if she's suddenly gone hard of hearing instead of choosing to dismiss me, and say, "Whether you approve or not, I need the house ready for Thursday. Can you see that it's prepared?"

"Sorry, everybody's busy. You'll have to do it yourself."

My temper is escalating again, but I know better than to take out my frustration on Glory.

She's easygoing on the surface but has an implacable will. She's also island to the core. I have no idea how old she is—her face is lined but not what you'd call wrinkled, her long hair is still raven black—but I do know she was already involved in the business when I was born. She's part of the Vinland Council, the small group that makes the decisions, creates the bylaws, and rigidly controls the tourism trade.

I like and respect her, and her opinion of me matters.

"Care to tell me why somebody 'needs' to be on the island?" She swings the chair around, her eyes boring into mine.

"The guest's grandmother died," I say warily. "The woman wanted her ashes buried here, apparently."

Something flickers in Glory's eyes, gone before I can place it. "Name? Did you do a background check or were you too focused on keeping Savannah away from the house to bother?"

The interrogation stings and I retort, "Obviously I'm not Frieda, but I do know to do a background check. Her name is Blythe Harmon. Totally clean. Not so much as a speeding ticket."

"A body would need a reason to want to be buried on the island," Glory muses. "Rather an unusual request. Who was she?"

"Didn't ask. Don't care. I just want to keep Savannah out of that house."

"I want to see the background check," Glory says, turning back to her computer. "Forward it to me, would you? And you'll have to get the house ready. Here's a checklist with the stuff you'll need to take out with you. Grab a spare cart and drive out there now to check on our girl. After you break the news, she can help you finish up the house."

Our girl. Not your girl. And really, it's surprising that Glory granted me even that concession. When I left the island, I went into exile, becoming an outsider who belongs here no more than the summer workers and the tourists. Savannah, on the other hand, is all island. The whole community will have her back, no matter what. Vinland is part of her and she is part of it. And since I'm the only real family she has left, that means I have to stay here until she's eighteen, another six long years of fake treasure hunting and limited horizons, and inescapable reminders of things I've spent my life trying to forget.

Man up, Flynn. I square my shoulders and try to get my head into a better space. I can do this for Savannah. But the memories that were relatively easy to brush off when I was out in the world in a constant whirl of excitement and activity, moving from one adventure to the next, are everywhere now. Worse than the memories, every now and then Frieda herself shows up, not exactly in the flesh but way too real for my sanity.

She materializes in the cart beside me when I head out of the storeroom toward Improbable House. She's wearing the clothes she died in, jeans and a flannel shirt, bloodstained and torn. Her hair, as dark as mine is blond, hangs in a single braid over one shoulder, her eyes, so much like Savannah's, are fixed on my face.

"Do you have to wear those clothes? It's disturbing." I don't say it aloud; I haven't strayed that far into madness yet, but she answers anyway.

"You have to wear what you died in. Those appear to be the rules."

I keep my eyes trained on the road, hoping she'll disappear. When we pass a cart full of summer students, they all wave, and I watch their gazes closely to see if they're just waving at me.

"They can't see me," Frieda says softly. "There are rules about that, too."

"Never did like rules much," I mutter under my breath.

And just like that, a memory hits me, as vivid as if I really am sitting in our old fishing boat under cover of darkness, instead of driving a golf cart on one of Vinland's back roads.

My brain and body are so saturated with adrenaline, I can't think, can't feel, can only act. I'm only dimly aware of the horror of what just happened, the fear of what I have to do.

Frieda stands on the dock looking down at me. There's blood on her face, her shirt, her hands. Only some of it is mine. "You're really leaving me, Flynn?" Her voice falters, and I feel her sob catching in my own chest. She looks small and fragile, shivering in the cold wind that whips her dark hair around her face.

"One of us has to go," I say, gazing up at her with one eye, the vision in the other obscured by my T-shirt, balled up in one hand, pressed against the line of fire burning down the side of my face. The part that touches my skin is hot, the balled-up part under my hand is clammy and cold. My stomach is twisting and twisting and I'm afraid I'm going to vomit.

"And one of us has to stay," she sobs. "I know it. I'll go, Flynn. Mom will—"

"Fuck her." I mean to sound tough and hard, but my voice breaks as the adrenaline fades and the first harbinger of the emotional reaction that is waiting for me breaks through. "If she'd protected us like she was supposed to, none of this would have happened."

"You know it wasn't that easy . . ."

"Well. It's over now."

"I don't want you to go," she says, small and quiet.

"I want to go," I profess, digging deep for bluster. "There's nothing for me here."

"I'm here," she says, and the catch in her voice hurts more than my face.

"We'll both go. Get in the boat. Come with me."

She shakes her head. "We have to follow the plan. Too many questions if we both disappear. Besides, somebody's got to stay with Mom." Again that tremor in her voice. The moon sails out from behind clouds and glints off tears on her cheeks. Frieda hardly ever cries. I'm bigger and stronger, but she's tougher by far and we both know it.

I need to go before I lose my resolve. I rev the motor, my one-eyed gaze sweeping over the moonlit water, looking for any signs of other boats. All clear, as far as I can see. When I turn back to Frieda, she's already walking away from me, set on the course that fate has determined for us. A gust of wind tears my last goodbye from my lips and carries it away. If she hears, she doesn't acknowledge.

"I'm sorry," I say now. We've left town behind and there's nobody to hear me but the trees, so I say it out loud, but when I glance at the seat beside me, it's empty. Which figures. The rules are sure to include not accepting apologies offered too late, and no ghost in any book I've ever read haunted somebody in order to say, *Hey, buddy. What you did to me wasn't all that bad. Let it go.*

"Bah, humbug," I say, quoting Scrooge, even though I know how well that phrase served him in the ghost-banishment department. I try to convince myself that my sister's apparent materialization is just a matter of a guilty conscience paired with grief and an overactive imagination, but all my resolve vanishes as I near the house and a dark swirl of ravens rises into the air.

I pause in the clearing in front of the house, thinking maybe I've got it wrong, as I don't see my golf cart anywhere. But then an enormous raven detaches himself from the others, drifting down to land on my shoulder, cronking inquiringly. "Hungry," he says.

"Sorry, Norman. Didn't bring you anything," I tell him. "Where's Savannah?"

He swears at me and doesn't answer, so I drive around the house to the back, and there, sure enough, is my cart, a wagon full of black potting soil hitched behind it.

Savannah is on her knees in the middle of a small patch of scarlet geraniums, which were most certainly not here before. She looks up as I park. Her hair is soaking wet. Mud smudges her cheeks. Her gaze is fixed not on me but on my vehicle.

"What's this?" she asks.

"You took my cart."

It's a lame excuse for driving a fully loaded housekeeping cart all the way out here. I can see that she isn't buying it.

"You rented out the house!" Now she does look at me, and what I see in her face makes me wish she would turn back to her flowers.

I take a breath, trying to channel somebody wise and kind, like Yoda, maybe, only without the pointy ears and green skin and backward way of speaking. But I've already rushed in where angels fear to tread, so there's nothing for it but to tell it straight.

"Yes. I've rented the house. Our guest will be arriving on Thursday and possibly staying all summer."

"I can't believe you did this!" Savannah's eyes narrow almost to slits, her face white with fury. She looks so like her mother in that moment that my flesh quivers at the memory of Frieda's well-placed fists. She was the boss of me until gender differences reared their unfair heads and her body softened while my muscles grew harder and my growth accelerated.

"This is a rental property. It needs to pay for itself."

"Money is all you care about! Money and your stupid treasure hunts. Why are you even here?"

"Because you're here," I begin, but she's not having it.

"You should leave," she says.

"I'm staying."

"Why?" The word sounds torn from her throat, her eyes a challenge.

"Because your mother was my sister and I loved her. I love you—"

"Do not!" She's wild with grief and fury now, her face shiny with tears, her voice breaking. "You never visited us. We never visited you."

"It's complicated," I say, which is true, but not a good answer for a twelve-year-old.

"Whatever."

"You can believe what you want. I wouldn't be here if I didn't care. No matter what you overheard, I'm here because I want to be here. Now, whether you like it or not, the house is rented. I'm going to make up the beds and get it ready. Want to help?"

"How will I visit Mom?"

I look at her—so small, so alone, so defiant, kneeling in the middle of the flowers she's planted in the place where her mother died, and my heart feels too big for my chest.

"How about we go plant some flowers on her grave?" I suggest. "I'll go with you. We can—"

"But I can't talk to her there." Savannah tries to snarl the words, but her face crumples up; the tears flow faster and she doubles over, weeping, utterly broken.

I cross the distance between us, scoop her up out of the bed of flowers, and hold her. Her arms go around my neck and she buries her face against my chest. Her tears soak into my shirt, her thin, wiry body shaking with the waves of grief. Tears burn in my own eyes and I blink them back. Something warm and protective and fierce flares up inside me. I'm searching for words to tell her what I feel, to maybe even tell her that I do love her, whatever she might think, but before I can find the words, her body stiffens.

"Put me down."

I do, and she steps back away from me. "You've ruined everything," she says, drawing her arm across her eyes. Then she turns and stalks over to my cart and drives off without looking back.

"Nice job, Flynn," I tell myself. "Utterly brilliant."

"To be fair, she might have a difficult streak," Frieda says, hands on her hips, head cocked to one side, a hint of a smile on her lips.

"I don't suppose you can help me with the house," I mutter.

"Are you kidding? Totally against ghost rules."

"Seems like I should be able to make up the rules for my own hallucinations," I retort, driving the housekeeping cart around to the front door and lugging a clipboard and a sack full of towels and bedding into the entryway. I can do this. Get the house ready, install the guest, keep Savannah away.

Once the house loses its hold on her, maybe the two of us can figure out our relationship.

Chapter Ten

BLYTHE

"How do you get lost on an island?" I inquire of Nomi's ashes. Confining her to the suitcase seems disrespectful, so she's ridden shotgun for the entire trip, belted in just in case of a sudden stop.

Nomi doesn't answer, not that I expected her to, and I peer out my windshield at the narrow, winding highway, hoping that I'm going in the right direction. Orcas Island is bigger than I thought, and less inhabited. The roads are not particularly well marked, and the heavy forest keeps me from using the water as a landmark.

Siri doesn't answer, either, because I lost cell service shortly after turning onto this road. Not another car in sight. No gas stations where I can stop and ask directions. Just me and Nomi and the trees. The beginnings of anxiety flutter beneath my ribs. What if I screw this up?

The water taxi is the only way I can get to Vinland, and it only makes the trip on Thursday at nine a.m. Only people who have booked a vacation rental are allowed on the island, and they can only come in on Thursdays on the water taxi. Charters aren't supposed to take you there, so unless you have your own boat or seaplane, have a personal connection to somebody who does, or have a whole lot of money, you're out of luck.

There's always next Thursday, of course, but that's a whole week of time wasted—time for which I'm paying—or Mr. Wilcox is, anyway, out of my supposed trust fund—for an unused rental. Besides, I can already hear the critical commentary I'm going to have to listen to if I screw this up.

Kristen: *I knew I should have come with you!*

Mom: *Honey, you're really very bright. If only you could learn to focus . . .*

Alan: *We could be getting married today.*

And then Nomi's voice chimes in. *Blybee. It's an adventure! Think of it like a game.*

Right. A game. One that requires a sense of direction, which has never been my strong point. I've already been driving too long.

"Should I turn around? Did I miss it?"

Again, Nomi doesn't answer. Just as I start looking for a wide space or a pullout so I can turn back, I see a sign for the Doe Bay Marina. Thank God. I've found it. I've still got plenty of time. The trees thin, revealing the bay, the docks, a bevy of boats.

My relief lasts for as long as it takes me to turn off the highway and follow a short, bumpy road into the parking lot for the marina, where I'm at a loss once again. There's no obvious sign saying something helpful like VINLAND PASSENGERS, LINE UP HERE. The only things in the parking lot, besides me and a few parked and empty cars, are two kiosks. One is covered with buoys and floats and has signs that read WHALE WATCHING and KAYAK RENTALS. It's closed. The other appears to be a pirate-themed coffee kiosk. Somebody is in it, thank all the powers that be. I can get coffee and information in one fell swoop.

When I step out of my car, the tang of salt water fills my nostrils. The air feels softer than it does at home. My inner child jumps up and down in excitement. I'm on an island! This is an adventure! And soon I'll be on another island, one with a treasure hidden on it somewhere.

The coffee kiosk is inhabited by a girl, maybe twenty but probably younger, eyes heavy with sleep, a tricornered pirate hat not quite straight over shoulder-length chestnut hair. There's a badge on the hat that reads VINLAND ISLAND, and up close I now see the hand-lettered sign on the kiosk that says: VINLAND WATER TAXI, MEET HERE.

"Coffee?" the girl asks, attempting to adjust the hat and getting it more crooked in the process.

"Probably. But first, I was wondering about the taxi to Vinland."

"You have to get your ticket online," she says accusingly, as if I've breached some ethical protocol. "There's a process. You can't just show up here and ask for one."

"It's in the car."

She just stares at me, and with a long sigh, I retrace my steps and come back with a printout of my ticket.

"And your vacation rental agreement," she says, apparently unimpressed.

"I already had to email proof of that to get the ticket," I protest.

She shrugs. "You want on the boat, you follow the code." And then she adds, belatedly, "You savvy, matey?" in what I assume is meant to be a pirate growl.

"Fine." I go back to the car again, dig out the rental agreement, and show her that as well.

Her eyes widen and she stares at me with a whole new respect. "Improbable House? By *yourself*?" She looks over my shoulder, apparently searching for the group that ought to be traveling with me.

"It was available. Why? Is it usually only rented to groups?"

"It's haunted," she says, pulling the cap off a thick marker and printing my name on a shiny piece of card stock. "Viking or pirate?"

"I'm sorry?"

"For the Vinland experience. You get to choose whether you want to be a pirate or a Viking."

"Oh, for a minute there I thought I was choosing what kind of ghosts I want in my rental." I laugh. She doesn't.

"That would be kind of ridiculous, don't you think?" she asks. "There's a carload just pulling in, so if you could hurry?"

"But which is better?" I ask, glancing over my shoulder to see a minivan parking next to my car. It looks like it's got about twenty kids in it plus a rambunctious dog.

"Obviously, I'm partial to pirates," the girl says. "But tastes vary."

She says it in the same way my mother talks about people eating at McDonald's when they could be enjoying a nice vinaigrette salad with radicchio and poached salmon.

"Viking, then," I say, not so much to be contrary as out of a desire to balance things. Yin and yang. Pirate and Viking. Besides, the original Vinland was a Viking island, and I have no idea what pirates have to do with anything.

"Suit yourself." She folds the card stock and shoves it into a black plastic pouch with a clear window and clips it to a lanyard featuring a raven perched on a horned helmet. "Wear this. Don't lose it. Hope you didn't want coffee, because I don't have time now. It's going to take forever to deal with that lot."

A swarm of kids are running around the van, shouting and chasing each other. The dog, a large mixed breed that could obviously use some training, lunges at its leash and barks.

"But I did want coffee."

"Don't be difficult. Please. Here, don't forget your hat." The girl hands me a plastic Viking helmet, horns and all.

"Really? Is it required?"

"Absolutely. Put it on."

I smash the helmet down over my hair, which has gone feral in the humidity, and return to my car yet again.

"Sorry, Nomi, but you're going to have to ride in the suitcase from here."

I zip her in, then lean against the car for a bit, watching while the pirate girl processes the family with the kids and out-of-control dog. Next in line is an elderly couple, both of whom choose to be Vikings. When they head toward the pier, I follow.

Our progress is hampered by the kids, who run wild, chasing each other up and down the pier, perilously close to falling off the edge into the water, and the dog, who has never been informed about leash laws and is currently running free. The parents, both belonging to Team Pirate, are oblivious.

The pair of Vikings I've followed share my annoyance, if not my concern. "Must they be so loud?" the man complains.

"Some parents should not be parents," the woman says, glaring pointedly at the father and mother, who stand, heads close together, chatting calmly and making no effort whatsoever to rein in their unruly offspring.

"Surely somebody on the boat will make them sit down," I offer.

"Maybe they will all fall overboard," the man mutters. I laugh and he glares at me in a way that makes me edge away from him.

More people arrive and cluster in groups on the dock. Two young men are speaking what I think is German. There's a group of four, Chinese I think, laughing and chatting. A retired couple jostles their way through the crowd and plants themselves next to me. The woman, her Viking hat in stark contrast with a pair of white shorts and a striped sailor top, grins at me, her eyes sparkling. Her husband, holding a pirate hat in one hand, has his shirt buttoned all the way up to the top and is wearing a tie. His face is tight with disdain, and he shouts at the woman, to be heard above the clamor, "Vikings. Ridiculous. There is no evidence whatsoever that they ever made it to the West Coast."

"There is the Vinland map," she says, adjusting her helmet. "And that ship they found in California. Besides, it's all in good fun. Does it matter?"

"Of course it matters! I don't know why I agreed to this. We should have just done the cruise."

"Because you love me," she says calmly. "Now, be a good sport and put your hat on." She gently tugs the pirate hat out of his hand and stands on tiptoe to plop it on his head.

"We'll both end up with head lice," he mutters. "I look ludicrous."

It's true. The pirate hat in conjunction with his pinstriped shirt and tie, his polished shoes, and the expression on his face is irresistibly funny.

"Never mind him," the woman says, beaming at me. "I'm Gail. He's Gene. He's not nearly so grumpy as he seems."

"Blythe," I say.

Before things have time to get awkward, Gail points to the water and crows gleefully, "Here's our boat!"

There is, indeed, a boat heading in our direction. It flies a skull-and-crossbones flag, and below it another flag, red with a black raven, that I assume represents the Vikings.

Our motley group, about thirty people strong by now, raises a shout of excitement. Gene puts his hands over his ears and mouths something that I think is "damned hearing aids," but I can't hear a thing over the uproar.

The pirate girl from the kiosk shows up with a bullhorn, clears a couple of kids off a small platform, and climbs up on it, waving her arms. Nobody pays any attention whatsoever and she raises the bullhorn to her lips and bellows, "Treasure hunters! I need you in a line, over here on the right-hand side!"

The girl deserves a medal. Somehow or other she wrangles us all into a ragged line, and explains to the family with the dog that he has to be on a leash.

A young man in full pirate regalia and a stern-faced woman, who is apparently not buying into either Team Viking or Team Pirate and is dressed in blue jeans and a flannel shirt, take their places on either side of the gangway.

The man blows three sharp blasts on a whistle, then cups his hands around his mouth and shouts, "Listen up, treasure hunters!"

When relative silence descends, he goes on. "I'm your first mate, the Dread Pirate Travis. And this here is Captain Vickers. Shout 'Aye, aye, Dread Pirate Travis,' if you've heard me."

"Aye, aye, Dread Pirate Travis!" most of the passengers shout.

"Can I go home now?" Gene asks.

Gail, who shouted louder than anyone, elbows him. "Hush. Listen."

Travis puts a hand to his ear. "That sounded like a pathetic bunch of landlubbers to me. Let's hear it again, louder this time."

"Aye, aye, Dread Pirate Travis!" This time everybody joins in, except for Gene, who complains, "Travis? You've got to be kidding. What kind of name is that for a pirate?"

Travis stabs a finger in our direction. "What's yer name, matey? Yes, you, in the accountant getup."

Gail hollers, "His name is Gene!"

"Well then, Gene. Not precisely a pirate name, either, is it, me hearty?"

The crowd laughs and turns to stare at Gene, who glowers at everybody. Gail looks vaguely worried and lays a restraining hand on his arm.

Captain Vickers raises her voice and intervenes. "Time to sail! All hands on deck. Don't precisely care what anybody is called, so long as we get this boat underway. Come on. You there. What's your name?" she asks, pointing at a middle-aged blond woman.

"Michelle Richardson, Captain."

The captain nods and makes a checkmark on her clipboard. As Michelle steps on board, Travis takes her bag and hands her a life jacket. "Step right on up to the front of the ship and have a seat."

The family with the kids and the dog is next. A little girl looks up at Travis. "How come you're not the captain?"

"Because Captain Vickers is the captain. One captain per ship, lassie."

"She doesn't look like a captain."

The woman looks up from her clipboard and levels a steadfast gaze on the child. "And what should a captain look like, precisely?"

"Well, she should be a man, maybe?" The little girl is uncertain now, but still standing her ground.

"Really," the captain says. "I hadn't realized that only men can drive boats. Trust me. You don't want Travis in charge." Her gaze shifts from the child to the sky and a low bank of clouds out over the water. "There's weather coming in. Let's get moving, shall we?"

Travis shrugs and grins good-naturedly.

The little girl's mother nudges her forward. It's my turn.

"Blythe Harmon," I say, and my heart does a little tap-dance routine as the captain runs the pen down her list. Maybe I'm not on there. Maybe that Flynn person didn't add me and I'll have to wait another week before I can get to the island. Her pen stops moving and she glances up at me. "Did you say your last name is Harmon?"

The tap-dance routine in my chest picks up its tempo. "That's me. Is there a problem?"

"You look like somebody else," she says, but she makes a check mark with her pen and calls out, "Next! Let's keep moving, people."

"Don't mind her. Takes her responsibility serious, does our captain." Travis tugs at my suitcase.

"Is that necessary?" I ask, tightening my grip and tugging back. "I'd rather keep it with me."

"I promise it will be safe and secure and you'll get it back on the other side."

"Not so sure I should trust the word of a pirate," I say, trying to relax, but reluctant to let Nomi's ashes out of my sight.

"It's protocol. Kind of hard to lose a suitcase on a little boat," he says, a hint of frustration creeping into his voice. Gene and Gail are now waiting behind me with their bags. I'm creating a traffic jam and making Travis's job more difficult, but still I cling to the bag as if it's my last lifeline.

"Problem?" The captain's cool gaze sweeps over me.

I feel the heat rising to my face. She probably thinks I'm smuggling drugs or something. Travis takes advantage of my distraction to yank the bag out of my temporarily relaxed fingers, handing me a life jacket in exchange and gesturing toward an already crowded bench, right next to the family with the dog.

Theoretically, I'm in favor of children. In books and movies, they are delightful—innocence and creativity and seeing the world with new eyes and bringing people together and all that. But up close they are unpredictable and irrational and either whiny or loud.

This gang is not only loud, highly mobile, and rather dirty, their innocence and love for humanity are questionable. They keep churning around, changing places, climbing up on the bench to get a better look at the water, and shouting at one parent or the other to look at this, that, or the other thing. The parents don't bother to glance up from their respective phones, issuing warnings and reprimands in a way that makes it clear they have no expectation of being obeyed.

I'm seated beside the quietest of the bunch, a girl who is probably thirteen or so. She's made an effort to look older—thick foundation in the wrong color, smoky eyes with eyeliner that wanders a little from its intended path, and a bra that is trying hard to create cleavage but doesn't have much to work with. She peers up at me briefly through clumpy eyelashes, then returns to her phone, texting as if her life depends on it.

Travis moves to the front of the boat, microphone in hand, and his voice cuts through the hubbub, amplified by overhead speakers. "First Mate Travis here, mateys, but that's still Dread Pirate Travis to you," he says.

Polite laughter, mixed with a few groans, follows from the crowd.

"Time to put your life jackets on," Travis says.

"Is that really required?" somebody asks.

"Boat's not leaving the harbor until everybody is wearing them," Travis answers.

"Seems like you don't have much faith in the boat then!" somebody shouts out. But everybody jostles each other, trying to make room to put the stiff, uncomfortable things on. Everybody, that is, except the family next to me, none of whom is listening at all. The youngest child has gotten tangled up in the dog leash. The two middle boys are about to come to blows over some sort of Transformer toy. When the dog pulls the small child off the seat onto the floor and she wails loudly, the father finally tears his gaze away from the phone long enough to see what's going on and says, "Allison, help your sister."

"Oh my God," the girl beside me says. "Why do I have to do everything? I swear that dog is possessed."

The little girl sits on the deck, wailing helplessly, while the clueless dog makes things worse by running around her and tightening the leash. I drop to my knees and grab the dog's collar, giving the child a reassuring smile.

"You're kind of all tangled up."

Her eyes open wide and she stops crying right in mid-wail, making a little hiccuping sound.

"Brodie is a bad dog," she says in a wavering voice.

"He's not bad. He's just a little excited. Aren't you, boy?" The dog's tail wags furiously as he does his best to lick my face, an action that tightens the leash around the little girl and sets her crying again.

The child's mother sighs loudly, shoves the phone into her bag, and says, in a martyred tone, "Hold still, Violet, you're not helping. Brodie. Come here."

She grabs the dog's leash with a perfectly manicured, beringed hand and tries to drag him in the direction of disentanglement. Brodie obviously doesn't want to go anywhere with her and does his best to climb into my lap. I'm rendered useless by a fit of sneezing, not on account of the dog but because of the woman's overpowering perfume.

"Oh, for heaven's sake," the father says, joining the fray. "This will be easier." He bends over and unclips the leash from the dog's collar.

While his action does make it easier to unravel the still-whimpering child, now there is an exuberant dog freely darting from passenger to passenger, his bushy tail smacking into anything within reach and creating enough wind to launch a small sailboat.

Captain Vickers stalks over and says, "I need you to contain your dog and get yourselves and your children into life jackets. Now. Or get off my boat."

It's immediately clear from their shocked expressions that neither children nor parents are used to being spoken to in this way.

"I think you can see that we're doing the best we can here," the man says, pulling himself to his full height and puffing out his chest. "I don't care for your tone."

"You'll care for it a lot less when I escort you back onto the dock."

"You can't do that," the woman protests, standing beside her husband. "We paid."

"I don't give a rat's ass whether you paid or didn't pay. Life jackets. Now. And get that dog back on a leash."

Amid snatches of muffled laughter from some of the passengers, I grab the leash that is dangling from the man's hand and head over to Travis, who has the dog by the collar. Behind me, I hear the mother's voice saying, "I want to speak to your manager."

Captain Vickers laughs outright. "You're out of luck, ma'am. I own the boat."

"We have paid for a week on Vinland Island. You can't—"

"I can. This is the only boat that can or will take you there. So get your goddamned life jackets on or your vacation ends now."

"We'll be posting about this," the man says. "How dare you speak that way in front of our children."

"Would you just do what she says?" somebody demands. "The rest of us would like to go now." A spontaneous cheer goes up from the rest of the passengers.

Travis grins at me. "Think you might be persuaded to hold on to the dog until we get to Vinland? They are not exactly reliable dog guardians."

I look down at Brodie, who is now sitting at my feet, panting happily as he gazes up at me adoringly.

My heart melts. He's really very sweet. It's not his fault that nobody has bothered to train him.

"You don't think the family will mind?"

Travis snorts. "They'll be back on their phones in five minutes. Wait for the outcry when they lose the signal; that's always fun. Better go sit down; we're about to sail."

I look up to see that the entire family is putting their life jackets on. Captain Vickers strides across the boat and vanishes up a ladder marked KEEP OFF—STAFF ONLY. A motor roars to life and thrums beneath my feet.

As the boat begins to move away from the dock, Travis leads us in an off-key rendition of "A Pirate's Life for Me," then elicits cheers from Team Pirate and Team Viking. After that, he offers up facts about the small islands we sail by. When there are no islands at close range, he regales us with tales of the Spanish galleons that used to sail these waters and of Leif Erikson and the Vikings, and the mysterious historical Vinland for which the island is named.

I only half listen to his patter. Brodie sits quietly, pressed against my legs, and I stroke his head and rub his soft ears. The smell of the sea washes the perfume out of my nostrils. I lift my face to the wind, focus my gaze on the horizon, and let myself imagine that this really is a sailing ship and that I really am off on a search for treasure.

Just as I'm beginning to feel stiff and a little cold, my butt cheeks going numb from the hard bench beneath me, Travis shouts, "Land ahoy! Look starboard, me lovelies, and feast your eyes on the shores of Vinland!"

Our boat motors around the rocky point of a small island, revealing a forested shoreline that curves inward into a shallow bay. A road leads up toward what looks like a high-prowed Viking ship and a row of jewel-toned buildings with thatched roofs. A variety of houses and cabins are set into the trees along the shore. To my left, the island curves upward into a towering hill, the top of which disappears into clinging mist.

The boat angles toward a white pier stretching out into the bay. A line of people, some of them wearing pirate or Viking hats, stands waiting.

"Listen up, me hearties," Travis bellows. "When ye landlubbers set foot on Vinland, ye'll be met by those who control yer fate for the time ye inhabit these shores. Listen close to what they tell ye, and be ye back on the jetty in seven days' time, just as the sun marks midday, unless ye wish to be stranded on this forsaken isle. Shout 'aye, aye' if ye understand me."

A loud shout goes up, my voice joining with the rest. A wild surge of freedom washes over me, along with a dreamlike sensation that I'm entering a magical world where anything is possible—even finding a treasure marked on a map drawn by a six-year-old child.

Chapter Eleven

FLYNN

Thursdays on Vinland are the worst day of the week. Controlled chaos, if all goes well. Uncontrolled chaos if it doesn't. It's a lot like embarkation day on a cruise ship. Rounding up all the departing passengers, getting them to the dock on time to meet the water taxi, and dispatching workers to clean and restock their rentals is like teaching a herd of cats to swim.

And then there's the incoming. Sorting people into pirate and Viking teams and explaining the rules of treasure hunting is only the beginning. Nobody really listens, and we'll be explaining over and over again for the length of their stay. Then there's the matter of getting their attention long enough to match them up with their golf carts and giving them their maps and directions to their lodgings. Worst of all is fielding the innumerable questions and evading the requests for me to "talk like a Viking."

"Frieda always wore a Viking hat," Glory says as we stand on the dock with the outgoing guests, watching the Thursday boat chug toward us, its imprisoned and meaningless sails flapping in the wind.

"Frieda did a lot of things," I answer, surveying a batch of rambunctious kids and a redheaded woman trying to wrangle an overexcited dog.

Glory shakes her pirate-hatted head reprovingly. "We're all about creating an experience, Flynn. You need to play along." She practices what she preaches, I'll give her that. In addition to the hat, she's wearing giant gold hoops in her ears and an eye patch over one eye.

"I am not a Disney princess and I'm not playing dress-up," I retort. "The rest of this is bad enough."

Glory snort-laughs. "Now, that I'd like to see. You. As Cinderella dressed for the ball."

"Those kids are going to be trouble," I observe.

Glory shrugs. "Kids are always trouble. Hey, there's a girl more or less your age, Savannah."

Savannah just shrugs. She hasn't said a word to me all morning. Her eyes are scanning the passengers with an unusual level of intensity, probably looking for the woman who will be moving into Improbable House. I'm doing the same thing, only for different reasons. I want her to feel welcome. I want her to stay, whereas I'm pretty sure that if Savannah knew how to cast a hex on somebody, our guest would be breaking out with a bad case of boils right about now.

"Ready, Cinderella?" Glory asks.

"Forgot my tiara but I'll manage," I retort, still searching the faces on the boat.

It takes a minute for me to connect the driver's license photo of a reserved woman, maybe a little severe, her hair pulled tightly back from her face in a bun, with the woman being towed down the gangplank by a large and shaggy dog. But it is undoubtedly her—Blythe Harmon, here to help me keep Savannah away from that accursed house.

Blythe's face is vivid and expressive, alight with laughter. A riot of fiery curls spills out beneath a crooked Viking hat and spirals down over her shoulders. In a dramatically storybook moment, the clouds part and a ray of sunlight illuminates her.

Her head comes up. Her gaze meets mine. I'm not one to be spell-bound, especially not by a woman, but I have a weird sensation of being caught up out of time. One heartbeat. Two.

A seagull perched on a nearby piling takes flight. The dog lunges after the bird. The leash slips through Blythe's fingers. And then, in one giant leap, the dog is airborne. He sails over the edge of the dock and splashes into the water.

Time returns to its normal frenetic pace. Screams and shouts go up. Everybody runs to the edge of the pier. Blythe pushes through the crowd and drops onto her knees, leaning out over the water and shout-ing, "Brodie! Here, buddy!"

I stride through the throng, shoving people out of the way.

The dog is paddling frantically, keeping his head well above water, but he's not getting anywhere. There are no strong currents here in the bay, I have plenty of reason to know. Frieda and I used to sneak down here to swim, even though it was strictly against all of the island rules.

"I think the leash is snagged on something," Blythe exclaims, lean-ing precariously forward and peering down into the water.

My eyes follow the line of the leash. It should be floating, but there's a definite downward line of tension. The dog's eyes are wide in panic. Already his head is sinking lower in the water.

"He's going to drown!" Blythe says. "I'm going in."

I grab her shoulder and hold her back. "No you're not. The water is freezing."

She glares at me. "I'm not going to just sit here and watch him drown."

Still holding her back, I watch the dog, who is obviously tiring. Damn it. Savannah will never forgive me if I let the creature drown. Besides, if this woman goes in after her pet, I'll end up rescuing both of them.

"I've got it. Stay put."

I peel out of my clothes and my shoes and dive before I have time for second thoughts. The water in the sound at this time of year is still dangerously cold. My breath is driven from my body. My heart, shocked, thumps hard in my chest. When I get close to the dog, he tries to climb me to safety, his weight and motion shoving my head under the surface.

The water in the harbor is murky and the salt burns my eyes. I can make out only dim shapes—the struggling dog, the dark bulk of the pilings that hold up the pier.

I feel the sharp swipe of toenails across my arm and then my chest as I connect with the leash and close my hand around it. Already my muscles feel heavy and slow, my lungs burning with the need to breathe. Ignoring the churning paws, I fumble with the dog's collar, trying to unhook the leash.

My fingers are numb and awkward, the dog won't hold still, and I can't see what I'm doing. I collide with something solid, a pier piling probably, and feel a sharp pain slice across the back of my shoulder. Perfect. Another scar to add to the collection. Surfacing, still holding the collar, I finally manage to unhook the leash.

Free, the dog starts swimming toward shore, but he's tired and I'm not sure he's going to make it. A shout from the direction of the water taxi alerts me, and a lifesaver ring splashes into the water. I throw one arm over it, then swim after the dog. There's a dicey moment as he scrambles for safety, but once he's got his front paws hooked over the ring he settles enough that I can hold him there while the captain drags us in.

Waiting hands reach down to haul the dog up to safety. As I climb up the ladder onto the pier, a loud cheer goes up. If the water wasn't so cold, I'd go back in to escape the attention, but I know I'm close to hypothermia. My entire body convulses with violent shivers as the wind cuts through my skin.

Glory materializes like magic with my clothes and a blanket, which must have come off the boat. "You'll catch your death," she says. "Get dressed."

Somebody wolf whistles, one of the older women, I have no doubt. Old men do not hold the patent on lechery, I've discovered.

Glory laughs. "Sexy shirtless Viking man is infinitely better than the princess costume any day."

"Not funny," I mutter through chattering teeth, trying to drag my jeans on over dripping legs.

"Good for business," she says. "Pics all over Instagram as soon as they get a signal." But she has mercy and holds the blanket up between me and the onlookers, giving me privacy while I get into my clothes, and then throwing the blanket around my shoulders. "Go home and get cleaned up."

"I can help first."

"You're bleeding. You'll terrify the passengers."

I look down at my arms, thoroughly scored by the dog's claws, bleeding freely and burning with salt and the return of sensation. "Tell them it's part of the experience. Stop looking at me like that. I'm fine."

"If you say so. I'll go start rallying the troops."

I hear Travis doing his shtick, improvising a little to capitalize on the excitement and get his charges back into the holiday spirit while he loads up the outgoing crew. Our incoming guests are milling about, talking excitedly in small groups. Some are watching Blythe rub down the dog with a towel that has materialized from somewhere, probably the same place as my blanket. Savannah, who would normally be all over the animal rescue program, is nowhere in sight.

Glory heads toward land, waving her arms above her head and shouting, "Incoming treasure hunters, this way!"

Shivering, bloody, and furious, I wrap the blanket around my shoulders more tightly and stride over to check on the dog, who obviously thinks being toweled off is a game. He mock-growls, biting at the towel, his tail wagging enthusiastically. When he sees me, he squirms away from Blythe and leaps up, planting both paws in the middle of my belly.

"Hey, boy," I say. "Easy there. Feet on the ground."

He drops down, runs a circle around us both, then hightails it for shore, where he dives right into the middle of the group of kids.

"Oops," Blythe says, laughing. "Gonna need a new leash." She gets to her feet and looks up at me, holding the absurd Viking hat onto her head with one hand. She's tall for a woman, her eyes level with my chin, and while she peers intently at my face, I can't help but look into hers. A golden dusting of freckles over flawless white skin, delicately arched eyebrows, a slightly bowed upper lip. Her eyes are like sunlight through a wave, blue-green and luminous.

I catch a whiff of shampoo and sea and something less pleasant, wet dog, maybe, which sharpens my anger and brings me back to my senses.

"He really did a number on you," she says, her eyes dropping to my bleeding arms.

I draw the blanket more tightly around me in an attempt to both hide the wounds and stop the shivering. "Maybe you should go get your dog under control before it does any more damage," I growl.

"My dog?" she asks, as if she hasn't noticed that the animal is now terrorizing the guests.

"If you can't be bothered to train and control him, you shouldn't have brought him. I'll need to add a pet fee to your rental agreement."

"Wait. You think that Brodie belongs to me?" She stares pointedly toward the sulky teenage girl, who is now holding on to the dog's collar, and then turns back to me.

"Travis asked me to help out with the dog because those people couldn't manage him," she says. "So if you're done berating me, I'll go join the group, if that's okay. I don't suppose you know what happened to my bag?"

I look around. Glory is assigning people to their golf carts and checking names off her list. Travis is giving everybody on the water taxi the life jacket lecture. There are no bags on the pier or anywhere else that I can see.

"Brodie pulled me off the boat before I could grab it," Blythe says a little frantically, starting to run back along the pier to the water taxi.

I grab my radio. "Travis, hold up. Do you still have Miss Harmon's bag?"

"I'll check," he says into the radio. Into his microphone he says, for the benefit of his crowd, "We may have illegal booty aboard this here ship. Hold fast afore we set sail."

What a day. Only noon and I'm ready for a hot shower and a bottle of something fortifying and thoroughly inebriating. I've already rented this woman a house that is falling apart, accused her of being a negligent pet owner when she doesn't own a pet, and now we appear to have lost her bag. I've got scratches all over my arms and my chest and something on the back side of my shoulder that burns like a motherfucker. I can feel it bleeding, the wet heat instantly turning cold. Know it's staining my favorite T-shirt.

Even better, Savannah has taken advantage of the distraction and run off somewhere.

"Nice job, Flynn," I mutter under my breath.

"What's that?" Blythe asks.

"Nothing," I tell her. "Bad habit. Talking to myself. Wait here. I'll get your bag."

Travis hands over a roller bag, gushing apologies. "I'm so sorry," he says. "All that excitement with the dog! We've never gone off with a bag before. You're a hero, Flynn." He slaps me on my lacerated shoulder and it's all I can do to keep from flinching. "Well, better go before some vaporing person jumps overboard so they can be rescued by a Viking god," he says, laughing. "Turn it into a whole new paid attraction."

"You're a funny guy," I say between clenched teeth.

Just to top it off, the sky lowers and envelops me in a chill, drizzling mist.

Chapter Twelve

BLYTHE

I have been swallowed by a cloud. The shore has vanished. Even Flynn is little more than a dark shape at the end of the pier. I can hear his voice, and the voices of the travelers, and Travis apologizing profusely. There's a splash of waves against the pier. Seagulls' cries.

It all feels far away, a different world, as if I've passed through some invisible portal into another place where I am completely alone, unreached and unreachable by human hands. Shivering takes me, a quaking that begins deep at the center of me and spreads out into my arms and legs and shoulders. I feel wide-awake, alert, aware in a way that is new to me. As if mesmerized, I watch the mist swirl and re-form. Breathe in the scent of sea and tar and the exhaust from the boat. Feel my feet grounded firmly on the pier, its subtle movement, almost the spinning of the earth.

"Got it," Flynn's voice booms. I hear his footsteps, the sound of wheels, and he emerges out of the mist. For an instant caught out of time, he looks otherworldly, a towering god of the sea in a rough gray cloak, long hair streaming water, face marked by a magically inflicted scar. But then the trance breaks, and he's just a tall, scarred man in a blanket, towing a black roller bag with one hand.

"I'll take that." I grab the handle of the suitcase, partly because Nomi's in there, partly because I need the reconnection with reality, with something solid and familiar and mine. But Flynn doesn't let go.

"Least I can do after all of this disruption is handle your bag. I'm sorry your stay has gotten off to such a bad start. And now you've missed most of orientation."

"It's okay," I say between chattering teeth, aware that my own hair and clothing are damp and I'm chilled to the bone. If I'm cold, Flynn must be freezing after taking a swim in the icy water. "You should go somewhere and get warm. You'll catch pneumonia."

"If I was that fragile, I'd have been dead a long time ago," he says, moving out ahead of me. I half run to catch up to him. With a little thump of the suitcase that makes me shudder for Nomi, we move off the pier and onto the paved parking area. I can see the treasure hunters, all sitting in golf carts, and the dim shape of trees behind them, but everything beyond is obscured by the mist.

A woman in a pirate hat and a raincoat stands at the front of the carts, talking, her voice pitched to carry. "Any questions?" she asks.

Flynn leads the way to an empty cart and hefts the suitcase into the back. "What on earth have you got in there?" he asks. "Rocks? Weighs a ton."

"My grandmother," I say, picturing the urn broken and Nomi spilled out all over the suitcase. Or the snow globe, fractured down the middle, spilling out white flakes and magic onto my clothes.

His blue eyes widen and his gaze locks on mine. "Right. I forgot about her. Get in," he says, removing a sodden cardboard sign with my name on it from the windshield. He climbs into the passenger side. "Since you've missed the talk, I'll get you up to speed."

The mist has transitioned into full-on rain now, drumming on the tin roof, making it hard to hear the question shouted by the man who belongs to the kids and the dog. "Where's the best place to catch a cell signal?"

"Idiot," Flynn mutters, drowning out the answer as he goes on explaining things. "You know how to read, right? There's a folder on the kitchen table in your rental. Everything that has just been said here is written in that folder. There's a map to Improbable House right here in the console."

He unlatches the top of the compartment built into the seat between us and hands me a map of the island that is, unsurprisingly, more detailed than the one that marks my own personal treasure hunt. "We're here," he says, touching a finger to the map. "As you see, there's only one road that leads up from the bay here to Vinland Square. That's where you'll find everything you need—restaurants, coffee, groceries, and WiFi."

"And what is the thing with phone service?" I ask, looking at my own phone, which is searching for a signal.

"Isn't any."

"Oh, come on. Tell me the secret. What do the locals do?"

He shakes his head. "No signal on the island. There's a landline in your rental. You can get free WiFi at the Coffee Dragon." He gestures toward the misty blankness. "It's a great landmark if you're ever trying to find the square. Not now, of course, because we're all socked in and you can't see anything. But you can't get lost on Vinland, and all roads lead to the square eventually.

"Now, if you follow this one and only road, it will take you to the parking lot. Foot traffic only within the square, so there's lots of space there for carts. What you're going to do is drive through the parking lot and keep on going, all the way to the end of the island, where you'll find Improbable House. Key is in a lockbox on the porch. Code is 8888. Got it?"

He turns his head to look at me, fixing me with a pair of ice-blue eyes that, for some completely inconceivable reason, warm me. Maybe he no longer looks like the god of the sea, but he definitely fits the part of a Viking warrior.

One of the other carts drives away out of the lot, followed by another.

"So, they are all going to their rentals then?" I ask.

"Some are. There's a group lunch, if you like, but the houses are stocked with basics. Soups, bread, sandwich stuff. Some people prefer to eat on their own. You look half-frozen. You might want to take a hot shower and get into dry clothes."

I think about cramming into a restaurant with all these strangers. Making small talk. Hashing over the rescue of the dog. I'm damp, I'm cold. I want to unpack Nomi and make sure her urn isn't broken.

A violent shiver shakes my whole body. "That actually sounds like a good idea."

"Great. Make sure you come back in tomorrow morning for the metal-detecting class. You'll get your first clue."

"I'm not really here for the treasure," I remind him.

He shrugs, then swings out of the cart, bending back in to say, "You paid for the whole adventure. Might as well have some fun. You know how to drive one of these things?"

"Never golfed."

"It's easy. Turn on the key to start it, just like a car. Press the go pedal to go. There's your brake. Flip this lever to *F* for forward, *N* for neutral, *R* for reverse. See you in the morning?"

I feel myself nodding yes. Flynn vanishes, and again, even though there are still carts visible, I have that strange sensation of being adrift in some alternate reality. Shaking it off, I turn on my cart, step on the go pedal, and follow a line of carts up the hill. As Flynn said, at the top of the hill is another parking lot, bounded by a low stone wall.

A wooden archway is painted with the words WELCOME TO VINLAND in ornate purple letters. On one side stands a larger-than-life Viking, and on the other, a pirate. Both are garishly painted. The Viking wears a horned helmet and brandishes an enormous sword. The pirate wears an eye patch and a bandanna. Another large sign reads, NO GOLF CARTS PAST THIS POINT. PLEASE PARK IN THE LOT.

Following Flynn's directions, I keep going, through the parking lot and along a road that is almost immediately lined by the ghostly forms of towering trees. The pavement ends, so I'm driving on a graveled, rutted track pitted with mud puddles. Rain patters on the roof. The tires make wet, sucking sounds.

The trees begin to feel threatening, like they're watching me and resent the intrusion. Spokane is not exactly a sprawling metropolis, but I'm still a city girl, born and raised. My family was never into camping and outdoor spaces, and city parks are as isolated as I ever get. Now I'm all alone in the middle of nowhere with no means of protection and not even a cell signal. Every horror movie I've ever watched, every episode of *Criminal Minds* and *Law & Order*, comes rushing in. If I were a psycho killer, I'd wait here by the road. Grab my victim and drag her off into the trees where nobody would hear her scream.

I press my foot to the go pedal on my cart, but speed isn't exactly its strong point.

"Oh, Nomi. I hope you know what you're doing," I say, out loud so I can hear the sound of my own voice. It's a mistake. The trees are listening. If anything else is out there, anything predatory, it too will have heard me.

My own breathing is too rapid, too loud.

I try to slow it, grounding myself in logic. It's just this fog that's got me freaked out, that's making me feel so strange. Some people spend their whole lives off-grid. Even Aunt Bella has been known to spend weeks in a cabin where there were no phones and no internet, so she could get away from everybody and relax and think.

The road begins to climb and curve. *This is good, this is fine,* I tell my racing heart. The island's southern end is a higher elevation than the rest. This climb means I'm getting close. I hear a raucous commotion of birds somewhere ahead, and then see them circling above the treetops, big and black and apparently very excited about something. A murder of crows. An unkindness of ravens.

Just an expression, Blythe. Hold on to your Viking hat. I touch my fingers to the raven pendant riding between my collarbones.

Neither crows or ravens hurt people, and they aren't supernatural. But they do eat carrion. Am I going to drive around a corner and find something dead? Maybe the chainsaw killer was already here and has a victim. Or maybe they are somehow drawn to Nomi's ashes in my suitcase.

I remind myself that ashes have no odor. It's not like I'm dragging a dead body around with me. And birds can't be attracted to a dead soul, if there were such a thing. Still, my breathing stays rapid and shallow, my heart races. Around every curve I brace myself for the sight of some dead forest creature, swollen and bloated, or worse, a massacred human, or some man with a gun or a knife or maybe a bloody ax, waiting in ambush.

But of course there's nothing but more rain. More mist, more mud, more trees, more grass and bushes. It seems like hours before the cart rolls into a clearing and a house looms up out of the mist. The birds circle above it, shrieking their displeasure at my arrival, settling onto the peak of the gabled roof and then taking flight again with a rush of wings.

The house, tall and weathered and gray, appears to be not leaning, exactly, but slumped in on itself, as though it has grown weary and given up on standing straight. Up close, I can see that the shingled roof is green with moss. Ivy clings to the walls. All of the windows seem to be watching me.

I park at the edge of a neatly graveled lot, reluctant to go in, despite the promise of warmth and shelter from the rain. Then the front door opens, and a girl steps onto the rickety porch. Under the influence of solitude and mist, I have the uneasy sense that she is an apparition, a creature not of this world. She's no more than twelve or thirteen, I'd guess, her body still angular and boyish. A thick black braid hangs over one shoulder. A ball cap is pulled down low over her eyes.

"You shouldn't be here," she says, letting the screen door bang shut behind her.

"This isn't Improbable House?" I retrace the route I've taken in my mind. Did I miss a turn? I have to admit that if I did get it wrong, being redirected to a cozy, normal-looking little cottage of some kind, one without a flock of big black birds circling overhead, would be a huge relief.

The girl glares at me. "Yes, this is Improbable House. But it doesn't want you."

"And you are?" I ask.

"Savannah. Did Uncle Flynn tell you the house is haunted?"

Doubt and irritation give way to understanding. This is all part of the drama production that goes on here on Vinland. People dress up like Vikings and pirates. This house is supposed to be haunted. I suppose they can't summon a good spooky mist at will, but they can put a freakish child on the porch to heighten the mood.

Suddenly I feel the pleasure of surprise and delight. How fun to be part of a game like this! I get out of the cart. "Flynn is your uncle? You don't look like him."

"I look like my mother." The child descends the steps and brushes by me. "I'll get your bag."

"Wait, I'll get it."

But she has already dragged it out and dropped it heavily into the gravel at her feet. "What in blazes have you got in here?" she asks. "Rocks?"

"I said I'd get it." Grabbing the extended handle, I try to wheel the bag toward the porch, but the wheels won't roll properly in the wet gravel. Using both hands, I heft the weight and lug it up the creaking stairs, braced for the wood to crack and drop me with every step. It does feel heavier than it did this morning, but I blame it on fatigue and hunger and the shivering that just won't stop.

Savannah follows me. I set my bag down on the porch, gingerly, listening for the sound of pieces rattling around inside. Just as I reach out to open the door, one of the black birds swoops down and lands on the railing right beside me.

"Hello," it croaks in a shockingly human voice. "Welcome."

I shriek and stumble backward. The bird is extraordinarily large and so close I could reach out and touch him. He tilts his head and stares at me out of a glittering black eye.

"That's just Norman," the girl says disdainfully. "He won't hurt you. Probably."

"But he just . . . he talked."

"He's very smart," she says, her expression implying that this is a quality I am lacking.

"Can they all talk?" I ask, tipping my head back to look at the croaking black birds circling above me. "Also, why are there so many of them?"

"I told you the house is haunted," she says. "The ravens live here. They don't want you any more than the house does."

Norman hops closer, sizing me up in a way that affirms his superior intelligence. I'd rather he was a very stupid bird, honestly, and not quite so big and black and otherworldly. My mind goes uneasily and unwillingly to Poe and his spooky raven.

I'm more than ready for this unsettling child to leave and take her familiar with her, but she seems to have absolutely no intention of doing so.

"Well, I guess you might as well come in." She opens the door and I step inside, half expecting to see cobwebs hanging from chandeliers and to hear ghostly sounds of moaning and wailing. But inside, the house is sparkling clean, invitingly appointed with well-worn, comfortable chairs and gleaming antique tables and chests of drawers.

"That's the main living room," she says. "Here's the downstairs bathroom. The cold-water knob sometimes drips, but if you turn it hard enough it will stop. There are more towels in the cabinet. Here's the laundry room. You'll have to do your own laundry."

She announces this in a tone that suggests I would expect her to do the laundry for me. "All of the beds have clean sheets, of course," she goes on, in much the same tone, "but if I were you, I'd sleep in the one downstairs."

I'm about to ask why, and then remember her comments about the house being haunted and decide that I don't want to know.

"Come see the kitchen," Savannah says. "You'll notice that the fridge and pantry are fully stocked."

The kitchen is a large, high-ceilinged room with visible beams and plentiful windows. A rustic wooden table with six chairs occupies a nook that looks out on an overgrown garden. The child opens the refrigerator door, pointing out the basics—eggs and milk, bacon and bread, peanut butter and jelly, a couple of packaged salads.

"There's coffee in the cupboard to the right of the sink. Anything else you want, you can get from Old Nick at the trading post. He's mean, but he has to be nice to tourists."

"Unlike your uncle Flynn."

Oops. I've said that out loud instead of in my head. She whirls around to glare at me, and I brace myself for the backlash.

"Uncle Flynn is a professional asshole. He doesn't have to be nice to anybody. Are you coming or what?"

She stomps out of the kitchen and I follow in her wake, down the hallway and up a narrow, creaking staircase. I have an uneasy sense that somebody is behind me, strong enough to make me turn and look even though I know there is nobody there.

When I reach the top, Savannah is waiting, hands on hips. "Don't look at me like that. And don't bother to say it. Trust me, I've heard it a bazillion times."

"Heard what? Please, by all means, enlighten me as to what I was going to say."

She tosses her head, shifts her posture, wags her forefinger, and says in a voice that is obviously meant to mimic mine, "Do you really think you should use that word? You're a child."

"You *are* a child," I point out. "But which word?"

"Asshole. Uncle Flynn is one. So what are you going to do?"

"Noted," I say. "Fortunately I'm not the language police. What I was really wanting to ask is: What sort of ghosts are supposedly in this house?" I keep my tone light, not wanting to admit even to myself that I'm feeling jumpy and imagining invisible eyes watching my every move.

"Only two have been seen," she says in a low voice. "But we think there are more. They make noise at night. Bang the cupboards. Sometimes guests have heard music or voices. The Lady appears in white, moaning—she died here, long ago. This is her bedroom."

She opens the door to a large corner room, two walls of which are mostly windows. All I can see is mist, but the view must be beautiful on a clear day. An antique four-poster bed is made up with a lovely hand-made quilt in shades of blue and green. A vase of wildflowers adorns a chest of drawers crafted from a dark, glowing wood.

"Oh, these flowers are lovely." I bend down and inhale their fragrance.

"They're not for you," Savannah says darkly. "They're for the Lady. She doesn't like people sleeping in this room. Like I said, if I were you I'd sleep downstairs."

She holds the door, pointedly waiting for me to exit this space, and closes it behind me.

I follow her around as she points out the two other bedrooms, a full bathroom, and a storage closet with extra blankets, sheets, and towels.

"All of these rooms leak when it rains," she says. "Plus, there's the Dark Man to worry about."

I roll my eyes, feeling better at her description of these ghosts. The Lady. The Dark Man. Predictable and clichéd. I would have expected a little more imagination. Savannah sees me and shakes her head, lowering her voice to a tone suitable for ghost stories around a campfire.

"He's evil," she intones, her eyes wide, the pupils dark. "The Lady just wants to be left alone, but the Dark Man wants to hurt you. Well, that's it for the tour. I should let you get settled in."

She clatters down the stairs and I follow more slowly.

"I'll put your suitcase in your room for you," she calls up.

I speed my steps. "Just leave it. I'll do it."

But she's already towing my bag across the floor and into a downstairs bedroom. It's smaller than the rooms upstairs, and darker, with only one small window. It smells dank and disused and feels like it holds an extra chill.

Savannah tries to lift the bag up onto the bed, but her wiry little body can't quite manage it. "Damn. That's the heaviest suitcase ever," she says breathlessly. And then, in a different sort of voice, "Uh-oh. We've got a problem."

"What? What is it?" Imagining ashes or snow or both leaking out through the zipper, I rush over and heft the bag up onto the bed myself.

"Unless your name is Marc, this isn't your bag," Savannah says, fingering a leather tag attached to the handle. "See?"

With a shock of dismay, I do see. The bags are identical apart from the tag. I didn't even check when Flynn rescued this suitcase from the boat, due to mist and cold and that weird otherworldly sensation. I'd just assumed he had it right.

Denial makes me tug the zipper open, as if somehow the tags got switched but the suitcase will still belong to me. But no. I'm looking at an array of treasure-hunting books. *Getting Acquainted with Your Metal Detector. Buried Treasures of the Western States. The Secret: A Treasure Hunt.*

Savannah picks up *The Secret* and flips through the pages. "Wow, these are weird-ass pictures."

I look over her shoulder and have to agree, but that's beside the point.

My knees feel weak, all at once, and I sink down onto the bed. "This Marc person must have taken mine during all the confusion with that dog. Oh my God. Nomi's in my bag." I imagine her, frightened and alone, in the hands of some treasure-obsessed person named Marc.

"Who's Nomi?" Savannah demands. "Wait, did you put a pet in your suitcase? It could suffocate!"

"Nomi's my grandmother."

"Your grandmother is in your suitcase?" She's bewildered now, rather than accusing, and I take a deep breath before trying to explain.

"Only her ashes. She was cremated."

I pick up my cell to call the office so somebody can sort this out immediately, before I remember that there won't be a signal. Right. Landline. Flynn said the phone would be in the kitchen. I get up and run as fast as I can without spinning out on the slippery hardwood. Sure enough, a phone sits on the counter, a laminated sign stuck to the wall above it that reads NEED SOMETHING? JUST CALL.

But when I pick up the receiver and press the green talk button, there's no dial tone. Savannah stands in the doorway, watching me. When I look directly at her, she twitches her shoulders and seems to find something of great interest to look at on top of the counters off to the right.

"The phone isn't working," I say, standing there with the useless receiver in my hand.

She shrugs. "Told you the house is haunted."

I take a breath, hold it until I start to feel dizzy, then let it all out in a rush. "You're on your way back. Would you please tell your uncle that the phone isn't working and that I have the wrong bag?"

"I can't," she says.

"What do you mean, you can't?"

She bites her lip, not meeting my eyes. "I'm sort of not supposed to be here."

"Sort of?"

"Okay. I'm not supposed to be here at all."

"Well, you are here. You'll have to tell him and—"

"No," she begs. "Please. He can't know."

Her desperation makes me wonder uneasily about her relationship with her uncle and whether he could possibly be harming her.

"Maybe talk to Glory, instead of your uncle?" I suggest. "Or Frieda, even. When will she be back, do you think?"

The child's pupils dilate, all the color washing out of her face so fast I put out an instinctive hand, ready to catch her if she faints. "She's not ever coming back," she whispers, then turns and flees the house as if pursued by all the hounds of hell, slamming the door behind her.

Chapter Thirteen

BLYTHE

Great. Just absolutely fantastic.

Maybe I'm not happy about the child being here at the house, but I didn't mean to upset her. And now, instead of stepping into a hot shower or taking a good long soak in the tub, not to mention finding something to eat, I'm going to have to drive back through the mist and the fog, track down the rental office, and try to figure out what happened to my bag and to Nomi.

There has been nothing but one disaster after another ever since I set foot on Vinland. I can't even change into dry clothes or put on a warmer jacket. Cursing out loud, with an amount of fluency and vehemence that would shock my mother and surprises even me, I grab the handle of the outrageously heavy bag, drag it back out to the golf cart, and hoist it up into the front passenger seat, which is easier than trying to lift it into the back.

I reach for the key, already rehearsing an imaginary speech worthy of Kristen or my mother or maybe even Alan at his kingliest. I want the phone repaired immediately. I want Savannah to stay away. I insist on a discounted rate.

The key isn't in the starter. I was sure I left it there, but obviously not.

"Damn it!" I scream at the top of my lungs. My voice echoes back to me, a Greek chorus of "damn it, damn it, damn it" that sets the ravens, who had settled onto the roof, into a squawking flurry.

Get it together, Blythe. Where would you have put the key?

I go through my coat pockets. My jean pockets. Nothing and nothing. With a heavy sigh, I flounce out of the cart and up to the house, retracing my steps, looking on every flat surface in every room.

No key.

I take off my jacket and empty the pockets, even shaking it upside down. Nothing. I'm sure I didn't put it in my handbag, but I dump that out on the table, too.

Better and better and better.

Well, I can stay here and wait for somebody to check on me, or I can walk all the way back to town.

My body makes the decision for me. I'm starving. I'm cold. I feel weak and faint and weepy. Food and warmth first. Surely this Marc person will want his own bag and somebody will figure out the swap. Nomi will be fine. If nobody comes out here, then I'll have to go in, but it can wait.

I leave Marc's bag out in the cart. There's nobody here to steal his stupid books and I don't have the energy to lift that bag one more time. Locking the door, I go straight to the bathroom, strip out of my damp clothes, and climb directly into a hot shower. That at least seems to be working. The water is steamy and abundant and I stand under it for a long time, until the shivering stops and my skin is glowing and reddened from the heat.

The towels are gloriously big and fluffy. I wrap one around my wet hair like a turban and knot the other around my body while I walk to the linen closet, where I trade the towel for a warm and cozy comforter. I toss my clothes into the dryer. They need to be washed, but that can wait.

There's kindling and wood laid out in the living room fireplace, with matches on the mantelpiece. I've never actually lit a real fire before, but when I strike a match and touch it to the newspaper, the little flames spread hungrily, crackle on the kindling, and spread to the wood. The sound is comforting and the fire gives off a pleasant heat that my body greedily absorbs.

I place my damp shoes in front of the fire to dry, and then, still wrapped in my comforter, I venture into the kitchen and rummage through what's easily available, settling on a cup of ramen noodles—a quick and easy meal, thanks to the microwave. When the timer dings, I grab the container of noodles, pick up the orientation folder Flynn told me about from off the kitchen table, and carry everything back to the living room where I can toast in front of the fire while I eat and read and wait for somebody to bring me Nomi.

The folder features a garish, full-color illustration of a treasure chest heaped with golden coins and outsize jewels. Inside, I find another map of the island, this one with all the rental properties and businesses marked. I set this aside as potentially helpful with Nomi's treasure hunt.

Another sheet lists the food establishments. Meals at three of them—a pizza joint, a burger stand, and a diner—are covered by my rental fee. A fine-dining restaurant, which isn't included, looks like the sort of establishment that costs a fortune. If I prefer to cook my own meals, groceries are available for purchase at Odin's Trading Post.

A multipage, full-color flyer outlines the elaborate treasure hunt, which is the central reason for a vacation on Vinland. I'd known about the hunt, superficially, but since I was coming for an entirely different purpose, I didn't pay much attention.

Vinland guests receive a series of clues in the form of cryptic rhymes. The game is to solve the riddles, search prospective sites with a metal detector, and discover more buried clues that will lead to more prospective sites, and so on. Everybody, including me, will get one clue to start out with at the metal-detecting class tomorrow. The winner is the person who follows all the clues to locate a valuable treasure—five thousand dollars the first week of the season, increasing by another

thousand every week that it hasn't been located and unearthed. If somebody does find the treasure trove, then the game starts all over again at
five thousand.

My inner child stirs with curiosity and the promise of fun. Sure, I'm
really here to figure out where to bury Nomi, but there's no reason why
I can't play this game at the same time. The last item in the folder is a
gold-foil envelope with my name written on it in elegant calligraphy. I
open it carefully, withdrawing a photograph of Improbable House. On
the back is written:

> *A Viking's heart is always with the sea.*
> *If you search that elusive shore,*
> *You will find all that you are looking for.*

A little shiver runs through me—this time of excitement and
delight. How fun! I've always loved the ocean. I can't think of anything
I'd like better than to wander around the shores of this island waving a
metal detector and looking for treasure. Weird, though, that I already
have a clue when the instructions said we get the first one at the Friday-
morning class.

Maybe this one is just an example? But then, why the fancy envelope with my name on it?

My body is warm now, inside and out. Rain drums hypnotically
against the windows. The fire crackles comfortably. I can't seem to stop
yawning. Drowsiness begins to weight my limbs and my eyelids. Telling
myself that I'll just rest for a minute before I get my clothes from the
dryer and walk to the office to ask Flynn or somebody to look for my
suitcase and give me another key for my cart, I lie back on the couch
and close my eyes while I put together a tentative plan.

First, of course, I need to find my bag. And message everybody
at home to let them know I got here okay. And then tomorrow I'll go

to Flynn's metal-detecting class, and then I'll start trying to figure out which tree is designated by the treasure map that brought me here. There are a lot of trees on this island. I can't imagine how I will find the right one.

Gradually I drift into a half sleep, waking suddenly, stiff and disoriented. My fire has burned down to coals. The rain has stopped. And somebody is knocking at the front door. Still half asleep, I pad, barefoot, through the house, then pause with my hand on the dead bolt and call, "Who's there?"

"It's Flynn."

His deep voice jolts me wide-awake. My hand goes to my hair, knowing from experience that it will be a hopeless mess due to humidity and sleeping on it while it's wet. And then I remember I'm clad only in my undies and a comforter. My face heats with embarrassment as I realize how close I was to opening the door like this.

I should go get my clothes, but what if he leaves before I come back? Or worse, gets impatient and uses his own key and catches me basically naked?

"Just a minute," I say, wrapping myself up like a burrito. This leaves my shoulders bare but at least I'm not exposing anything important.

When I open the door, Flynn's eyes widen. I pretend that I'm properly clothed and combed and say, graciously, "Can I help you with something?"

"Apologies for disturbing your nap," he says, "but I thought you might be wanting your bag."

Forgetting my pretended dignity, I squeal with delight and dart past him to grab the handle, trying to tow it into the house while still holding the blanket in place.

"Marc was unsure what to do with a supply of women's clothes and was inordinately disturbed by being in the possession of what I'm guessing are your grandmother's ashes," Flynn says. "Figured you'd be worried about them. The phone didn't work so I headed right on over."

"I was worried about them, yes. Thank you."

Flynn's lips twist into a quizzical smile and he says, "Perhaps I could come in? It's still raining some and this porch roof leaks. I could, um, help you with the suitcase so you could manage your wardrobe."

I glance down to see that the comforter has come undone and let go of the suitcase to try to fix it.

His smile widens as he lifts the bag and carries it into the entryway.

"Let me get dressed," I say, trying to channel my mother's unruffled superiority, but it's a total fail and I turn tail and scamper down the hallway and into the laundry room. Slamming the door behind me, I lean against it, breathing and trying to regain a veneer of composure, before I pull on my now warm and dry, even if still dirty, clothes. When I return, at a more dignified pace, Flynn has moved the bag into the living room and hefted it up onto the couch for me.

"Figured you'd want to look and confirm nothing is missing."

"Yes, thank you so much." I zip it open, relieved to see the urn holding Nomi's ashes is intact. "Thank God you're okay," I say, hugging the urn to my chest.

Flynn's eyebrows go up. "One might think *dead* and *okay* were not exactly synonymous."

"She's here and undisturbed," I retort, setting her on the mantelpiece. I give her a little pat and then move on to the rest of my things. The snow globe is also safe and unbroken, and with a breath of relief, I set it beside Nomi.

"That's a beautiful item," Flynn says, coming to stand beside me. "Don't think I've ever seen anything like it."

I let my fingers rest on the cool glass. "Nomi used to say she could see things in it. Like a crystal ball."

"And could she?"

I glance up at him to see if he's mocking, but he's looking at the globe, not at me, his brow slightly furrowed. He looks as if he's listening to something I can't hear.

"I used to believe she could," I answer, laughing a little. "She told me she saw me on an island on my thirtieth birthday."

"And now here you are. Is it your birthday?" I feel him looking at me, now, and glance up to find his eyes intent on my face, as if I'm a puzzle he's trying to solve.

I'm suddenly dramatically aware of him and how close he is to me. How tall he is, the broadness of his shoulders. I don't need to try to imagine how he looks under his clothes; all I need to do is remember him surging up the ladder out of the bay like a vengeful god of the sea, water pouring off the well-defined muscles of chest and abs, the bloody scratches on his arms, those sculpted thighs . . .

The embers of the fire seem to be giving off a lot of heat.

"It is not," I say, retreating to the couch to zip up my bag. "But it was. Last week."

"I suppose I should get Marc his bag," Flynn says. "He was quite concerned about it. Books, apparently."

"It's in my golf cart. But before you go, could you take a look at the phone? I tried to call out, but the line is dead."

"I could," he says, but not with a reassuring level of enthusiasm. "Though I must warn you that repairs are not my strong suit."

"Also," I blurt out, "I'm afraid that I've lost the key to my golf cart. I was going to drive Marc's bag into town but. Well."

I brace myself for sarcastic comments about my ineptitude, but instead he looks aghast. "My God," he exclaims. "First I accuse you of neglecting a dog that doesn't belong to you, then we lose your bag, then you find yourself in this run-down old heap with no phone and no transportation. I can't believe you're even speaking to me."

"Well, it wasn't your fault, exactly," I say. "At least most of it."

He laughs. "Tell that to Glory."

"Is she the pirate woman who was running things?"

"Indeed. Okay." He digs in his pocket and hands me a key. "Spare for your cart. They are all keyed the same, by the way. It's difficult to steal things on Vinland, so we keep it simple. Why don't you unpack while I look at the phone?"

"All right." I start rolling my bag toward the bedroom Savannah designated as mine.

Flynn calls after me, "You're welcome to stay wherever you like, of course. But the rooms upstairs are much nicer. Have you had a look yet?"

"Aren't they haunted?" I ask lightly, not wanting to give Savannah away.

He laughs. "So the legend has it. Trust me, the views are worth the risk. Come on."

Picking up my heavy bag as lightly as if it's a child's toy, he carries it up the stairs. I follow. He leads the way into the corner room. I smell the fragrance of the flowers immediately when I step inside, a delightfully elusive scent. And then I forget everything as I take in the view.

The fog has lifted.

Off to the left is a magnificent oak tree, gnarled and twisted with age. To the right, a tangle of wild rosebushes, heavy with blossoms. Spreading out before me is an expanse of overgrown lawn and a small bed of scarlet flowers. The grass slopes away at a gentle incline, ending in a weathered wooden fence. Beyond the fence, cliffs drop off sharply down to what I persist in calling the ocean, even though I know it's either a strait or a sound or a bay. Waves break against the rock, throwing white foam toward the sky. Sunlight breaks through the clouds and sparkles diamond bright on placid blue-green water. In the distance I can make out the shapes of several small, forested islands, still partly wreathed in mist.

One of the windows is a slider leading onto a small balcony, and I step outside, breathing in the rain-scented air, tangy with the smell of salt and green things and roses.

I hear Flynn behind me, saying something about the roof leaking again, and buckets, but I don't turn around. He steps out onto the balcony beside me and leans on the railing, an expression on his face that is somewhere between longing and maybe even dread. And then it's gone with a blink of his eyes.

"Sorry about the leaks. This roof refuses to stay fixed, so we have buckets. I'll put them out for you. Right after I look at the phone. And that grass! I swear that was mowed two days ago, but you'd never know it. I'll send somebody over to do it again."

I hear his footsteps retreating and tear myself away from the glorious panorama below to unpack my things. It only takes a minute to stow my jeans and sweatshirts and underthings in the drawers of the antique dresser.

Flynn's footsteps on the stairs bring me back out to meet him in the hallway.

"Bad news," he says. "I'll have to get a telephone repair person out here from the mainland."

"How long is that going to take?" The dismay in my voice is loud and clear. I can't imagine being at this old house by myself, so far away from anybody else, without a phone. It's easy to scoff at the idea of ghosts by light of day, but tonight when everything is dark it will be a completely different story.

Flynn withdraws his radio from his belt and holds it out. "Take this. If you need anything, you just press this button to talk, release it to listen. Either Glory or I will be tuned in twenty-four seven. Better than the phone, honestly. That often just goes to voice mail."

"Are you sure? Won't you need it?"

"We've got spares. I can't have a guest out here with no means of communication. And I'll get a repair person in as soon as I can."

I take the radio, clinging to it like a security blanket while I trail after him, watching him set up buckets to catch the drips, muttering all the while about how this damned house refuses to allow itself to be repaired. When he's done, instead of immediately driving off into the distance, he lingers on the front porch, as if he has something to say but doesn't know how to say it.

"Was there something else?" I finally ask.

He straightens up from where he's leaning on a railing that looks like it could give way at any moment and drop him over the edge into the wild tangle of rosebushes, and runs a hand through his hair. "Remember to come to the metal-detecting class in the morning."

"How hard can it really be, the metal-detecting thing?" I ask.

"Harder than you might expect," Flynn answers, not taking offense. "More importantly, you'll want to get your metal detector and your first clue."

"Right. Okay. I'll be there, if I survive the night."

I mean it as a joke, but there's a flash of uneasiness in his eyes as he says, "This island is probably the safest place in the world you could be. The ghosts won't hurt you."

As he descends the steps and drives off in the cart, I stay where I am, staring off into the trees, my flesh all creepy-crawly and the hairs on the back of my neck standing on end.

He was just trying to scare you, I tell myself.

Well, he's done a good job, myself answers.

I lock and dead bolt the door when I go back inside, trying not to listen to the voice in my head that says doors are no use against ghosts, and even if they were, then I'd be locking them in with me, not keeping them out. Every time the old house creaks or groans, which it does frequently, I startle.

"Get your head together, Blythe," I say out loud. "The house is old. Not haunted."

Obviously, I'm just tired and hungry and unsettled. Food would be good. I weigh the draw of human companionship and a ready-made meal against the golf cart drive through the trees and the obligation to check in with my family, and decide to just stay where I am. A rummage through the pantry and the kitchen cupboards turns up the makings for tomato soup and a grilled cheese sandwich, comfort food from my childhood. Half an hour later I carry a tray up the stairs and out onto the covered balcony.

The sky has cleared and the water is calm and serene. There's a small table and two chairs, and I set myself up with the Vinland Island folder and Nomi's treasure map to look over while I eat. That X could be anywhere, beside any tree beside any house on the island. So I set it aside, after a fruitless attempt to superimpose it on an actual map of Vinland, which is entirely the wrong shape, and decide to focus on the treasure-hunt clue that was in my folder.

Only this time, when I pull the photo with the clue written on it out of the envelope, I notice another sheet of paper, folded in half, that I missed before. It looks old, yellowed, a little brittle. Nice touch, I think, aging the paper like that. I unfold it and read:

My love,
The house is grieving.
For you. For us. For the life that we were meant to
have here together.
It refuses to hold a coat of paint. The shingles fall off
as fast as they can be nailed back on. The lawn won't stay
mowed and the forest keeps encroaching, no matter how
hard we work to fend it off.
Your mother fainted dead away when we heard the
news that you were missing in action. She's still sedated,

months later. And your father has taken up drinking. Neither one of them can look me in the eye, as if somehow it's my fault that we've all lost you. Neither one of them can help me.

That was the day the ravens came. I was sitting on the balcony, holding a thought of you in my mind, believing, I think, that as long as I could conjure you in my imagination you must still be alive. I heard the croaking and the flapping of wings, felt a shadow fall over me. And when I looked up, there they were, swirling above me in a dark cloud.

And then down they came, landing in the branches of our old oak tree. Since then, they've never left. They roost on the roof, constantly muttering in a way that makes me think that if I only knew how to listen I would hear the words, and that maybe they have news of you.

I was strong, at first, despite the ravens and the grieving house. I hunted for you. I wrote to other men in your unit. But they all told me the same thing, that you'd gone out on a mission, that a land mine was triggered, that you never came back.

I thought I could stay here anyway, to wait as long as it takes for you to find your way home. Or for the proof of your death to do it for you. But as my belly swells with the baby . . . our baby, all that is left of you . . . the practical creeps in.

I have some realities to face.

This little person growing inside me, part of you and part of me, both, deserves a real life, not a half-life in this shadowed house. I can't do this by myself. The money that you left for me is gone.

If I sell the house, the money will support us for a time. There's a man who is interested in buying. But what if I sell it, and then you come home to find somebody else living here?

I do wish you could tell me what to do . . .

When I reach the end, I dash the tears from my eyes and read the whole thing again, my heart lodged in my throat. No wonder the handwriting looks familiar. The letter is signed, *Always and ever your Nomi.*

Chapter Fourteen

BLYTHE

I sleep badly, even though I'm exhausted.

The house is noisy. It creaks and groans, and once, just as I'm drifting on the edge of slumber, I startle awake with a gasp, certain that I've heard footsteps on the stairs. For a long time I lie wide-awake in the dark, listening. No more footsteps, but the groaning and creaking continue. There's a faint scratching and scuffling in the wall behind my bed. A rustling and murmuring sound overhead, accompanied by an intermittent moaning.

Old houses make noises, I tell myself. They settle, or something. There are probably mice in the walls and in the ceiling. Maybe there's a window open that's responsible for the moaning sound.

Or maybe the house really is haunted.

For a long time I lie there, awake, listening, hiding like a child with the covers pulled up over my head.

Where's my brave Blybee? Nomi's voice whispers, so clear I reach for her hand in the dark. Of course there is nothing there, but I feel safer, all at once. Protected. I grope for the lamp on the bedside table, but its dim glow just seems to create more shadows. So I get out of bed and scamper across the room to turn on the overhead switch. Better. Now that the shadows are banished, I check the sliding door to the balcony, making sure it's closed and locked. Then I go through the house, turning on all the lights, checking all the windows and doors.

I consider moving into the downstairs room, but then Savannah and Flynn might both know that their ghost story actually worked to scare me. Instead, I scoop up Nomi's ashes and the snow globe and carry them both upstairs with me, setting them on the dresser like a shrine, before climbing back into bed with all the lights still on.

I finally fall asleep with a pillow over my head to block the light.

A fuss from the ravens drags me into reluctant wakefulness. The sky outside my window is blue, and the sunlight streaming in is bright enough to make the electric light look dim. I wonder, drowsily, what's got the ravens all stirred up. Maybe they're like dogs, barking when somebody comes to the door. Anybody could be out there—the phone repair person, Savannah, Flynn.

The thought of Flynn jolts me wide-awake. My heart flutters wildly, my skin heating with something I refuse to acknowledge as anything more than embarrassment. He would be scornful of my slothful ways. My reaction has everything to do with that and nothing to do with the way his broad shoulders seem to fill up all the space in a room, the penetrating blue of his eyes, the way his lips twist into a half smile without going the full distance.

Once I'm out of bed and have confirmed that whatever the ravens are squawking over, it certainly isn't an extra golf cart parked in front of the house, I look at the time and realize I have a little less than an hour to get dressed and make it to Flynn's metal-detecting class—if I decide to go.

Discovering Nomi's letter tucked into an envelope with my Vinland Treasure Hunt clue has turned my brain into a kaleidoscope of ever-shifting possibilities and ideas and questions. The house she mentions fits Improbable House perfectly, and she's even mentioned the big oak tree in the yard—which means it could very likely be the tree on my map! But this also means that Nomi must have lived here once, that maybe she slept in this very room and looked out these very windows while grieving for my grandfather.

The thought of that breaks my heart at the same time as it fills me with excitement. If the big oak tree is the tree on my map, then I know where to start looking. Maybe I'll find the place today, lay Nomi to rest after all these years, collect a small fortune from Mr. Wilcox—and have a whole week to play the Vinland Treasure Hunt game.

But there are also questions. Who put Nomi's letter in the envelope, for instance? Did Mr. Wilcox pay somebody to hide clues for me? Could it possibly be Flynn? I didn't notice the letter in the envelope until after he was gone.

I'm torn between running out to the tree right now and starting to randomly dig, or going to Flynn's class to get my metal detector and learn how to use it properly. Just because I've found the tree doesn't mean I've found the treasure. Besides, if I do want to play the Vinland Island game, I need my clue.

Which is yet another question, because I could have sworn Flynn said the first clue would be found at his class, not in the folder.

I need to ask him about that. And I really do need to check in with my family and let them know I'm safe, and I should message Mr. Wilcox and let him know I'm close to finding the treasure.

That decides it. I'll go to Flynn's class. I'll stop by the Coffee Dragon for a much-needed dose of caffeine and use the WiFi to check in with everybody. Another glance at the clock tells me there's no time to take a shower or try to tame my hair. I gather it into a loose twist on top of my head, splash water on my face, pull on a pair of jeans and a T-shirt, drop a quick kiss on Nomi's urn, and run out to my golf cart. If I'm lucky, I'll have just enough time to grab something hot and caffeinated at the coffee shop and still make it to Flynn's class without incurring his wrath by showing up late.

This time, I enjoy the ride through the trees. They still seem mysterious, but no longer threatening, probably because the sky is blue and the sun is shining. A squirrel scolds me as I drive by. Birds twitter and sing. A bunny startles out of the grass at the side of the track and hops off into the woods.

Before I know it, I'm parking the cart in the lot provided, and passing under the arch into the Vinland Square.

I feel like I've crossed the portal into a different world. The square is a riot of voices and color. A young woman wearing a skull-and-crossbones kerchief plays a set of steel drums. Groups of people in pirate hats or Viking helmets wander in and out of the brightly painted shops.

The Coffee Dragon dominates everything, her dragon-headed prow and narrow stern rising high above the ground. The deck is full of people. Some chat animatedly in groups, others sit alone with laptops or phones, making use of the WiFi. The coffee smells fantastic.

Viking helmets, plastic parrots, ravens, and skulls and crossbones unabashedly mix and mingle in the ship's rigging above my head. The deck under my feet is surely made from old ship planking, and a faint whiff of tar mixes with the fragrant aroma of coffee. I enter an enclosed area with a roof, designed to resemble a ship's cabin. A wooden chest full of fake gold coins and jewels sits in the place where Starbucks would feature impulse buys. Even though I know the treasure has to be fake, it's hard to tear my eyes away from the soft gleam of the gold, the green fire of emeralds, the red flash of rubies. I reach my hand out to touch, and a voice instantly blares over a loudspeaker: "This treasure is guarded by a curse. Touch at your own peril."

I snatch back my hand, glancing around to see who has noticed. The other patrons, none of whom are part of the group I came in with on the water taxi, clap and cheer. Flushed with embarrassment, feeling as though I've been caught shoplifting on reality TV, I consider slinking right off the boat and never coming back, but the motherly-looking woman behind the counter waves me forward, smiling brightly.

"Never you worry, my dear. Every one of those people either fell for the treasure themselves, or saw somebody who did. You're in good company. Now. What can I get for you? Coffee? Breakfast? Information?"

The woman's warm smile and comfortably rounded body feel safe and inviting and I gravitate to her with relief, sinking down onto one of the barstools that line the counter.

"It shows that much?"

"Well, I haven't seen your face before, so you're one of the incoming. Vinland takes a little getting used to. I'm Giselle, and you just come and talk to me any time you're bewildered or overwhelmed. What's your name, my love? And where are you staying?"

"I'm Blythe. And I'm at Improbable House."

Giselle's beaming face stops beaming. "What is Flynn thinking?" she murmurs, as if she's talking to herself more than me. And then she shakes herself, as if suddenly remembering I'm standing there, and asks, "What can I get you, Blythe from Improbable House?"

I consult the menu. "Am I allowed to mix and match? Pirates and Vikings, I mean?"

"You can have whatever you like. Only you'll need to hurry if you want to catch Flynn's class."

"I'll have the Ragnarök Ruin and a Pirate's Breakfast. Do I have time?" The café is noticeably emptier than it was when I came in, with only a few solitary customers scattered at the outside tables.

"You've got fifteen minutes," Giselle says over the hiss of the machine as she pulls my espresso shots. "Flynn will talk for the first ten minutes or so. After that, it's hands on."

"What's the WiFi password?"

She points over her shoulder to a blackboard behind her where the password is neatly written: *blackbeard.* I enter it in, and my phone immediately begins to buzz with a barrage of incoming messages.

"Here's your coffee," Giselle says, distracting me from the onslaught. "If you want to sit for a minute, I'll bring over your sandwich."

"Yeah, thanks," I mumble, barely glancing up as I carry phone and coffee off to a table, scrolling through the disaster.

Kristen: Did you find the water taxi? Were you on time?

Kristen: Where ARE you? Talk to me.

Kristen: Were you body snatched? Mom is going ballistic and I'm the one who has to deal with her. Call me.

Kristen: Called the rental place. Left a message.

Kristen: This isn't funny. You need to check in.

"Oh God," I moan out loud, clicking open the string from Mom with the sensation that I'm voluntarily walking into a pit of starving rattlesnakes.

Mom: Did you make it to the island? Please call.

Mom: Where are you? If you would be considerate enough to check in, I would appreciate it.

Mom: If I don't hear from you within 30 minutes, I will call that rental place to check on you.

Mom: The police say I have to wait 24 hours to file a missing person report.

Kerry Anne King

"Everything okay?" Giselle's voice is concerned. She sets a breakfast sandwich and a scone down on the table in front of me, with a sympathetic smile. "Sounded like you needed some extra nourishment."

"My family," I answer, with a failed attempt at a smile. "Phone isn't working at Improbable House, and I didn't check in. They're filing a missing person report."

She laughs. "Family, right? You can't escape 'em, even on an island. Look at it this way—at least you have people who care about you."

"Well, if the sheriff comes looking for me, you can let him know I'm alive and well."

"Oh, lovey, we don't have a sheriff. Not on the island, anyway. They'd have to send somebody over from Orcas, and they'll call here looking for you before they do that."

There's some relief in her words, but I'm still cringing at the thought of Flynn listening to the messages from my family, and having law enforcement make phone calls checking on my supposed disappearance is humiliating. I'm a grown woman, not a child, but they're behaving as if I've been lost at sea for a month, when really I've only been out of contact for less than a day.

Handling the phone as if it's something that might bite, I text Mom back first.

> Blythe: I'm fine! No cell service and my landline was out. Call off the missing person people, I beg you.

Immediately my phone lights up again:

> How do I know this is you? Maybe somebody stole your phone. I want to hear your voice.

I glance up at Giselle and say, "She doesn't believe it's me texting. Too many movies and thriller novels."

142

"Call your mother," Giselle says. "Let her hear your voice."

"But I don't have service," I protest. I take a swallow of coffee and follow it with a bite of scone, crumbly buttery goodness with the tang of fruit, lightly sweetened. "Oh my God, this is amazing."

Giselle smiles. "Come with me. Call your mother."

I bring the coffee and food with me, following Giselle behind the coffee bar and into a snug, cozy room. It contains a round table with a stack of magazines. A bookshelf full of paperbacks. A comfortable-looking sofa with a soft throw. And a landline phone.

"It'll be long distance," I say, hesitating. She waves her hand at me. "Don't worry about it. I have kids on the mainland. I know about the worry."

She vanishes back out into the coffee shop and leaves me alone. Mom answers on the first ring. "Who is this?"

"It's me."

"Are you being coerced?"

"Mom. I'm on an island. It doesn't have cell service, and the phone line was down in my rental. Also, oh my God. You lived before cell phones. What did you do then?" I take a sip of my drink—coffee and chocolate and whipped cream in delectable combination.

"We worried!" Mom exclaims. "What kind of place is that, to leave you stranded without communication? Has your phone line been fixed then? What's the number?"

"No, it hasn't been fixed. I'm calling from a phone at the coffee shop, which is also the only place I can access WiFi. I promise you that I'm perfectly safe, and I will check in daily."

"I left a message with that vacation rental place, but nobody has called me back yet. I want you to come home, Blythe."

"They're busy, Mom. Besides, I can't leave until next Thursday." Then, instead of moving to hang up, I ask, "Was Nomi ever here, do you think? On Vinland Island?"

"What I think is that you should be focused on Alan and your career. Have you spoken with him?"

"I'm serious," I persist, ignoring the mention of Alan. That is one conversation I am not having with my mother over a long-distance line from Vinland. "Do you think maybe your father was from here?"

There's a brief silence on the line. "She wouldn't talk about him. All I know is that he died in Vietnam."

"You must have had grandparents. Where were they from?"

"They died when I was just a baby. I never met them and she never talked about them, either. What does it matter?"

I shove my hand into my pocket and touch the letter, as if it's a talisman, a connection. "I just think she might have been here, is all. Could you maybe ask Aunt Bella?"

"You want to talk to Bella about this, you call her yourself."

"Mom. There's no phone—"

"Blythe. Come home."

"I will when I'm ready. Call off the missing person thing, Mom. And stop calling the rental place. I'm perfectly safe here. Is Daddy home?"

"He's at work. Not worrying about you at all. Just like him."

I smile to myself. My calm, easygoing father is a wonderful ballast to my mother. I have a feeling they've both grown more extreme over the years by pushing against the opposite in each other.

"Be careful," Mom says. "And call Alan!"

I hang up and take a bite of my now lukewarm breakfast sandwich. And then I look at the time. Damn it. Only two minutes before Flynn's class. No time to catch up with Kristen. Which is fine. Mom will already be on the phone with her, filling her in. And as for Alan, I plan to ignore the other text message on my phone, the one from him that says: We need to talk. Call me.

"You should scoot," Giselle says, sticking her head into the room. "Leave the food here. Come and eat after class."

"But it's so good." I take a bite of the sandwich and put my hand on the scone, protectively. "So I'm a few minutes late. What's he going to do, throw me off the island?"

Giselle laughs but says, "You don't want to miss your first clue."

"My second clue, you mean," I correct her. "The first one was in my welcome packet."

She looks puzzled. "Huh. They must have changed the game. Well, any clues then, first, second, or other. And until they get your phone fixed, you just feel free to come in here anytime. This wouldn't have happened when Frieda was running things. Flynn means well, but . . ." She shrugs and lets her words trail away.

"Is there something wrong with the house?" I ask. "Besides it being 'haunted.'" I make quotes around the word, laughing a little.

Giselle doesn't laugh. "It's not the house itself, so much, I guess. Although, in my opinion, the whole thing should just be torn down. It's more what happened to Frieda."

"Is that why she's on vacation?" I ask, my hand stopping with the coffee halfway to my lips. "Because of something that happened at the house?"

"Vacation?" Giselle gasps. "Who told you she's on vacation?"

"Flynn."

"Good heavens. Something wrong with that boy," she gasps, one hand going to her heart in a way that makes me start running imaginary CPR protocols. I've taken the training but never had to use it, and I can never quite keep it all straight in my head.

"Are you all right?" I ask.

She gathers herself together and nods. "I'm perfectly fine. Just . . . surprised, is all."

Giselle hesitates, as if she's not sure whether to speak or not. Then she leans forward, drops her voice, and says, "Frieda, she is, or was— God, this is so horrible." Her hand covers her mouth, her kind brown eyes brimming up with tears. "Frieda is dead. She died right there at that house. An accident. Her daughter saw it happen. Flynn hadn't been on the island since he was sixteen, but he's Frieda's brother. He came back to care for the child and take over the business, but you can tell that his heart isn't in it."

I stare at her, frozen in a moment of horror, remembering the question that sent Savannah running from the house yesterday. A memory from my own childhood washes over me.

Strangers have come to take Nomi away. I'm not at all sure we should let them put her in their long black car. I've been told to stay in my room, but I need to tell Nomi that I understand she's not dead, just asleep, so I dart into her room to whisper in her ear that I've completed the ritual she assigned me and that I know everything will be well.

But the people from the black car shake my faith. Mom is still crying, and the woman says, all solemn, and sad faced, "I'm sorry for your loss."

Nurse Lisa, who has been coming to the house to take care of Nomi, lays her hand on Mom's shoulder. "It's good that she went easy. She's not in pain anymore."

The black car people slide Nomi off the bed onto the wheeled cart they brought with them, and then they pull a sheet up over her face.

I try to pull it back. "She can't breathe like that!"

"She's all done breathing, sweetheart," Miss Lisa says, putting her arms around me. "This is a sign of respect."

I'm only six, but I know putting a sheet over somebody's face isn't respect. It's because nobody wants to look at her, with her face the color it is now, and her eyes staring, and her not breathing. She doesn't look at all like Sleeping Beauty in the picture book. And she smells bad, like Kristen when she has a potty accident, only worse.

Even so, my faith in Nomi is absolute. Everybody will be so surprised when she wakes up again. "Where are they taking her?" I ask, as the strangers drive Nomi away in the black car. "Who will take care of her?"

I look up at the three adults. None of them are looking at me. Their eyes are fixed on the place where the black car was, before it turned the corner.

"Where are they taking her?" I ask again.

Mom puts her face in her hands and doesn't answer.

"She's going to a special place where the dead are cared for," Lisa says.

Horror strikes me, as the use of the word dead *finally hits home. I've had three encounters with dead—a goldfish, a bird that hit the window, and Whiskers, my cat. All three are buried in the backyard. I picture Nomi, shoved into a hole and covered with dirt. She'll suffocate for sure. All at once the adults looking down at me are not comforting, but terrifying. How can they allow this? Even my father isn't going to stop it.*

Daddy tries to put his arms around me, but I break away and run to my room, hiding under the covers. I refuse to come out for dinner when Daddy comes to get me. He strokes my hair and leaves me alone.

What really happens is worse than burying. When Aunt Bella comes to the house, I run to her, pleading, "Tell them she isn't really dead! Tell them we were playing a game."

"I have no idea what you're talking about, child," Aunt Bella says. "Nomi went to sleep shortly after your mother left. You went outside to play. I was downstairs in the kitchen when she died. There certainly weren't any games."

"But—"

"Hush," she says, stroking my hair. "I know it's hard to let her go. But she isn't coming back, Blythe. She's gone forever."

"Are you all right?" Giselle asks, dragging me back into the present. "I didn't mean to upset you."

"I'm fine. Just—I'm going to kill Flynn. He said Frieda was on vacation, and yesterday I asked Savannah when she was coming back. What a terrible thing to say to the child!"

Giselle sighs. "You had no idea. Savannah will be okay. Precocious thing, she is. Helped Frieda out with all sorts of maintenance. Now she pretty much haunts that old house, trying to hold on to the memory of her mother, poor lamb. Who can blame her? No father, no other family.

And Flynn, God love him, I'm sure he'd die for her, but he's about as comforting as a grizzly bear. Two of 'em lock heads something fierce." She stops to smooth both her hair and her composure. "Well, now. I reckon I've told you far more than you were needing to know. From a practical point of view, there's no reason not to rent out the house, I suppose."

I have so many questions clamoring for answers, but Giselle is done talking. She pinches her lips together tightly, an expression ill at ease on her round face, and says, "If you want to catch that class, you'd best be running along. Go all the way down to the end of the square, until you can see Ragnarök Mini Golf on your left. Take a left turn and you'll find your group."

I run out of the coffee shop, carrying my fury with me. Nobody gave me what I needed when I was a child and Nomi died. I'm about to explain a few things to Flynn.

Chapter Fifteen

Flynn

If I hate Vinland Thursdays because of the chaos and intrusive energy stirred up by outgoing and incoming tourists, I hate Fridays because I've inherited the job of teaching the introduction-to-metal-detecting class.

"Better get started," Glory says, looking at her watch. "Nobody here is on vacation time yet."

"Yeah, yeah. Since I'm supposed to be a Viking, can I quaff a horn of mead first?"

She laughs and strides off to our football-sized practice field to make a few adjustments. I look around for Savannah, who is supposed to be helping but is nowhere to be seen. She's been avoiding me ever since yesterday, when I confronted her with the interesting information that the phone line to Improbable House had been cut through by some sort of sharp object.

"There are mice," she said, all wide-eyed innocence. "And squirrels in the attic. I could go over with some live traps—"

"The line was not chewed through, Savannah. It was cut. With a knife."

She gasped, clutching her chest theatrically. "Oh my God. A robber? A serial killer, maybe? On the island?"

Praying for patience, not wanting to accuse her outright, I'd settled for a command. "You stay away from that house. You hear me?"

She rolled her eyes and made a quick escape, diving into helping the team with maintenance requests at the other rentals with a diligence and enthusiasm I found as suspicious as her current absence.

The fact that a certain vivacious face and mane of red curls is also missing gives me a very bad feeling, which I don't have time to indulge.

I lift my arms above my head and wave, semaphore style. "Okay, treasure hunters. Gather round!"

A motley group drifts in my direction, talking excitedly as I distribute the inexpensive and not very effective metal detectors that come "free" with their vacation rentals. Two overachievers have brought their own. One of them is Marc, the guy who brought a suitcase full of treasure-hunting guides. The other is the man who belongs to the family with the dog. But their fancy detectors and treasure-hunting books aren't going to help them. The truth is, the winner of the grand treasure generally stumbles over it out of pure dumb luck. Equipment and strategy have little to do with success.

"Pirates over here." I gesture to my right. "Vikings on my left."

Laughing and chattering, the groups separate into two more-or-less even teams. A few retired couples. A handful of singles, more interested in finding a special somebody than they are in finding treasure, except for Marc, of course, who has nerded out to the max and donned a full-on pirate costume. And, of course, the family with the dog. The teenage girl looks sullen and bored. The other kids are chasing each other around in circles while the dog dashes around them, attempting to trip them up with the leash that drags freely behind him. The father of the family unit is completely fixated on his expensive metal detector, while the mother tends to the crisis of a damaged fingernail.

My job right now is to convey the rules of the game and teach these people the rudiments of metal detecting. Oh, and entertain them in the process. This is mandatory, Glory impressed upon me as she helped me write my script.

"But this isn't really treasure hunting," I'd objected when she explained what needed to be included.

"They know it's not real. They are paying for an experience," she'd said. "Like when people visit Alaska and pay to pan for gold. They don't really think they're prospecting. It's all just one big game of 'let's pretend.'"

"Which they are paying for."

"Which they are paying for. Listen. Tell me how this is any different than Disneyland? At least here they have to learn how to operate the detectors and actually go out and look for clues. And whether they find the grand treasure or not, they have a lot of fun, and they always get something to show for it. You want a bunch of retired people and families with kids to swim with the sharks or wander around in the desert in an attempt to find real treasure? Come on, Flynn. They get a tiny taste of the real thing. How is that so bad?"

"It's the principle of the thing," I told her. She told me what exactly I could do with my principles and suggested that I get busy memorizing my spiel. Which I've done, because I owe Frieda, and Savannah needs me. So I gather my charges and begin.

"Once upon a time, ladies and gentlemen, Vikings sailed these waters in their dragon-prowed ships—"

"Do you have actual evidence of that?" an elderly man queries. He's not wearing a hat, either Viking or pirate, and I guess that he's here because of the small woman beside him, who looks embarrassed by his challenging tone. There's one in every crowd, and I'm happy to get this over with. He has no way of knowing that the two of us are on exactly the same page.

"If you mean have we found a Viking cache on the island, or seen a Viking ship anchored out in the bay, the answer is not this week, but a pirate craft was spotted yesterday morn." A wave of laughter rises at this response and I ride it to the finish. "If a cache had been found, obviously we wouldn't be looking for it! However, there is a historical record of an island the Vikings called Vinland. The descriptions around this elusive landmass indicate it was located somewhere in this part of the Pacific. And we do have evidence that they sailed this coast. Take, for instance, the Viking ship discovered in California."

"Are you a Viking?" one of the younger women calls out. The Viking hat carefully perched on her head is her most substantial article of clothing. She's dressed in shorts so short that her butt cheeks aren't quite contained, her breasts presented like an offering in a low-cut halter top. It's not exactly warm out here, and she wraps her arms around her body to control her shivering, using the action to nudge her already impressive cleavage toward the danger point of a wardrobe malfunction.

An unasked-for comparison presents itself to my mind's eye: Blythe's sensible T-shirt and jeans, muddied by the dog, her make-up-free skin, with that sprinkle of gold-dust freckles over the nose, the directness of her gaze.

"Depends which day you ask me," I answer, lowering my voice to gravel and assuming a pirate drawl. "As fer the pirates, mateys, we know that Spanish galleons sailed these waters and that there were pirates among 'em. Have ye heard of the cursed Oak Island?"

Most of the group cheer. The skeptical gentleman, naturally, shouts out, "That's on the other side of the continent! Wrong ocean! We're in the Pacific, not the Atlantic, last I checked!"

"Indeed, you are right, matey. This is the Pacific. My point about Oak Island is that treasure can be found in unlikely places. All right, everybody. Let's get to the class. I've prepared a practice field for you over there. Each of you will take one of the squares marked out by pegs and string and search for buried objects.

"But first, the rules of this game. While you may find clues located in and around your rentals, the grand treasure will not be found there. Anybody caught digging up the lawn in their rental will be put to work refilling the canyon and laying sod. And if you make holes in the walls of houses or businesses, you will be responsible for the cost of repairs."

I know damn well they are all going to dig at their rentals, I just want to restrict the damage, which leads me to my next bit.

"We also don't want Vinland so full of holes that somebody breaks a leg or a colony of prairie dogs moves in. Today I'll show you how to use your detector to pinpoint treasure, and how to dig a small hole rather than a trench. We'll also discuss filling in your holes and cleaning up after yourselves.

"Please note—rentals other than yours are off-limits to you, unless you're invited in by the renter. And the homes of the people who live and work on Vinland are off-limits as well. Please respect our right to privacy.

"Now. Let's talk about the game. Hands up if you've heard about *The Secret.*"

About half the hands go up. I ignore Marc, who is clearly an enthusiast, and pick the man who ought to be responsible for the dog currently sniffing around the practice area. "You, sir. What is *The Secret?*"

"It's a load of magical malarky about how what you think and believe impacts what happens to you in life. Like, you can just think about being rich and poof! Wealth comes to you."

"If that were the case, I'd be living on a private island about now with an entire staff to wait on me," I say. "I'm talking an entirely different secret. Anybody else?"

The woman with the skeptic waves enthusiastically and I choose her. "It's a treasure-hunting book!" she says. "The author buried treasures in parks. In the book there's a picture and a poem that tell where each one is buried, but you have to decipher all the clues. If you get it right, you dig up a small box with a key in it and trade that in for a treasure."

"Bingo!" I smile at her. "The Vinland Treasure Hunt follows a similar model, except we don't have any mystical and mysterious pictures, and you'll get a series of written clues to decipher. You will find your first clue in the practice field today."

"Can we just bribe you?" the half-dressed woman asks. "To tell us what the clues mean?"

"Depends on the bribe," I reply with an exaggerated wink, and then backtrack, quickly, remembering a situation where a woman did try to get me into bed in exchange for information leading to the treasure. "Only one person on this island actually knows where the treasure is hidden, and that person is not me. So you're on your own."

This is the truth. Glory and Frieda wrote out clues and planned this year's game. I've seen the clues that I've planted in my field, but that's it. Now that Frieda is gone, Glory is the only one who knows the answers, and there is absolutely no danger that she will ever tell.

I go on.

"As you already know, everything on the island is run in teams—Vikings versus pirates. Let's have a cheer and see who is stronger! Team Viking, let's hear it!"

The Vikings squeal and shriek and roar. I'm supposed to pretend to stagger backward under the force of the outcry with my hands over my ears, but I'm not going to do it. A man's got to draw the line somewhere.

"Now Team Pirate!"

Both teams are loud and earsplitting. I choose Team Pirate just so as not to be judged as biased by those who think I'm a Viking because of how I look.

"Team Pirate! Ten points!"

They cheer even louder while the Vikings complain good-naturedly. I raise my hand for silence and go on.

"You'll be working with the other members of your teams who have stayed over from previous weeks and know the ropes. Check the schedule in your folder for time and place of team meetings. Team points will be posted on the chalkboard outside Odin's Trading Post every evening at nine p.m. Members of the team with the most points for the day get extra clues."

Everybody cheers again. Either they don't know or don't care that the bonus clues will lead them to local businesses where they will be invited to buy things. The entire system is designed to separate the visitors from as much of their money as possible. Glory says if they are not bright enough to recognize that, then that's their problem. She has a point, and it's not like any of these people are in danger of starving, but still.

"Are we done here?" It's the teenage girl that belongs to the family with the dog. "Can I, like, go back to that ship place?"

"Nope," her father says, far too cheerfully. "You just want to get into your social media or whatever. We came here to get away from all that."

"Can I please die now?" she asks.

The dog, possibly considering this a real cry for help, jumps up and plants his paws on her chest, swiping her face with his tongue. "Gross, Brodie!" she squeals, pushing him away. "Get down! Ewww. Mom, can I at least go fix my face?"

"Let me wipe you," her mother says, pulling out a tissue. "You look fine."

Brodie gambols in my direction. I brace myself for the onslaught—but the dog stops in the middle of a bound, coming down stiff legged with his snout lifted, nostrils flaring. With a sharp bark, he veers off course, careening through my carefully constructed practice field, trailing his leash behind him. It catches, briefly, on a stake. His paws get tangled in the string that separates the squares, but he keeps moving until he runs directly into the arms of Blythe Harmon, who drops onto her knees to receive him.

While he licks her face, she holds on to his neck, laughter bubbling up out of her. "Oh my God, I can't breathe," she declares. "Could you sit, do you think?"

Surprisingly, the dog sits.

"Well, you're certainly a mess, aren't you?" she says. She holds his leash with one hand, trying to untangle string trailing off him with the other.

"Perhaps we could get on with the class?" I suggest, realizing I'm not the only one staring in her direction. "I'll hold the dog."

"I've got him." Savannah miraculously appears at this moment, as if she's just poofed out of thin air, but obviously she's been hanging out somewhere, observing, staying out of my sight just so she can say, later, *I was there the whole time! Don't be such a grump.*

And then, because this class isn't screwed up badly enough already, Old Nick hobbles over and leans against a tree off to the side, his one sharp eye focused on Blythe. When Frieda materializes, perched on a branch above his head, swinging her legs like a child and grinning at me, I feel like the whole lot of them, alive and dead, are out to get me. I bring my gaze back where it belongs, clear my throat, and say, "Blythe, if you'd like to join us, I'm just about to explain how the detectors work. Savannah, I'm delighted to see that you could make it. Perhaps you could issue Blythe her detector?"

I'm pretty sure I've missed something I was supposed to say, but nobody really listens anyway. I might as well teach them what it is they really want to know.

"Your metal detector has an on-off switch and a volume control. Find that now." This part, at least, most people can figure out. As expected, as soon as they've got their machines turned on, most of the crowd starts swinging them around like golf clubs. A chorus of different-toned beeps fills the air as the detectors predictably pick up the metal in the other detectors.

"They are machines, not baseball bats, ladies and gentlemen, if you please. No points are awarded for home runs, or concussions, so please lower your detectors to the ground." While I talk, I walk over to an elderly couple, who hasn't figured out how to turn theirs on yet, and quietly demonstrate the on-off switch without breaking my patter.

"You want to sweep your detector from side to side, keeping it flat to the ground, not lifting it like a golf swing." I demonstrate, but nobody is looking at me, except for Frieda, who is now hanging upside down from the branch by her knees, laughing, her hands brushing over Nick's bald head.

He runs his own hand over his scalp, as though he's felt her touch, and I freeze in the middle of a sentence, my heart thudding erratically. If Nick felt those fingers, it means Frieda is more than a figment of my guilty imagination. The long-buried past stirs restlessly in its grave and a full-body shudder runs through me. If Nick has sensed Frieda, though, the awareness is not enough to pull his attention away from Blythe.

I can't fault him for that. She stands out from the others as if they're two-dimensional cutouts and she's the only one alive and real. That bright hair, escaping from a messy bun on top of her head into a wild cascade of spirals. Her vivid face. Laughter that runs through me like a perfect chord of music.

"Were you going to tell us where to go, or do we just pick a square?" the skeptical guy, Gene, asks, gripping his metal detector with determination and purpose. I suspect he looks at this as a necessary but unpleasant task he's bound and determined to complete in order to make his wife happy.

"I'm glad you asked," I answer, walking backward toward the practice field. "Follow me, treasure hunters. Each of you has been assigned a square on this grid. You will notice that each square is marked by a post and labeled with a letter of the alphabet. As I call your name, please proceed to the appropriate square. As it happens, Gene Alcott, you are in *A*, but please wait one moment before you begin. All of you—remember to move across your square from one side to the other and back again, sweeping your metal detector side to side. If you think you've found something, shout and wave and I'll come over and show you how to pinpoint and dig."

Leaving the dog with Savannah, Blythe follows the others over to the practice field. When I call her name, she steps onto square *D* as instructed, carrying the detector Savannah hooked her up with. I'm busy then, keeping an eye on organized chaos, redirecting people over and over to follow a pattern that will make it improbable that they'll miss anything.

"Flynn! I think I found something!" It's Blythe. My steps speed of their own accord as I move toward her, but she isn't looking at me. Her head comes up and turns toward the tree, and for a distracted instant I think maybe she, too, can see Frieda.

"Who is that old man?" she asks uneasily. "He keeps watching me."

I can see why she'd be bothered. Nick's scarred face looks both hard and hungry, his one good eye undeniably focused in our direction.

"Odin, the one-eyed god," I say lightly. "Can't you tell?"

"Seriously, Flynn."

"That's Old Nick. He owns Odin's Trading Post and has lived here longer than I can remember. He's harmless. Now, let's see what you've found."

She glances up at Nick one more time, and then waves her metal detector over the ground, eliciting a medium-range tone that I know means she's located her clue.

"Smaller movements," I tell her. "You want to zero in on the spot. Good. Now, press your pinpoint button. Move the detector again. Perfect. You are ready to dig."

I hand her a small gardening trowel. "No need to dig a giant hole, which would actually be counterproductive. You can totally miss a small object like a coin or a ring if you move too much dirt at once."

She gets down on her hands and knees without any concern for getting dirty and digs, following my instructions until she lets out a squeal of childlike delight. "I found something."

I can't help smiling at her excitement, watching as she unearths a small wooden box and plunks down on her butt right there in the dirt to open it. Inside is a silver dollar, old and tarnished, the same thing that we put in all the boxes to trigger the detector, and also the folded piece of paper that contains a clue.

Blythe unfolds the paper and reads aloud:

> *Where ravens gather*
> *And the lone wolf howls*
> *The world tree whispers secrets*
> *Under the elusive moon.*

I must be losing my mind, because even though I personally planted every clue in this field, I've never seen this one before and have no idea what it's referring to.

"Now what?" Blythe asks.

"Don't you know how a treasure hunt works?"

"I wander around waving my magic wand until it beeps?"

"Pretty much. Good luck!"

"But I have no idea what this refers to. Where do I start? Wait! There's something else in the box, maybe that will help."

She withdraws a small key, heavily tarnished, and a folded, yellowed sheet of paper. She runs her fingers over the key and shoves it in her pocket before unfolding the paper. She reads, silently, then fixes a glare on me and demands, "Where did you get this letter? And what else do you know about my grandmother?"

I take the paper from her hand, feeling like time has slowed. Maybe I'm capable of forgetting a clue, but I know absolutely and positively that I'm the one who filled these boxes, and that I did not put anything in any of them other than the coin and a clue.

"Flynn! Over here!" a voice calls.

"In a minute!"

The paper, so old and brittle it nearly cracks along the fold lines, is written over in black ink, and reads:

My love,
I'm not going to sell Improbable House after all, although my parents pressured me to do it. It's heartbroken already, poor thing. Besides, what if I sold it, and then you did come home? You'd find me gone and the house gone and it would be almost as if our love had never been. I'm turning it over to a property rental service to take care of. I don't like the man who runs it. His wife always seems to have a black eye or a broken rib or whatever from walking into doors. But he's a good handyman, so everybody says. And he's "island." Being island (which I'm learning more and more that I am not and can never be) is everything here. You know how they are. If I lived in our house with you for the next twenty-five years, I might be accepted in the end. But not now. Not here on my own.
If you were with me, it wouldn't matter what anybody thought.
But you are not island, either, not anymore. You are nowhere. And so I've arranged to rent out the house. I'm moving back to Spokane tomorrow. I'm leaving these letters for you, in our secret hidey-hole, in case you come back.
Please, come back.
Love, Nomi

I stand there, trying to read it again while the lines blur and cross and the dead stir restlessly in their graves. I know exactly who the property manager was that Nomi talked about in the letter, and the brutality he was capable of.

"You can't run forever," Frieda whispers.

"Well?" Blythe demands, and I try to get my face and my emotions under control.

"I wonder who this Nomi person is," I say, moving in what seems to be the safest direction.

"My grandmother. As if you didn't know."

"The one you're here to bury?" Startled, I shift my gaze to meet hers. Her eyes are clear and searching and guileless, but it wouldn't be the first time in my life I've read somebody wrong.

"Hey, Flynn! Are you coming?" the voice from behind me calls again, this time with an unmistakable edge of annoyance.

Another voice says, "Chill, dude. The girl is a hell of a lot prettier than you. What do you expect?"

"Watch your language, there are children present," a woman snaps.

Blythe reaches for the letter. "You've got some explaining to do, Flynn."

She's the one with some explaining to do, but instead of telling her that, I try, for once in my life, to go for tact and strategy. "Listen, can we talk about this later?"

"I'm holding you to that. Talking later, I mean." Her eyes search mine for answers that she's never going to get from me.

"Wait for me after class," I tell her, turning away to do my job. I glance over my shoulder as I walk away to see her still sitting there in the dirt, poring over the letter in her hands as though it holds the answers to the questions of life itself.

Chapter Sixteen

BLYTHE

The old man, Nick, is still watching my every move. I know that in Viking lore Odin is the one-eyed god, but Old Nick is a much better name for this man, who is as scarred and twisted and angry looking as the devil himself. His ongoing scrutiny makes my skin crawl. Defiant, I lift my head and return his stare, thinking he'll back off when he sees that I'm aware of him, but he meets my gaze with increased intensity, if anything, and I'm the one who looks away.

I return my attention to Nomi's letter, reading and rereading. Who was she writing to? How did it end up in this practice field with my Vinland clue? I'm so focused on the letter that I completely miss the disaster headed in my direction. Too late, I hear the sound of galloping dog feet and glance up just as Brodie barrels into me, nearly knocking me flat. He licks my face, then makes a grab for the letter.

"Savannah! Do something!" I squeal, holding the letter above my head.

"I'm trying! He's stronger than I thought! Brodie. Come away," she scolds, managing to drag him to a safe distance. "What's that? It doesn't look like a clue."

"It's not." I tuck the precious piece of paper back into the little box for safekeeping. "At least, I don't think it is." I get to my feet to put a safe distance between me and the excited dog. "This is my real clue: *Where ravens gather, and the lone wolf howls, the world tree whispers secrets under the elusive moon.*"

"I don't know that one," she says. And then her face lights up and she asks, "Let me help you. It's not cheating since I don't know what the clue means. Please? I never get to play."

"Sure. Why not? Where do you think we should start?"

"Mini golf! Absolutely mini golf. We can play this afternoon."

"What's this about mini golf?" Flynn's voice asks.

"Blythe wants to play," Savannah says. "I'm going to take her."

Flynn looks skeptical. "Don't you have something you're supposed to be doing right now?"

"I'm holding on to Brodie. In case you didn't notice." She glares at him defiantly.

"I'm sure Blythe has things she'd rather be doing than playing mini golf with you," he says.

"Actually, if Savannah can be spared from work, I'd love to play. Would you believe I have never played mini golf before, ever?"

"You really don't need to feel obligated," Flynn says slowly. "You're a guest here."

"Not obligated. I'd really like to do this." I wink at Savannah.

Flynn scowls, then says, "All right, but Savannah needs to help clean up here first. And I believe the Williams family is done, so you can give them back their dog."

Savannah frowns. "They don't take care of him. Probably don't even feed him. He keeps scratching; I think he has fleas."

"He doesn't exactly look like he's starving," Flynn says quietly. "And we've got enough animals already, don't you think?"

"I checked his tag earlier. He's registered and his rabies are up to date," I say, to make myself feel better. I agree with Savannah that the Williams family are terrible dog owners.

Savannah drops to her knees and throws her arms around the dog's neck. "I bet they beat him and starve him."

Brodie pants happily, obviously loving the attention.

"You have no evidence of that," Flynn says. "Overindulgent with him, if anything. Come on, Savannah. They are guests. Return the dog. Now."

I see the mutinous set of her lips and jaw and intervene. "We'll keep an eye on him, right? And if we see any signs of abuse, then we'll do something." I shift my attention to Flynn and ask, as sweetly as I can, "So it's okay if I borrow her for a round of mini golf after lunch?"

"It's not like she's forced to labor in a salt mine and deprived of meals," Flynn retorts. "If she's really not bothering you, she can certainly take the time to play a round of golf. Although, this wouldn't possibly have anything to do with helping a guest solve their clue, would it?"

"I know the rules," Savannah says, all big-eyed innocence. "One o'clock? I'll meet you at the golf course."

"Okay."

"Sorry about that," Flynn says as she stalks away, Brodie at her side, toward where two of the Williams children are wrestling, while the teenage girl looks mortified and the youngest child whines loudly about being hungry.

"What you should be sorry about is telling me her mother was on vacation," I retort. "Yesterday I asked her when Frieda was coming back! I feel horrible!"

"Yesterday? Damn it. She was out at the house, wasn't she? I specifically told her to stay away from there." His jaw tightens, his eyes focusing on Savannah, who is saying something I can't hear to the other girl as she hands over the leash. Whatever it is, it earns her a full-on mean-girl toss of the hair and look of disdain.

"Well," he says, his expression impassive, his tone cool. "We need to talk about your unusual find. And I'm starving. How about an early lunch? The Smuggler's Cove Café, maybe? So long as you don't have any allergies and you're not a super clean food freak with an objection to meat."

My hackles rise, both at his evasion of my attempt to confront him about his lie and at the tone of his remark, but I hold on to my temper. He must know more about Nomi's letter, for one thing, and if I blow up at him now, he'll never tell me anything. For another, I've got growing concerns about Savannah, and I can't help her if I totally piss off her uncle.

"I'm not picky," I say, a little stiffly. "I'll eat whatever."

"Come on, then," he says, and we walk down the street in silence, Flynn apparently deep in thought, leaving me to take in the brightly colored buildings and what they have to offer. There's Loki's Puzzles and Gifts, which is like every tourist-trap store anywhere, except that the T-shirts and mugs and games on display in the windows are all Viking or pirate themed. We pass Valkyrie Burgers "for Viking-sized appetites," the outdoor tables filled, ironically, by people in pirate hats. There's Midgard Pizza and Thor's Mead Hall.

An elegant-looking storefront reads, THE WORLD TREE: A FINE DINING ESTABLISHMENT FIT FOR THE GODS. Remembering my clue, I note the depiction of a world tree, a raven, and a wolf in the picture on the sign and promise myself to come back later to investigate. Brokkr and Eitri's Gallery offers beautiful, artisan-crafted jewelry and art. Even the tiny, one-roomed post office has a thatched roof and a stuffed raven perched on a sign above the door.

As we pass a long, low building that looks like a Viking longhouse, I see the one-eyed man again, and a shiver scurries up and down my spine at the intense way he watches me. A hand-lettered sign on the building reads, ODIN'S TRADING POST—PLUNDER AND SUNDRIES. Flynn places a hand protectively on my back and speeds his pace a little. Before I can ask him to tell me more about Nick, he says, "Here we are," and I let my question go for now.

The Smuggler's Cove Café is marked by a worn wooden sign, the name of the establishment carved into the wood and then painted in red. On the arch-shaped door, painted black like the entrance to a cave, a hand-lettered sheet of paper reads, *Let it be known: You'll eat what we serve ye, or ye'll not eat at all.*

Inside, it's so dark it takes a moment for my eyes to adjust enough to see clearly. There are no windows. The low ceiling is crisscrossed by heavy beams, from which dangle naked light bulbs that provide a dim, red-tinted glow. Rough wooden tables are interspersed with barrels and crates. Flynn leads the way to a shadowy corner and we sit across from each other in surprisingly comfortable leather chairs.

A weathered-looking woman clad in a flannel shirt and baggy, camel-colored trousers strides over to our table. Her gray hair is cut short around a heavily lined face, and the expression she wears is much closer to *go ahead and make my day* than *what can I get you, honey?*

Her eyes on me seem particularly keen, as if she's trying to puzzle something out. "You're with Flynn, so I presume you already know how this works," she says in a gravelly voice. "Denny's made beef stew and sourdough bread. Water's there, if you're thirsty." She gestures at a stoneware jug at the center of the table. "Food'll be right out." And with that, she turns, back ramrod straight, and heads for the kitchen.

I turn a questioning gaze on Flynn and he grins. "Meet Clair. She and Denny are island born and island raised. Don't like outsiders much, and definitely don't like the foolishness of this whole Vinland business."

"They've certainly gone along with the decor."

Flynn lifts an eyebrow. "You see any evidence of either Vikings or pirates anywhere? There were actually smugglers in the area, so they've stuck to facts. Also, Denny cooks whatever she feels like making on any given day. No substitutions, no special requests. Like the sign on the door says. Eat, or don't eat."

"An unusual business plan."

"They've got a captive audience. Anybody who wants a sit-down lunch instead of a burger or a hot dog or pizza is coming here." He pours us each a stoneware mug full of water, adjusts the jug so it's in the center of the table, then leans forward on his elbows and says, "Now. About your unconventional treasure finds."

"You've really never seen the clue before?"

He shakes his head. "And I certainly haven't seen the letter."

I watch him for any sign that he's lying, but his face is in the shadows and I can't be sure.

"Could I see them both again?" he asks.

I lean back in my chair, lifting my mug and swallowing ice-cold water, before I ask, "Why does it matter to you?"

"The game is carefully controlled. People pay to play. Some of them are powerful types with lawyers in their pockets. Or they *are* lawyers. Any hint of preferential treatment or altering of the rules and terms is going to raise a fuss and possibly set a lawsuit in motion. The game is Vinland's only source of income, and the islanders can't afford any aberrations."

"Are you not 'island,' then?" I ask.

"Left when I was sixteen and never came back."

"Until now."

"Until now."

"But Frieda was your sister. So I'd guess you were born and raised here. Doesn't that count?"

"Can we leave the question of my islander status out of this and talk about your unconventional clues?" he asks quietly, but even in the shadows I can see the increased tension in his posture, the tightening of his jaw.

"Just pondering the bit in the letter about Nomi not being 'island,' and wondering what it means," I say, which is only half the truth, because my curiosity is fully activated. Why did Flynn leave while his sister stayed? And why is he still here now, instead of scooping up Savannah and moving her somewhere else?

"It means that she wasn't from here," he says, his tone guarded.

Seeing that I won't get anywhere on this front, I shift gears, hoping to throw him off balance.

"Let's talk about Savannah and why you told me that ridiculous lie."

"How about we don't."

He touches the scar on his face, lightly, then rests his hand on the table. "Look. Renting you the house in the first place was out of line. Telling you that thing about Frieda . . . Well, Glory would say I'm so far from the line I can't even see it from here. I apologize for both."

"Why *did* you rent it to me? I thought maybe you felt sorry for me about my grandmother."

"I thought it would stop Savannah from going there. I was desperate. You offered yourself up at the perfect moment."

"Like a lamb to the slaughter," I say.

His lips twist into a half smile, self-deprecating, rueful, charming. "I keep wanting to blame somebody for this mess," he says, "but obviously none of it is your fault. I'll try to keep her away. She's not exactly . . . receptive to either requests or commands that come from me."

"Why?"

Now it's his turn to look confused. "Why doesn't she listen to me?"

"Why keep her away, if that's where she wants to be?"

"It can't be healthy for her, can it? She's there constantly. She's the one who planted the geraniums, right in the place where Frieda fell. She's avoiding the other kids. She needs to be around people. Living people. She needs to show up for work."

"How old is she, twelve? A little young to be part of the workforce, isn't she?"

He bristles. "Feel free to report me to the island authorities."

"Oh, come on. There are no island authorities. What about the mainland authorities?"

I sound like my mother. I sound like Kristen. What is it about this man that brings out this side of me? I have no intention of reporting him to anybody. Savannah might not exactly adore him, but she hasn't given any indication of being beaten or neglected or overworked.

Flynn lays both hands flat on the table between us, as if bracing himself, as he leans toward me. I can feel the anger radiating off of him, and mine sparks to meet it, ready for a shouting match, if that's what he wants.

Instead, he draws a deep breath and says, evenly, "She grew up in the family business and used to help her mother. I'm paying her to keep her busy. And to try to keep her away from her obsession with Improbable House. You were supposed to help with that."

"My apologies. I must have missed the clause in the rental contract that said I'm responsible for controlling your niece."

Flynn tenses. But then, instead of bellowing with anger, his lips twist into that utterly disarming half smile. "That clause was right next to the one where you agreed to be responsible for other people's dogs," he says.

I feel myself melting but refuse to be derailed. "I don't understand why you'd want to keep her away from the house. Of course she wants to be there. What do you expect?"

He stares at me blankly for a moment, and then sort of seems to cave in on himself. "I was thinking that being at the house must be a horribly painful reminder for her."

"Well, of course it's painful! You can't expect her to just go on with life as if nothing has happened."

"You're probably right," he says. "Giselle and Glory both say the same thing. Now you. Maybe the house is one more thing I'm getting wrong."

I search his face for sarcasm, finding instead weariness and a deep and abiding sadness. For the first time it dawns on me that he's obviously also grieving, and how difficult and painful this situation must be for him. My anger melts away and I open my mouth to say something consoling and then shut it again, knowing from experience that well-intended words often hurt more than they heal.

"I don't know, Flynn. Grief is a lonely business, don't you think? Maybe she needs that right now."

When he speaks again, his voice is so quiet I have to lean toward him to hear. "She saw her mother fall. She tried to do first aid; can you imagine? Radioed for help. Glory said she wouldn't talk to anybody for hours, except to say that it was her fault. How is she ever going to get past the trauma if she keeps revisiting it day after day after day? She won't talk about it. She hardly ever cries. She just haunts the place as if she's a ghost herself."

Another memory bubbles up into my consciousness.

I'm curled into a tight ball on Nomi's hospital bed. The sheets and blankets have all been stripped away and it's cold and slippery and smells like bleach. But this is the last place I saw her, the place she will come back to when she proves everybody wrong and wakes from her fairy-tale sleep. Mom is standing beside me.

"What on earth are you doing, Blythe?"

I just curl tighter into myself, doing my best armadillo impression ever.

"Get up, now."

170

I ignore her.

"Blythe!"

When I still don't answer, she tries to pick me up and my armadillo explodes into a screaming and kicking fury.

Over the sound of my own screaming, I hear the door slam behind her as she leaves the room and I think I've won.

Until the men come to take the bed away. The next day, Mom removes every single thing that was Nomi's from the room. A desk replaces the bed. Bookshelves line the walls. My own grief is all that remains, locked up tightly in my chest with nowhere to go.

"Lunch is served," a woman's voice says, dragging me back into the present.

Clair sets two giant, steaming bowls on the table, along with a platter of bread and a bowl of butter. The smell of beef and spices and fresh baking fills my nostrils, and my mouth begins to water.

I lean over my bowl, breathing in deeply. "That smells amazing."

"Good girl. You can stay," Clair says.

"Perfect response, and the highest possible seal of approval," Flynn says after she walks away to another table, where a man and a woman have just seated themselves.

"I'll just have a salad," the woman says, when Clair explains the menu.

"No salad today, sorry, only stew and bread," Clair says patiently. "You can get salad at either Valkyrie Burgers or Midgard Pizza."

"Oh, for goodness' sake. You can't be serious," the woman says.

"There was a sign on the door," Clair says calmly.

"We'll eat the stew," the man says. When the woman opens her mouth again, he tells her, "Eat this. Then we can stop for a salad at one of those other places if you like."

Flynn rolls his eyes at me and I can't help grinning back. I take a piece of bread and spread butter on it.

"My Nomi died when I was six," I say, watching the butter melting into the still-warm bread, keeping my voice even. "I couldn't fathom her being gone, and all I wanted was to be in the place I last saw her, to try to hang on to the essence of her even though she herself was gone. But my mother erased everything that was Nomi from that room."

"And?"

"It was the worst thing she could have done. I needed time. And maybe Savannah needs that, too." I let my eyes flicker upward to meet Flynn's to see how he's taking this. "None of my business, of course," I add, to soften the irritation I see on his face.

"This is a completely different situation," he says.

"Of course it's different. No loss is ever the same for any two people, is it? Have you asked her why she hangs out at the house?"

"Let's talk about your grandmother," he says—his turn to change the subject.

"How about we eat while the food is hot?" I say, as my stomach reminds me that I didn't finish my breakfast. "It smells fantastic."

"It *is* fantastic."

I try a bite, chewing with great appreciation. The stew is every bit as good as it smells, savory and rich and delicious, the beef so tender it practically melts in my mouth.

"Good?" Flynn asks, watching me.

"Amazing."

The two of us clean our plates without any further talk, observing an unspoken truce. When the bowls are empty and there's nothing left of the bread but a few crumbs, Flynn wipes his mouth with a napkin, folds it neatly on the table, and waits while I do the same.

"If your grandmother died when you were six," he says, "why do you need to bury her ashes? That's a weird amount of urgency over somebody who has been dead for years."

"Says the guy who told me his dead sister was on vacation," I retort.

"Touché." He raises his glass in my direction and then takes a long swallow, as if drinking a toast. "But to be fair, Frieda's only been gone a few months. What are you really doing here?"

"Burying Nomi's ashes, like I said. You saw them."

"There could be anything in that urn. Campfire ash for all I know."

My anger flares. "Are you accusing me of lying?"

His glacier-blue eyes are intent on mine. "You can't seriously expect me to believe that you're here to scatter ashes twenty years after the fact."

"Twenty-three years. And you can't expect me to believe that you know nothing about how letters that my grandmother wrote over fifty years ago are turning up as clues in a fake treasure hunt."

At that, he leans back in his chair and softens his gaze, looking more thoughtful and less like he's interrogating me. "How that letter ended up in the practice field is a mystery I intend to solve," he says slowly. "I can see how you wouldn't believe me, but I swear I know nothing about the letter or your grandmother, or how or why it got there."

"What about the other one?"

He looks at me blankly, his face a question. "The other what?"

"The letter in my welcome folder. In the gold-foil envelope with my first clue."

Again he shakes his head, his forehead creased in a frown. "We don't put an envelope in the packets. The first clue is always buried in the practice field, so people will show up and hear the rules about how the game works."

I want to believe him. I want to soften the worry that is carved into his face. I want to see that half smile curve all the way into a full one, to see it warm his eyes.

But for once in my life I'm not going to be naive and gullible and sucked in by a good story told by a liar. I push him. "Your practice ground. Your rental company. You see how it looks."

"I do," he says. He runs a hand through his hair, surveying me thoughtfully. "Somebody is up to something. I'll start asking questions, but it would be helpful if you'd consider telling me what you're really doing here."

"Burying my grandmother's ashes." I fling my hands up in frustration, then let them settle back on the table with a sigh. "The only way you're going to believe that is if I tell you the whole story, I suppose. It's a long and strange one."

"Why does that not surprise me?" he says.

Clair appears at our table just then with a carafe, two mugs, and two slices of peach pie. "Seems the two of you are going to be a while. Denny sent this out for you."

"Tell her thank you," Flynn says, smiling affectionately.

She pats his shoulder and bends down to kiss his forehead. "You look tired. Are you sleeping?"

He shrugs. "Not so much."

"Denny says bring Savannah over for dinner one night."

"I will."

The door opens and two women walk in and head for a table. "Gotta go," Clair says, with another pat on his shoulder.

I take a bite of pie and embarrass myself by making a little moaning sound out loud. Flynn smiles. "Perfect, right?"

"Absolutely." I take another bite, and then I tell him the whole story. Turning thirty, and Alan's proposal and the balloons and the ashes and even the job I didn't want and didn't earn on my own merits.

When I'm done, he doesn't say anything right away, obviously thinking. "So you were sent on a treasure hunt, to an island you thought you made up as a child. But it seems that your grandmother must have been here, a long time ago. Have you considered that maybe she'd also planned this whole thing? What would happen when you got here, I mean? Left the letters with somebody and asked them to add them to your clues?"

"It's possible." I think about Nomi writing down the longitude and latitude from the numbers I drew from the card deck. I'd assumed she was writing down the numbers I gave her. But then another thought comes to me, and I ask, "But when did Vinland become Vinland? Turn into a treasure-hunt game, I mean?"

He thinks for a moment, then says, "Not until 2004."

I shake my head. "She was already dead. She couldn't have known about the Vinland Treasure Hunt. And I don't think she meant for me to read the letters. They were private, for some man she was in love with."

"Not just some man. Your grandfather," he says.

My eyes widen and I stare at him, absorbing the truth of this.

"Unless your mother had an older sibling."

I shake my head. "Mom was Nomi's only child. My grandfather died in Vietnam. She must have been writing the letters to him. And that means he *was* island. He had to have been from here."

We're both silent, then, my brain so jumbled with contradictory thoughts and beliefs and ideas that I feel like it might explode.

"I'll ask around," Flynn says. "Both about him and the letter. There are not a lot of people who could have put the envelope in your welcome packet. I mean, it has to be somebody who knew you were coming, right? Has to be somebody with access to the guest list."

"I'll talk to Nomi's lawyer. I bet he knows something. And my aunt Bella. She was in on all of Nomi's secrets."

"I'd like to see that other letter, if you don't mind," Flynn says. "And the first clue."

"They're back at the house. I promised to play mini golf with Savannah."

Before he can answer, a woman's voice comes through his radio. "Flynn, Margo here. We've got a situation at Lost Cove."

"Be right there," he says before turning his attention back to me. "Maybe tomorrow? I'll radio you." He gets to his feet and stands, looking down at me. "Thank you for that, by the way. Hanging out with Savannah."

"I really don't mind."

He smiles, then, the full-on smile I've been imagining, crooked because of the scar. It softens his face, makes him look younger, easier. I watch him stride away, feeling like the whole world has shifted around me, completely altered by a single smile.

Chapter Seventeen

BLYTHE

When I step out of the café into Vinland Square, my old life feels far away and flimsy. The light seems brighter, the air smells cleaner, the colors look more vibrant, as if I've been viewing the world from behind a dusty pane of glass and have just stepped outside, as if I've been under a spell and am only now awakening. Even my body feels different— lighter and freer and full of vitality.

Anything—even magic—seems possible, maybe even probable. Of course I'll figure out Nomi's treasure map. And then I'll have enough money to create a whole new life. I'll quit my real estate job. Maybe I'll go back to college and become a vet, or start my own rescue shelter, or travel, beginning with an extended stay here on Vinland. There's no need to rush.

Riding the wave of this new buoyancy, I drift toward the golf course and my appointment with Savannah, browsing the shops as I go.

I stop at Loki's Puzzles and Gifts to buy a T-shirt for Kristen, choosing a particularly tasteless image of half-naked Valkyries I know she'll hate. Dad gets an oversize mug that features Thor's hammer as the handle. I browse the window of the art store, thinking maybe I'll find something pretty for Mom and promising myself I'll come back and look over the wares later. Right now, I'm almost late to meet Savannah, and I speed my steps in that direction.

Ragnarök Mini Golf is situated on an island in the middle of an artificial lake. There's a boat landing area just outside the square, adjacent to Flynn's practice ground, which features plastic seagulls and a canned soundtrack that gives them voices. A rusty anchor and chain lean up against some old wooden barrels, and Viking and pirate automatons swig imaginary mead and rum from a drinking horn and a brown bottle, respectively.

Five pedal boats sit empty on the beach—two decked out with fake rigging and sails and a miniature skull-and-bones pirate flag, three with high prows and dragon mastheads. Savannah is already sitting in one of the Viking boats, chatting with a dangerously dapper young pirate. The girl, still all childish innocence, seems oblivious to the nature of his attention, but I suspect that Flynn would not approve of the way the boy's eyes follow her every move, the expression on his face in the unguarded moment before he sees me.

"Here I am," I call out, to give them both warning. Savannah waves, and the young pirate very nearly upsets the boat in his hurry to scramble out, arranging his costume sword to hang properly at his side.

"Ma'am," he says, then stops. "I mean, ahoy there, lassie. Your ship sails in three shakes of a lamb's tail."

"You're such a dork, Sy," Savannah says. He flushes beet red and puts a hand up to adjust his hat, managing only to knock it off into the water. Up close, I can see that his mustache is drawn on and that he's not much older than Savannah. Another island child with summer employment, from the looks of things. I smile at him encouragingly.

"Oh, shit, I mean shoot, I mean damn me eyes for a clumsy oaf," he stammers, fishing the sodden hat out of the drink, his skin glowing with humiliation.

"So, do I buy a ticket or something?" I ask, trying to shift the moment.

"Just get in the boat," Savannah answers for him. "Sy will push us off."

The boy's brown eyes meet mine, miserable and furious, and I refrain from smiling, realizing any sympathy would just be salt in the wounds of a damaged ego.

"Metal detectors not allowed," he says, not to me but to Savannah. "You know better."

"Chill, dude," she says. "We'll leave it with Steven."

"Why can't we use the detector?" I ask.

"No detecting, no digging," Sy says. "Interferes with the golfing."

I allow the young pirate to help me into the boat, even though I don't need help, since I figure he needs to feel useful right about now. His hands are still wet, and water trickles down his face and neck from the hat he's shoved back on his head.

Once I'm safely in, he gives the boat a little shove and we're in open water. "May ye find the treasure," Sy calls after us. "Beware Odin's spies!"

As if summoned, a raven circles overhead, swooping down to land on the gunwale next to Savannah. "There you are," she scolds. "I was worried about you."

Norman squawks derisively and hops sideways to get closer to me. "Hungry," he says.

"Oh my God, Norman, you're such a mooch," Savannah reprimands.

"You should be nicer to him," I say, as we both put our feet on the pedals and begin pumping.

"Who, Norman?"

"No, Sy."

"He looked ridiculous!" A peal of laughter follows, and I can't help but join her.

"Tell me the clue again," she says, and I recite it:

Where ravens gather
And the lone wolf howls
The world tree whispers secrets
Under the elusive moon.

"Definitely here," she says, gesturing toward the mini golf course. I see what she's getting at. Beyond a curved bridge, painted in rainbow colors, stands a tree that dominates the small island. Its branches are full of stuffed ravens, and I'm willing to bet that when we get close there will be a representation of Odin's wolves somewhere in the vicinity.

"We're not here under the moon," I object. "And if we can't use the metal detector, then how are we supposed to look for a clue?"

Savannah shrugs, trailing her fingers in the water. "I like riding the boat. And the mini golf course is fun. And the world tree is cool, you'll see."

I suppress a burst of impatience, thinking about the real tree waiting for me outside of Improbable House. I'm certain that's where my treasure is, and I can't wait to get back to it.

You can spare a couple of hours for a grieving child, I remind myself, looking askance at Norman, who has been staring at me, unblinking, ever since he showed up.

We approach the landing, an exact copy of the one where we got our boat—rusty anchor, seagulls, the whole thing. Another attendant, a female Viking this time, late teens or early twenties, moors our boat.

"Hey, Savannah," she says. "Are you going to have me over sometime, or what? It's been ages. And your uncle is kind of—"

I clear my throat, pretty sure what's coming next, and the girl interrupts herself in midsentence. "Lady," she says to me, with an attempt at a rough sort of curtsy. "Welcome to Asgard, home of the gods. Cross the rainbow bridge at your own peril. Enter through yon humble establishment."

She gestures toward a low wooden building, the entrance of which marks the only way off the dock.

"Later, Jeanie," Savannah says, then leads the way into the mother of all tourist traps, so crammed with mugs, T-shirts, postcards, pictures, costume jewelry, and a bewildering array of other souvenir items, displayed in wooden treasure chests and barrels and baskets, that it's difficult to find a clear path through to the golf course.

Savannah, of course, knows her way, and I follow her through the maze to where a tall, thin man stands, scowling, behind a checkout counter. Next to him is a barrel full of multicolored golf balls and a rack of clubs. And next to that is an electronic gate that leads out of the store and to the golf course beyond.

The entire Williams family, including Brodie, mills around in front of the counter. One of the kids tests the gate, which doesn't budge. Mr. Williams has a firm grip on Brodie's leash, for once, but the dog's wildly wagging tail is dangerously close to a display of mugs and other breakable objects.

"You can't take the dog onto the golf course," the man says. "It's against the rules."

"It's against the rules to leave the dog alone in the rental without a crate," Mr. Williams protests. "Come on, man. We just want to play a round of golf."

"Fine. But somebody will have to sit it out and stay with the dog."

Mrs. Williams presses up against the counter, leaning forward to read his name tag. "Steven, is it? Listen, Steven, we want to play as a family, so nobody is going to sit it out with the dog."

Steven doesn't flinch. "Then I guess you should have brought a crate, ma'am. The rules were given to you with your rental agreement."

"We couldn't carry a crate onto that tiny water taxi," she protests. "You should offer some for sale at that trading post place."

"You feel free to chat with Nick about that," Steven says. "Now, if you'd just step aside, there are people behind you, without dogs, who are trying to get onto the golf course."

Mrs. Williams shoots me a venomous glare over her shoulder, as if this is all my fault somehow. And then she smiles, drops her voice, and says, "Brodie is a service dog. If you don't let him in, I'll call my attorney and we'll sue you for violating our rights."

"What kind of service does that creature provide?" Steven asks, exuding skepticism.

"We are under no obligation to tell you that," she declares loftily. "Now, are you going to let us through, or shall we go back to that Coffee Dragon place and call our attorney?"

"Just let them go, Steven," Savannah says. "It's not worth it."

"Fine," he snaps. He pushes a button and the gate buzzes and unlatches. The kids troop through, grabbing balls and clubs and clattering out the door, followed by the parents and the dog.

"If that creature poops on my golf course," Steven calls after them, leaving the rest of the threat empty. Then he picks up his radio.

"Flynn, this is Steven. We've got a situation."

Flynn's voice crackles over the radio at once. "What's up?"

"Those people with the dog insisted on taking him on the course. Called him a service animal. Threatened a lawsuit."

"On my way."

"It will be okay, Steven," Savannah says, patting his arm. "Blythe and I will watch the dog, right, Blythe?"

I nod. "And if he makes a mess, we'll clean it up."

This doesn't appear to make Steven feel better.

He sighs dramatically. "Which color of balls, ladies?"

"Ruby and emerald," Savannah says. "And we're gonna leave Blythe's detector with you, okay?"

He selects a red ball and a green one out of the barrel and hands us each a club. I hand him my metal detector. Then he buzzes us through the gate and we step out of the cluttered store and onto the Ragnarök Mini Golf course.

"Wow," I say, trying to take it all in.

Savannah giggles at my reaction. "Trippy, right?"

"That's one word for it," I murmur, pretty sure that when the designer was a child, they must have had a lawn full of gnomes and ceramic frogs and pink flamingos in summer, and inflatable Santas and reindeer and snowmen in winter, and then somewhere along the way fallen in love with Viking mythology.

A rainbow bridge, painted in garish colors no self-respecting real rainbow would ever wear in public, arches up over a winding stream, bluer than any water has a right to be. Farther along the course I can see, among other attractions, a pirate ship, a Viking ship, and the tall tree with spreading green branches. Two mechanical wolves circle the trunk, emitting hair-raising howls.

It's a big course, and it's going to take a long time to reach that goal if we play through. Especially since we're stuck behind the Williams family and Brodie, a scenario that is playing out about as expected. The kids are whacking balls all over the place, randomly, without any concern for the rules. Brodie is barking and straining at the leash, trying to chase them, while Mr. Williams yells at him to settle down.

"Hold this damn dog while I play the first hole, would you?" Mr. Williams says to his wife.

She frowns but takes the leash, jerking it sharply. "Get over here and sit down, okay?"

Brodie doesn't sit. He yips loudly, leaping and lunging as Mr. Williams's bright yellow ball rolls up and over the rainbow bridge, stopping just short of an oversize figure bearing a sword in one hand and a ram's horn in the other. The paint is peeling off the side of the figure's face, making him look like he has a terrible skin disease. An attached label reads, **HEIMDALL, GUARDIAN OF ASGARD**. Norman perches on his shoulder, surveying all of us with an expression of disdain.

Mrs. Williams yanks Brodie back so hard he falls over onto his back, emitting a sharp yelp before cowering at her feet as she berates him. "Oh my God, you are the worst dog ever."

"Maybe if you stop shouting," I suggest coldly, trying to hold on to my temper. "He just wants to play, and you're agitating him further."

"How about you mind your own business?" she retorts. Then she turns to the sulky teenager standing nearby and snaps, "Here, hold him while I play."

The girl accepts the leash, holding it as if it's coated in some noxious substance, and when Brodie leaps after the green ball now rolling over the bridge, it slides easily through her fingers and the dog runs after the ball and grabs it before it gets anywhere near Heimdall.

"I thought I told you to hold on to him!" The woman snarls at her daughter, who rolls her eyes, unfazed.

"Whatever, Mom. Chillax. He's not hurting anything."

"Well, I can tell you this," Mrs. Williams says. "When we get home, he's going right back to the shelter I let you kids persuade me to take him out of. Not one of you lifts a finger to take care of him, and I am *done!*"

She strides across the bridge, yelling, "Come here, right now, you stupid dog, or you'll be sorry." Brodie wisely stays well out of her reach, the ball firmly in his jaws.

Savannah runs across the bridge and puts herself between the dog and the angry woman. He immediately drops the ball at her feet, inviting her to play. "You don't deserve to have a dog," she says, getting a grip on the leash.

"Listen here, young woman," Mr. Williams says. "We aren't interested in your opinions. Give me the dog." He takes a step toward her. Brodie cowers down at her feet and whimpers.

"No," Savannah declares. "You're going to hit him or something. He's scared of you. Look."

"What's going on here?" a deep voice booms, and Flynn strides over the bridge to join us, looking much more like Asgard's guardian than the derelict Heimdall. He stops beside Savannah and rests a hand on her shoulder, clearly indicating where his protective instincts lie.

My heart picks up speed and then develops a weird magnetic property that draws me toward him. I want to keep going until we stand as close as it's possible to get, heart to heart, with my arms around him and his around me, his lips . . .

I manage to stop myself next to the Williams people, who have aligned under duress into a cohesive unit.

"What's going on," the woman says, "is that your daughter is interfering with our golf game and with our dog."

"Really," Flynn responds. "Because what I heard is that you insisted on bringing a dog onto the golf course, and what I see is that you've not been able to keep him under control." His voice is quiet, his face impassive, but if the Williams people have any common sense at all, they'll notice the dangerous thrumming of anger just below the surface of his words.

But they are not common-sense-type people.

"Just give us the dog and leave us alone." Mr. Williams takes another step forward and grabs the leash, yanking it—and Savannah, who refuses to let go—toward him.

Flynn makes a soft sound that resonates through me like a growl, and before I know what I'm doing, I've stepped into action.

"I have an idea," I say brightly, circling around to stand between Flynn and Mr. Williams. "Adopting a dog always seems like such a good idea, doesn't it?" I flash a full smile at Mrs. Williams and the children. "But then it turns into hard work. Maybe you have a dog that isn't so very well trained—"

"Try a dog that is a monster," Mrs. Williams interjects.

"A dog that seems like a monster," I agree.

"He's not!" Savannah protests, outraged. "He just needs—"

"So very difficult to care for and manage," I go on, ignoring her. "Which, especially given your very good intentions in adopting, is hard to deal with, isn't it? You'd think the dog would be grateful and obedient, but no! Instead he runs around destroying things and grabbing balls and . . . making messes in inconvenient places."

All of our eyes go to Brodie, who is doing exactly that, dangerously close to Heimdall's sandaled foot.

"And nobody will help," Mrs. Williams says bitterly. "I'm going to be expected to clean that up now. And it wasn't even my idea to bring him on this trip."

"Listen, Louise," her husband begins, but she silences him with a glare and the words, "Are *you* going to clean it up?"

"How about this?" I suggest. "I'll clean it up. And there's no need to wait until you get home to take him to a shelter. As it turns out, I work with an animal rescue organization in Spokane, and I'd be delighted to take him for you. Right now."

The man and woman exchange a look, and I hold my breath, waiting.

"Mom!" one of the boys protests. "Dad. You can't just give Brodie away."

"Are you going to clean that up?" his mother asks.

"I don't have a bag," he says, horrified. "You didn't bring one."

"Like I thought. Well, you know what? I'd like to be able to hunt for treasure and maybe even eat in the restaurant without having to worry about the mutt." She turns to me and says, "Looks like you've got yourself a dog."

Spurred on by a clamor of protests from the kids, her husband says, tentatively, "Lou, do you really think—"

"I do think. And now, I am going shopping without worrying about that furry engine of destruction."

"Oh, thank the goddess," the girl says. "Me too."

The two of them vanish back into the shop, leaving her husband to deal with the three younger children. The littlest girl starts to wail, loudly. He picks her up, looks helplessly from the dog to the boys, to Flynn, to me, and mutters, "Maybe it's all for the best. Come on, kids. Who wants ice cream?"

A silence descends in their wake, broken only by Brodie's panting and the distant mechanical croaking and howling of the ravens and wolves at the world tree. Savannah collapses onto the ground and throws both arms around Brodie, looking up at me to say, "You're not really going to put him in a shelter, are you? I mean, you couldn't. He's so cute. Look at this face."

Brodie looks up at me with big brown eyes, and as I lean down and rub his floppy ears I know, as clearly as I've ever known anything, that he will not be going anywhere other than home with me.

Flynn clears his throat. "Well, then," he says. "Anybody got a bag?"

Savannah and I both stare back at him, wide-eyed, because of course we do not. He laughs and shakes his head. "Naturally."

Before I can offer to go find something, he says, "Tell you what. I'll get a bag from Steven and take care of the mess, and then I'll take Brodie out of harm's way while the two of you play your golf game."

Five minutes later, Flynn and Brodie and the little bag of dog poop have vanished into the store, leaving me and Savannah to play our game.

"Maybe we should forget golf and go straight to the world tree," I say, worrying about Flynn stuck babysitting my new dog.

"I think you need to play through. Sometimes there are clues in the holes," she says. "Besides, maybe if Uncle Flynn falls in love with Brodie, he'll let me get a dog."

I don't point out that Brodie isn't necessarily the sort of dog that inspires somebody to go get one of their own, and Savannah hits her ball up over the curve of the bridge and scores a hole in one. She's obviously played the course frequently and has a score above par, while mine is so far on the other end it's not even worth trying to keep score. But it's more fun than I expected, and our bursts of laughter follow my ball into all the nooks and crannies I manage to send it to.

"Since when are there pirates in Valhalla?" I ask, as my ball wanders off into a display of barrels and treasure chests on the deck of a ship flying the skull and crossbones.

Savannah snort-laughs. "Since the town council decided that pirates and treasure are connected. And that tourists would like pirates. That's what my mom says anyway." She whacks the ball, then adds, fiercely, "Said."

She stomps off and I follow, soberly now, her grief overshadowing our lighthearted mood.

"Here we are," she announces, as if I can't see the huge tree in front of us for myself.

A sign informs me I'm looking at Yggdrasil, the world tree, and that the two ravens sitting in its branches are Muninn and Huginn, which translates as Memory and Thought, and they are both spies of Odin. The two wolves sitting beneath it are Odin's companions, Geri and Freki, otherwise known as Greedy and Ravenous. A hidden speaker in the tree emits recorded raven calls. The wolves howl. Odin leans against the trunk, looking altogether too much like the old man, Nick.

With a rush of wings, another raven descends and alights in the tree. "Hello there," he croaks.

"Hey, Norman," I say. Then I hit my ball, too hard, and it pops over the hole and smacks into one of the wolves, rebounds, and nestles up against a hollow at the base of the trunk, where there's no way I can get a proper swing at it. Norman squawks a protest. Savannah taps her own ball easily into the hole.

The mechanical ravens croak. The wolves howl. A man's voice, distorted by a tinny speaker, intones, "You are blessed of the gods. Your place at the table is assured."

"What about *my* place at the table?" I mutter, wedging my club between the ball and the tree and giving it a little flick that sends it rolling away into the grass. "Also, how do you suggest we look for a clue?"

"I haven't the faintest," Savannah says. "But I just won a dinner at the World Tree Restaurant. That's what that recording means."

"Doesn't everybody get that?" I tap my own ball into the hole, finally, waiting for the ravens and the wolves and the announcement. Silence.

"It goes off, like, every ten times a ball rolls in, or something," Savannah says. "Steven is always switching it up. Winners get a guaranteed reservation and eat for free. Otherwise it's super expensive, and if you don't make a reservation early in the week, you never get in. But you can come with me because I get to bring a guest."

"Awesome. But. What about me finding a clue?"

"Well, the last one did say something about the tree under the moon," she says.

I glare at her, but she is utterly unfazed. "Also, it says to listen. So you might try that, I guess."

Looking around to make sure nobody is watching, I step up to the tree, taking the opposite side from the figure of Odin, and lean my ear against the trunk. I hear my own breathing. The rustling of leaves. A faint electrical hum. But no words of wisdom are imparted to my listening ear.

"Maybe you need to hug the tree," Savannah suggests. "Trees need love, too."

"You are a crazy girl." I hesitate, visions of Mom and Kristen popping into my head. But they're not here, and I honestly don't care what anybody thinks. Laughing, I do as Savannah says, reaching my arms around the smooth trunk, laying my cheek against it. My heart lightens with the action, and the memory that comes with it. Nomi and me, in the city park, hugging trees with abandon. She never even seemed to notice the odd looks from passersby.

"You can't worry about what people think, little Bee," she would say. "Where's the fun in that?"

In honor of Nomi, I turn my face into the tree and kiss it, wrapping my arms around it more tightly, pressing my hands against the bark. My pinkie finger senses an unevenness on the back of the tree, and I move my hand to explore it, letting out a startled squeal of discovery.

"Savannah, there's a knothole in this tree."

She comes running and we both move around to get a better look, my heart hammering with excitement. Surely there will be a clue for me in that unexpected hollow. My questing fingers brush against the edge of a piece of paper. I pull it out and unfold it, holding it where both of us can see.

It reads:

You've uncovered the key to treasure. Take 25% off any purchase made at Brokkr and Eitri's Gallery.

"Cool!" Savannah exclaims, as if I've just found the key to a great treasure rather than a coupon to a tourist shop. "Most people never find that hole in the tree, so if anybody asks, I didn't coach you. Brokkr and Eitri has awesome stuff. I'm going to sell my paintings there someday, just wait."

"Are all the clues like this?" I ask. "Gift certificates and whatnot?"

"Everything on Vinland is about selling stuff. Don't tell anybody I told you that; it's supposed to be some big secret. That's why the clues you've been getting are so unusual. This one is totally Vinland standard. Come on. Let's make our reservations and go find Brodie."

Chapter Eighteen

Blythe

As I drive my cart out of the trees and into the clearing with Brodie on the seat beside me, I have a strange sense of déjà vu, as if I'm coming home to a familiar and well-loved house, rather than a decaying wreck in which I've spent only a few hours. Brodie, who has ridden this far surprisingly quietly, is now on his feet, whining with excitement. I'd love to let him off leash but have no reason to believe he'll come when I call him, so I park the cart and walk him around the yard. He puts his nose to the ground, sniffing as if this is the first time he's ever smelled gravel or grass or bushes in his entire life. After he's had the chance to water several bushes, I lead him up the steps onto the porch.

He bounds ahead, straining at the leash, while I follow more slowly, noticing the way my feet instinctively move to the right to miss a loosened nail on the third step. My hand curves around the railing smoothly, easily, as if it's made this climb a hundred times. When I walk through the door, I hear a faint whisper that sounds almost like *welcome home*.

I let Brodie off leash, and he begins an enthusiastic exploration of the house, while I dig through the cupboards for dishes that will do for his water and food. Flynn has promised to come by later with dog food. Once I've set the bowls in the entryway and Brodie has had a good, long, slobbery drink, I go straight upstairs to check on Nomi.

"Sorry to leave you alone so long," I tell her. "But guess what? I've acquired a dog!" A square of warm light shines in the window, making a prism out of the snow globe and casting a rainbow at my feet. I pick up the globe and shake it, hoping that maybe I'll catch a glimpse of something otherworldly. As usual, all I see is snow.

Then I carry the urn over to the bed, sit down, close my eyes, and try to erase time so I can see things through her eyes. If I were Nomi, where would I want to be buried? What did this house look like when she moved through it? What about the yard?

If she was pregnant with my mother when she wrote those letters, then it was fifty-six years ago. What was going on in the world back then? The Beatles and bra burning and Vietnam. Martin Luther King. I try to imagine a young Nomi, living in this house in the middle of a world in chaos, pregnant and alone, with her lover lost in the jungle and presumed dead. Fretting about the news, worrying about the future of her unborn child, wondering how she would manage to make a life for both of them.

I can't conjure her up. The only two versions of Nomi I have are the fun-loving, mischievous, game-playing Nomi, and the bald-from-chemo, sick, and in-pain Nomi. And even then she lived life as if it was a magnificent game, an adventure, right up until the end.

Proof of that is this treasure hunt, which she must have planned when she knew that she was dying. With the weight of the urn resting in my lap, my palms flat on its cool, smooth surface, I sink into the memory of the day she died.

Mom is out running errands and Daddy is at work and Aunt Bella is downstairs in the kitchen. We don't really need Aunt Bella, 'cause Nomi and I can watch each other, and Mrs. Maxwell is right next door and ready to help out if we need her for the tiniest little thing, but when I told Mom that, she said if I wanted to be difficult I could just come along with her and Kristen.

Of course I said I'd stay, because I was really hoping maybe Nomi would feel well enough to play with me. But she's been sleeping all this time while I read aloud to her from my latest library book, or at least I think she's sleeping until she interrupts me right in the middle of an exciting battle between two knights.

"Blybee," she says, "you know I love you, don't you?"

I stop reading and look up at her. Her eyes are open, staring up at the ceiling. Of course I know she loves me. It's a fact, like the way the sun comes up every morning and Daddy goes to work and Mom fixes us cereal and fruit and makes me drink my orange juice.

The question makes a funny feeling in my belly, like maybe she's going to forget who I am, for real this time, so I don't argue or anything and just remember she's sick and that Mom says she's not quite right, whatever that means. So I put down the book and get up and kiss her cheek and say, "Of course. And I love you, too."

"I want you to promise me something," she says, looking at me now, and smiling a little bit, almost like her old smile before she got sick, except that her eyes are all shiny with tears.

The tears make that funny feeling in my belly even stronger, so I don't talk, I just nod my head.

"Promise me, when you turn thirty, you really will go find the treasure we marked on our map."

I feel like one of my beloved knights accepting a sacred quest. "I promise," I tell her.

"That's my Blybee. I have another one. Ready?"

Again, I nod my head.

"Don't let your mother tell you who you are. She means well, but she'll get that part all wrong."

"I don't even know what that means," I whisper, a little bit scared now. I'm me. Why would Mom tell me anything different?

"You don't now, but you will later," she says. "Promise."

"I promise."

"Good girl. Let's play a game, shall we?" Nomi says. "One where I send you on a quest. Like the knights in your book. You must be quick. You must be secret. You must be like a shadow of the night."

I jump up and down and squeal a little with excitement. "Are you feeling better, then?" I ask.

"So much better," she says, with a little smile. "And about to be marvelous. Are you ready?"

I nod, pressing my hands together and trying to look sober and brave like a knight.

"Before we play, I want you to promise me one more thing. You must never, ever tell anybody about this game. Even your mom or your dad. No matter what. That might be hard, but I know you are very brave and that you can do it."

I start to think this isn't a game at all, and the funny feeling turns into full-on scared. Reading about quests is one thing. But I'm not good at keeping secrets and I know, even if Nomi doesn't, that I'm not very brave. I'm afraid of shadows at night, and I'm afraid of Mom when she gets mad, and I'm even afraid of other kids at school sometimes.

"I don't know if I can," I whisper.

"This is important," Nomi says. "Of course you can."

"If it's important, maybe you should ask Mom to play."

Nomi shakes her head, and says in her make-believe voice, "This is a task that can be undertaken only by Blybee the Magnificent. Blythe Beatrice Harmon, do you solemnly swear to undertake this quest and to tell no one, ever?"

A thrill runs through me, head to toe. I feel solemn, and excited, and maybe a little bit brave. "I accept the quest," I say. "I promise not to tell."

She frowns a little, looking me over. "You need a costume, I think. But it would take too long to make armor."

"I'm in dis . . . disguise anyway, right? So armor would be wrong." I look around the room and grab up a small blanket folded neatly in the chair that she no longer sits in. I put it over my head and gather it at my throat, trying to glide around the room like a cat burglar in a movie.

"Your first task," Nomi says, laughing a little, "is this. Go to my dresser. Open the top drawer on the right side."

I follow her directions, thinking carefully for just a minute about which hand is my right one, but not wanting to ask. The other kids at school all seem to know this but I can't ever remember.

"You eat with your right hand," Nomi says calmly, as if she totally understands the situation, and I feel so much love I want to run back over to the bed and hug her. She always knows exactly what I need. Now it's easy to know which side is right, and I open the drawer, then wait for what comes next.

"In the back of the drawer you'll find a small velvet box. Open it, take out what you find, and bring it to me."

I dig into the drawer, like she says, pushing aside underwear and socks, and at the very back I find the box. Snatching it up, I run back to her bed.

"Well done, faithful Blybee," she says, with an approving smile. "Approach."

I climb up on the bed beside her, trying not to breathe too deep, because there's a smell about Nomi that is a little bit like something gone bad in the fridge.

She opens the box and draws out a beautiful pendant on a silver chain. A bird, carved from some shiny black stone, with a bright green eye, sits in the branches of a silver tree. Nomi clasps the chain around my neck. It takes her a while. The fingers of her good hand are shaking, and the other hand is clumsy and stiff. I'm afraid maybe she'll poke me by mistake, but I bravely stay still and don't move.

"Tell your mother, when she asks, that I wanted you to have it."

"Thank you." I should be excited but I feel a little bit worried instead. Something isn't right with Nomi. She looks very tired and her face isn't quite the right color. *"Did you want to rest now?"*

Her eyes open and she tries to look stern. *"There is more to your quest. Go ask Aunt Bella to bring me a healing draught from the crystal fountain. And then, while she does that, you must follow these directions very carefully. Are you listening?"*

"I'm always listening."

"So you are, my beautiful girl. Okay. Here is your quest. First, send Aunt Bella up to me with the healing draught from the crystal fountain. Then go out to the yard and walk all the way around it five times in one direction. Then stop and walk all the way around it five times in the other direction. When you've finished that, put your arms around the oak tree, close your eyes, and count to one hundred three times. Then go tell Mrs. Maxwell you have earned a glass of milk and a cookie. Can you do that?"

"I don't know if I can remember all that. It's a lot."

"Of course you can. Let's practice it."

She gives me my directions again, and I repeat them back to her.

"Now go," she says. *"When you return, you will find me in an enchanted slumber."*

I'm not sure that I like this part, and instead of running off, I ask, *"How long will you sleep? Will there be a prince?"*

"A very long time," she says. *"And there will be no way to wake me. You must be brave and never speak of it to anyone. Do you understand?"*

I nod, but whisper, *"I don't want you to sleep for a very long time."*

"It's the only way to heal the pain, child," she says. *"You're my brave and beautiful girl, Blybee. Give me a hug and a kiss, and then off you go."*

She holds me extra tight with her one good arm, and whispers, *"Remember."*

I run off to follow her directions to the letter. It takes a long time, and then Mrs. Maxwell is slow about getting the milk and the cookie out for me, and on second thought she gives me two cookies, because she says she's sure I need them. It would be rude to grab them and run, so I eat politely and finish my milk. By the time I tell Mrs. Maxwell thank you and run back home, Mom's car is in the driveway.

I find Aunt Bella in the kitchen. Her eyes are all red and her nose sounds snuffly. She tries to stop me, but I slip away from her and run up to Nomi's room. Mom is sitting by Nomi's bed, with Kristen in her arms. Mom's face is all wet with tears. She opens her other arm to me and I run to her, looking over her shoulder at Nomi, who lies so deeply and soundly asleep that I can't see her breathing. I want to tell my mother not to cry, that it's only part of a game and that Nomi is just in a fairy-tale sleep. But I remember just at the last minute that I must not tell.

"Oh, Nomi," I say now, tears sliding out from under my still-closed lids. My hand goes to the well-worn pendant, tracing the lines of the tree and the raven sitting in its branches.

All these years, whenever I thought about the day Nomi died, I'd thought it a coincidence that she died while I was outside on a quest, with Aunt Bella in the kitchen. Now, in the middle of this whole elaborate treasure hunt, I realize that even her death was planned. The gift, the goodbye, the ruse to get me out of the house. Not to mention that Aunt Bella was the one who showed up with the urn full of ashes that weren't Nomi. She's been in on this from the beginning.

She has some explaining to do. Later. Because I'm pretty sure I know the spot marked by the X in my map.

It must be a place with a special connection for Nomi, which means Improbable House is the house on the treasure map. And that means the only possible tree is the big oak out in the yard. The ravens, far from being a bad omen, are a sign that I'm on the right track.

Filled with excitement and certainty, I clip the leash back onto Brodie's collar, gather up my metal detector and trowel, and head out to the tree, almost expecting to see a giant X marking the spot. Of course there's no such thing, but there *is* a heart carved into the bark, which is maybe even better.

I decide to risk letting Brodie loose, figuring that if he runs off, the worst thing that can happen is he'll go back to town. It's a small island; it's not like he's going to get permanently lost. Then I turn on my metal detector and begin working the area under the tree, carefully following Flynn's instructions and searching in long, overlapping sweeps.

Two hours later, Brodie has fallen asleep under the tree, and all my optimism has vanished. My efforts have yielded me two dollars and twenty-six cents in change, an old necklace that might be silver, a pocket full of aluminum pop tops, five bottle caps, a seriously sore arm and shoulder, and a feeling of deep discouragement. I'd been so sure this was the place, but obviously my quest isn't going to be so easy.

A throbbing at my temples warns of a headache threatening to get in on the muscle-pain action. My stomach growls, and I realize I'm starving. I'm also grubby and exhausted and don't want to go eat in a restaurant or talk to anybody, so I pack up my equipment and my loot and head back to the house.

Cooking has never been my thing, so I go for the tomato soup and grilled cheese once again. It's the last can of tomato soup in the pantry, so in the future I'll need to either change up my program or stop by Odin's Trading Post, the one store in the town that I'm not excited about visiting.

Brodie nudges me with his muzzle, looking up at me expectantly while wagging his tail. "Flynn is bringing you something," I tell him. "Or at least he said he was."

The dog whines and gazes up at me out of those big doggy eyes. I bend down to pat his head and rub his ears. "Don't worry. I won't let you starve. Let's see what we can come up with."

I open a can of tuna, stir in an egg, and Brodie slurps the mess up with great delight. "Well, at least you're not a picky eater," I say, heating a pan for my grilled cheese. My mind wanders to the treasure map and the tree and Nomi's ashes. I'd been so damn sure about that tree. Maybe I've just failed to find whatever she buried there. Maybe it's not metal and the detector won't pick it up.

If that's not the right tree, then I'll have to start asking around. There must be people on the island who remember Nomi; definitely they would remember my grandfather. As for Aunt Bella, obviously she knows something. The trick will be getting her to tell.

But I can't shake my belief that whatever I'm looking for is near Improbable House. The answers are probably right in front of me and I'm not seeing them because I'm not looking at things the right way. I open the front door and step out onto the rickety porch. Norman, sitting on the railing, cronks at me.

"What are you doing here?" I ask him.

He ruffles up his feathers and hops sideways, his eyes glittering. "Nevermore," he croaks.

I shiver at the reference, then mutter, "Very funny, Savannah." I turn my back on the raven and stand facing the door, one hand closed around the pendant as if it's a magical talisman. I close my eyes, take a deep breath, and try to focus. Be Nomi. See it through her eyes.

When I step back inside and walk through the empty rooms, I feel like the house is trying to talk to me, if only I knew how to listen. I stand in the living room, eyes half-closed, letting images come and go, floating in and out of my brain. I'm missing something, but I can't think what it is. I climb the stairs, wandering through the upstairs rooms.

I step onto the balcony, looking down at the yard. The bed of scarlet geraniums. The neat little garden shed. The uncut grass, the rosebushes, the cliffs. The water, glimmering like silk under a clear blue sky. The distant islands, hazy, mysterious.

A loud, repetitive blaring startles me half out of my skin. Brodie's barking adds to the racket.

I catch a smell of burning. For a moment I freeze and then I remember.

"Oh my God. Dinner."

By the time I reach the kitchen my eyes are watering and I hold my arm over my nose and mouth to make it easier to breathe. Thank God nothing is actually on fire, but the soup has boiled over and the sandwich is charred beyond recognition. Turning the heat off the burners, I move both pans to the middle of the stove and open the window. Most of the smoke is billowing up from what was going to be my grilled cheese sandwich, so I grab a potholder and run for the porch with the whole horrible fail.

The minute the door opens a caustic voice demands, "Are you trying to burn down my house?"

I startle so violently that I drop the pan, just managing to jump back fast enough so the cast iron doesn't land on my bare feet. It rolls and clatters, spilling the charcoaled bread onto the weathered wood.

Nick stands at the bottom of the steps, glaring at me, looking for all the world like a malevolent genie. For one confused minute I think he's here in response to the fire alarm, and then I remember the long drive from here to anywhere and that this is impossible. I remind myself that Nick is just a badly scarred human, that the raven is just a bird, that nothing here is otherworldly or mysterious.

The old man hobbles up the steps and shoves past me and into the house, sniffing like a bloodhound and following the burning smell directly to the kitchen. Brodie follows on his heels, barking and growling, either at Nick or at the smoke, or both.

As for Nick, he scowls at my pot of scummy soup, the smoke, the burnt and blackened burner on the stove, and then at the dog.

"I want you out," he shouts, over the blaring of the smoke detector and Brodie's barking. "Tomorrow."

Chapter Nineteen

FLYNN

I smell the smoke before I can see it.

Improbable House is still obscured by trees, but obviously something is horribly wrong. The ravens are swirling and squawking and throwing up a fuss in the sky above me. Pressing my foot harder on the go pedal, I urge the cart to go faster, but it's already topped out at its twenty-five-miles-an-hour limit.

Goddamn golf carts. I miss my car, a sweetly restored '67 GTO, currently stashed in a garage on the mainland. Press the accelerator on that baby and you can get somewhere in a hurry. Hell, even a Prius would give me a welcome little burst of speed. But the only gasoline engine permitted on Vinland belongs to its one and only fire truck, which is unfortunately several miles away, tucked away into the garage from which it emerges only for trainings and regular maintenance.

When I reach the clearing, black smoke is pouring out of the open kitchen window, but to my relief I can't see any flames. Grease fire, maybe. Something manageable. The alarm is bleating and that insane dog is barking, so if Blythe is in there, she should have warning to get out, unless she's injured or unconscious. I have a not entirely unwelcome vision of heroically rushing in, scooping her up in my arms, and carrying her to safety.

Except, there's already another golf cart parked beside hers in the lot. I'm out of the cart before it stops moving, picturing in my mind the location of the fire extinguisher, hoping I won't have to radio for the fire truck. Nick is already in a snit over this property; the last thing he needs to know is that his unwanted tenant has lit the house on fire.

Before I make it to the kitchen I hear the shouting and know it's too late to head off that particular disaster—Nick is already here and knows everything.

Through a haze of smoke I make sure that nothing is actively burning, then reach up over my head and yank the batteries out of the smoke detector. Brodie immediately stops barking, running over to me to be petted. The blessed silence lasts for all of about ten seconds before Nick says, "Glad you're here, Flynn. I was just telling this tenant that she needs to be out by tomorrow."

I look from his angry face to Blythe's stricken one, both of them streaming tears from the smoke, and suggest, as calmly as I can, "How about we take this conversation outside where we can breathe?" Without waiting to see if they follow my advice, I make my way through the house, opening all the windows and turning on the bathroom fan.

When I'm done, I join the combatants outside. Blythe sits on the porch next to Brodie, stroking his head. "It's not like I brought a dog *with* me," she's saying, in a soothing sort of voice. "I rescued him from some people who weren't taking good care of him."

"You're still in violation of the contract," Nick growls.

"Couldn't you possibly make an exception, given the circumstances?" She looks up at him with a pleading and hopeful expression that would make me give her anything she asked for, but Nick is built of tougher stuff.

"No, I could not make an exception. No dogs. Flynn here should never have rented this house in the first place. It's not even on the rotation."

"But I can't leave yet," she protests. "I have something I need to do before I go."

"Bury your grandmother's ashes, you mean?" Nick's voice, always harsh, takes on a threatening tone. "Oh yes, I heard about your little mission, and let me tell you this—you will not be burying human remains on my property."

"Come on, Nick. It's only—" I intervene, but he cuts me off.

"There's a law about that. Put those ashes anywhere on public property that you want. Private property requires permission and you do not have it. You should be thankful I'm not kicking you out tonight, you and that fleabag mongrel."

Blythe ducks her head, but not before I see the sheen of tears in her eyes. It makes me want to hit him, old man or not, but I manage to hold on to my temper.

"Renting the house was my mistake, not hers," I say, as evenly as I can. "And she certainly wasn't planning on the dog. She signed the contract in good faith, Nick."

The old man scowls. The smooth parts of his face flush red with anger; the scars blanch white. "Fine. I'll honor the contract, which is up next Thursday. It will not be renewed. She will not bury ashes anywhere on this property. And I want a pet deposit paid immediately."

"All right, Nick. I'll take care of it," I say.

Blythe glances up at me, tears tracking down her cheeks. I shake my head at her, a silent warning not to say anything, and she clasps her knees and leans forward, hiding her face against them.

"See that you do." Nick stomps off down the stairs and to his cart.

"Hey," I say, sitting down on the step beside Blythe. She doesn't move, doesn't look up.

Her vulnerable pose and the little snuffling sounds she's making do something dangerous to my heart. I put an arm around her shoulder. "Don't let that old asshole make you cry."

With a little sigh, her body softens and she lets her curly red head rest against me. "Is there any way he might let me stay?" she asks.

I want to lean my head against the softness of her hair. I want to cup her face in my hand, tilt it up to mine, and wipe the tears away. And, God help me, I really, deeply want to kiss her.

"I'll get Glory to talk to him. Or maybe Savannah. Even Nick has a hard time saying no to her. In the meantime, I come bearing dog food and training treats, and, fortunately for you, pizza. Because I'm guessing that whatever dinner was meant to be, even Brodie and Norman aren't going to eat it. And Norman eats anything."

"You're failing to live up to your asshole reputation," she says, sitting up straight and looking at me. My heart accelerates, sending heat through my body to all the inconvenient places. It's probably a good thing Nick is refusing another contract. This woman is already too much under my skin.

"Couldn't let the dog starve." My voice sounds hoarse, and I clear my throat, getting to my feet to put some distance between us. "Of course, that's probably how Nick found out you had a dog, but he would have found out anyway, island gossip being what it is."

I heft the bag of dog food out of the back of my cart and carry it up the steps. The third step makes a creaking sound and gives a little under my weight, and I make a note to get somebody to have a look at it.

Blythe opens the door for me and I carry the dog food in and drop the bag in the kitchen. The smoke is clearing. I notice the empty bowl on the floor beside the dish of water and smile a little at the fact that Blythe has managed to feed the animal but not herself. Which reminds me of the pizza, rapidly cooling out in the cart.

I hear the door slam and the sound of quick, light footsteps and the click of dog claws. Blythe comes in, holding the box high out of reach of Brodie, who is sniffing enthusiastically.

"He was going to help himself," she says, as she sets the food on the counter. "Definitely needs to learn some manners."

"Savannah would say his manners are better than those of the people he belonged to."

"I agree," she says, opening the box and sniffing nearly as enthusiastically as Brodie. "Mmmm. That smells delicious. You're going to have some, too, right?" she asks. "Beer in the fridge if you want one."

My mouth is watering, but I hesitate, for a whole bunch of reasons. One of which is that every minute I spend with Blythe beguiles me toward a temptation I know I need to resist. Another is the specter of Frieda, sitting in one of the chairs at the table. I want to ask her what she's doing here, what kind of unfinished business is holding her to this place, but of course I can't with Blythe here. Besides, I'm afraid to hear the answer.

Blythe shivers as she sets the plates on the table. "Cold in here," she says.

"Must be the open windows," I answer, with another glance at Frieda. Maybe it's the windows. Maybe it's the presence of a ghost.

Brodie sits down square in the middle of the kitchen and fixes my dearly departed sister with an intense stare. Then he lifts his muzzle and utters a forlorn and spine-tingling howl.

"Oh, what's the matter, baby?" Blythe drops down beside him and caresses his head. He stops howling, but stays tense, alert, his gaze fixed unwaveringly on Frieda.

"Well, that's not creepy or anything," she says. "Maybe the house really is haunted."

"It's an old house," I say, as casually as I can manage. "I suppose it's possible. Maybe it's your grandmother."

"No way," she says, but not very convincingly. And then, "Do you believe in ghosts?"

"I believe I need a drink," I say, opening the fridge. "Want a beer?"

"I'm having wine."

"Sorry, we only stock beer. Wine means a visit to Nick's."

"Thank God I brought some with me, then," she says with an exaggerated shudder. "I was saving it for when I bury Nomi. If I bury Nomi."

"I'll have a glass, then, if you're up for sharing." I get out two glasses while Blythe wields a corkscrew.

"Never been a fan of the wimpy pour," she says, filling both goblets nearly to the top. She raises hers in my direction and then takes a long swallow. "Mmm. That should pair well with pizza."

"Everything pairs well with pizza."

She crosses to the table and I'm relieved to see that Frieda has vanished. Brodie sniffs at the chair where she was sitting, then collapses on the floor with his chin on his paws and gives our food his full attention.

Blythe opens the pizza box and grabs a slice, then stops with it halfway to her mouth and lowers it back down again. "What if a week isn't long enough, Flynn? And what if the place I'm supposed to bury her is on Nick's property? What am I going to do?"

Her eyes start to fill with tears again and I say, quickly, "Right now we're going to eat pizza and drink wine. And then, when you've got some food and liquid fortitude in you, we'll strategize. Don't worry about Nick. We'll figure something out. And if the place to bury Nomi is at Improbable House somewhere, you'll just scatter the ashes and then what is he going to do about it?"

"I dunno. Send me to jail?" But she laughs as she says it, and the tears recede again. "Tell me about you, Flynn. What do you do when you're not playing Viking Treasure Master here on Vinland?"

"I'm a mild-mannered archaeology professor who secretly hunts for ancient treasures during the summers."

"And has a fear of snakes, I suppose. Very funny, Indie. Come on. You did a background check on me and I told you everything at lunch, and I know nothing about you. It's not fair."

I find myself wishing my glass was full of whiskey, but I settle for the wine, taking a long swallow while I arrange my thoughts.

"Okay. I'm not a professor. But I did go to college for a year, planning to be an archaeologist, and yes, I was influenced by Indiana himself. I had a taste for adventure and pictured myself swinging on vines through the jungle and discovering magical artifacts at great risk to my life. Imagine my dismay when I realized archaeology is more about math and statistics and red tape. Not for me."

"I get that," Blythe says. "I always thought my life was going to be full of adventure. And then it wasn't. Is that why you left the island? Bored? Looking for excitement?"

Her elbows are on the table, chin propped on her hands, eyes intent on my face. It must be the wine, or the influence of the house, or maybe Frieda whispering in my ear, because I very nearly tell her all of it.

But the habit of silence is too thoroughly ingrained.

"Something like that," I say, evading. "But it turns out the excitement to be had by a runaway sixteen-year-old isn't all it's cracked up to be."

"What did you do?" she asks.

"Got a job on a fishing boat, for starters." I shrug, glossing over those first terrifying nights on the streets of Seattle, both hoping and fearing somebody from the island would come and find me. "I owe my life to the captain who took me on, but at the time I didn't see it that way. Hard, mind-numbing, exhausting work. Not enough sleep. Everything smelling of fish. No adventure about it. But I had a place to sleep and a roof over my head, of sorts, and a way to earn my keep."

"And college?"

"I was bored. Got my GED, tried college. Lacked the necessary discipline, hated staying still. So I tried fishing in Alaska. Worked in the cannery for a year. Decided I'd had enough of fish, so thought I'd do something more glamorous."

"Gold," Blythe guesses, emptying her glass.

"Gold," I agree. "Got a miner to take me on. Season was a bust, but I met a guy who had the treasure-hunting bug. Chased that for a while but kept coming up empty."

"And then what?" she asks.

"Aren't you bored yet?" I ask, conscious that I'm talking about myself much more than I usually do.

"Not even close." She gets up and brings the bottle to the table, refilling both of our glasses. "Tell me about what you do now."

"Or, you could tell me more about you."

She laughs at that, tossing her head so her curls fly up around her face, then settle. "Trust me, I'm boring," she says. "Talk."

"Okay. Well. Saw something on TV about divers and sunken ships, and that was the next quest. I always did love the water. So I got my scuba diving certification, figuring I'd just waltz right onto some expedition as a diver. It doesn't work that way, of course. Nobody wanted an inexperienced overeager idiot to go diving on a big, public expedition, and all of the private ones were kept on the down-low, and I didn't have the contacts to break in.

"Spent a season back in Alaska on the underwater end of a dredge in the Bering Sea, but that was monotonous and not as lucrative as you'd like to think. But I like diving. A lot. So most recently I've been doing odd jobs. I teach. Sometimes I do dives for law enforcement, recovering evidence. And I had just, finally, signed on to an expedition going after an actual sunken galleon when Frieda died, and now here I am."

"For Savannah."

"For Savannah. And because . . . Let's just say I owe my sister. Big."

"I admire what you've done," she says.

"Living to this age without ever learning how to be a responsible, upstanding citizen, you mean?"

"Exactly. Not letting society and its conventions tell you how to be. Exploring the world. Staying free."

I want to tell her that I'm not free at all, that everything I've done has been about trying to outrun my memories and my demons, that being unencumbered means being always alone. But I've already said too much, let down way too many of my defenses.

"Well, that's all done with," I tell her. "Now I'm having a crash course in responsibility. Adulting 101. How about you show me those letters and that first clue now?"

She surveys my face for a long moment, then nods, as if I've answered a question. She gets up and leaves the room, coming back a minute later with a gold-foil envelope, two sheets of yellowed paper, and two clues.

I start with the envelope, holding it by the edges, just in case at some point we need to check it for fingerprints.

"Well?" she asks.

"I don't recognize the handwriting. And, in the six months I've been here, I've never seen one of these envelopes."

I set it aside and read the letters, the one I haven't seen and the one that I have. And then I look at the clues, the one that was buried in the practice field about the world tree, and one that reads:

> *A Viking's heart is always with the sea.*
> *If you search that elusive shore,*
> *You will find all that you are looking for.*

"This is a clue I haven't seen before, either," I say, laying everything out before me and narrowing my eyes, as if somehow the objects will yield up their secrets if I just stare at them hard enough.

"What do you think it means?" Blythe asks, dropping to the floor to give Brodie a belly rub.

"That you should wave your metal detector around down by the water. Probably at the bottom of the cliffs here, since your grandmother appears to have lived in this house at some point."

"Well, right," she says. "That's what I was thinking. I meant, about everything. The weird clues. The letters. What's up with that?"

"I have no idea. Glory will know if anybody does. Nick has owned the place for as long as I can remember, but he's not about to tell us anything."

My radio crackles and Glory's voice comes on. "You checking in sometime, Flynn? You're past time."

"Be there in fifteen," I say into the radio, shoving back my chair. "Speak of the devil," I say to Blythe. "Gotta go. She's waiting to debrief the day."

Blythe looks up at me from the floor, and on an impulse, I reach my hand down to her. She takes it, and I pull her to her feet, which brings her right up against me. I hear the soft intake of her breath, see the way her lips part, ever so slightly. And then, before I know what I'm doing, I kiss her.

She kisses me back, her lips warm, questioning.

It's that, more than anything, that brings me to my senses. I break it off, almost immediately. Her eyes are startled, wide, a reflection of what I feel.

"I need to go," I say, but for once I'm not in a hurry to run away, and I just stand there, still holding her hand, looking into her eyes. I'm about to kiss her again when Brodie gets jealous. Whining, he forces himself between us.

Blythe laughs and releases my hand. "Right. Probably not a great idea, anyway," she says, and she's right, of course. Although my logic circuits are trying to convince me that it's perfectly safe. She's only here for a week, and then gone. No chance of really getting entangled in that much time, is there?

She follows me to the door, Brodie barking and running back and forth as if the two of us walking through the house is the most fun game ever. As soon as the door is open, he bursts out onto the porch, skids to a halt, and runs back in.

I stop short. Uh-oh.

Frieda is perched on the railing, Norman beside her. Both are looking at me.

Blythe collides with my back. "What's up?"

"Nothing," I say. "Sorry. Brodie is not shaping up to be a reliable guard dog." A minute ago I didn't want to leave. Now I can't wait to get away from here. I begin to run down the stairs. The third one, the one I felt creak and give on the way up, cracks and breaks and I only avoid putting my foot all the way through it by sitting down hard on my butt.

"That's not good," Blythe says.

She has no idea. This couldn't be less good. I can't get my breath. My heart is pumping, my vision black at the edges.

It happened here. The wood has been painted so many times, but I can still see the blood. Can still feel the panic. The pain.

"Oh my God. Are you hurt?" Blythe asks. Her hand rests on my shoulder.

"Fine, fine," I say, trying to shake off the moment. But I'm not fine. Not at all.

"Trust me," Frieda whispers, vanishing. Norman ruffles his feathers and croaks.

"Well," I say, getting to my feet. "That's not safe. I'm not the best repair person in the world, but let me at least fix it so you don't fall through."

I radio Glory. "Broken step on the porch. Gonna be a bit."

"Got it," she says. "Patch it. We'll make it pretty later."

"Understood."

"Do you have to go get supplies and stuff?" Blythe asks.

"Nope. All in the shed in the backyard."

She walks with me to the shed. I wish she'd leave me alone now, but at least she's quiet, not expecting me to talk.

Get it together, Flynn. It's a broken step. You know how this house is, has always been.

But I can't shake a feeling of dread and impending doom, can't get my panic to settle. I enter the code on the keypad lock and open the door, waiting a minute while my eyes adjust to the light.

"You wanna grab the hammer and the saw?" I gesture toward tools hanging on a pegboard wall. I move to the small stack of wood left over from previous repairs and select a length of two-by-ten. Then I find a handful of nails and a crowbar.

It's okay, I tell myself. I can hold it together until this is done. I'm even starting to believe it by the time we walk back around to the rickety porch.

"Whole thing needs to be rebuilt," I mutter. "Sorry about this. I knew I shouldn't have rented this house to you."

"It's fine," she says. "No harm done. Nobody hurt, right?"

"Right." Using the crowbar, I pry the nails up and remove the splintered pieces of wood. I set the crowbar on the step above, a place where it is level, secure, stable. Or should be. When I stand up to pitch the discards over the rail, the damn thing dislodges itself and falls down through the missing stair.

"I'll get it," Blythe says. Before I can stop her, she's on her knees, reaching in for the crowbar and handing it up to me. "There's something else here," she says. "Just a minute. Wow. Somebody must have lost this a long time ago."

When she surfaces, she's holding a large hunting knife, the blade extended.

I know that knife. I know the elk-antler hilt, worn from use. I know how it perfectly fits my grip. And I know exactly when and how it was lost.

Last time I saw it, that perfectly balanced steel blade was dripping with blood.

The world shifts beneath me as the fault line that runs through the core of me breaks wide open.

Chapter Twenty

BLYTHE

"Let's play a new game," Nomi says.

She holds out her hand, but when I reach for it she drifts away from me, backward, floating like a balloon.

"Is it flying?" I ask, looking down at my own feet, which are firmly planted on the floor. I spread my arms out wide and flap them once, but nothing happens.

Nomi laughs and begins to drift away from me, up, up, up. "You have always been able to fly, Blybee. You just have to let it happen."

I lower my arms and will my body to rise but it feels heavier, not lighter, being sucked down by a gravitational force I can't resist. Meanwhile, Nomi has floated to the top of a long, circular staircase, and panic strikes that I'm going to lose her again. Giving up on flying, I run up the stairs after her, or at least I try. My feet are so heavy and slow that by the time I finally reach the top of the stairs she is nowhere in sight.

I look in empty rooms, tears pouring down my face. I've lost her again. And then I see a ladder leading up, up, high into the stars. I begin to climb it, even though I tell myself it's dangerous because if I fall I'll be falling through space, falling forever.

"Nomi!" I call, my voice breaking.

My own voice wakes me, calling out into the darkness. I sit up, tears streaming down my cheeks, my hand over my thudding heart. For a moment I am disoriented and lost. I'm not in my childhood bed. Not in the luxury king beside Alan. Strange noises come from overhead. A rhythmic scratching, a rustling, a murmuring of voices.

A mournful howl follows, and then a weight settles in beside me, a cold nose nuzzles into my neck.

Brodie. I put my arms around him, whispering soothing words, orienting and grounding myself.

I'm in the upstairs bedroom of Improbable House. Which may or may not be haunted. Uneasily, I remember Brodie's weird behavior last night, the way he howled and stared at something invisible. I think about finding that knife, and how Flynn went so pale when he saw it that I thought he was going to pass out.

I think about Frieda dying here, and Savannah's obsession with the place, and Nomi's ashes, and the ravens, and the way the house persists in falling apart.

Finally, I summon up the courage to reach for the light on the bedside table. The dim light pushes the shadows into the corners of the room, but doesn't dispel them. Outside the window, the sky is beginning to lighten and trees loom against it, dark, silent, watchful. I rest one hand on Brodie's warm back, stroking his fur, and clutch my pendant with the other.

Sucking in a deep breath, I remind myself I'm supposed to be the brave and adventurous Blybee, then get up and run across the room, flipping on the overhead light and banishing the shadows. This should make me feel better, but it doesn't. The creepy noises continue. The back of my neck prickles. Brodie settles down on his haunches and looks up at the ceiling, tilting his head to one side, listening.

And it finally occurs to me that a house like this must surely have an attic. It's so obvious I ought to have thought of it before. From outside, I've even seen a third tier of windows. I've just been too distracted to investigate. What I'm hearing is probably rats or squirrels or maybe even bats.

And if the house has an attic, what better place would there be for Nomi to hide something away? A surge of curiosity competes with my fear. Maybe whatever I'm looking for is right above me. No way am I falling back asleep without taking a look.

Step one, find the door.

Out in the hallway, the noises are even louder, ghostly and strange. I'm almost certain I hear voices, along with a wailing, moaning sort of sound, and a rhythmic banging. I pause, my breath caught in my throat, my heart loud in my ears.

Maybe I should radio Flynn, tell him there are strange noises in the house. He'll come and . . .

And what, Blythe? Rescue you from your own overactive imagination? Kiss you again?

I have to admit that I liked being kissed, but I'm also aware that things are now awkward and complicated between the two of us, and that being alone with Flynn in a dark house is *so* not a good idea. I'm just going to have to rescue myself.

Logic says that if there's an attic, there must be a way to access it. A trapdoor, maybe. I tilt my head back, scanning the ceiling, and I see it—a slight recess, squared by a wooden frame. There's even a large brass ring at one edge. How have I missed this?

More importantly, how do I reach it?

There was a ladder out in the shed, but I can't imagine that the practical Vinlanders who run this place drag a ladder up the stairs every time they need to access the attic. Something prickles at the edges of my memory and then falls into place. Opening the door to the linen closet, I lift down a long rod with a hook on the end from where it hangs beside the ironing board. I'd noticed it when Savannah gave me the tour and wondered vaguely what it was for, then I'd forgotten all about it.

The rod is long enough to allow me to easily hook the ring in the trapdoor. I give it a good, firm tug, and it opens down toward me. A folding ladder is attached, and it only takes me a minute to figure out the mechanism to release it and set it up.

But then, I hesitate. The whispering, murmuring sound stopped the moment I opened the door, but the mournful wailing and the banging continue.

As I put my hands and feet on the ladder and begin to climb, I remember my dream, following Nomi up an endless ladder that leads to the stars. Shivers run up and down my spine as my fear returns. I'm reluctant to poke my head and shoulders up into that darkness above. I wish I had a flashlight. But I've come too far to back out now.

Brodie lifts his muzzle and does the howl thing again. I do wish he'd stop doing that; it's a sound that sets my teeth against each other and makes all my hair stand on end.

The attic is not entirely dark. Light from the hallway below sheds a weak glow around the trapdoor. Large windows on all four sides reveal the sky moving toward dawn. A window seat has been built in all the way around and topped with comfy-looking cushions. Dangling from the slanted ceiling right above me is the string for a single light bulb, and when I tug on it, the room is instantly illuminated.

It's smaller than I'd expected, no bigger than my bedroom. There are no cobwebby boxes or old cedar chests or forgotten treasure stashes. Just a low coffee table, a cozy nest made up of pillows and blankets on the window seat that looks out toward the sound, and a raven.

"Hello," Norman says. He cocks his head, eyeing me keenly, then flies over and lands on my shoulder. I feel his weight settle, the sharpness of his claws against my bare skin.

"Good morning, beautiful," he says.

Fear recedes, replaced with a feeling I can't quite describe. I feel honored and a little awed by the fact that this magnificent bird has decided to trust me. At the same time I'm still spooked a little by his size and the weirdness of hearing a human voice come out of his bird body.

"Norman. You scared me half to death! What on earth are you doing here?"

A cold gust of wind, accompanied by banging and wailing, answers for him. A window is open. Wind whistles through the opening, setting a wooden blind rocking.

Cautiously I lift my right hand and touch the raven's head. He leans into my fingers, for all the world like a cat who wants a chin rub. I smooth his feathers while taking in the panoramic view. From here, I can see not only the yard and the cliffs and the sound, but also the road, and the forest that it winds through.

Norman flaps off of my shoulder and launches himself through the open window, off and away. I watch him fly out of sight before closing it and securing the latch. I'm shivering, with cold this time, rather than fear or shock.

Brodie barks, and I cross to the trapdoor and call down to him. "You're okay. I'm okay. Lie down. Just chill."

To my surprise, he settles onto his belly and rests his muzzle on his paws.

I return to the window seat and wrap myself up in the blankets.

Did Nomi snuggle up into this space and watch the sunrise turn the water red and gold? Did she sit here in the evening and watch the stars come out? Maybe this was where she wrote the letters, gazing out into the world, waiting for her lost lover to come home to her.

If so, there's no trace of her, but somebody else has certainly been here. The coffee table is stacked with books. Several are time travel novels. One is about modern Wicca. Another is a guide for mediums. There's also a drawing pad and pencils. On the open page is a sketch of the panoramic view laid out below me. In all the drawings, a woman is either falling, or lying broken on the ground below, approximately where the bed of scarlet flowers is now. Behind it, the lawn, the shed, the cliff, the shoreline are meticulously and accurately rendered.

"Oh, Savannah," I whisper.

I feel like I've violated her sanctuary, seen something I'm not supposed to see, but at the same time I feel comfortable and at home here, like the space has always been waiting for me to find it. Setting the disturbing drawing pad aside, I snuggle deeper into the blankets. The bench is surprisingly comfortable, and as my body warms, drowsiness overtakes me. I lie down, watching the color of the sunrise fade as the sky turns to blue, my eyelids growing heavier and heavier until I gradually drift into sleep.

Chapter Twenty-One

Blythe

I wake to the smell of bacon and coffee.

For a moment I think I'm imagining it, but then I hear the distant clatter of pots and pans. A glance out the window that looks out on the front yard reveals a blue bicycle leaned up against the porch.

Brodie is no longer at the foot of the ladder where I left him. Groggy with sleep, my brain feeling muddy and slow, I make my way down the ladder, visit the bathroom, and splash cold water over my face in a futile attempt to wake up and clear my head. The house is cold, and I grab a sweatshirt from the bedroom and pull it on over the tank top and lounge pants I slept in, before going downstairs.

When I enter the kitchen, Savannah turns away from the stove, spatula in hand. "How do you like your eggs?"

Brodie lies on the floor next to her feet, clearly well aware of the bacon sizzling and hissing in a big pan. Butter is melting in another.

"Hurry up before the butter burns," she says impatiently.

"Over easy," I say, because I have to say something, and she swivels back to the stove and breaks four brown eggs into the skillet. The toaster pops up four slices of toast.

"Butter that, would you?" Savannah orders.

"I'll never eat all this," I say. "Although I bet Brodie likes toast. And he definitely loves eggs, only he'll take them raw."

Brodie thumps his tail and whines, signaling his agreement.

Savannah snorts. "I happen to like toast. Also eggs. And I already fed Brodie, anyway."

I need coffee, and I reach up into the cupboard for a mug, then get a second one down for Savannah, filling both from the coffeepot on the counter. "I don't remember seeing anything about breakfast service in the rental contract."

"This is a bonus service," she says. Then adds, "Honestly? I wanted to come see Brodie. And I was hungry. So I made food for both of us."

The radio in a holster at her hip sputters and hisses, reminding me that mine is currently up in the attic. Flynn's voice comes through. "Savannah. Check in, please."

She ignores it, rearranging the bacon with a pair of tongs.

"Savannah!" Flynn's voice says, loud and clear.

With a gusty sigh, she pulls the radio out of its holster and responds, "I'm busy."

"I'm sure you are. Doing what? And where?"

"Working," she says. "You're interrupting." She turns her radio off before shoving it back into the holster. She flips the eggs with the spatula, more successfully than I've ever managed.

"Maybe you should just tell him where you are," I counter, getting out knives and forks. "He's worried about you."

"He doesn't want me here," she says. "If I don't talk to him, I don't have to lie."

"I think, maybe, he has a point," I say, thinking about the drawings in the attic.

"Don't you start!" She whirls around and glares at me, waving her spatula. A bit of egg white drops off and plops onto the floor.

Brodie makes short work of it. If I want to talk to her about her drawings and those books I saw in the attic, I'll need to tread carefully and not antagonize her.

"You're right. Absolutely none of my business," I agree.

She was all primed for a fight and my response disarms her. She stands there, staring at me, trying to think of a comeback.

"Your eggs are burning," I point out gently.

"Oh, shit." She swings around and moves the pan off the stove, poking at the eggs with her spatula. "They're not burnt, exactly," she says. "But definitely not over easy. Hope you're not picky."

She rattles two plates out of the cupboard, slides two of the eggs onto a plate, and hands it to me, then fishes the bacon out of the pan with a pair of tongs and lays it on a paper towel.

"Some guy called for you last night," she says, sliding her eggs carefully onto her toast. "Alan. After I got home." Her eyes dart up to meet mine and then away again. I get the feeling there's something more on her mind than Alan, but I figure I'll wait until she's ready to tell me rather than asking questions.

At the same time, I'm aghast at the idea of Alan talking to Flynn. I add a couple of pieces of bacon to my plate. Brodie whines and puts his front feet up on the counter. "No!" I tell him firmly, glaring until he puts his feet back on the floor, fixing me with a pleading gaze.

"Did Alan leave a message?" I ask casually, as if it doesn't matter to me one way or another.

"Nope." Savannah puts the mug I got out for her back into the cupboard and drags out a bigger one, filling it half full with cream, topping it off with coffee, and stirring in three teaspoons of sugar. I watch the spoon go round and round, clinking against the stoneware, waiting for more. But more doesn't come. She carries the mug over to the table and comes back for her plate.

"Are you going to eat?" she demands. "Your eggs are getting cold."

"Maybe I should call Flynn and get the message," I say, my eyes straying to the radio.

"He doesn't know anything," she says with her mouth full. "I'm the one who talked to him." She takes a long swallow from her mug, watching me over the rim.

Yep. Something is definitely on her mind. "Savannah . . ."

"Uncle Flynn doesn't even know he called. He likes you, you know."

"Alan? We've known each other a long—"

"No. Uncle Flynn."

I sit down and begin neatly dissecting my toast with my knife and fork. Brodie rests his muzzle on the table and I make him lie down. He crawls under the table, waiting expectantly for me to drop things.

"How about one thing at a time," I suggest. "What did Alan have to say?"

"Nothing. Just to call him."

"There's something else. What?"

She looks down at her plate and shoves eggs around with the remnants of her toast. What I can see of her face is tight and unhappy.

"Savannah, whatever it is, you have to tell me."

"It's not about Alan or messages."

She drops her toast on top of the remains of her egg and shoves her plate away. Then she takes a deep breath, folds her hands on the table, and looks directly into my eyes. "I need to confess."

Her expression reminds me of a soldier on his way to battle.

"What exactly have you done?" Fear flickers in my belly. Maybe she really did do something that contributed to her mother's death. If she tells me a thing like that, then what am I supposed to do? I'd have to break her confidence and tell Flynn.

"I didn't want anybody in the house," Savannah says. "And Uncle Flynn rented it anyway. So I . . ." She pauses and her gaze drops to her folded hands. In a small voice she says, rushing the words so they tumble over each other, "I cut the phone line. And I took your golf cart key, and I tried to make you think the house was haunted. So maybe you would leave right away."

And then, eyes downcast, she awaits my judgment.

"Let me guess. You left the attic window open and put some food in there for Norman so he'd come in and make spooky noises."

She stares at me with her mouth open, then finally says, "How mad are you?"

"I'm not."

"You're not?"

I shake my head. "I think I understand, actually. You want to be close to your mom. Maybe you even feel a little bit guilty about how she died."

"How do you know that?" The combination of naked grief and hope in her face nearly breaks me.

"I think everybody feels guilty after something like that," I say, thinking about Nomi. "Like we should have stopped it somehow. Or saved them."

I've said the wrong thing. The hope in her face vanishes. "You don't understand anything," she says.

"I saw your drawings. Up in the attic."

"You weren't supposed to be up there!"

"I went to investigate all the spooky noises that you arranged for me," I say, a little bit sharply.

"I thought you weren't mad!" she retorts.

I sigh, and count to ten in my head before speaking again. "Okay. Maybe a little bit mad. But good news for you—Nick wants me out. I'm only here until next Thursday, and then you'll have the whole place to yourself again."

"Oh no!" she wails, eyes wide with dismay. "You can't leave!"

"I thought that's what you wanted."

"That was before! Now I know you. And besides, you can't take Brodie!"

She looks like she's about to cry, so I say hastily, "Well, we still have lots of time to solve the treasure hunt, and you can come see Brodie every day while I'm here."

"But that's not long enough," she says. "Why won't Nick let you stay longer?"

"No dogs at this house, apparently."

"Oh my God. Who could object to Brodie? Besides those horrible Williams people. I'll talk to Nick. I bet he'll let you stay if I ask him."

She shoves back her chair and carries our plates over to the sink. "I'll wash these later. First, I'm going up to set live traps."

"Traps for what?"

"I might have brought some mice over. Don't you dare kill them. It's not their fault."

"Wouldn't dream of it." I get up and start running hot water into the sink. "And I can wash the dishes."

"Most people hate mice," Savannah says. "Uncle Flynn would kill them. He says they carry germs."

"Well, they do. But they're cute little critters. Not their fault that they like warm places and they carry diseases. Go set your traps."

Savannah grabs her backpack and I hear her feet, and Brodie's, running up the stairs.

I take my time washing the dishes and putting them away. Then I wipe down the counters and the table and sweep the floor. When I'm done, Savannah hasn't come down, so I climb the stairs to see what she's doing.

Brodie is curled up on my bed, while Savannah stands in front of the dresser gazing into the clear glass of Nomi's snow globe.

"It's beautiful," she says, when she hears me behind her. "Can I shake it? I'll be very careful."

"If you like."

I move up beside her as she lifts the globe with both hands, remembering the awe and wonder I felt as a child when Nomi let me do the same thing. Both of us stare, mesmerized, into the glass, watching the swirling white flakes drift and settle.

"Nomi used to see visions in it, like in a crystal ball," I tell her. "Or, at least, at the time I thought she could. She was probably just playing make-believe."

"What did she see?" Savannah asks, her voice hushed as if we're in church.

"Me, here on this island on my thirtieth birthday, for one thing."

"You're making that up."

I shrug. "Believe it or not. That's what she said she saw, anyway."

"Is it your birthday?"

"Nope. That was last week."

"Make-believe, then," she says, turning back to the dresser, this time looking at the urn. "What was she like?"

"She was . . . my person, if that makes sense. She loved games of pretend. She made me believe that magic was real. We laughed a lot. I still miss her."

"What did she die from?"

"She had cancer."

"My mom fell," Savannah says, her voice small and tight. "Off the ladder."

I feel helpless and inadequate. I want to say something comforting, but don't really have anything comforting to say. "It gets better," I tell her finally. "I used to hate it when people told me that, but it's true. It won't always hurt so much."

"I want it to hurt," she says fiercely. "It's supposed to hurt."

"I remember feeling that way," I say. "For a long time. I thought maybe it was my fault that she died."

"Was it?"

"It was not. But I didn't figure that out until I was all grown up."

"If she died from cancer, how could that be your fault?" Savannah demands, turning around and glaring at me.

"I was six. I didn't really understand what was happening."

"And these are her ashes?"

"Yes."

Savannah makes a small sound that reminds me of a wounded animal. "I'm glad they didn't burn Mom. But they locked her in a coffin and stuck it in a hole and piled dirt on top." Her voice goes all squeaky when she says, "I have these dreams where I'm the one that's buried and I can't get out. And sometimes I dream I'm falling."

For a moment I stay perfectly still, and then I dare to put an arm around her and rest my hand on her shoulder. She stiffens and I think she's going to pull away, but then she grabs me as if she's drowning and I'm her only hope of survival. I make soothing noises, rocking her a little, while she weeps. Tears pour down my own face.

When the shuddering of her body slows and eases and she pulls away to mop her face with her sleeve, I want so much to do something to make her feel better.

"So hey," I say instead, "would you maybe be up for helping me solve a little mystery?"

"I'm already helping you."

"I mean another one. The real reason I'm here. It has to do with my Nomi and what she said she saw in that crystal ball, and there's even a treasure map."

"Seriously?" She mops her face again with her sleeve and sniffles. I fetch the box of tissues and she blows her nose.

"There is intrigue and some kind of shenanigans going on. I came to find the place where she wanted to be buried. There's something hidden that I have to find, here on the island somewhere."

Savannah looks at me, her eyes red and swollen but now alight with interest, and I keep talking.

"There was an extra clue in my welcome folder. And a key. And somebody has left two letters for me that my Nomi wrote, I think to my grandfather, and I'm pretty sure she used to live here, at Improbable

House. Your uncle Flynn says he doesn't know anything about the letters or the clues, so I honestly don't know where they came from. Come downstairs. I'll show you."

I lead the way back to the kitchen, where I pour us each another cup of coffee. Then I tell her about the balloon man, and even Alan. I lay out the letters and the clues and the treasure map and the little key on the table between us.

"It's not much of a map," she says doubtfully. "I mean, it doesn't really tell you anything about where to look, does it?"

"That's because I drew it when I was six. Nomi's lawyer kept it all these years for me and brought it to me on my birthday."

"Maybe it's that oak tree in the yard," Savannah says. "It even has a heart carved into it!"

"That's what I thought! But I already looked there. Scanned all around under the tree yesterday."

"Maybe you missed it. No offense, but you're kind of new to metal detecting. I could look. Or we could maybe even ask Uncle Flynn. He's the best at that sort of thing."

A knock thunders on the door. I startle.

Savannah scowls. "We've summoned him." She tromps over to the door and flings it open.

Sure enough, Flynn's blond hair and broad shoulders are framed in the doorway. His face is a thundercloud. "What are you doing here?" he demands. "And why did you turn off your radio?"

"I'm helping Blythe with something."

"I don't really think Blythe needs your help," he says. "Come with me, right this minute."

"She made me breakfast," I say, walking up behind Savannah and resting a hand on her shoulder. "And she's helping me with my mystery."

His eyes meet mine, piercing and blue, and I feel a flush rising in my cheeks, remembering the kiss.

"You don't need to cover for her," Flynn says. "What was it? Releasing mice? Snooping through your things?"

"I don't snoop!" Savannah protests.

"You have work to do, in case you had forgotten."

"Fine," she says, in a martyred tone. "Dinner tonight at the World Tree, though, right, Blythe? You'll be there?"

"I'll be there. And then, maybe tomorrow you could help me search along the shore, since that one clue talks about the sea."

"The sea caves!" Savannah exclaims. "We need to look in the caves, for sure."

"There's an official tour of the caves; Blythe would probably rather wait for that," Flynn says in a repressive tone that has the same effect on me as it does on Savannah.

I feel her shoulder stiffen with rebellion, feel my own irritation rise at being told what I'd rather do.

"Actually," I say, "I'd rather explore them with Savannah. If it's all the same to you."

"It's not all the same to me," he says, his tone matching mine. "I've been thinking about those oddball clues, and the letters. I asked Glory, and she doesn't know, either. Which means somebody on the island has an agenda, and until I know what it is, I'd rather the two of you don't go running off into dangerous locations on your own."

"The caves aren't dangerous," Savannah objects scornfully.

"People have drowned in them," Flynn says.

"Only if they're too stupid to pay attention to storms and super high tides."

"Also," he says, ignoring her objections, "you'll both be alone, and well away from others. If whoever is leaving Blythe clues wanted to hurt her—"

"You could come with us," I say impulsively. "As security. Not to help me solve the clues."

He hesitates, and I immediately wish I could call my words back.

"Nobody will know," Savannah says. "We'll go down the ladder right here at Improbable House. So nobody can think you're giving Blythe the extra advantage."

Flynn's eyes meet mine and I feel the heat rising through my body again with the memory of his kiss and all that it awakened in me.

It's too soon after Alan. Flynn is not the right man for me. Why didn't I keep my mouth shut?

"With your permission, Blythe, I'd like to tag along," he says formally, as if he's talking to a total stranger. Which, I remind myself, I nearly am.

"Awesome!" Savannah says. "Dinner at five, Blythe. I'll see you then."

She darts off, Brodie at her heels, leaving Flynn and me in an awkward silence. "Well," he says, clearing his throat. "I'd better be off. Lots of work to do today." He gives me a half smile, then descends the steps, carefully, and begins securing Savannah's bicycle to a rack on the cart. While she waits, she tilts her head back and calls, "Norman! Here, Norman!" To my surprise the raven comes as obediently as a dog, more obediently than Brodie, if I'm honest, flapping into view and circling above the cart.

Without another word or a backward glance, Flynn starts the cart and drives away.

Chapter Twenty-Two

FLYNN

I have been bewitched, bespelled, mesmerized, cast under a glamour, all of which is of course impossible and illogical, but it's the only explanation for my desire to turn the cart around, run up those dangerously rickety steps, sweep Blythe into my arms, and kiss her again. Worse, I want to know her. I want to talk to her, find out what she thinks about things. I want to hold her hand and take walks by the beach and under the stars. I want to tell her everything about my own life.

The vision of her as she stood there on the porch looking after me, wearing a too-big sweatshirt and flannel pajama pants with bunnies, her glorious hair disheveled and wild, was very nearly too much for my self-control. Maybe, if we hadn't found that goddamn knife, I would have gone back to her last night after my meeting with Glory. Maybe she'd have taken me into her bed, and I would have buried my face in her hair, traced the line of those gold-dust freckles on her beautiful skin, and kissed every inch of her, not just her lips. Never have I encountered a woman who got under my skin the way Blythe has done in such a short space of time.

But we did find the knife, and my life is what it is, and commitment is not on my radar. Romance is not for me. I keep myself to nonexclusive, easygoing, practical friends-with-benefits arrangements without commitments or strings attached. Getting close to anybody feels dangerous. Besides, adventure is always calling.

"I'm actually glad you're coming tomorrow," Savannah says, way too casually. "It's not like these are real clues, so it's not like you'd be interfering with the game if you help."

She's up to something. Her face is so much like Frieda's, and I know that scheming look all too well. Of course, with Frieda I was usually in on the plan. With Savannah I am completely shut out.

"I'm sorry I snarled," I tell her. "Believe it or not, I have great intentions, pretty much always. It's just that I worry when I don't know where you are. So maybe you could start telling me?"

She shrugs one shoulder and looks down at her hands, twisting in her lap.

"Listen. I'm new to all of this. Maybe you could cut me some slack? I haven't the first clue how to be a parent."

"I don't have any parents," she spits out. "So maybe you could just try being my uncle for a change."

"I don't know how to do that, either."

"What *do* you know how to do?" The words are sarcastic, but maybe I'm listening better than usual because this time I catch the crushing grief and loss that underlie her anger.

Rather than lecturing her on having some respect, for once I tell her the truth. "I'm really great at being irresponsible, running off whenever I feel like it, and having shallow, meaningless relationships."

She snorts softly, a sound that could be agreement, or a smothered sob, or even reluctant laughter. Her face is turned away, and I know she wants to keep whatever she's feeling from me.

A silence stretches between us, full of so many things that need to be said, and finally I offer, "I'm sorry I wasn't here. That I didn't get to know you before. This would have been easier for both of us."

If I thought an apology was going to get me off the hook, I was misguided. She levels a devastating gaze at me and demands, "Why weren't you? You never visited. Not even once. Not even when Grandma died."

I turn my gaze back to the road, away from the accusations in her eyes. "It's complicated."

"What's so complicated? Family is supposed to stick together."

Wide open as I am, my defenses blown apart, the words drag me deep into a childhood memory.

"Family sticks together, Flynn," my mother's voice says. "Always. No matter what."

Her hands are cool on my forehead, smoothing back my hair. They feel good, soothing, but the words burn more than the oozing circles on my skin and I pull away so she can't touch me. My head spins when I try to stand and the floor wobbles, but I brace myself and hold steady until my vision clears.

I look at my mother, sitting quietly on the edge of my bed, tears flowing silently down her cheeks. She looks small and frail and broken, but the bloodstain on the sheet just beside her workworn hand hardens my heart. She's supposed to protect Frieda. She's supposed to protect me. Why does she insist on staying here, with him?

I can't breathe, as if there's an iron band constricting my chest at the same time as pressure builds from within. I'm going to explode, like a bomb, if something doesn't give.

"Honey, think," she whispers, those quiet tears ever flowing. "We can't leave. Where would we go? What would we do?"

"Anywhere off of this fucking island!" I scream at her, trying desperately to release the pressure in my chest before it blows me apart.

"Oh, Flynn," she whispers. She reaches for my hand, but I shake my head and stumble backward, half aware that if I let her touch me I'll succumb, as I always have—let her soothe me into some form of quiescence.

"Just a little longer," she pleads. "Look how much you've grown. You're nearly as big as he is now." And that's when I see it in her face, when I hear

the words that she hasn't said. It's your job to protect us, Flynn. It's your job to make him stop . . .

I can't tell Savannah any of this. How things were with our family. What Frieda and I did. She can't know any of it.

And neither can Blythe. I can't tell her, and I can't have a real relationship with her if I don't let her into the heart of who I am. Any moment, behind any corner, under any loose board, I could run into something that unravels the whole web of lies that is my existence.

My skin flashes hot and cold. The old burn scars flare with pain signals as if they are new. I try to breathe despite the pressure growing in my chest.

"How did you get that scar, anyway?" Savannah asks, and I catch myself in the old habit of running my index finger over the long white line, eyebrow to eyelid, that small and blessed hop over my eye, down over the cheekbone. I drop my hand to the steering wheel, focusing in on the smooth solidity of it. I anchor my feet on the floor of the cart, register the temperature of the air, the smell of the trees, the sound of Savannah's breathing beside me.

And I remind myself of why I live the life I live, and why I can't afford to fall into a relationship, even one that is bound to end next Thursday when the water taxi comes to take Blythe back to wherever she came from. Her family. Alan.

"It was an accident." The lie comes out harsher than I mean it to, thanks to the unrelenting pressure in my chest.

"An accident like you ran into somebody's knife while treasure hunting?"

"An accident like it's none of your business."

"You could tell her," Frieda says, materializing on the seat between us. "You should tell somebody. It would be good for your soul."

"Not happening," I mutter out loud.

"What's not happening?" Savannah asks, and I realize that I'm talking out loud to somebody who is definitely dead.

"How about we talk about you hanging around in Improbable House when there's a guest there? You know it's against the rules."

"Blythe doesn't mind," she says. "I like her. I'm helping her with her treasure hunt."

"I thought you didn't want anybody in the house."

"I changed my mind. I'm allowed." Savannah crosses her arms over her chest and stares straight ahead, daring me to argue with her.

"Sure. You're allowed. A gazillion times a day, if you like."

She glances at me suspiciously, obviously expecting an argument. "Hey, I'm always changing my mind. No reason why I should be the only one."

"You need to talk to Nick," she says, then. "Tell him to let Blythe stay past Thursday."

"I don't know that he'll listen," I say grimly.

"You have to try! I don't want Brodie to leave. Or Blythe." Her voice breaks and tears well up in her eyes.

Savannah's tears have the impact of a fist to my solar plexus, followed by a thickening in my throat and a prickling behind my eyes, which almost immediately gives way to the desire to land a right hook on the jaw of anybody who has hurt her. She's had enough grief and I don't want her to have more. I picture myself striding up to Nick's counter and laying him flat.

Which, of course, I can never do because he's an old man, disabled and frail. I could talk to him, though. Maybe make him see reason. Because if I don't? Just a few more days and Blythe will be gone. An emptiness opens up inside me at the thought. If I feel this way about her already, where will I be if she stays two weeks? Three? A month?

"Maybe it's better if she does go," I mutter.

Which is utterly the wrong thing to say. Frieda shakes her head and vanishes.

"Oh my God. You don't understand anything," Savannah cries. We drive the rest of the way in a silence charged like the air before a thunderstorm, and the minute I stop the cart, she runs into the house, slamming the door behind her.

Chapter Twenty-Three

Blythe

Brodie and I take a leisurely walk, investigating the property. He alternates between sniffing at everything, marking his new territory, and running in ecstatic circles. We start with the old oak tree, and I stand there, tracing the lines of the heart carved in its bark, gazing up at its spreading green branches, and wondering what I'm missing until Brodie lets me know he's had enough and wants to move on.

We explore the wide expanse of shaggy grass, thick with golden dandelions. Beyond the rosebushes, heavy with blooms and bees, a weathered wooden fence marks a safety perimeter well back from the cliffs. A small gate is flagged with a sign that reads, **Danger. Proceed at Your Own Risk.**

I make Brodie sit and stay, while I slip through the gate and cautiously approach the cliff. Down below, the tide is coming in, eating away at a narrow strip of rocky beach between the waves and the cliff. The only access is an aluminum ladder bolted to the rock. Brodie barks frantically from the other side of the fence.

"Take it easy, buddy," I say, deciding to put this adventure off until tomorrow and go with Savannah and Flynn. If there are clues down there, they are all underwater right now.

So we go back to the house and I spend a couple of hours searching for hidey-holes and secrets, assisted by Brodie, who sniffs busily in corners and closets and under furniture and is completely unreliable as an assistant. I wander around tapping on walls, running my hands over the backs of the closets, even checking behind paintings to see if they might be hiding secrets.

Nothing. Even the attic reveals nothing more surprising than built-in storage under the window seat bench, containing extra pillows and blankets.

Savannah radios me at about three. "Don't forget about dinner."

"I won't forget."

"Remember to dress nice!"

"Right. Got it."

I try and fail to picture Savannah dressed for fine dining, then abandon that and take care of getting my own self ready to go. Fortunately, I did pack one dress—just a casual sundress, but it will have to do. I leave my hair loose on my shoulders and put on a touch of makeup. When I look in the mirror, for a minute I hear Alan and Kristen and my mother all running commentary.

> Mom: *Maybe put your hair up? It always looks uncombed when you leave it down like that.*

> Kristen: *Is that really your only dress? Maybe some jewelry?*

> Alan: *You're gorgeous, as always, but maybe not the outfit for a five-star restaurant?*

Brodie comes up and nudges me, liberally shedding fur all over the front of the dress. I start to brush it off, then stop, look in the mirror again, and say out loud to the array of critics in my head, "I'm on a theme park island, going out for dinner with a twelve-year-old so we can look for clues to a fake treasure hunt. Honestly, I should probably wear the Viking hat."

The idea of that sets me laughing so hard I decide to do it. I'll embrace the island experience, maybe even coax a laugh out of Savannah. Brodie is not at all happy when he understands that he'll be staying alone at the house. I give him a leftover piece of bacon and admonish him, "Listen up, Brodie. You are the dog of the house while I am gone. It is your job to keep guard, manage the ghosts, and if somebody sneaks in here with another letter or clue, you need to tell me who it was. Got it?"

He woofs, once, dog language for something that is obviously not agreement, because after I close the door I can hear him whining and yipping. I cross my fingers that he won't have an anxiety fit and tear the house apart, but then I remind myself that Ted Wilcox is paying a hefty pet deposit on my behalf. What can Nick do about it? Kick me out? I'm already being evicted earlier than planned.

When I park my golf cart in the lot at the edge of Vinland Square, it's only 4:30, which is perfect. I have time to stop by the Coffee Dragon. I hear my phone start to chime with messages even before I climb the steps onto the deck, but I don't look at them yet. I have another mission in mind.

Giselle, disheveled and flushed, smiles at me from behind the counter. "Blythe, right? What can I get you?"

"I was hoping I might use your phone."

"Yours not fixed yet?"

"Apparently it requires somebody coming out from the mainland."

"You poor thing." She lowers her voice. "And then Old Nick being so difficult on top of everything else. You must just think we're all horrible."

"Actually, most of you are lovely." I flash her a smile. "But I do need to make one quick call, if I could?"

"Of course. You know where the phone is. Go on ahead. Anything else I can do for you, you just let me know."

"Thanks, Giselle." I start to walk around the counter, then stop and come back. "There is one thing. I've just discovered that my grandmother used to live here, or at least visited here. I don't suppose you would remember her? Her name was Naomi Balfour."

Giselle busies herself mopping the counter as she answers, "Oh, honey. I see so many people! I'm sure I wouldn't remember."

"This would have been before Vinland was Vinland. Over fifty years ago. You would have been a child, if you were even born."

"I'm sorry," she says. "You're right, I was just a little thing. Only a few of the old ones left—most of them have either passed on or retired to the mainland. Old Nick would be your best bet."

I snort. "I don't exactly think he's going to trade stories with me about my grandmother. Well, if you wouldn't mind asking around, if it's not too much trouble? I'd love to talk to somebody who knew her then."

"Of course," Giselle says cheerfully. "I'll do some asking and let you know." She turns away to get coffee for a guest, and I slip behind the counter and into the small, cozy room with the phone.

Aunt Bella answers on the second ring. "Update me," she says, moving directly past hello.

"It's Blythe," I say. "And hello to you, too. Is that how you answer the phone these days?"

"Blythe!" she crows. "What a delightful surprise. No, I was expecting a call from somebody entirely other. How are you? How is the island? Your mother is in quite a state."

"She tried to declare me missing and send out the National Guard."

Aunt Bella clucks. "Your mother has always been a worrier. Even when she was just a little bit of a thing. Maybe especially then. Well, I'm so honored that you'd make time to call me while you're on your little adventure."

"What do you know about all this, Aunt Bella? The truth now."

"I have no idea what you mean. I was as surprised as you were when that man showed up with Naomi's ashes."

"No you weren't. You were in on it."

"Blythe, darling, I think—"

"Listen, Aunt Bella. I've been thinking a lot and remembering a lot. That day Nomi died—you helped her."

"What on earth makes you—"

"Don't even try. It was all so neat and coincidental, wasn't it, that she died while everybody was away from the house? She made up this elaborate quest game to get me out of the way. You helped her plan that, and you helped her plan this."

There's a long silence on the other end, and I think she's either going to hang up or keep lying, but instead she says, "You always were a smart girl, Blythe. I told her you'd figure it out."

"Not until recently." A lump swells in my throat, choking off my voice. I swallow hard, take a breath. "I thought for years that it was my fault she died. That I'd made a mistake in the quest she sent me out to perform, and that's why she never came back from her enchanted sleep."

"Oh, Blythe!" Aunt Bella sounds horrified. "I had no idea."

"I can't believe you helped her kill herself!"

"I'm so sorry that you suffered that way, as a child," Aunt Bella says. "But now that you're grown-up you must be able to understand. She was suffering. She'd had an episode where she'd forgotten who you all were. She told me she could handle pain, and even losing the use of her body, but not losing her mind. She didn't want all of you to see her that way, especially you, my girl. She was already too dependent and disabled to be able to take care of it herself, so she asked me."

"Why not just send me out to play? She asked me to keep the 'quest' a secret! All those years I thought I'd somehow killed her and couldn't say anything!"

The tears ambush me, unexpected but overpowering, flowing silently down my face. I can't stop, even though I know the mascara I just carefully applied is smearing, even though if Giselle walks in she will see.

"Oh, honey. She would feel so terrible if she knew. *I* feel terrible! I didn't realize. She wanted to be sure to get you safely out of the way, give you a fun last memory, and be sure you wouldn't say anything. She never dreamed you'd think it was your fault!"

"What would have been so awful if I'd told Mom that she sent me out on a pretend quest?"

"The insurance money, child. Naomi was worried your mother would put the pieces together and say something to the authorities, and you and Kristen wouldn't get the money. Life insurance doesn't pay out for suicide."

"But that's insurance fraud!" I'm suddenly struck with an attack of conscience. If I do find Nomi's hidden treasure and bury her ashes and inherit the money she set aside for me, am I breaking the law?

"That's exactly the reaction she was afraid of," Aunt Bella says calmly. "But it's not fraud."

"How is it not?"

"Because she was going to die anyway. If she'd suffered another month, it would have been all legal. Because she decided to exit early, under her terms, suddenly it's not? Bullshit."

I sit quietly, not bothering to wipe away the tears that are running down my face, letting all of this sink in.

"Are you going to do something stupid like try to give it back?" Aunt Bella asks.

"I wouldn't even know who to give it back to!"

"Exactly!" Aunt Bella says. "That's my girl. Now. Are you having fun?"

I know I'm going to forgive her completely, but not just yet. I'm not ready to admit that yes, I am having fun. That I have been kissed and have adopted a dog and fallen in love with an old house and do not ever want to come home.

"You owe me some answers," I say ruthlessly. "For letting me suffer alone all those years when I was a child."

She answers with silence, but I press on.

"I've been presented with letters that Nomi wrote to my grandfather. What do you know about him?"

"He was lost in Vietnam."

"Oh, come on. Something I don't know."

"I didn't know him, honey. But how interesting about the letters!"

"I'm staying in the house she used to live in. The one they were going to live in, when he came home from the war."

"That's lovely! That should help you."

"Don't tell me you don't know all about this treasure hunt!" I say. "You planned it together. Just like you planned her death."

"Not true, I'm afraid," Aunt Bella says. "The treasure hunt thing was all hers."

"But why? Why me, why now? If she really wanted her ashes buried here, you could have done that for her right after she died. Sending me to the island—the treasure map, the bequest on my thirtieth birthday— it's all so elaborate."

Again there is silence on the other end.

"Aunt Bella. You owe me. Damages for pain and suffering."

"All right. I'll tell you this. It all started with that snow globe thing," she says, after another long pause. "Naomi was . . . She had . . . We used the term 'second sight' back then. She could sometimes see things that were going to happen. And she told me she saw something in that globe when the two of you were playing pretend.

"'Blythe needs to go to the island. But how can I be sure she gets there, if I'm dead?' she asked me. And I told her that if you were meant to be somewhere, then that's where you'd be. And she said that she was worried your mother would do her best to make you so reality-bound you'd never allow yourself to follow fate unless she helped things along. She knew you loved treasure hunts, but she didn't think the promise of fun would do it. But, she said, 'If I ask her to bury my ashes and make fulfilling the quest a prerequisite for inheritance, then I'll have buy-in from Blythe and also from my beloved but practical and rather mercenary daughter.'"

"You can't believe she actually had a vision, Aunt Bella." But I say this more like a question than a statement. I want the magic back. I want to believe.

"Fortunately, what either one of us believes doesn't matter," she says. "You're right where and when she wanted you to be."

"Aunt Bella, what did she tell you she saw?"

"Sorry, darling. Another call coming in. Have fun. Call me when you find the treasure."

"Aunt Bella—"

But the line is dead.

Momentarily forgetting where I am, I let loose a scream of frustration, and slam the phone down onto the table.

"Everything okay, dear?" Giselle asks, poking her head in through the door.

"Fine, thanks." I plaster on a smile that isn't fooling either of us.

"Well, good then," she says. "Maybe you'd like to wash your face before you go to dinner? You can use my private bathroom. Go through that door on the opposite side of the room and it will take you into my house. There are makeup remover wipes in the top drawer on the right. I'm afraid I don't have any makeup, though."

"Thank you. You are an angel." I get up and start toward the designated door, then turn back to her, suspicious now of everything and everybody. "Wait. How did you know about dinner?"

"Savannah told me all about it, my dear."

What I see in the bathroom mirror is not a pretty sight. I'd forgotten about the Viking hat, askew on my head. My face is smeared with black streaks, my eyes are red and swollen. I owe Giselle mightily for not letting me go out in public this way. I try to repair the damage, but removing the smudges of mascara also removes circles of foundation from under my puffy eyes, and in the end I just wipe it all off, splash cold water over my face, and settle for a touch of the lip gloss I've got in my purse.

"Much better," Giselle says approvingly when I emerge back into the Dragon. "You'd better hurry, now."

"Oh God. What time is it? Am I late?"

"Just the right amount of late," she says.

I have no idea what she means, but there isn't time to ask, or to check all the messages lighting up my phone.

I arrive at the doors of the World Tree out of breath and brimming with apologies. The young woman behind the reception desk, dressed in a flowing white sheath with flowers in her hair, more Greek goddess than Viking maiden, acts as if she has all the world and time at her disposal.

"I'll be with you in a moment," she says, glancing up, then goes on making notes on what looks like a spreadsheet.

I scan the tables, all full, for Savannah, but if she's beat me here she must be on the other side of a giant wooden pillar, carved to resemble the bark of a living tree, that rises from floor to ceiling in the center of the room. The ceiling and walls are painted to resemble boughs and branches and leaves, giving the effect that all of us are beneath the canopy of an old and mighty oak.

"Listen, I have a five o'clock reservation," I say, when the girl fails to look back up after a good long minute. "Or, at least I'm with somebody who has a reservation. She might be here already."

"Oh." She puts down her pen and looks up at me, suddenly giving me her full attention. "Are you Blythe? I'm sorry. Right this way."

She leads me around the giant central tree and gestures toward a candlelit table for two. The other chair is occupied not by the twelve-year-old child I was expecting, but by Flynn, dressed to the nines in a suit and tie. He gets to his feet and pulls out my chair. Surprised, I sit and allow him to slide it up to the table before asking, "Where's Savannah?"

"Savannah," he says, "has been taken suddenly and inexplicably ill."

I stare at him in dismay. "Oh no! What's the matter? Shouldn't you be home with her?"

"Sudden onset of a headache and sore throat. I was going to radio you to cancel, but she proclaimed that it was vitally important that I meet you for dinner. 'Blythe was so looking forward to the World Tree! And one of her clues might be there. You have to go in my place, Uncle Flynn.' Her actual words, whispered, because of the throat. So here I am, and here you are, and you look lovely. The Viking hat is a nice touch with the dress." His lips twist up into a smile, his eyes lit with what might be laughter.

"You too. I mean, not lovely, but . . ." I wave my hands, searching for the right word. *Handsome* isn't it, although it's difficult to take my eyes away from his face. *Exotic. Delightfully dangerous.* Like Thor in a tuxedo, pretending to be less than himself. My entire body thrums in response to the flash of his smile.

"Savannah told me you were looking forward to getting all dressed up and having the five-star experience, so I have, at her urging, donned the one coat and tie in my possession."

My hand goes self-consciously to the skirt of the dress, smoothing it with one hand, as I glance around and see that the other diners are wearing casual attire.

A toga-clad young waiter glides over to our table with a bucket of ice and a bottle of champagne. My eyes widen as I read the label and I glance back at Flynn, who says, "That looks wonderful, Zak, but we didn't order it."

The young man, whose melting dark eyes, tangled curls, and charming smile probably earn him an entire living in tips, proceeds to open the bottle. "Consider it a gift." He pours golden, bubbling wine into our glasses and asks, "Are we ready to order?"

"We haven't even looked at the menu yet," Flynn says. "We'll need a minute."

"Perfectly fine, take your time. A selection of appetizers has also been ordered, compliments of the house, and will be out shortly."

He inclines his gorgeous head, then glides away toward the kitchen, leaving the two of us to look at each other awkwardly across the table.

"What's with the whole Greek vibe?" I ask, avoiding all of the more interesting questions. "I thought everything was supposed to be Vikings and pirates?"

Flynn laughs. "Amazing collision of stereotypes on Vinland, isn't there? If asked, the owner of the World Tree will tell you the servers are dressed as the servants to the gods must have dressed. The truth is, he wanted a classy joint, and wasn't about to staff it with pirates and half-dressed serving wenches. This was his compromise."

"Well, it's really very beautiful," I say, looking up at the painted ceiling, and wondering if maybe this is the location designated by the clue about the world tree. There are no ravens or wolves, of course, but maybe that bit was merely theoretical.

"Well, no point wasting this excellent champagne," Flynn says, raising his glass. I look down at mine, remembering the last time I drank champagne, an evening that launched me on this whole improbable adventure. When I lift the glass and look back into Flynn's eyes, I have an odd sense that I'm engaging in a ceremonial gesture.

"To treasure," he says. "May it be easily found and may there be joy in the finding."

I touch my glass to his and we both drink. The bubbles dance delicately on my tongue. Flynn's face is softened by the candlelight. There's a faint line between his brows. His eyes look into mine as if he's seeking something, an answer of some sort, even though all I have are questions.

"I guess we should look at the menu," he says, his gaze not moving from mine.

"I guess we should." My voice sounds dry and raspy and I clear my throat and lower my eyes, feeling the heat rising to my cheeks and grateful for the dim light. "What's good here?"

"Everything," he says. "Although I'm really rather surprised that somebody hasn't ordered for us."

"Savannah's not really sick, is she?" I ask.

"I have my suspicions. She's a scheming little creature. Too smart for her own good. Way out of my league, that's for sure."

"And mine," I say, laughing. "She was quite creative with her plans to get me out of Improbable House. That, at least, I understand. But why fake illness to get out of dinner? It was all her idea. She made the reservations. She radioed me this afternoon to remind me that dinner dress was required, which I see is not the case. What do you suppose she's up to?"

"At first, I thought she just wanted us occupied so she could go back to the house. But given that she's recently decided that she doesn't want you to leave, and then looking at where we are sitting, all dressed up, with a bottle of champagne and appetizers on the way . . ." He quirks an eyebrow and his lips curve in a wry smile.

"Ohhh," I breathe, understanding flooding in. "She thinks that . . . you and me . . . oh dear." I gulp champagne, probably not my smartest move given the situation. Flynn refills my empty glass. "Would the restaurant really do all this for her, though?" I ask.

"The people of Vinland will do anything she asks them to right about now."

He says it lightly, but I see the lines of grief settle into his face and say impulsively, "Tell me about her mother. About Frieda. Were you close?"

He refills his own glass, takes a long swallow before meeting my gaze again. "The answer to that should be simple, but it's really terribly complicated."

"I get that. I have a sister. Half the time I'd like to strangle her, but I can't imagine life without her."

"Kristen, right?" he asks. "The one who calls expecting me to relay messages about how you need to make sure I comp you heavily in exchange for your inadequate accommodations?"

"That's the one." I push past his evasion and ask, "Was Frieda a schemer, like Savannah?"

The waiter appears just then with a tray of appetizers. Panfried oysters. A shrimp cocktail. Crab cakes. Warm rolls with herbed butter.

"Are you ready to order?"

"I don't think I'll need to if we eat all this," I murmur.

The waiter laughs, as if I'm being witty. "The Alaskan king crab is very good," he suggests.

"Sounds good to me," Flynn says, handing over his menu. "Blythe?"

"I can't," I say, shuddering at the memory of a disastrous occasion when Alan took me to a seafood restaurant for crab.

"They are a little messy," Flynn says. "But Zak here will bring you a giant apron."

"It's not that . . ." I laugh a little, remembering Alan's over-the-top reaction to my squeamishness. "It's just so . . . violent. Wrenching the legs off, cracking them open. I know they're dead, but I feel like those eyes are watching themselves be dismembered."

Instead of scoffing, Flynn gives me one of his rare full-on smiles, the one that lights up his eyes and changes his whole face. "Savannah can't do it, either," he says. "Animal lover to the core. I'll have the blackened rockfish, instead," he tells the waiter.

"If you want the crab, don't let me stop you."

"I've been meaning to try the rockfish for ages," he says. "Plus, we've got crab cakes already, so perhaps enough crustaceans have sacrificed their lives for our pleasure. What are you having?"

"Perhaps the salmon?" the waiter suggests.

"Sure, the salmon sounds great," I agree, not because I'm particularly fond of salmon but more because I don't want to keep them both waiting while I work my way through the menu.

"You were going to tell me about your sister," I say, when the waiter is gone.

He glances up from the roll he's buttering. "Was I?"

"Yes," I reply firmly. "You were. You were just telling me how your relationship was complicated."

His brow furrows. He lays aside both the butter knife and the roll and sits looking down at his plate for a long moment before he says, "We were twins. She was the other half of me—the stronger, smarter, and better half, to be honest. We were inseparable. We worked together, went to school together, got in trouble together. And then . . . I ran away from the island and never saw her again."

"Ever? But why?"

"I told you it was complicated," he says. "I wouldn't come back to the island. There were . . . reasons. And I was all over the planet so she couldn't easily come to me. We talked on the phone. Exchanged emails and pictures. It wasn't much, but that twin bond we had—I was deep under the ocean when she died and I felt the shock of it go through me. I knew before I got the phone call."

He shrugs both shoulders, as if he's trying to shift a weight, and takes a bite of a crab cake. "These are amazing. You should try one."

I do, and they are. While I eat, I wonder what Flynn is not telling me. About why he really left and why he never came back. But he obviously doesn't want to talk about his childhood, so I ask more about Savannah instead.

"Where is Savannah's father?"

"Who knows?" He smiles, a little grimly, and I realize that this isn't an easy subject, either. "Frieda wouldn't tell us, but I suspect he was a summer worker. The island transformed from Calvert to Vinland when we were fifteen. Quite a shift, I'm sure you can imagine. Up until then we were isolated from society, incredibly sheltered from everybody but island people. We grew up and went to school with a small group of other kids, no more than fifty in kindergarten through tenth grade. Some homeschooled for high school, most went to high school on the mainland.

"Frieda and I had only been off island for a handful of days in our entire lives. All of a sudden there were people coming in. The visiting kids, the college students who came to work, seemed exotic and worldly and highly desirable. I had a super crush on a college girl that first Vinland summer, but I was still a spindly, awkward kid and she had no interest in me. Frieda, though—she looked twenty-one and the incoming guys were all over her.

"And then, I abandoned her. She was sixteen, more alone on this godforsaken island than she'd ever been. A few years later when she called to tell me she was pregnant, she wouldn't give me a name. She said only that she figured both she and Savannah could do perfectly fine without him. I should have been here for her. For both of them. I wasn't.

"The first time I laid eyes on Savannah was the day before Frieda's funeral. I regret," he says, softly. "So many things I regret."

His big hand rests on the table, palm up, and I'm moved to lay mine over it as I say, "You're here now, Flynn."

His fingers close over mine, gently, and then to my astonishment, he lifts my hand and kisses it. I can't look away from his searching gaze—don't even want to. With my free hand, I reach up and trace the scar on his face with my index finger, and ask a question I know I should leave alone. "Why did you run away? Did it have to do with this?"

There's a flare of pain in his eyes, an instant of heartbreaking vulnerability, and then I feel his body go still, rigid. His eyes seem to grow opaque, his face impassive. He smiles a wooden smile and releases my hand. "We should finish these appetizers before the food arrives. More champagne?"

He pours me another glass. I load up my plate and we eat in silence for a moment. When he speaks again, he's retreated into his shell.

"I'm still trying to get somebody to come and fix the phone, but it might not be before Wednesday."

I shrug. "No worries. I've gotten kind of fond of the silence, to be honest. A little escape from my own family."

His smile is the automatic half smile, the one that doesn't reach his eyes. "Yes, well. If we get it fixed, they can stop leaving messages for you on my office phone."

"I have messages?"

He rolls his eyes. "Your mother would like you to know that she thinks you should end this wild-goose chase immediately and come back to civilization. Your sister, as I mentioned, suggests that you consider suing me for damages, unless I refund your money and pay you for your pain and suffering. Your father says to tell you to just enjoy your time. Alan requests—no, demands—that you call him immediately."

"King Alan," I say wryly. "I know that tone."

"He doesn't sound so much like he thinks the two of you are over," Flynn says casually, popping a shrimp into his mouth.

"That's because he hasn't met Brodie yet," I say lightly. "Alan doesn't do dogs—even clean, well-behaved expensive little dogs." And then, because it feels important to be all the way honest with Flynn: "We're definitely over. I have no idea what I'm going to do when I leave Vinland, but I won't be going back to Alan."

His eyes focus in on my face, maybe even on my lips, as if he's remembering our kiss in this moment as vividly as I am. And then his own lips part and I lean forward to hear what he's going to say, only he says nothing because the waiter arrives with our food. By the time our plates are on the table and the last of the champagne has been poured into our glasses, the moment has passed.

"Once you've solved this little treasure hunt your grandmother set you on, it sounds like you could go pretty much anywhere you like," Flynn says. "Start a new life somewhere."

"If I solve it," I say, forking up a bite of perfectly flaky salmon. "I was one hundred percent certain it would be under that oak tree somewhere. I scanned the whole area and found a bunch of junk, but nothing close to what I'm looking for. Not that I actually know what I'm looking for, but still."

"I can bring my scanner over, if you like," Flynn says. "It's not breaking any rules to help you with *that* treasure hunt."

"That would be great. Tomorrow, maybe? But you're also coming to the caves with us. Can you spare that kind of time?"

"I think I can get away with it. I could always pull a Savannah and turn my radio off."

We both laugh at that, and then, remembering, I sober and say, "I hope she isn't really ill."

"I'm pretty sure she's fine. Physically, anyway. Emotionally? I haven't a clue."

"There's something you should probably know," I say, with the uneasy feeling that I'm betraying a trust. "I stumbled over some pictures in the attic. Drawings of her mother's death. Falling, fallen, about to fall. She didn't want me to tell you."

"God," he says, setting down his fork and staring at me in dismay. "What should I do? Does she need a counselor? Oh God, you don't think she would . . . that she would ever . . ."

"End her own life? I don't think so, Flynn. It's almost more like she's trying to process, or make sense of it all somehow. She's a brilliant artist, if you didn't know."

"I didn't." He pushes away his plate and leans back in his chair. "I am in so far over my head."

"You're doing better than you think," I tell him. "She knows you love her. That counts for a lot."

"You think? I'm not at all sure of that. Listen, Blythe. I know it's a lot to ask. But she seems to have opened up to you. Can you ask her?"

"Ask her what, exactly?"

"I don't know, anything and everything. About what happened. Whether she's had thoughts of self-harm."

"Whatever I can," I promise.

Our waiter returns with dessert—one giant hot fudge sundae with two spoons. He sets it on the table between us. "Before you ask, I know you did not order dessert. This comes from the same source as the champagne and the appetizers. Enjoy."

He moves on to another table, leaving Flynn and me alone with our single dessert.

"Makes you wonder where the camera is hidden, doesn't it?" he asks. "Like we're on some reality TV show."

"Or wandered into a remake of *Parent Trap*," I say, laughing. I pick up a spoon and take a bite. "Not gonna waste it just because somebody might be watching."

Flynn picks up the other spoon and joins me. I'm enjoying the last creamy, delicious bite when I notice the writing on the paper snowflake doily between the silver bowl and the plate it rests on.

"What's this?" I draw it out and hold it close to the candle flame. Handwritten words read:

Treasure comes in many forms.
Look for these things:
What has been and is not
What is forgotten, remembered
What is lost, found.

"What is it?" Flynn asks.

"I thought it was another clue, but if it is, it's the worst one ever." I hand it over to him and watch while he reads.

"This is getting ridiculous." He waves an arm over his head to summon our waiter. "What's this?" he demands, holding out the message as soon as the young man arrives at the table. "And don't tell me you don't know."

The young man shrugs. "What do you want me to say? I don't know. I picked up your dessert and brought it over here. Just like this."

"Who gave you the instructions about the champagne and the dessert?"

"Chef. Is there a problem, Flynn? Am I in trouble?"

"No, Zak, you are not in trouble. I just need some information. Who has been in the kitchen tonight?"

"Nobody! I mean, obviously people have been in the kitchen. But nobody unusual. Just Chef, and Jenny and Chris and the rest of the waitstaff. May I go now, Flynn? I've got tables waiting."

"Right," Flynn says. "Don't mean to get you in trouble. Thanks for the chat. A little something extra to make up for lost time." He holds out a twenty, and the young man, still obviously flustered, takes it with a nod of thanks and scurries off to another table.

"Can we go talk to the chef?" I ask.

"Are you kidding?" Flynn says, with an expression of exaggerated horror. "More than my life is worth, or yours, to interrupt Victor during dinner service. I'll try to catch him later. Right now, my lady, I fear that I must leave you. I should check on Savannah, and there is still work to be done. I'll walk you to your cart."

When we're clear of the restaurant, he takes my hand and we walk in a companionable silence. I stop when we're passing the Coffee Dragon. It's closed, but there are people at tables on the deck, checking phones and laptops, so apparently the WiFi is still working.

"I should check my messages," I say. "So maybe they'll stop bothering you."

"They're not bothering me so very much," he says. And then, despite the watching eyes, he leans down and kisses me, a gentle, lingering kiss that makes me close my eyes and think of starlight. "Good night, Blythe," he whispers against my hair.

When he releases me and walks away, I feel unmoored, a small boat adrift on a vast and uncharted sea. Feeling, more than seeing, curious eyes on me, I pretend that being kissed like this hasn't taken my breath away and make my way up the steps onto the deck of the Dragon, where I settle myself at a table near the railing and pull out my phone.

I do not need Alan making any more calls to Flynn, so I check that thread first.

> Alan: I'm sorry.

Wait, what? I stare at that message in shock, wondering what on earth he's done. Alan isn't big on apologies. On the few occasions during our relationship when he really thought he was wrong, he sent flowers with a handwritten card, but he has never actually said the words.

I keep reading.

> Alan: Kristen helped me understand why you were so upset about my arranging that job for you. I didn't mean to make you feel inadequate. It's just that I'm an arranger. It's what I do. Who I am.

> Alan: Speaking of which, the opportunity of a lifetime has come up. I'm meeting with an international acquisitions team in Paris. It was sudden. I'm flying out on Wednesday. This Wednesday. I have two first-class tickets.

> Alan: Come with me, Blythe. Get yourself off that island and to Sea-Tac by 6 a.m. Don't worry about clothes, we'll go shopping. In Paris! You can charm the team at

a little soiree they are planning. And then you and I can
fall in love all over again in Paris. Say yes.

For a long time I sit there, staring at my phone, considering the offer, and realizing that I don't want any of it. I would trade all of Paris—a shopping expedition, a first-class hotel, the museums, and the Eiffel Tower—for the chance to locate Nomi's treasure.

Or for another kiss from Flynn, Nomi's voice whispers inside my head.

"Flynn is just an island adventure," I object. "All part of the Vinland fantasy. When I leave in another few days, he will rapidly become a pleasant memory."

Blybee, lying to yourself is a dangerous thing.

In any case, I'm not going to Paris. I tap my response into the phone:

> Blythe: Thank you for understanding, Alan. That means
> a lot to me. But I can't go to Paris. I suggest you take
> Kristen. She'll do a much better job of charming your
> potential business partners. And I know she'd love to
> go shopping.

And then I message Kristen.

> Blythe: Go to Paris with Alan. He needs a helper and I'm
> still tied up on the island.

> Blythe: By the way, it's definitely over between us.

Chapter Twenty-Four

FLYNN

When I get home, Savannah is pretending to be asleep.

She's a little too slow turning off the bedside lamp and I see the thin stripe of light under her door go dark just as I'm hitting the top of the stairs. She lies on her back, eyes closed, her breathing too rapid for sleep. I go along with the charade, drawing the covers up over her shoulders, touching my hand to her forehead to check for a fever. She is perfectly cool.

With an overly dramatic little sigh, she turns onto her side, away from me, and buries her face in her pillow. I bend over and kiss her cheek, then leave her to believe she's fooled me.

It's no great surprise when she shows up for breakfast in the morning and announces that she must have had a very short virus, either that or her body has an amazing immune system, because she feels perfectly fine.

"I don't think you should go out," I tell her, straight-faced. "We don't want to infect anybody else with whatever you've got. I'll let Blythe know the caves are off—"

"But I'm fine!" she cries, aghast. "Maybe it was just allergies. See? You can look at my throat if you like."

She opens her mouth wide and sticks out her tongue. I fetch a flashlight and have a look. Then she digs up a thermometer, which of course declares her temperature as perfectly normal. My actions began as gentle revenge for last night, but I find myself considering following through with my threat.

The caves, like Improbable House, are fraught with memories. As if that's not bad enough, I've kissed Blythe again and now I don't know how to act when I see her. But I can't bring myself to disappoint Blythe or deprive Savannah of this expedition. So I let her off the hook and we load up in the cart and head for Improbable House.

Savannah chatters about the sea caves and the tide charts and asks endless questions about last night's dinner. What did we eat? What did we drink? Did Blythe have a good time? Was there another clue?

I tell her all about the evening, watching her carefully for reactions. She seems genuinely surprised by the message on the doily, exclaiming, "But that's so weird. What does it even mean, do you think?" and then launches into a chain of conjecture that leaves me, blessedly, to my own thoughts.

I can hear Brodie's barking joining with the croaking of the ravens before we round the final corner and drive into the lot of Improbable House. Blythe is out front waiting for us. She's dressed practically, in jeans and a sweatshirt, and she's prepared for the expedition, with her metal detector in one hand, a trowel in the other.

Savannah flings her arms around Brodie, hugging him around the neck, and then the two of them take off at a run toward the cliffs.

"Obviously, she's not sick," Blythe says, as the two of us follow at a more sedate pace.

"Nope. Not remotely."

"Were you able to find out anything else? From Glory or the chef?" She turns her head to look at me, stumbling over an uneven spot in the terrain. I put out my hand to steady her and it lights on her lower back and settles there. I let it stay as she looks up at me, eyes wide and startled. Up close, in the bright morning light, I see that her irises are mostly blue, with flecks of golden brown, not green. Her lips part as if to ask a question but she says nothing. Her pupils expand. My breath catches in my throat.

We are caught out of time, with something between us that will break if I try to name it, and I'm about to abandon the last shreds of sanity and kiss those parted lips right here and now, Savannah or no Savannah, danger to my heart or—

"Are you two coming or what?"

Savannah's shout reverberates through me. I drop my arm to my side and return to Blythe's question as if there had been no pause between its formulation and my answer.

"Glory claims to know nothing. Chef expressed outrage that any-body would dare to meddle with the presentation of his dessert. I honestly haven't a clue."

Savannah has already vanished over the edge of the cliffs and I feel a by-now-familiar shudder of anxiety go through me. I would like her to be cautious. To wait for me to double-check the ladder, to go down first so I can steady her if she loses her balance. But she's been monkeying up and down that ladder for years without interference and there's no way I'm going to change that now.

Blythe stops when she reaches the edge of the cliff and I move forward with the intention of offering reassurance and then descending ahead of her, so I can be there to ensure her safety. I know well how disorienting and dizzying that first moment of standing on the cliff's edge and looking down and then out onto the vast expanse of water and sky can be.

But rather than expressing the smallest uncertainty, she says, "What about Brodie? I should have left him in the house. If he tries to come after us, he'll fall."

An excellent point, one I would have thought of myself if I wasn't so distracted by the combination of her presence and our destination that I can't seem to hold two thoughts together at a time.

"I'll run him back," I tell her. "Wait for me. I'll carry the detector." But she doesn't, of course. By the time I come panting back, she's already vanished over the top and is halfway down, metal detector in one hand, climbing as easily as if she's done this a million times.

When she reaches the bottom, she cries out, "That was amazing!" She sets down the detector, stretches out her arms, and spins like a child, laughing with wild delight.

"You weren't scared?" Savannah asks admiringly. "We had a guest who got stuck in the middle, one time. Too terrified to move up or down."

"Oh my God, no. How much time have I wasted already, not coming down here?" Blythe asks. "That view! And just hanging in the air like that. I can't . . . just wow. I am doing this every day until I leave." She stops spinning and moves drunkenly across the sand to sink breathlessly onto a large rock.

"The ladder is generally not quite so enthusiastically received," I say as I descend the last few rungs and set my feet onto the wave-packed sand. I'm dazed by her enthusiasm, by the way she seems to shine, like sunlight reflected off the water.

"Can I see the clue again?" Savannah asks. "The one about the sea. You brought it, right?"

"I thought you weren't helping," Blythe teases, digging a slip of paper out of her pocket.

"I never said that," Savannah gasps. "That was all Uncle Flynn with the not helping. Honest to God, I have no idea where the clues are buried, and even if I did, this one isn't part of the Vinland hunt, I don't think."

"So why the caves, then?" Blythe asks.

"There are always notes hidden in the caves," Savannah urges.

"But this isn't an official note," Blythe argues. "You've both said so. So maybe it means the shore, exactly like it says."

"Good point," I say, seeing an opportunity to avoid the caves altogether. "Maybe we should work the shoreline instead."

"You're not helping, remember?" Savannah says repressively. "Come on, Blythe. The caves are super cool." She grabs Blythe's hand and tows her down the beach at a run. With a sigh, I pick up the metal detector and follow more slowly, giving myself an internal lecture with every step.

You're a grown man, Flynn, not a child.

Nobody is here to harm you.

The tide is low and getting lower.

The caves never were the danger, even then.

Still. A cold sweat breaks out on my body, my palms slick with it. The waves drown out the sound of my pounding heart, but I can feel it, shaking my body, can feel the adrenaline flood through my muscles, recognize the instinct to run far and fast.

Savannah and Blythe are waiting for me outside the first of the caves and my heart lurches, breaking its rapid but regular rhythm as I realize they'll expect me to go in.

Looking for something to say that will cover my illogical fear, I resort to tour-guide mode.

"Ladies, you will find two caves here at the base of this cliff, both of them largely man-made. Once, they were little more than shallow impressions made by the relatively gentle tides of the sound. You may have noticed that the waves here don't have the power of those from the open ocean. Men came along and saw opportunity. They carved the tunnels deeper and angled them upward, above the level of incoming tides, creating a space where a fugitive could hide, where a stash of gold and silver ingots could be stored to be retrieved later."

"You're such a dork, Uncle Flynn," Savannah says. "They're super cool, Blythe, no matter how they were made. Come on!"

I'm not about to admit to either of them that I'm beset by irrational fear. I take a deep, steadying breath, unclip the flashlight I carry on my belt, and shine it into the darkness. Savannah has her own light on, and darts through the entrance, Blythe following. I take one step, then another, entering the natural hollow, just barely tall enough for me to stand upright. Savannah is already vanishing into the smaller tunnel, large enough for a child to walk upright, for a man to crawl.

I take another step, and the memory hits me, completely immersive, wiping away everything besides pain and terror.

My body is suddenly small and thin, easily able to stand upright in the tunnel, facing the tall figure standing in the cavern beyond, blocking my exit.

"Don't leave me here. Please. I'll do anything." Pleading will make it worse. It feeds him. But I can't seem to stop.

"You're a sniveling little coward. This will teach you courage. You'll stay here until I come back for you."

"Please. Let me come with you."

"If you leave before I give you permission, I'll introduce your sister to this." He flicks his lighter and holds it to a cigarette between his lips.

My own back screams with pain in the places where he marked me, only a few minutes ago. Mostly he leaves Frieda alone, and I can't let it be my fault that he hurts her.

"I'll stay," I say, making my voice as steady as I can.

"Good boy." There's an unaccustomed note of approval in his voice. But then he's gone, taking the light with him, leaving me alone in the dark. My back is afire from the cigarette burns, the rest of me shivering with cold and terror.

The tide was already rising when we came in, before he made me take off my shirt and stand with my hands on the cavern wall while he pressed a lighted cigarette to my back, again and again.

"A man needs to be able to withstand pain, son. No screaming. No crying. No flinching. We'll do this until you learn."

Alone in the dark I can hear the water moving, rattling stones at the mouth of the cave. I know that the tides are relentless, know that the water will keep rising, rising, for hours yet. It's too dark to watch its progress. How high will it rise? Will it drown me?

Fear overtakes me, dissolving even my will to protect my sister.

I stumble through the darkness for the exit, but take only a few steps before I am standing in water, before a wave washes in, up over my knees, and I know that I am trapped, that the water has already reached the cliffs.

Scrambling back into the cave, tripping over stones in the dark, falling onto hands and knees, getting back up again, over and over, I make my way to the end of the tunnel, turning to press my burning back against the clammy stone, waiting for death.

Blythe's voice brings me back out of the abyss.

"Cool! So the smugglers kept things here? Wouldn't the water wash it away?"

"The water doesn't come all the way up to the very end, at least not more than a few inches. See the waterline?" Savannah answers.

Their voices are distant, a little muffled, both of them out of sight up the tunnel. I'm standing near the entrance. I can see the sunlight and an expanse of rocky beach. My body is big, strong, my tormentor long dead, even though it feels like just moments ago that he burned me and trapped me alone with my fear.

"Is this where they found the treasure cache?" Blythe is asking.

"Naw, we've never found anything interesting here. You can only get to the real treasure cave with a boat, and it's too dangerous for tourists. Wait a sec, that's new."

"Let me see," Blythe answers.

And then silence.

"What is it?" I call.

"Hang on. We're coming out."

Savannah emerges first, her face dirt-smeared, hair tangled. Blythe follows, a small wooden box in her hands.

"Let's take it outside where we can see," I suggest, leading the way before Savannah can propose that the box ought to be opened inside the cave for a more mysterious ambience or something.

Outside, all is clear and bright. The tide has turned, but we've got at least a couple of hours before it will reach us. Farther out, two sailboats skim along with a brisk wind, so light and easy they seem to me to be flying. I breathe in the salt air, ground myself in the reality of the rocky beach, the sunlit sky. The adrenaline in my body is receding, leaving me shaky and tired. I want to sit down, close my eyes, maybe sleep for a week.

Fortunately, neither Savannah nor Blythe notice anything amiss with me, both of them fascinated by their discovery. The box looks like all the others that we use for hiding Vinland clues: wooden, shaped like a treasure chest, with a curved lid and metal hinges. They're mass-produced, and cheap, but the treasure hunters seem to like them.

Blythe opens the box and reveals what appears to be a standard Vinland find—a silver coin and a paper clue. But when she hands the coin to Savannah and removes the note, there's another piece of paper still in the box. "It's a photo," Blythe says, digging out the stiff paper and turning it over.

Curious, I move to stand behind her. Savannah edges in on the other side and the three of us stand there, staring at an old black and white of a man and a woman. It doesn't take me long to figure out who the woman is, since Blythe is almost a carbon copy. The young man, his arm around the woman's waist, looks like he owns the world. His chin is lifted, his face glowing with a combination of love and pride.

"Who is it?" Savannah asks.

"Well, that's my Nomi. I don't know the man. Do you think it might be my grandfather?"

Savannah glances from the photo, to Blythe, and back again. "You look like her. Not like him at all."

"My mother and my sister look like him, though," Blythe says. "Nomi never showed us any pictures of him. I wonder why?"

"What does the clue say?" Savannah asks.

Blythe replaces the photo in the little box, unfolds the clue, and reads:

> *The Allfather sees all*
> *Knows all*
> *Has it all.*
> *Including 25% off all items in the store.*

"That one's easy!" Savannah crows. "Odin! We need to go to the trading post."

"Old Nick's place, you mean?" Blythe asks. "That's the one place on the island I've been avoiding. Maybe he'll change his mind and kick me out early."

"He's not so bad when you know him," Savannah says. "I'll go with you! And I'll tell him you're helping me . . . recover from my grief."

"You're awfully quiet, Flynn. What are you thinking?" Blythe asks, looking up at me out of those big blue-green eyes.

I'm thinking that I can't breathe when I think about her leaving. I'm thinking that I want to go knock some sense into Nick myself. What I say is "I'm thinking it's weird that this standard Vinland get-tourists-to-spend-money clue is packaged with a picture of your grandmother."

"We need to go see Nick," Savannah says. "Right now."

"You and I have work to do," I tell her.

"Aw, come on, Uncle Flynn! You're no fun! And we can't make Blythe go there by herself."

"Life is hard."

"Could you let me borrow her?" Blythe asks. "Tomorrow, maybe, since she has work to do? I need her to protect me when I go to Odin's." She gives me a meaningful look, the kind that reminds me that she promised to try to talk to Savannah. There is, of course, no arguing with that.

"I guess, since you need a security detail," I concede. "And because if anybody can talk Nick around, aka manipulate him, it will be Savannah."

Savannah flings her arms around my waist and squeezes, a move so unexpected that she's gone again before I can hug her back. She scrambles up the ladder like a monkey, followed by Blythe, and I'm grateful for the space of time to breathe and get my emotions under control.

But Blythe is waiting for me at the top, with an enigmatic little smile that turns my heart inside out. We walk to the cart in silence, but just as I turn to get in, she lays a hand on my arm. "You said you might help me scan under the tree today?"

"Right." I look down at her, knowing I don't dare spend any more time alone with her if I want to still have half a heart when she leaves. "I'm sorry. I've got a busy day. I'll try to clear some time tomorrow, but no promises."

"Understood," she says, snatching back her hand as if stung.

As we drive away, Savannah says, "You can be such an idiot, Uncle Flynn."

Frieda, materializing on the seat beside her, nods agreement.

I don't argue. They are absolutely right.

Chapter Twenty-Five

BLYTHE

I leave Brodie at the house when I drive into the village to meet Savannah, given that Nick's earlier reaction to the dog wasn't exactly enthusiastic. We've spent the morning outside, searching the property with the metal detector, and he seems good and tired and ready for a nap.

While I drive, I allow myself to daydream. What if I had the whole summer in this glorious old falling-down house? A whole summer away from failing to live up to Mom's expectations, away from the demands of a job I'm not really fit for.

A whole summer to get to know Flynn.

No, no, Blythe. Do not think about Flynn, who has made it perfectly clear that he doesn't want to spend any extra time with you. You'll be leaving the island on Thursday, and going back to real life, a life that doesn't happen to include a large, scarred Viking with incredibly blue eyes and surprisingly sensitive lips, and a voice that makes you trembly all the way down to your toes . . .

The not-thinking-about-things isn't working so well, so I'm grateful to see Savannah leaning against the statue of the pirate when I pull into the parking lot on the edge of Vinland Square. Norman is perched on the pirate's head, looking baleful and superior. He ruffles his feathers and croaks, "Nevermore."

"Did you have to teach him to say that?" I demand as a chill chases itself up my spine.

"That was Mom," Savannah says. "It's out of some moldy old poem or something. Did you remember the photo?"

"I did."

"And the discount coupon clue thing?"

"Check."

"I was thinking, we should have a code name, don't you think? For our mission?"

I don't think. Talking to Nick does not feel remotely like a game to me; he is creepy and unpleasant and there is too much riding on this. But Savannah's face is alight with energy and excitement. It won't hurt me to play along. Maybe it will even take the edge off the dread congealing in my stomach with my lunch. "Mission Improbable?" I suggest. "Ride of the Valkyries?"

"Valkyries are fun," she says, but then she hums the first few bars of the theme from *Mission: Impossible* and intones, "Your mission, if you choose to accept it, is to face Allfather Odin and ask of him a boon . . ."

Norman flutters down onto her shoulder and starts poking his beak into her hair, as if searching for something. She giggles. "See? Norman likes it. Definitely Mission Improbable. Come on. Let's go!"

She sets off, Norman riding along, and I fall into step beside her. When we reach the trading post, she stops outside the front door, turns to me, and says, "I'll do the talking. Follow my lead."

I lay a restraining hand on the shoulder that doesn't have a raven attached to it. "Wait. I'm not sure this is a good idea. Maybe it would be better to get Flynn to talk to him again."

She wilts, visibly, like an unwatered houseplant set out in the desert sun, and turns two big, innocent eyes up to me. Her bottom lip quivers. "Whatever you think, Blythe. Only, I had everything all planned . . ."

"The theatrics aren't working, Savannah," I say. "Save them for your uncle."

"Nevermore," Norman croaks.

"God have mercy," I mutter. Even as the words leave my lips, I have an uneasy sensation that calling on God right outside Odin's Trading Post is going to summon the wrong deity.

Savannah hums "Mission: Impossible."

I can't help laughing at the absurdity of it all. "All right, mission leader," I say. "I'm right on your six."

She flashes me a brilliant smile, opens the door, and leads the way across the threshold.

The light is dim, and I have the disorienting impression that I've both entered a cave and stepped outside of time. The mouthwatering aroma of sausages fills my nostrils, carrying undertones of sage and cinnamon, coffee and tea, plus something bitter and smoky I can't place.

Wooden shelves are lined with cans and boxes that would look commonplace in a grocery store, but here somehow seem exotic and mysterious. Barrels hold staples like flour and sugar and yes, coffee beans, tea, and spices.

Savannah leads the way to the counter, calling out, cheerfully, "Hey, Nick! We are famished! We need lunch."

Nick leans on the counter, glaring at us . . . no, not us, me . . . and says nothing until Norman flutters off Savannah's shoulder and alights on his.

"You know you can't bring that bird in here," he growls. "Health regulations."

"Everybody knows Odin has ravens, Nick," Savannah says. "If anybody comes in, they'll think it's all part of the setting. So, can we get some dogs? Blythe has a coupon and everything!" She elbows me. "Give it to him, Blythe."

I lay the clue on the counter and he leans over to peer at it.

*The Allfather sees all
Knows all
Has it all.
Including 25% off all mercantile items.*

He grunts and then glares at me. "Playing the Vinland Treasure Hunt after all, then, are you? Thought you were here to bury your grandmother."

"I talked her into it," Savannah says. "Because I wanted to play. She's letting me help. Which is why we're here, for the next clue. Only we're also really truly starving, Nick. Two Viking Dogs, pretty please."

"This infernal bird has got to go before I touch food," he says. "Take him outside."

"Yes, Almighty Odin," Savannah says. "Your word is, of course, my command. Come on, Norman."

The raven cocks his head and peers at her, but doesn't offer to move from his current perch.

"Get off, you," Nick says, shrugging his shoulder, but Norman isn't budging.

"Nevermore," he croaks.

"Norman. Come here right now." Savannah whistles and holds out an arm, and the bird grudgingly exchanges his perch on Nick's shoulder for her arm. She carries him off, leaving me alone with Nick, which was definitely not part of the plan.

"That dog totally destroy the house yet?" he asks. "Pee in the corners? Poop in the kitchen? Tear up the carpets and chew the furniture?"

"Brodie has been very good," I say stiffly, holding on to my temper. The last thing I need to do is offend Nick. I can be polite, even if he's being an asshole.

"And how is your grandmother?" he asks, his voice thick with sarcasm.

"Still dead," I retort.

Savannah comes trotting back and settles herself beside me, delivering a sharp elbow to my ribs. "About those dogs, Nick? We are seriously going to die of starvation in a moment." She flops forward onto the counter, eyes closed, head turned to the side, tongue lolling out.

Nick mutters something I don't catch, which is probably for the best, and limps over to the food preparation counter. "What do you want on them?" he asks.

"Allfather Dogs, for both of us!" Savannah tells him. Then stage whispers to me, "Go look around and find something else to buy."

I roll my eyes at her but do as she says, moving up and down the aisles, loving the store despite my uneasiness with Nick. If there's a system to the way things are organized, I can't figure it out. It's like a magpie stocked the shelves. Cans of soup are lined up right next to a selection of screwdrivers, a couple of hammers, and some small barrels holding a selection of screws and nails. Pain relievers and cold medicine share a shelf with dog and cat food. The expected Vinland tourist claptrap is entirely missing—the only mugs and T-shirts I can see are plain and practical. This store is more for the island locals, I realize, with the Viking Dogs being Nick's main concession to the tourist trade.

I return to the counter carrying a bag of dog treats and a couple of cans of tomato soup. Savannah's expression tells me that I should have done better in my item selection, but it's too late. Nick lays our Viking Dogs, in their little paper Viking boats, on the counter, then positions himself behind an old-fashioned cash register to ring them up, along with my extra items.

Savannah grabs up her dog and takes a huge bite. "Oh my God. This is so good," she says, with her mouth full. "Try yours, Blythe. Allfather Dogs are so awesome."

I'm not feeling remotely hungry, but I did promise to follow her lead, although I am not about to enter into an overly dramatic hot dog–eating act the way she is. I take a bite, and make a little humming sound involuntarily as my mouth encounters the perfect blend of savory sausage, homemade bun, mustard, mayo, and ketchup and whatever else it is that he's put in here.

"Amazing," I say, sincerely, after I've swallowed and grabbed a napkin off a stack on the counter to wipe my mouth.

Nick finishes ringing up my purchases and gives me a total. While I'm digging cash out of my purse, Savannah leans her elbows on the counter and says, in a confidential tone, "There was something so weird in the box with Blythe's clue! Uncle Flynn doesn't know how it got there, or Glory, either."

The old man says nothing as he takes my money and gives me change.

"Could you look at it, Nick, maybe? I figure if anybody on the island would know, it would be you."

"I'm not pretending to be the all-seeing Odin with you," he growls. "You want a make-believe game, go see somebody else."

"It's not make-believe," she says. "Show him, Blythe."

I lay the picture on the counter in front of him. He gives it a cursory glance, like a reluctant witness on a cop show, but then I see him do a double take. His body stiffens. He bends over to look at the picture on the counter, his hands well away from it, as if touching it would contaminate him.

"So, do you know who the people are?" Savannah asks.

"This young lady here is the spitting image of the woman in the photograph," he says, "so I'd hazard a guess that's the grandmother who requires burying. As for the man, can't say as I've ever seen him. Now, if the two of you would excuse me, I have work to do."

"You're sure?" Savannah presses. "You've been here longer than anybody."

"You want to play a game of identifying tourists from the past, I suggest you talk to Glory. Or Captain Vickers."

"None of them is old as you, Nick."

"*Nobody* is as old as me, child," he says. "Shoo now."

He sounds more weary than angry, though, and I signal Savannah to ask about extending my stay.

She looks up at the old man, eyes wide, somehow making herself look younger and more vulnerable, and says, "I read this thing online last week about grieving kids, and you know what it says? It says pets are, like, the best therapy. Especially horses and dogs. And dolphins."

"And I bet ravens," Nick says. "Good thing you've got Norman."

"Norman is not cuddly," Savannah protests. "He can't sleep in my bed with me, or—"

"Neither could a dolphin or a horse," Nick says, smart enough to see where this is going.

"Which leaves a dog as the best option!" she crows triumphantly.

"You should talk Flynn into getting you one then," Nick grumbles. "Now, I'm busy, so if you ladies would excuse me."

"Well, but, we'd have to go to the mainland, and you know how tourist season is," Savannah protests, summoning up tears and a touching little sniff. "So I was thinking, maybe if Blythe could stay, and keep Brodie, I could—"

"The dog is not staying in my house beyond Thursday," he says.

"I'll just have to keep him myself, then," Savannah says. "That way Blythe won't have to leave."

"I'm taking the house off the rotation," Nick says. "That's final, Savannah. No more pestering. The old eyesore should be burned down. Maybe I'll sell it to somebody who can demolish it and build something new."

"No!" Savannah and I both cry together.

"You wouldn't, Nick, would you?" Savannah is no longer pretending grief and dismay. She reaches across the counter and grabs his good hand, her eyes wide and beseeching.

"It's my house, and I'll do whatever I like. Now, both of you out of my store!" He's shouting, his scarred face twisted with anger. Even Savannah retreats, apparently recognizing that persisting will just add fuel to the fire. I scoop up the photo, my purchases, and the rest of my hot dog and scurry for the door, heavy with foreboding.

There is no possible way this man is going to let me stay.

Chapter Twenty-Six

BLYTHE

Even before I open my eyes, I know three things with utter clarity:

One, today is Tuesday, which means I have only today and tomorrow to solve Nomi's treasure hunt.

Two, even if I do figure out where Nomi wants to be buried and earn the money she left in trust for me, on Thursday morning I will have to leave this old house where I feel so close to Nomi, where I have been allowed to be myself without interference from my well-meaning family, and go back to the real world.

I will have to say goodbye to Savannah and Flynn.

I've never really connected with kids, maybe because I haven't been around them much. But Savannah has wormed her way into my life. Even when she's annoying me, there's a little warm glow under my skin, a softness under my rib cage, a nurturing, protective drive, more powerful, more intense than what I feel for unprotected animals. How will I ever know if the child is okay, once I'm gone? Will Flynn ever open up enough to share his grief with her so she can unload hers on him?

Speaking of Flynn, the third thing I know is that I have fallen, ridiculously and improbably, in love with him. All the logic in the world doesn't work to change that.

My eyes open and I try to ground myself in reality—the feel of the mattress beneath me, the water stains on the ceiling above me, the sound of dripping into the bucket in the bathtub, which lets me know it's raining again before I even look out the window to confirm. I get out of bed, registering the shock of the cold hardwood floor beneath my bare feet, pad over to the window, and wrench it open.

Fresh, damp air wafts in, smelling of roses and grass and the sea. The world is shrouded in mist, and I can't see the cliffs or the big oak tree or the lilac hedge or the waters of the sound. The ravens, unbothered by the rain, croak and squawk and mutter, some of them flying off on mysterious raven missions, others returning. The sound of wings is becoming as expected as the sound of the waves lapping against the shore.

The old house, the misty, magical scene outside my window that looks for all the world like a movie set for some fantasy, the presence of the ravens . . . all of this does not help bring me closer to logic and reality.

I try to tell myself that I hardly know Flynn, that it takes time to really fall in love. I remind myself that on his side I'm obviously no more than an island dalliance, one he can easily do without. I try to apply other words to what I feel: infatuation, lust, intrigue, but none of them quite fit. I make myself think about Alan, and how I once thought I was in love with him, but no matter how hard I try, I can't remember feeling this way about anybody before.

The idea of walking onto that boat on Thursday morning, of standing there on the deck and watching both Flynn and Savannah grow smaller and smaller while I sail away forever, turns me inside out.

Obviously, I need more time. Time to figure out where to bury Nomi, time to get Savannah to talk about her mother, time to make Flynn fall in love with me. Unfortunately, time is one thing I don't have, and I don't know how to make more of it.

"Nomi," I say, stroking the urn full of her ashes. "I don't know if I'm going to be able to pull this off. I'm not the brave and adventurous Blybee you always told me I was. I'm really Blythe the inadequate and disappointing. You should have probably sent Kristen, if you wanted to make something happen."

But the words of the old story that I've been telling myself for years feel awkward and untrue and misshapen as they leave my mouth. They sound self-pitying and martyred, and I realize, with a little shock of surprise, that I don't feel at all like either a failure or a martyr.

I've done a lot of courageous things in my life, especially in the last week. I turned down a job and an offer of marriage and came to Vinland for an adventure. Maybe I'm not great at high-powered real estate deals, but I'm excellent with frightened animals, and I really am good with people. Maybe I haven't figured out where to bury Nomi yet, or talked Nick into letting me stay, but I've rescued Brodie and befriended Savannah and apparently managed to fall in love.

Not bad for five days. Rather than wandering about bemoaning my fate, I need to solve Nomi's puzzle. Then I'll have money enough to come back next summer, or maybe even later this season if something opens up.

An hour later, showered, dressed, and full of determination, I clip the leash onto Brodie's collar and the two of us head for Vinland Square. The Coffee Dragon is the first stop, obviously. I need breakfast. I need coffee. And I need advice from somebody who is island and has a sympathetic ear.

Brodie is excited and keeps pulling at the leash, stopping to say hello to everybody who passes us. Most of them are more than happy to stop and pet him and scratch his ears, and his tail is getting a full-on cardio workout. It takes nearly half an hour to make our way to the Dragon. When we get there, the tables on the deck are all taken. Gail waves me over to theirs, and even Gene smiles. He's wearing a T-shirt, in place of the button-up shirt and tie; his expression is more relaxed and his shoulders not so tight.

He offers Brodie a piece of bacon and then lets the dog lick his fingers.

"Are you okay, dear?" Gail asks, with a worried pucker between her eyebrows. "We haven't seen you since Friday, and we heard about that nasty old man making you leave."

"I'm perfectly fine," I tell her. "I've been around—I guess I've just missed seeing you. Do you think maybe you could hold on to Brodie for me while I run in and order?"

"I'll hold him," Gene says, getting a good firm grip on the leash. "I like dogs."

There are only two people in line in front of me at the counter and they move quickly because Giselle has help today—Savannah, of all people, pulling shots and fetching pastries. Which kind of throws a wrench in my plans to talk to Giselle.

"Blythe!" Savannah squeals, as if I'm her long-lost best friend. "Are you treasure hunting?"

"Right at the moment I'm caffeine hunting. And I need breakfast."

"You also need an apple turnover," Savannah says. "Trust me. They are ah-mazing. Where's Brodie? Did you leave him behind?"

"Nope. Gene's got him for a minute. I'll take the Shipwreck Breakfast and the Captain Blackbeard Coffee. And an apple turnover."

There's nobody in line behind me. While Savannah bustles around getting my order ready, I lean forward on the counter and catch Giselle's eye.

"What is it?" she asks when I gesture for her to come over. "You look worried."

"I am, a little," I confess.

She makes a clucking noise and pats my hand. "Is it about burying your grandmother and those weird clues? You'll figure it out."

"How do you know about all that?"

Giselle laughs. "The only thing faster than the speed of light is gossip on Vinland. Everybody knows all about your business, I'm afraid."

"Do you think you might . . . Would you talk to Nick for me? Put in a good word, maybe, see if he'd let me stay longer?"

"He's a stubborn old man, Nick is. Once he's taken a position, he's unlikely to change it. But I'll have a word with him."

"If he doesn't come around, do you know of any other options? Somewhere else I could stay? At least for another week?"

She frowns, thinking. "I assume you've talked to Flynn?"

I nod.

"Well, if he says there's nothing, I'm sure there's nothing. You might have a word with Glory, see if she'd let you stay in the dormitory with the summer help, but I think that's also full. I really don't know what's to be done. We're already overbooked. I've got somebody in my guest room or I'd ask you to stay with me."

Giselle's words deflate the optimism I'd worked up this morning. She's so sympathetic, I'd been sure she'd have an idea. She smiles brightly at me now.

"You just keep on following clues, dear, I'm sure you'll figure it out. You've got two whole days."

"Plus, I'm helping!" Savannah says.

"See? You can't possibly fail."

"One more thing," I say, withdrawing the photo from my purse and laying it on the counter. "You'd have been a child when this was taken, but do you remember either of these people?"

She wipes her hands on her napkin and picks up the photograph by the edges. After a moment, she slowly shakes her head. "I'm afraid not. The woman looks familiar, but that's because she looks like you, I imagine. Your grandmother?"

"Yeah, that's Nomi. You're sure you don't recognize the man?"

"I'm so sorry I can't help you," she says, handing back the photo. "Anything else? I should get back to work." She turns away, even though there's still nobody behind me and Savannah is completing my coffee and putting everything on a tray.

"Trees," I say desperately. "I think what I'm looking for is buried under a tree. Are there any landmark trees on the island that I might be missing?"

"There's that big oak tree by Improbable House," she says.

"Yeah. That's what I thought. There was nothing there."

"Hmmmm," she muses. "There are a lot of trees on the island. It would have to be a noticeable and memorable one, wouldn't it?"

"We've already checked the world tree in mini golf, and Blythe went to the World Tree Restaurant," Savannah says, bringing over a tray with a whipped cream–topped coffee, a plate of bacon and potatoes and eggs, and the recommended apple turnover.

"I'm afraid I have no other ideas," Giselle says. "Enjoy breakfast!"

"I could come over later," Savannah says, her chirpiness all gone, her thin face intense and pale. "To go over all the clues. I could bring pizza."

"Let's do it," I say, picking up the tray. "Radio me before you come, okay? In case I'm outside looking around."

Back out on the deck, Gail is nowhere to be seen, but Gene sits quietly, bent forward to pet Brodie's head with both hands.

The dog erupts into barking and whining as soon as he sees me. Gene laughs. "He loves you."

"He thinks I've brought him treats. Where's Gail?"

"Bingo. Team bingo, can you believe it? Vikings against pirates. Whichever team wins gets clues to the treasure."

"I'm sorry to make you late," I say, setting down my tray and getting my hands on Brodie's leash.

"It was a mercy. Sure you don't need a dog holder while you run more errands?"

"I'm sorry to say that I think I can manage."

He sighs. "Well, only two more days, I suppose. Better go join the games."

"Oh, come on, Gene. Admit it. You're having fun."

"And ruin my reputation as a first-class grump? Come on now." But he grins as he says it, and actually runs down the steps from the deck like a man at least half his age.

Which leaves me alone to drink my coffee and eat my breakfast. Brodie begs for a while, but finally lies down at my feet, ever hopeful that I'm going to drop something.

Optimism flows back into me with the caffeine and sugar, as I drink my coffee and eat the perfectly flaky, lightly sweetened turnover. Savannah coming over later means another chance to talk to her about her mother. Plus, Flynn still hasn't scanned under the oak tree, and he's almost sure to find something if I've missed it. Plus, I still have my clue and coupon for the gallery. Maybe the proprietor will recognize the man in the picture, or maybe I'll find another clue.

I check my messages, firing a quick response off to Mom to say that I'm still alive, still not kidnapped, definitely not in any sort of trouble. I message Dad to let him know I love him.

There are no messages from Kristen, or from Alan.

I wonder if she's going to go with him to Paris, and check to see if I feel jealous at all. Nope. Not even a twinge. I open my email, mostly spam and social media notifications. There's one from Blake and Lomax, acknowledging that I've declined the position. There are a handful of requests from people wanting to view some of my houses, and I forward them all to Bonnie, the receptionist at my office, so she can pass them on to one of my coworkers.

And then I pull out my last remaining clue and spread it on the table in front of me.

You've uncovered the key to treasure. Take 25% off any purchase made at Brokkr and Eitri's Gallery.

As clues go, it's not much, just a generic Vinland clue designed to make me spend money, but hey. Worst-case scenario, maybe I'll find a nice gift for Mom. Brodie and I make our way to the gallery, stopping frequently for him to receive pets and treats. When we finally stand outside the shop, looking in the window, I realize a little late that taking Brodie into a place full of pottery and glassware is a very bad idea.

I'm about to turn around and retrace my steps to the Coffee Dragon and ask Savannah to watch him for a bit, when the door opens and an old man shuffles out, pushing a walker. His head is bald as an egg, all the missing hair apparently displaced to a pair of eyebrows so long they must get in the way of his vision. He's dressed in knee-length breeches, with silver buckles, red hose, and a golden doublet. I figure he must be one of the tourists and am trying to guess whether his costume is meant to be Viking or pirate, when he says, "You just go on in and look around, my dear. I'll hold the doggy for you."

"That's okay," I say. "Thank you. But aren't you wanting to get to the bingo game?"

He lets out a belly laugh that forces him to lean harder on the walker so as not to fall over. "I can't play, bless you," he says. "This is my shop. Did you think I was a treasure hunter, then? That's a good one." He gestures at his outfit. "I'm dressed like the dwarves, don't you see? You just leave the doggy here with me, we'll be fine."

"Brodie's a little rambunctious. I'm afraid—"

But the old man has already gotten a hand on the leash. "I'm not an invalid, my dear. Not yet."

Against my better judgment, mostly because I don't want to make him feel bad, I leave the old man with Brodie and enter the store.

In complete contrast to the owner's outrageous costume, the shelves are full of beautiful items, tastefully displayed. I browse samples of pottery and stoneware, vases and ornaments in rainbow-colored glass, throw rugs woven on a loom, carvings of seals and killer whales and birds. Baskets, wind chimes, and suncatchers dangle above my head.

The walls are hung with photographs of the island and the sea, and one wall, in the last room I visit, is hung with landscape paintings that remind me of Monet.

They are all about light, and most of them feature the sound and the islands in the distance. High tide and low, mist and full sunlight, the waning light of afternoon, the moment just before dusk when the sky is moving toward the colors of sunset but isn't there quite yet. There are no sunrises or sunsets, so either the artist has declined to paint them, or tourists have already snapped them all up.

All are beautiful, but what draws my eye is a more limited series, hung in a row, that features a single tree. The sound is visible beyond, but the landscape and the water are blurred and indistinct, so the focus is always on the commanding presence of the gnarled trunk and twisting branches. As with the other paintings, much attention has been paid to light. Shifting shadows, from morning through evening, gradually changing color gradients, exquisite attention to the details of bark and branch and leaf.

Something about them is familiar. I cast through my memories for a minute and come up with that huge, luminous painting in Ted Wilcox's office. Could these possibly be the same artist? They are all much smaller, but the more I look at them, the more I think they have to be.

The final painting in the series is different from the others, and the most compelling.

It's a little larger, in a rough wooden frame. It's painted in shades of black and gray, capturing the magic of moonlight. The tree is leafless, its twisting boughs in dramatic contrast to the full-moon sky. A raven sits on one bare branch, watchful, foreboding. In the grass at the base of the tree a silvery wolf lifts his muzzle in a silent howl.

Words have been skillfully woven into the moonlight and shadows, so that I have to study them to read what they say. When I make it out, the fine hairs on the back of my neck lift in recognition:

What has been and is not
What is forgotten, remembered.

These lines were written on the doily at the World Tree Restaurant. Plus, they fit with the other clue:

Where ravens gather
And the lone wolf howls
The world tree whispers secrets
Under the elusive moon.

Elation fills me. I'm on the right track. This painting is obviously an important part of the puzzle, and will direct me to the next clue, or maybe even let me know exactly where to bury Nomi. Carefully, I lift it from the wall and carry it over to the counter, laying my coupon for 25 percent off on top.

As I head outside to find the gallery owner, I remember Brodie and speed my steps, afraid that I'll find the old man laid out on the sidewalk from a bad fall. But he's sitting on the little seat on his walker, Brodie lying calmly next to his feet.

"Find something you like?" the old man asks.

"Those tree paintings . . . They are brilliant. Who is the artist?"

"That I can't tell you," he says, stiffly rising to his feet with a little grunt of pain. "Did you want to buy one?"

"Yes, I've set it by the cash register. But it's really very important that I know who the artist is! Are you sure you can't tell me?"

"I expect you could persuade me, if only I knew," he says, smiling warmly. "Our artist is quite reclusive and doesn't want his identity known. Or hers. It's a secret, even from me."

"But—how do you get the paintings? How do you pay the commission?"

"All through a go-between, my dear. I could ask for you, but I've asked before and still don't know."

"Would you ask again? And right away? I'm sorry to be a bother, but it's really quite urgent. My rental agreement expires on Thursday, and I need to find a tree, very possibly this tree, before then. I don't suppose you know where this tree is, do you?"

"Whoa there, young lady. Hold up. Maybe you'd better start at the beginning. Talk slowly, my hearing's not what it once was."

I take a deep breath and then another, reining in my impatience. Then I dig in my purse for the gold-foil envelope, in which I've been collecting all the clues. I remove the photo first, and show it to him.

"This is my grandmother, when she was young. I don't know who the man is, but I'm guessing it might be my grandfather. She came to the island sometime before my mother was born, so well over fifty years ago now. I don't suppose you remember her?"

"Well, now," he says, taking the photo out of my hands and gazing at it speculatively. "Did she have hair the color of yours, then? Black-and-white photos remove so many details, don't you think?"

"I look just like her," I breathe, afraid to hope that he'll actually be able to help me.

"I do remember her," he says slowly. "Hard to forget a woman like that; it was like she had a light inside her. Ted Wilcox brought her home for a visit, if I remember right. That's not him in the photo, though. I wonder whatever happened to old Ted. Never did know if the war took him or he just moved somewhere." He says this as if the two fates are equivalent.

"Wait a minute," I gasp. "Ted Wilcox is *island*?"

He glances up at me, his previously pleasantly confused gaze now keen and focused. "How do you know old Ted? And what does your grandmother have to do with the paintings?"

"That's what I'm trying to figure out! Look." I show him the trea-sure map, the letters, the clues, explaining all about the bequest and the map, and the unusual Vinland clues. He listens quietly, looking at everything I show him, absorbing my story without saying another word. When I'm done, he says slowly, "Reckon you'll just have to keep on following the clues. You'll figure it out. Now, how about you give me a credit card and I'll go in and ring up your painting?"

"But don't you see?" I cry desperately. "Please. That picture is a clue. That has got to be the tree I'm looking for. It could be anywhere on the island! If I could just talk to the painter, or if you could relay a message? Ask where the tree is located. That's all I need to know. Please? Tomorrow is my last full day. I can't possibly check out the whole island for a matching tree in one day!"

"I'll ask," he says. "Where are you staying? I'll call if I hear anything."

"Improbable House," I tell him. "But the landline isn't working. Can you radio me?"

"Don't have one of those."

"If you could let Flynn or Savannah know? Both of them are up on what's going on."

"All right," he says. "I reckon I could do that much for you. You just wait here with that sweet dog of yours. I'll be right back."

I wait impatiently while he shuffles into the store, leaning heavily on the walker. Brodie, who acted as calm and well-behaved as a service dog while the old man was here, reverts to his usual self, tugging at the leash in all directions, jumping up on me, yipping and whining to get moving.

I have sympathy. Standing here, waiting, is hard. I want to look the painting over more closely. Take it out of the frame and see if there's some secret message on the back. I also want to call Mr. Wilcox and ask him what the hell he knows that he's keeping from me. He could have told me so many things, been so helpful. The minute I have this painting in my possession I am definitely getting him on the phone.

A long fifteen minutes later, I'm making my way across the square, an excited Brodie pulling on my right hand, a paper-wrapped picture tied up with twine growing heavier and heavier in my left. When I finally reach the Coffee Dragon, I bound up the stairs, weave between the tables, and go directly to the counter, bringing Brodie with me. I'm hoping Savannah is still here and will watch him for me, but there's no sign of her.

Giselle is busy making drinks. Her face is flushed and she looks tired and older than I'd thought she was. I call out to her, "I have to make a call."

She nods, gives Brodie no more than a glance, and goes back to work. I drag him into the back room and shut the door to contain him, setting the picture down on the table and shaking out my hands and arms to ease the aching muscles. Then I pull up Mr. Wilcox's number from my contacts on my phone, and dial it into the landline.

Two rings, and a woman's voice answers. "Arden and Wilcox, attorneys at law. How can I help you?"

"I need to speak with Ted Wilcox, please. It's urgent."

"He's not available just now. If I could have your name and number, and he could call you back?"

I give her my name and Giselle's number, then say, "Could you ask him to call right away? Or could he possibly be disturbed? I don't have access to a phone where I'm staying."

"Oh dear," she says. "No, I'm terribly sorry. Could Ms. Arden help you, do you think? She could probably call back in, say, half an hour?"

"No, I most definitely need to speak to Mr. Wilcox. I can call back later, or I can give you a number where he could leave a message."

"If it's urgent, you'd be much better speaking with Ms. Arden. He's on vacation, you see. Won't be back until next week. Ma'am? Are you still there?"

"I'm here. Listen. You know that painting in his office? You wouldn't have any idea where he got that from, would you? Or who the artist is?"

"Ma'am, I'm sorry, but I'm actually new here. Is there anything else I can do for you?"

"Give me Mr. Wilcox's personal cell?"

"I'm sorry, I'm not permitted to do that. If you'd like to speak to Ms. Arden—"

I hang up. The number I called was his work cell, so he's obviously got it forwarded to the office and is not taking calls. Damn it. I'm certain he has the answers that I need. How dare he go on vacation this week, of all the times in the world? I'm so close to solving the puzzle, and I'm being blocked in all directions.

A sneaky, ugly little thought creeps into my brain. Maybe Mr. Wilcox doesn't want me to succeed. I wonder what happens to my trust money if I don't? Maybe it reverts to him. If he lived on the island once, he'd have influence. Maybe he's instructed everybody not to help me. He could have even asked somebody to dig up whatever I'm supposedly looking for so I'll never find it.

Nomi trusted him, though. And he took the trouble to bring the balloons and sing the song and interrupt Alan's proposal. And then he explained everything to me. Alan is the one who leaps to the conclusion everybody is cheating him or out to get him. I am not that person. I don't want to be that person.

I just need to keep following the clues. Maybe this picture will tell me everything I need to know.

Chapter Twenty-Seven

Blythe

As it turns out, when the picture is removed from the frame it looks exactly like it did inside the frame. There's no secret message written on the back of the canvas, no note tucked in between the protective paper backing and the painting itself. The frame is nothing special, either, made of some sort of unvarnished wood, weathered a silvery gray.

There is no signature, which is strange. If this person doesn't even sign their work, they must really not want anybody to know who they are.

I sit back and stare at it, willing it to give me answers. It just sits there, looking like a painting, revealing nothing.

My hand goes to the pendant Nomi gave me, also a tree with a raven in the branches. I take it off and lay it on top of the painting. I add the treasure map and the clue that talks about the tree by moonlight.

Damn it. I'm sure this is a painting of *the* tree, the one I need to find. And I don't think it's a picture of the oak tree outside the house. This artist is very detailed and meticulous, and would surely have included the heart. And the background, even though it's blurred and out of focus, doesn't seem right.

Well, there's one way to check that. I take the painting, whistle for Brodie, and the two of us go out to the oak tree to take a look. Sure enough, no matter which way I look at the tree, there is no background that matches up at all. Which doesn't mean a thing, of course. The artist could have made up a background. Or a tree, for that matter. There's absolutely no hard evidence that this painting is a real-life rendering of a tree somewhere on the island. It could be a tree in Boston or Kentucky, for all I know. Maybe it was drawn from a photograph.

Except there is that study of light, like Monet and his haystack. Surely that means something?

My brain hurts. I'm not getting anywhere trying to reason this out, and none of the islanders seem to know a thing. I take Brodie and the picture back to the house, then climb down the ladder to the rocky beach below. It's quiet, all by myself, just the waves splashing rhythmically up onto the shore and the cries of seagulls. The cloud cover thins and watery rays of sunlight reach down to warm me.

But if I was hoping for a sudden burst of illumination to clarify my problem, it doesn't come. I'm just as stuck as I was. My radio crackles and Savannah's voice comes on.

"Where are you? I'm at the house."

"Down at the beach. I'll be right up. Wait for me."

She was supposed to radio me before she came over, but I should know by now that "supposed to" and Savannah are not on speaking terms. I scramble up the ladder, thinking about all the items I left out on the table. The painting, the clues, the letters, the pendant, the knife we found under the porch, which I'd used to cut through the paper backing on the painting. Nothing there for me to worry about her seeing, but I feel uneasy and find myself hurrying. The child is unpredictable.

When I enter the house, she is nowhere to be seen and doesn't answer when I call her name. I follow the aroma of cheese and sauce into the kitchen, where a large pizza rests on the table. The box is cold to my touch, which means she was here for a while before she radioed me.

The painting and the other items that I left on the table are missing.

"Savannah!" I shout again. Brodie barks and comes tearing down the stairs to jump all over me, leaping up to try to lick my face. I pet him enough to calm him a little, before I climb the stairs. The attic is open, the extendable ladder blocking the hallway.

Savannah's voice floats down to me. "Up here! I'm almost ready for you."

"What on earth are you . . ." I break off as my head clears the trap-door and I see *what* she is doing, although I can't come up with a *why*.

The drawings of her mother, falling, about to fall, lying dead, are tacked up on the available wall space. At the center of the room, she's created what resembles an altar. A white tablecloth covers the coffee table. In the center, the tree painting is propped up against Nomi's ashes. A variety of other small objects are on display. The snow globe is positioned directly in front of one of two chairs.

Norman is perched on one of the cushions of the window seat. He turns his head to stare at me out of one beady black eye, but says nothing.

Before I can come up with words, Savannah lights a match and touches it to the wicks of three tall white candles.

"Ready!" she says, as if what she's up to is perfectly obvious. "Come up and have a seat."

"I thought we were eating pizza," I say, climbing the rest of the way up into the loft and looking around to see if any other transformative wonders have taken place in my absence.

Down below, Brodie yelps and puts his front paws on the ladder, as if he's going to climb after us.

"You're fine," I call down to him. "Sit. Stay. Lie down."

He does none of the above and I turn back to Savannah. "I'm a little uneasy about candles in this old attic," I say.

She rolls her eyes. "There's a fire extinguisher right there. See? And we're not going to knock over the candles. It's fine."

Letting go of the vision I'd had of Savannah and me eating pizza and maybe drinking cocoa with marshmallows in front of the fireplace while I entice her into confiding in me, I approach the table, surveying the array of objects. Nomi's ashes and the snow globe. The painting, the clues, and the letters. My pendant. The tiny key and the knife I found under the porch. My treasure map.

"Tell me what we're doing?"

"Looking into the crystal ball, just like you used to with your Nomi!" she says.

"Of course we are. And we're looking for . . . ?"

"Whatever it wants to tell us! Where to bury your Nomi." She's not looking at me now, her head bent so I can't see her face. Her fingers roll and unroll the hem of her T-shirt.

"What else might it tell us, do you think?" I ask, suspicion stirring.

She shrugs a shoulder, still not looking at me.

There are two items on the table that she didn't borrow from me. A raven feather. A folded piece of lined notebook paper. Maybe the feather is incidental, left behind by Norman. Maybe it's on purpose. The paper is something else entirely. When I reach for it, she puts her hand out to stop me.

"Not yet," she says, glancing up and then quickly away again. Her eyes are bright with unshed tears. "I'll tell you when."

"All right." I stand where I am, settling into the moment, waiting for her to direct this scene she has created.

"You sit there." She points to the chair in front of the snow globe, and I settle into it.

She sits across from me, her face drawn and tight. "This would be better in the dark," she whispers.

"We could eat pizza first and do it later."

She shakes her head. "Uncle Flynn. I told him I needed to stay late, or even overnight. He said no. He wouldn't even let me ask you."

"So he doesn't know you're here."

She shakes her head.

"And he'll come looking for you."

She nods.

"What about if I radio him and ask him?"

"Please," she begs. "Don't tell him. If we're quick, then he won't—"

The ravens alert us that we haven't been quick enough. There's a croaking and flapping as dark bodies fly past the windows. Norman spreads his wings as if about to take flight, but then settles himself again. Savannah and I both stare out the window at where a golf cart emerges from the woods and parks in the lot, an annoyed-looking Viking at the wheel.

"Shit," Savannah says, as Flynn gets out of the cart and strides toward the door.

Brodie explodes into a frenzy of barking and takes off down the stairs as Flynn begins to climb onto the porch.

A moment later, a knock thunders at the front door.

Savannah and I stare at each other across the table, neither of us moving.

"We could close the trapdoor," she says hopefully.

I'm pretty sure that a childish prank like hiding in the attic with Savannah and pretending we're not here isn't something that will endear me to the man of my dreams.

"He knows we're here," I remind her. "Both of us. My cart. Your bike. The pizza."

"The pizza!" she says, suddenly recovering the power of motion. "We go downstairs and eat pizza. He loves it, so he can eat too, and we'll get him to drink a couple of beers, and then you can persuade him to let me spend the night, since I'm already here and all. This ritual would be way better done at midnight, don't you think?"

What I think is that I don't like the words *ritual* and *midnight* uttered together in a house that can't possibly really be haunted but certainly sometimes feels that way. And I think that I want Flynn to stay, and Savannah to tell me what's bothering her, and I really, really want to figure out where to bury Nomi, for all the reasons.

"We're too late for that," I warn Savannah as she scurries for the ladder.

Brodie has stopped barking.

Flynn's voice calls out, "Savannah? Blythe? Everybody okay up there?"

Dog paws scamper up the stairs, followed by heavier footsteps. A moment later Flynn's head emerges through the trapdoor, his mouth already open to utter what I'm pretty sure is going to be a *Why the hell didn't you answer me?* comment.

I watch him take in the drawings on the walls and the details of the makeshift altar. When his eyes finally meet mine, I hold his gaze, trying to silently telegraph that something delicate hangs in the balance.

"You've found our secret conclave, you might as well come on up," I say lightly. "Savannah, do we have another chair?"

Her eyes are wide with shock and what might be betrayal as she registers my suggestion. "No!" she exclaims. "Only two chairs."

"I'll just go get one from the kitchen, then," Flynn says, vanishing back down the ladder.

"We have to stop him," Savannah pleads. "Make him go away."

"He loved her, too," I say, very softly. "I think he should be here."

Her hand reaches out and covers the folded piece of notebook paper. She tries to hold my gaze but her eyes drop away and her bottom lip trembles.

I put my hand over hers before she can remove the paper from the table. "Let it stay," I say. "We won't read it unless you want to."

Flynn is already back, shoving a chair up through the opening. Savannah, frowning, refuses to touch it, but I get up and take it from him, shifting the two chairs already at the table to make room for his.

"Uncle Flynn can't stay. He won't understand. It won't work if he's here," she protests. But I see, with relief, that the folded piece of paper is still on the table.

Flynn settles himself into the chair he's brought and looks askance at the candles. "Don't you think a séance should happen at midnight?" he inquires.

"Oh my God! You are impossible!" Savannah says. "I asked if I could stay over and you said no. And it's not a séance!"

"Well, at the very least, the lights should be dim, don't you think?" He gets back up and pulls the string on the attic's only light bulb, plunging us into, if not darkness, at least a more suitable murkiness that makes the candle flames glow brighter. Outside the windows, the sky has closed back in, surrounding us in a wall of gloomy and impenetrable mist.

"Now, might I inquire into the purpose of this gathering?" Flynn asks. "Are we summoning spirits or evicting them?"

I'm beginning to wish I'd listened to Savannah. His presence is tantalizing and distracting. His knee presses against mine under the small table. A masculine scent of soap and the outdoors mingles with melting wax and the dusty, ancient smell of the attic.

"We are asking Blythe's Nomi to tell us where she wants to be buried," Savannah says with great dignity.

"I see." His eyes move around the room, taking in all of Savannah's drawings. I can feel the impact of them slamming into him. He draws a breath, recovers himself, and turns his attention to the table, letting his gaze rove over the items with feigned casualness, until he sees the knife. He stiffens. He reaches out, his open hand hovering above it, as if a single touch will burn him. "This doesn't have anything to do with Blythe's treasure hunt," he says, low.

"I suspect there's a tiny bit more going on here than consulting the snow globe about Nomi's burial wishes," I suggest, very gently. I keep my eyes on that incongruous piece of notebook paper, which I've begun to suspect is actually not incongruous at all, but rather the reason for this whole elaborate scenario.

"I can't imagine what my old knife has to do with anything."

My breath catches in my throat at the pain in his voice. We are crammed together so close at the tiny table that I can feel him begin to tremble.

"It's not yours. It was Mom's," Savannah protests. "Look." She opens it, pointing at a monogram engraved on the blade. "See? FRJ. Frieda Renatta Johansen. She has a locket that looks exactly the same."

"So that's it," I say, leaning closer. "I tried to make it out earlier and gave it up as maybe a trademark."

"The monogram stands for Flynn Richard," Flynn says. His breathing is too rapid. Even in the dim light I can see that he's too pale. A sheen of sweat dampens his forehead.

I put my hands on Nomi's snow globe to ground and calm myself. The glass feels cool and smooth beneath my hands. I find myself looking into the curved glass as if maybe it does really hold answers. All I see is the distorted reflection of my own face and the room around me.

But Nomi's voice whispers, *So many secrets. Time to tell them all.* An inexplicable breeze blows through the room, rattling the folded paper.

"I think you've both got some big secrets," I say, surprised by the calm authority of my own voice. "And I think this would be a great time to share them."

Two pairs of horrified eyes meet mine.

"You have no idea what you're suggesting," Flynn rasps, his voice hoarse with suppressed emotion.

Savannah says nothing, but her hand darts toward the folded piece of paper. I get to it first, holding it up for both of them to see.

"I suspect that there's something written here," I say. "Something Savannah wants to share but is afraid to. And I think, maybe, if her uncle Flynn was to tell his own deep dark secret first, it might help her to say what she needs to say to her mother."

It's all wild surmising, and I wait, breath held, for Savannah to retort that I have absolutely no idea what I'm talking about, and for Flynn to bellow at me to mind my own business.

But Savannah sits quietly, head bent, hands twisting in her lap.

Flynn glances at me, then at her, and asks quietly, "Is that true, Savannah? Because I will do anything, say anything, if it will help you."

She glances up, her face a mask of misery, all her usual bravado totally melted away. "I'll tell if you do," she whispers. "Tell why you really ran away and didn't come back."

Flynn hunches forward as if somebody has punched him in the gut. His right hand goes to his face. He traces the scar with his index finger, once, twice, three times, before he twitches his shoulders and lowers his hand to rest, fisted, on the table.

I shiver with a presentiment of what is to come. All at once I want to freeze time, right here, to stop what I've set in motion. Some secrets, maybe, are better left unspoken. But it's too late.

"God help me," Flynn says. He picks up the knife and closes it, his knuckles whitening around the handle. "I'm pretty sure this is a story you should never hear, Savannah. For all sorts of reasons. None of it is what you think."

"I will still love you," she says tightly. "Whatever it is."

Flynn draws a deep breath, lets it out, and then, to my utter surprise, lets go of the knife and reaches for my hand instead. I can feel the tremors running through his frame, the dampness of his palm. I squeeze, hard, channeling support and strength, grounding my feet on the floor, asking Nomi to please, please, guide us all if she is able.

"Our family, growing up, wasn't so healthy," Flynn begins slowly. "My father died when we were toddlers. We never knew him. My mother wasn't the sort of woman who could manage on her own. She moved back in with her father, my grandfather. My grandmother had died long ago, so it was just the four of us."

He clears his throat, and his fingers tighten around mine. I dread what's coming but squeeze back encouragingly.

"Granddad used to hurt my mother. And me. Sometimes Frieda, but fortunately he mostly left her alone."

Savannah's eyes widen. "So you didn't really run into a wall with your face," she breathes.

"No. I was clumsy back then, but not that clumsy. And yes, he marked me, more than once. That scar happened the night I ran away."

He sits for a moment in silence, his face remote, as if he's far away from us in another place and time. "It happened here, at Improbable House," he finally says. "It was about a year after Calvert became Vinland, and Granddad was just figuring out the rental and maintenance business. Glory had come on board to do a lot of it, but they hadn't figured out the summer worker program and all. Frieda and I helped out a lot. She was good at it. I wasn't.

"Granddad always had a short fuse, but as the business got more chaotic and stressful he'd been getting . . . erratic. Unpredictable. Came close to killing my mother once, before Frieda and I pulled him off her. He'd always taken his fists to me, but it was getting worse."

Flynn sucks in a breath and goes on. "Mom wouldn't press charges, and she wouldn't leave the island, so there wasn't much anybody could do; none of them knew what he did to me and Frieda. She was his favorite, so she hardly ever got hit.

"Granddad hated Improbable House. It would never hold a repair, and he sometimes said he was sure it was falling apart on purpose.

"We were working on the front porch. It was late evening and none of us had had dinner. We were all tired. I never was good at the repairs, like Frieda was. And I was clumsy and always tripping over my own feet. Anyway, he got pissed about me moving too slow, started spewing his usual invective. I talked back to him. Knew better; did it anyway. He hit me in the face with the edge of a board.

"Didn't quite knock me out, but it put me on the ground, half-conscious and spouting blood. It's like . . . that brought out the animal in him. Once I was down, he came at me with his fists and his boots. I couldn't see to fight back, and I was dizzy and my hands wouldn't work properly anyway, and then Frieda . . ."

He stops. His breathing is loud, ragged, as if he's been running.

Savannah's mouth is half-open. When Flynn doesn't go on, she whispers, "What happened? What did she do?"

"She was on her knees beside me, begging him to stop, trying to shield me with her own body. I wore the knife in a sheath at my belt. She grabbed it and stabbed him. He staggered backward, his eyes all wide and staring, his mouth open, and then he just . . . fell down."

"Mom was such a badass!" Savannah exclaims, her face glowing with excitement. "Was he dead?"

"It took a couple of minutes for him to die. Long enough for both of us to think about trying to save him. But then he just sort of gurgled and stopped breathing."

"I'm glad she killed him!" Savannah cries.

This is obviously not the response Flynn is expecting. He stops with his mouth open, staring at her with an expression that would be funny if the story wasn't so absolutely tragic and awful.

"Don't you see?" he asks, recovering himself. "It was my job to stop him, to kill him if he was going to be killed. I was the man of the family. It was my job to protect her, to protect my mother. But I let him push me around. I let him hurt my mother. And so Frieda had to step up and do what I should . . . what I couldn't . . . I was a coward and a weakling."

"You would have done the same for her, I bet," Savannah says. "If he was killing her, you would have stopped him."

I can tell by the electricity that runs through Flynn when she says it that he hasn't ever considered this.

"You would have," I echo. "The whole protective instinct is hardwired into you. But I still don't see why you ran away from the island."

"Well, we figured when the old man disappeared that there would be questions. If I left Vinland, everybody would think maybe I'd killed him and take the suspicion off Frieda. I begged her to come with me, but she said it was better if one of us stayed. So she ended up stuck on the island, and I had my freedom—"

"Not freedom so much, if you were always looking over your shoulder," I say softly.

"I did think, for a long time, that they might come after me. Frieda and I didn't dare communicate at first, except sometimes I'd call from a pay phone. But nothing ever came of it. They didn't have a body. And they all knew what sort of man he was. I'm told that nobody even reported him missing to the mainland authorities."

"So why didn't you come back? Like when I was born and stuff?" Savannah asks.

He shrugs. "I'd gotten into the habit of running, I guess. From one thing to another. And I . . . was afraid to come back. The memories."

"I understand about memories," Savannah says, her eyes wandering over her drawings on the walls. And then, "Don't tell me that mean old man is buried here somewhere."

Flynn's gaze goes to the window that looks out toward the sound, still obscured by mist.

"We let the ocean take him," he says. "The two of us dragged him to the cliffs and threw him over. It was high tide. I guess he was never found."

"I bet she was glad she was the one who killed him," Savannah says fiercely. "She missed *you*. She wanted you to come back."

"I'm here now," he says.

"But you're not staying. Not when I tell you . . ." Her voice quavers and she stops, her lower lip trembling.

"I'm staying as long as you need me," Flynn says. "No matter what."

"Your turn," I say gently, wiping tears from my face with one hand, and sliding the folded paper toward her with the other.

"I wrote it down," she says, her face white and strained. "Read it for me, Blythe."

Chapter Twenty-Eight

FLYNN

I feel—I don't even know how I feel. Now that the huge, deep dark secret that has shaped the course of my life has been spoken, I can see that it was never really as deep or as dark as I thought it was. The death of my grandfather wasn't murder; it was obviously self-defense. We could have reported it and Frieda would have been cleared. Everything would have been so much different. Easier. Lighter.

I've missed seventeen years with Frieda and twelve with Savannah, all out of some misguided sense of chivalry. Savannah is right—her mother was a badass. She saved my life. And Blythe is right—I would have saved hers had the roles been reversed.

Of course, Frieda is here in the room with us, only she's no longer wearing the clothes she died in. She stands behind Savannah's chair, hands on her shoulders, her expression reminding me that I'm here, now, in this time, and that rather than burying myself in regret I have an opportunity to help Savannah unload secrets of her own.

"There is nothing you could do, or say, that would make me not love you," I tell her. Her big eyes flick toward me, then back to the paper that Blythe is unfolding. She gnaws at her lower lip, her face a mask of misery.

I wish she was a few years younger so I could scoop her up in my arms and hold her, but she wouldn't welcome that right now and all I can do is sit here, be with her, bear witness to whatever it is she needs us to know.

Blythe begins reading out loud in her clear voice:

> *Dear Mom,*
> *I'm sorry. Sorry, sorry, sorry. I know holding the ladder is important and I didn't mean to let go. You always told me I needed to pay attention and I was, only then I wasn't because I was thinking about something else.*
> *So you fell and it was all my fault and I'd take it back if I could, only I can't. I tried to time travel but it didn't work.*
> *Again, I'm sorry, but sorry doesn't fix it.*
> *Love, Savannah*

Savannah has both hands pressed over her mouth now, holding back sobs.

Frieda, behind her, bends down and kisses the top of her head, looks directly at me, then dissolves into the shadows.

"Savannah," I begin, but my voice betrays me. I get out of my chair and kneel down beside her, cupping a hand under her chin and tipping her face up to mine. The tears flowing down her cheeks, the naked pain in her eyes, breaks something open inside me and I gather her thin body against my chest and stroke her hair.

For a moment she resists, holding herself tight and still, her hands fisted. Then all at once she lets go, burying her face in my shirt, arms clasped around my neck, and breaks into keening wails. I sit down and draw her into my lap as if she's a small child, rocking her, my cheek pressed against the top of her head.

When the sobs racking her body begin to ease, I start to talk. I tell her that accidents happen, that nobody can pay attention all of the time. I remind her that she is still a child, that she was only eleven, and shouldn't have been expected to be responsible for anybody's safety. When it feels to me like she's listening, I ask, "How did it happen? The ladder should have been stable."

Savannah sniffles and I peel off my T-shirt and offer it up as a handkerchief.

"Gross, Uncle Flynn," she says, which is an encouraging sign. But she does as I say, wiping her face and blowing her nose. Blythe tosses me a blanket to wrap around my bare shoulders and brings another for Savannah, who is shivering more with reaction than cold.

"Tell me," I say. "I've always wondered."

"She was repairing the roof," Savannah says. "You know how it's always developing leaks. She was tired. We were almost done. And then she said, 'Damn it, I don't want to move the ladder again.' I wasn't watching her, there was a sailboat out on the water and I was looking at that . . ."

She sobs again, but takes a breath and goes on in a wobbly voice. "I felt the ladder start to tip and I tried to grab it but it was moving too fast and then it just . . ." She stops and burrows into me again.

In my mind, I can see exactly how it played out. Most ladder accidents happen due to a stupid mistake when somebody is tired. Eyes closed, I can see my sister on the ladder, confronting one last small stretch of work just out of a safe reach. Not enough to be worth moving the ladder. All she has to do is lean, reach . . . and overbalance.

I hold Savannah tighter, imagining the horror of that moment— the ladder tipping dangerously, Frieda clinging on, providing the weight that upset the whole thing and sent her swinging out over the earth. The inevitable scream. The thud of a body, the clatter of a thirty-foot ladder.

And then I take a breath and talk to Savannah about physics—how tall that ladder is, how much it weighs, how much Frieda weighed, how once Frieda overbalanced there was no way Savannah's slight weight could ever have stopped it.

She grows quiet. I feel the tension going out of her as she allows herself to relax against me. A sharp intake of breath from Blythe makes me glance up. She's still sitting at the table, her hands on the snow globe. Quietly, she says, "Your mother wants you to know that she loves you, Savannah. And that she doesn't blame you the tiniest bit for what happened."

"You saw that?" Savannah asks, in a quavering voice.

"I absolutely did."

With a soft little sigh, she nestles back down into my arms. "Can we have hot chocolate?"

"We can," Blythe says. "Also, I think Brodie would like to kiss you."

"Hungry," Norman croaks, stirring on the perch where he has been sitting quietly all this time.

We all laugh, a little wildly, still right on the edge of tears.

"Hot chocolate for Savannah, but I need something a little stronger if we can find it," I say. "Also, I'm apparently too old to sit on the floor. I don't know that I can ever get up again."

Savannah gets off my lap and holds out her hands, and we make a production of her dragging me onto my feet.

Blythe picks up the painting of the tree that sits in the middle of Savannah's altar. "While we eat, maybe the two of you can help me brainstorm who on the island might have painted this."

"That's easy," Savannah says, already descending the ladder. "It's Nick."

Chapter Twenty-Nine

BLYTHE

"Are you sure?" Flynn asks, holding a slice of cold pizza in one hand, and a can of beer in the other.

We've all agreed that cold pizza is better than microwaved pizza, probably because all three of us are too wrung out to want to get up and down for the microwave. Savannah has her hot chocolate, which I did microwave, Flynn is nearly at the bottom of a can of beer, and I'm not far behind him.

Norman has been removed to the porch, where he is eating his own slice of pizza. Brodie, who refuses to leave Savannah's side, whines and whaps his tail on the floor, and she breaks off a piece and gives it to him.

"Please don't feed him from the table," I tell her. "He's a terrible beggar already."

But she grins at me with a spark of her usual impertinence, and I can't even begin to get properly annoyed.

The alcohol is already working its magic, making me feel warm and fuzzy, while the cheese and meat and once-crispy crust provide much-needed energy. Pizza contains all the food groups, Nomi used to say. Vegetables, protein, carbohydrates. All there in one delicious package.

Savannah's eyes are red and swollen, her face blotchy, and she looks utterly exhausted, but she's not ready to crash quite yet. She takes a big bite, then says with her mouth full, "I'm sure. He's got a workroom at the back of his house. Usually locked, but I'm there a lot. He's the one who taught me drawing, after he saw me trying to sketch something once. I'm not supposed to look at his paintings, but I do."

"Of course you do," Flynn says.

"He's been doing other things lately, the sound and the islands and all that. But I saw a tree painting at the back of a stack of others, leaned up against the wall. It's like the one Blythe bought, only there's not even a moon and you can barely make out the tree. I thought it was a painting of the dark. Because, dark." She takes a swig of hot chocolate and tears back into the pizza, as if she's famished.

"I can't believe it," I say slowly, trying to shift the image of the mean old man I hold in my head to encompass an artist capable of that kind of beauty. Also, how did Ted Wilcox get his hands on that painting in his office? Is there a connection between the two of them, beyond the coincidence that they both come from the island?

I feel like I'm trying to listen to a piece of music with half of the notes missing.

"I wonder . . . ," Flynn begins, but his voice trails off and his eyes go distant, his pizza still in his hand, seemingly forgotten.

"What?" Savannah and I both ask, bringing him back to now.

"Oh. It might be nothing. But, I've seen that series of paintings in the gallery, always loved them. And I've been sitting here trying to work out in my head where that tree would have to be to line up with the sound and that little island the way it does in all those paintings, and it seems like it could have been painted from the backyard of Improbable House."

"The oak tree doesn't line up," I say, leaning back in my chair. My eyelids want to close. My whole body feels like it wants to melt, like the marshmallows in Savannah's hot chocolate.

"There used to be another tree. I think," Flynn says. "I hadn't realized how many memories I'd locked away by trying not to think about what happened . . ." He clears his throat, takes a swig of beer. "Anyway. There was another big old oak tree in the backyard. It had to be cut down. That was a long time ago; we had just started school, I think. The branches were too high to reach for me to climb it, anyway. So I was still a little kid."

I stare at him, suddenly wide-awake. "But it would have been there when Nomi was here."

He nods. "Yes."

"Do you think you know where it was?"

"I can make a pretty good guess."

Savannah is already on her feet. "What are we waiting for? C'mon."

"Maybe Blythe would like to rest," Flynn says, glancing at me. "We could—"

"Now," I say. "Tomorrow's my last full day. I'd sleep so much better if I knew we'd found it."

"All right then." Flynn shoves back his chair. "Treasure hunting by moonlight it is, then."

"Just like the clue," Savannah squeals. "The world tree by moonlight. We've got the raven, and Brodie can be the lone wolf."

"Don't get your hopes too high," Flynn says, but I can hear the excitement in his voice and I suspect he's talking to himself.

She runs for the door, Brodie on her heels. Flynn begins to follow, then turns back toward me, his eyes deep with emotion.

"I can't begin to thank you," he says.

It's a good thing for me and my pride that he's all the way across the kitchen, or I would fling myself into his arms and kiss him, whether he wants me to or not. But there is not only physical distance between us, but also the weight of too many things unsaid. So instead I just smile and say, "Find me the place I'm looking for, and we're more than even."

"I don't know that we can ever be even," he says, in a rough sort of growl, then turns and follows Savannah into the night.

I stay where I am for a moment, pulling myself together. It's all so much to take in—the emotions that have been unleashed here tonight, the secrets that have been revealed.

One thing at a time, Nomi's voice whispers. I grab a coat and my metal detector and step out into the moonlit dark, breathing deeply, letting the salt air fill my lungs. The moon rides high and serene above my head, a few early stars keeping her company. The water spreads out in the distance, wide and free. I can feel the pull of it, the hunger for faraway lands and adventures. At the same time, I feel rooted to this place and don't want to leave.

Brodie gambols over, demanding attention and shaking me out of my reverie. Flynn is already working the metal detector out past Savannah's flower bed. She watches, holding a spade. As I approach she looks up and grins at me. My heart expands with love for this indomitable child.

"What do you think we'll find?" she asks.

"I have no idea. Possibly nothing."

"Uncle Flynn will find it," she says. "This is it. I know it is."

"It would help if I could remember exactly where it was," Flynn says. "I'm walking a grid in the general vicinity."

When his detector beeps I try not to hope, remembering all of my own false alarms.

He slows the sweeps he's making and goes over the same spot, again and again.

"Got something," he says.

"Pop top?" I ask lightly. "Tinfoil?"

"I think it might be gold."

"What?" Savannah squeals. She dashes over to him, carrying the spade. I'm not far behind. We both stare down at the grass around

Flynn's booted feet, as if whatever we're looking for will be lying right there in full view.

He slows the sweep of the detector, making smaller and smaller passes until he says, "Right here." He marks the spot with the toe of his boot and turns to Savannah. "Okay. The way I taught you now, remember. A little at a time. Blythe, could you get the hand scanner out of my cart? And we'll keep checking as we go."

Even though I'm dying of curiosity and want to drop to my knees and get my own hands in the dirt, I run to the cart for the hand scanner. When I get back, Savannah has already cut through the grass and turned over several shovelfuls.

"Go ahead and scan what she's turned up," Flynn directs, "just to be sure we're not missing something."

There's nothing in the small pile of dirt, but Flynn continues to get a signal from the hole.

"Deeper," he says, "but not much, I think. Use the trowel."

Savannah does as he says, down on hands and knees. "I hit something, I think."

That's it for my self-restraint, and hers. Both of us are digging with our hands now, like a couple of dogs. Brodie runs circles around all three of us, barking incessantly.

And then I feel something with my fingers. Smooth. Hard.

"We need a light," I say.

Flynn sets aside the scanner and shines a flashlight down into the hole. Savannah and I both clear away dirt from a small, rectangular shape, and I see that it's the top of a small box.

Disappointment floods me.

It's going to be another one of those Vinland clue boxes, not a thing that Nomi buried here. But still, we work it free.

"It's your treasure," Savannah says, putting the box in my hands. She drops down onto her butt in the grass and hugs a squirming Brodie.

I lever myself up onto my feet. Flynn redirects the flashlight, and I see that what I'm holding is not a Vinland box at all. This one is made by an absolute craftsman. The wood is dirty and decaying in places, but I can still see the perfectly crafted dovetail joints, an inlaid heart on the top.

It won't open.

"What's in it?" Savannah asks, bouncing up onto her feet to get a look.

"It's locked."

Flynn takes the box from my fingers, turning it over and over. "I could break it, I suppose, but I hate to do it."

"The key!" I exclaim. "It might fit."

We all troop back up to the house. Savannah runs up to the loft for the key and brings it to me. "Hurry up! The suspense is killing me!"

"As long as it's been buried, the key might not work," Flynn cautions. "Dirt, rust, you name it."

I sit down at the table with the box and carefully insert the key. It slides in easily, then grinds a little as I try to turn it. But then I feel the click as the mechanism gives, and with reverent fingers I lift the lid.

Nestled inside, next to a folded piece of yellowed paper, is a golden ring.

"Whoa," Savannah breathes. I pick up the paper, unfold it, and read aloud:

> *My darling,*
> *The time has come to admit the truth. I've never been fond of reality, but even I have to face up to the facts this time. You are not coming home. We will never be married and I will raise our child alone. I've rented out the house, and tomorrow I'm going back to the mainland to move in with my parents until after the baby is born.*

My love, when you asked me to marry you, right here by this tree where you kissed me for the very first time, could we ever have dreamed it would all go so wrong? When we created our own ceremony and exchanged our own vows right here, before you went to war, I was sure we'd have our real wedding before a year was up.

But it was not to be. The wedding ring feels like a lie, and it hurts my heart to wear it. I'm burying it here, hoping somehow even on the other side, wherever it is your spirit has gone, you'll feel me always with you.

I'll never stop loving you.

Nomi

The three of us are silent, those last words resonating through us. Then Savannah wipes her hands carefully, as clean as she can make them, on her jeans, picks up the ring, and holds it to the light.

"It's engraved," she says reverently. "Look."

I take the golden circle from her and slide it onto my own ring finger. It fits, perfectly, as if it was made for me. Flynn holds my hand up where we both can see and read, together, the words etched into the band: *Improbably Yours.*

"Are we going to bury her now?" Savannah asks. "That has to be it, right?"

"That has to be it," I agree. "We need pictures. I'd confirm with her attorney, but he's apparently gone on vacation."

"Well, if it's not right, we'll just have to dig her up again and you'll have to come back," Savannah says. "Let me take the pictures."

I hand over my phone, and she takes pictures of the box, both open and closed. One with the ring in it. A picture of the letter.

"What about a pic of where we found it?" she says.

The exhaustion has overtaken me and it's all I can do to sit up sort of straight and keep from resting my head on the table. I can see lines of fatigue on Flynn's face, and I have a feeling that Savannah will be asleep the minute she stops moving.

"I think tomorrow," I say. "Let's wait for daylight."

"I still have so many questions," Flynn says. "But I'm with you. Tomorrow. Come on, my little secret keeper. I'm thinking hot bath and bed."

Savannah doesn't argue. She drops to her knees to hug Brodie and then hugs me. Flynn puts an arm around her shoulders and she tucks herself against him, sheltered and safe. Something in his eyes as he holds my gaze across the kitchen makes my heart speed up. "Good night" is all he says, and then the two of them are gone.

"So many questions," I say out loud, echoing Flynn. But they will wait for morning. I don't want to leave the ring alone, now that it's been found after all these years, so I slip it back onto my finger.

"Good night, Nomi," I whisper as I crawl into the bed. Brodie jumps up after me and I don't object as he lies down on my feet.

Chapter Thirty

BLYTHE

I wake out of a deep sleep to a repetitive, rhythmic banging, accompanied by frenzied barking. It takes me a long minute to put the pieces together.

I'm in a bed and the bed is in the big bedroom in Improbable House. Yesterday I found Nomi's wedding ring. Flynn told us why he left the island. Savannah confessed that she thought she'd killed her mother. And I saw something other than snow in the snow globe.

None of that explains the banging and barking. Pale light filters in through the windows, letting me know it's daytime. Wednesday. My last full day on the island. The banging must be Flynn and Savannah at the door, although that child would just come in.

I climb out of bed, throw a sweatshirt on over the tank top I slept in, and make my way down the stairs, holding on to the banister to support my sleep-drugged body.

When I yank the door open, Nick is standing on the porch.

He looks almost as shocked to see me as I am to see him, probably because I'm totally uncombed and have pillow lines on my face.

I find my voice first. "Couldn't wait until I'm gone?" I ask. "One more day."

"Right," he says dazedly. "You're leaving." Then he seems to pull himself together and growls, in his habitual tone, "Came to make sure you're leaving. And that you haven't buried somebody on my property without permission."

I'm wide-awake now, and the possibility that he could actually stop me from burying Nomi, when I'm so close, sends a spike of adrenaline through me that transforms, almost instantly, into anger.

"Are you always like this?" I demand. "You're a horrible, nasty little man. I can't believe Nomi was in love with you."

His face goes so pale, I'm afraid he's going to pass out or have a heart attack or something.

"Where did you get that?" he rasps.

I look around, confusedly thinking that maybe we brought the painting back downstairs and he's referring to that.

Nick grabs my wrist. It takes me by surprise and he's stronger than he looks. Before I know it he's holding my hand up close to his eye, inspecting the ring.

"Dear God," he says. "I think . . . I think I need to sit down."

Maybe I'm mad at him, but he's still my grandfather. I take his arm to steady him and he doesn't try to fight me off. I support his faltering steps into the kitchen, where I seat him in a chair and get him a drink of water. While he drinks, I notice the band on his left ring finger. It's engraved. Even as I lean closer, before I can make out the words, I know what they are going to be.

"Why did you lie to me?" I ask. "You were the man in the photograph."

He shakes his head in denial. "That man died a long time ago."

"I need to show you something," I tell him. I run up the stairs and then into the attic, gathering all the letters. I'm half afraid that he will have left already when I return to the kitchen, but he's sitting where I left him. I search his ruined face, looking for the resemblance between him and the photograph, between him and Mom and Kristen and me, but all I can see are the scars and the bitterness.

"These are for you," I say, laying the letters on the table in front of him. "I suspect there were more, but these are the only ones I have."

He glances up at me, then down again. One finger touches the paper. "Her writing," he says softly.

"Yes. And written to you."

Before he reads more than halfway through the first letter he makes a sound like a wounded animal.

"Where did you get these?" he asks.

"They were in clues that looked like Vinland treasure clues but weren't," I say, hardening my heart. "You need to read them all."

He gasps, as though surfacing from a long time underwater, bends his head, and keeps reading. By the end of the second letter, tears are flowing from his good eye. He wipes at them, impatiently, then says, hoarsely, "I can't see. Read the last one."

He licks dry lips. Shakes his head in denial of a question nobody has asked.

As I read, a wintry sound escapes him, the scrape of dry leaves over frozen ground. The flexible parts of his face crumple, the tight burn scar unmoving.

"God," he says. It's a cry, a prayer, a sound of utter anguish.

When I'm done, he stares at me, his face that of a man who is in a hell of his own making. "No, no," he pleads. "She left me. She married another man. She had somebody else's baby."

"She always said our grandfather died in Vietnam," I say softly, moved by his obvious pain. "She loved you. Only you. All these years, she thought you were dead. She sent me here to bury her ashes under that tree, beside the ring."

"I *was* dead," he bursts out. "I *am* dead. The man she fell in love with died in that war, everything that was good in me burned away. When I came back, I was no more than a ghost. Lived on the streets for a year after I got out of the hospital. Trying to drink away what I'd become. How could I go back to her looking like this?

"Wound up in a psych ward . . . pain and booze and what I saw in the war . . . the things I did . . . I only wanted to die. But this doc talked me around. Told me I owed my girl a chance to love me still. That home was still home and people would still care about me. So I came back to the island.

"And she was gone. Pregnant, the gossip said. And I thought. I thought . . ."

A choked sound, part sob, part expletive catches in his throat. Brodie whines and rests his chin on the old man's lap.

"What did I have to give to her, to anybody? I was young, but already I was Old Nick, a monster to scare children with, that's what I'd become. So I didn't look for her. Tried not to think of her.

"When I saw you that first day—I thought I was dreaming. That she'd come back to me, finally. And then I realized I was awake and did the math and saw who you must be. And heard you were here to bury your grandmother. To me she was always alive, always young. It was like finding her and losing her again, all in the space of a breath. It was more than I could handle. I wanted to destroy anything and everything that reminded me of her. You had to go . . . It hurt too much to have you here."

The old man falls quiet. The only sound in the room is his labored breathing, and mine. My throat feels tight and raw. My eyes are dry, burning with his all-consuming pain and my anger.

"Obviously you didn't really know Nomi at all!" I hurl the words at him, a weapon. "She loved you. She wouldn't have stopped loving you because you were hurt! How shallow do you think she was? So you got wounded in the war. So did a lot of other people. That doesn't give you the right to pretend to be dead. You hurt her horribly."

"I was a fool." He sits up straight and looks me directly in the eye. For the first time, I catch a glimpse of the man he might have been, can see a faint resemblance to my mother, to the handsome young man in the photo.

"I don't deserve to know," he says, with quiet dignity. "But my child? A daughter or a son?"

"A daughter. My mother. Nomi named her Lyndsey. I have a little sister, too. Kristen."

"I regret," he says. "So deeply I regret."

I look across the table at my bitter, tormented grandfather, who has kept his secret all these years. I think of Frieda and Flynn, suffering over a secret that didn't need to be kept. And I think that the healing has to start somewhere, and maybe that somewhere is me.

"I don't know that I can ever call you Grandfather, but do you think, maybe, I might hug you?" I ask.

Chapter Thirty-One

BLYTHE

I make my grandfather coffee and breakfast.

He has questions about Nomi and how she died. About Mom. I've talked until my throat is hoarse by the time Flynn and Savannah show up.

They are not alone.

"I should have figured," I say, stepping out on the porch to greet them.

Aunt Bella hugs me. "Hello to you, too, darling. I understand that you've figured it all out, and just in the nick of time, too."

"How long have you been here?"

"A few hours longer than you. I came in last Thursday just before dawn on a private boat. Best if nobody knew I was here, Glory and I both thought. Less likely to spill the secrets."

"Glory knew?" Flynn asks. "That woman can keep a secret."

"So can somebody else around here." Aunt Bella ruffles Savannah's hair.

Savannah grins and bounces into the house before I can warn her. Then she bounces right back out. "Nick is in your kitchen."

"And who might Nick be?" Aunt Bella asks.

I grin at her. "You're not the only one with secrets. Hey, wait just a minute. I called you. We talked on the phone."

"Yes, of course."

"But I called your cell."

Aunt Bella waves that away. "Left it at home, forwarded to a landline."

"And Mr. Wilcox? Is he here, too?"

"Ted?" Aunt Bella exclaims. "Goodness no. He is bound and determined never to set foot on the island again."

"Well, where is he then? He's gone missing."

"No, I just made him promise not to talk to you. He's having a staycation, I believe. Now. Could we go in? I'm an old woman. I'd rather sit."

"Fine." I open the front door and lead the way into the kitchen. "Aunt Bella, meet my grandfather. Nick, this is Nomi's best friend, Bella."

"You?" she says, her hand on her heart. "You're Nomi's long-lost lover?" I see Nick's face begin to close down, but then Aunt Bella redeems herself. "Where on earth have you been all this time? She cried herself sick over you."

Savannah runs past me and hugs Nick. "Yay! If you're Blythe's grandfather, you have to let her stay! Right?"

"I reckon," he says gruffly, but now that I'm looking for it, I see his face soften, notice that he hugs Savannah back.

"Let's go in the living room," I suggest. "So we can all sit down and Aunt Bella can explain things."

Once we're all seated, Savannah and Brodie on the floor, Bella and Nick in armchairs, me and Flynn side by side on the couch, she beams at us all. "Well, isn't this lovely."

I clear my throat. "Explanations, Aunt Bella."

She laughs. "There's not all that much to tell. Nomi and I of course hatched the whole scheme together. She got you to draw that map,

Blythe, and wrote that first letter and made Ted swear to deliver everything to you on your thirtieth birthday. He'd been in love with her, you know, and even though they were old and he'd married somebody else by then, he never could refuse her.

"The problem was that we hadn't foreseen quiet Calvert Island becoming Vinland. Or the old tree where Nomi buried the ring being cut down. So I thought it best if I came on over and lent a hand. Ted set things up with Glory, and she was lovely about hosting me and helping me plant clues for you."

"But how did you get the letters?" I ask.

"Ah, that." Aunt Bella is enjoying herself. She smiles at us all, a born entertainer with a rapt audience. "Apparently Savannah's mother had found the letters in the attic of this house. She was reluctant to disturb them, but also didn't want some guest to get their hands on them. So she had given them to Glory for safekeeping. And once Glory learned what I was up to? She immediately shared the letters with me."

"I should be mad at you," I say. "I almost didn't figure it out!"

"Oh, it never really mattered," she says complacently. "You would have gotten the money in any case."

"What? Oh my God. How could you?"

"It was never about the money, child. You knew Naomi better than that. Ted has already opened an account for you, if you must know. Naomi just needed to get you here. Had to make the stakes high enough to do it. Here. I have one more letter for you."

She holds out a by now familiar piece of yellowed paper, written in Nomi's hand. I open it and read:

Dearest Blybee,
If you're reading this, everything has gone according to plan—a small miracle, given how many ways my scheming could have gone wrong.

Did you find him, darling girl, the man I saw in the snow globe? Are you happy? Did you fall in love? More importantly—are you YOU?

Goodbye, my darling girl. Thank you for laying me to rest.

Nomi

I feel the telltale heat rising to my cheeks, glancing up to see if Flynn, sitting beside me, has also read the letter. He's looking at me, not at the writing, but there's an expression in his eyes that makes me flush even deeper.

"Read it!" Savannah commands, from her place on the floor.

"I think I'll keep this one to myself," I say. And then I get up, so very calmly, and walk out of the room.

Water. I need water. I walk into the kitchen and am standing at the sink, filling a tumbler, telling myself how calm I am, when I look down and see that I'm still in my pajama pants and oversize sweatshirt. A reminder that I've never combed my hair or washed my face or even brushed my teeth.

And oh my God, Flynn has likely just read a letter from Nomi that pretty much says the whole reason she sent me on this wild-goose chase was so that I would fall in love.

With him.

Okay. So maybe I am not calm. At all.

"Blythe?"

Flynn stands across the kitchen, his eyes burning into me, his face unreadable.

With a completely inarticulate and undignified sound of dismay, I run past him, down the hall, and lock myself in the bathroom.

Flynn knocks on the door. He doesn't say anything, but I know it's him. I hold my breath and stay perfectly still, as if I can pretend the room is empty even though he obviously saw me run in here.

"Blythe. Please come out," he says.

"I can't."

"Tell you what. I'll wait for you outside. By the ladder to the beach. Okay? Please say something."

"Okay," I croak.

I listen for his retreating footsteps, then come out and dart up the stairs, where I change into jeans and a decent shirt. I comb my hair and brush my teeth. Putting on makeup at this point would be way too obvious, so I settle for just a touch of lip gloss.

A metallic thud makes me glance out the window to see that a ladder now rests against my balcony. When I open the slider, Flynn puts a hand over his heart and calls up, "But soft, what light through yonder window breaks?"

Laughter bubbles up inside of me, so much that it can't be contained.

Flynn holds the ladder while I descend, giggling helplessly. As soon as my feet are on the ground, I try to curtsy. "Thank you, Romeo. Thou art a true gentleman."

He laughs. "Figured you didn't want to see anybody else right now."

"You're a veritable mind reader."

"I kinda liked the bunny pants," he says. "A lot, actually. Very sexy."

I snort.

"You think I'm kidding?" He looks like he's going to kiss me, but then he grabs my hand and breaks into a run, towing me along behind him. "Hurry. Maybe we can get down over the cliff before they know we're missing."

When we reach the ladder, there's still no sign of anybody behind us. Flynn insists that he go first, so he can break my fall if I slip, and

I let him. Once we're down on the rocky shore, we start walking, by unspoken agreement, away from Improbable House and in the direction of the square.

All of my senses are tuned to the man walking beside me, looking untamed and a little wild with his long hair blowing in the breeze, the scar on his face, those farseeing eyes. And yet the hand that holds mine is strong and steady, the hand of a man who follows his own moral code and keeps his own promises.

"You know Savannah is my first priority," he says, after a long silence.

"Of course," I answer. "How could it be otherwise?"

"And you?" he asks. "What will you do?"

"Since Nick isn't going to kick me out immediately, I guess I'll stay another week. Bury Nomi. Get to know Nick, a little. And then, I don't know."

"You might stay." Flynn stops walking, tugging on my hand so I'm turned to face him.

"What would I do?" I ask, looking up into his eyes. "There's nothing for me here."

"Savannah's here. I'm here." His eyes, intent on mine, are doing something to my heart that is beyond the pales of reason. It surges in my ears like the waves. Time contracts and expands, then ceases to exist.

There is only this moment, this man, this one chance.

"Stay with me, Blythe." His voice is husky, his head bent so low I can feel his breath warm on my face. "With us."

I lay my hand on his cheek, against the line of the old scar, and lose myself in his eyes.

Nomi's voice whispers, carried on the wind, *Follow your heart, Blythe.*

"Is that a yes?" Flynn asks.

"Yes," I say, the word coming so easily now that I say it again. "Yes. A million times yes."

A low growl escapes him, and then his lips are on mine, his arms around me, gathering me in, gathering me *home*.

My last conscious thought for a very long time is *Ohhh, so that's what was missing . . .*

Epilogue

BLYTHE

"How's that?" Flynn steps back to survey his work.

"Perfect." The painting on the wall is as luminous and magical as the first time I saw it in Ted Wilcox's office: the bent and twisted old tree, the expanse of grass, the cliffs, and the water stretching like a promise beyond.

"It's crooked, actually," Savannah protests. "You need to use a level and a measuring tape to hang pictures."

Both of us laugh at that, Flynn's arm circling my waist, my head resting on his shoulder. It's a good thing we have Savannah to organize us and keep us in line, because neither one of us are measuring-tape-and-level kind of people. Brodie barks, once, then remembers the manners he's been taught and flops down onto the floor, panting, instead of running around wreaking havoc.

The painting is a housewarming gift from Ted, who says it's mine and he was only keeping it for me. I've bought the whole tree series and they are already hanging in the hallway.

Kristen and Mom have been to visit. Once she got over being furious with Nick for not being around for all of her life, Mom bullied my grandfather into doing things for his health and well-being, including getting a realistic-looking eye and a top-of-the-line prosthesis to replace that hook. It's easier for him to do things now, and it's also harder to be a total curmudgeon when you don't look so much like one.

He's still plenty crusty most of the time, but Savannah can melt him with a smile and has him completely wrapped around her little finger. I was going to buy Improbable House from him with the money from my trust fund, but he insisted on gifting it to me instead. For some reason that has nothing to do with logic, it has stopped falling apart. It looks like a different house with a coat of gray paint and a newly shingled roof.

The ravens, with the exception of Norman, are gone. None of us have any idea where they went. It's not like there's a sudden influx of ravens into any other area on the island. We've planted a new tree where the old one used to be, and buried Nomi there, along with both of the wedding rings. Nick has asked that we put him there, too, when his time comes, and we've agreed. I'd thought it might be sad, having Nomi right outside the window, but it's really kind of nice to have her always near.

Tomorrow we're moving new furniture in. And the week after that, we're getting married, right here at the house. It's Vinland off season, so no tourists. Glory has gotten the authority to marry us through some church or other, and Giselle and Clair and Denny have put their heads together to plan all the food.

Mom and Dad and Kristen are coming, of course. Alan too. He called a couple of weeks after we buried Nomi to have a long conversation and do something I don't think he'd ever done before, which was to say that he was wrong. What I'd said about him only wanting to marry me because he'd locked onto it as a goal was actually true, he said, and got him thinking about a lot of other things in life he thought he wanted.

He's definitely still on track to become a millionaire, but Kristen is keeping him balanced and reminding him about other important things. I'm pretty sure that next time he asks her about her opinion on an engagement ring, it will be going on her finger.

As for me, I have a position as a property manager after all. I've been helping Glory and Flynn with the business, and sometimes I even take over Flynn's metal-detecting classes. I think it's fun to get into character and pretend to be a Viking shield-maiden every now and then. Savannah and I have added a dog-sitting business to the island's attractions, which gives both of us plenty of opportunity to spend our time with the animals we both adore.

"Can we go?" Savannah asks. "I'm hungry. Brodie's bored. We don't want to stand here and look at a picture all day."

"Cool your jets," Flynn says, but he's laughing. He pulls me in closer and kisses the top of my head. "Ready?"

"Ready."

We're almost late for a surprise party at the Smuggler's Cove Café, a secret that has been spilled to us from at least three different sources. Flynn takes my hand and we follow Savannah and Brodie out of the empty house, so soon to be a home.

Norman is sitting on the porch railing, waiting for us. "Nevermore," he says, and this time I take the word as a prediction and a promise. Never again will I forget who I really am or how to keep my eyes open to the magic all around me.

"Thank you, Nomi," I whisper, and climb into the golf cart with my improbable new family.

ACKNOWLEDGMENTS

Once upon a time I believed that a book was something created by a single person, probably while starving in a garret somewhere, writing away by candlelight. But with every book I write (not one of them in a garret so far, and all fueled by plenty of coffee and snacks) I've become increasingly aware that every book is created by a multitude.

It's impossible to sort out which character trait, plot point, or idea was born out of which encounter with which person, event, or book. So I want to begin this page with thanks to all the people I have encountered, to all the books I have read, and to the many and varied experiences that have made up my life.

Thanks to Barbara Samuel for suggesting that I play with an escapist setting for my next book—this inspired the invention of a whole new island and sent my Viking (yes, I have my own Viking!) and me off on a fabulous vacation—ahem, I mean research trip—to the San Juan Islands.

Thanks and all my love to said Viking for watching *The Curse of Oak Island* and the other treasure-hunting shows that helped inspire the idea for Vinland. Also for buying me a metal detector and continuing to love me when I turn into an angsty, touchy human when the writing isn't going well.

Sandi, my dear friend, our regular check-ins feed my creativity, receptivity, and joy, and your support totally kept me going through the rough spots. I am ever blessed to count you as my friend. Also, I may have been just a tiny bit (or a whole lot) influenced by your books and let their magic flow into mine.

Chuck—even though, in the end, I decided not to burn Improbable House down after all and the chapters you helped me with have been relegated to my Darlings Graveyard file—I'm ever grateful for your time, expertise, and assistance on creating plausible fire-and-rescue scenarios.

To the valiant and brilliant editing team involved in shaping the sprawling draft I first submitted into the final, polished product, thank you a million times over. Jodi Warshaw, it has been a privilege and an honor to create another book with you. Jenna Free, your love for this book kept me from succumbing to dark despair during the Great Thanksgiving Rewrite of 2021. Thanks so much again for your awesome insights into character arcs and plot structure, and your willingness to help me kill and bury my darlings when I got carried away with my own ideas.

Deidre, my marvelous agent—thank you for always having my back and being there when I need you. Along with, you know, getting the contract and doing your usual brilliant agent thing.

Last, but certainly not least, thanks to the characters who volunteered to be written into this story. Blythe, Flynn, and Savannah, especially—I love all three of you and it's been a pleasure hanging out.

ABOUT THE AUTHOR

Photo © Diane Maehl

Kerry Anne King is a *Washington Post* and Amazon charts bestselling author of compelling and transformational stories about family and personal growth with elements of mystery, humor, and an undercurrent of romance. She was voted the 2020 Writer of the Year by the Rocky Mountain Fiction Writers. Her novel, *Everything You Are*, was a finalist in the Nancy Pearl Book Awards hosted by the Pacific Northwest Writers Association, and *A Borrowed Life* was a finalist in the 2020 Authors on the Air Book of the Year Awards. In addition to writing, Kerry supports other writers through motivational coaching and speaking. She is the host of *Tell Me Your Secrets*, a videocast/

podcast featuring lively, informal interviews with authors and other people involved with bringing books into the world. When not absorbed in creative pursuits, Kerry hangs out with her real-life Viking on their little piece of heaven in rural northeastern Washington. For more information visit www.allthingskerry.com.